MUSHROOM CLOUDS AND MUSHROOM MEN

The Fantastic Cinema of Ishiro Honda

By Peter H. Brothers

authorHOUSE®

AuthorHouse™
1663 Liberty Drive
Bloomington, IN 47403
www.authorhouse.com
Phone: 1-800-839-8640

First published by AuthorHouse 10/12/2009

ISBN: 978-1-4490-2772-8 (e)
ISBN: 978-1-4490-2771-1 (sc)

Printed in the United States of America
Bloomington, Indiana

In Memory of . . .

Guy Mariner Tucker

and

John Rocco Roberto

. . . they carried the torch.

For me, the most wonderful fragrance in the world is new film. You open the canister for the first time and breathe deeply. That night, the same wonderful fragrance fills your dreams. It's grand!

—Ishiro Honda to Stuart Galbraith IV, *Monsters Are Attacking Tokyo*, 1998.

TABLE OF CONTENTS

SECTION IV: "THE WORLD IS STILL FULL OF WONDERS!"

SECTION V: "STILL A YOUNG SOLDIER."

SECTION VI: "CHILD'S PLAY!"

SECTION VII: "THE DIE IS CAST!"

ACKNOWLEDGMENTS

I owe it all to my grandmother.

You see, when I was about seven years old, my grandmother Tillie Schultz (a blessed memory) was babysitting me when she turned on the TV to Los Angeles area's Channel 9, KHJ, so I could watch a program called, "The Million Dollar Movie." As it happened, the movie being broadcast was *Godzilla, King of the Monsters!* To put it mildly, I was hooked then and have been hooked ever since. Growing up in the late fifties and early sixties, I was fortunate enough to see the American versions of Honda's *Battle in Outer Space, Mothra, King Kong vs. Godzilla, Godzilla vs. the Thing, Atragon* and *Varan the Unbelievable* during their initial showings in movie theaters.

Deep bows of gratitude go to: Armand Vaquer, August Ragone, Brant Elliott, Brett Homenick, C. Francis Carnicelli, Carolyn Kamii, Chris Elam, Curtis Weaver, Daisuke Ishii, David Kalat, Diane Le Moine, Etsuko Miyajima, Greg Clausen, Jim and Akiko Firgurski, Jon Skocik, Jolyon Yates, Kiromi Aoyama, Larry Tucynski, Marina Kitagawa, Mark and Kiyo Charnow, Oki Miyano, Ray Malus, Reed Greele, Richard Pusateri, Ron Ford, Ronnie Burton, Ryan Eden, Susan Abouaf, Tami Miyashita, Toho Kingdom, Video Daikaiju, Yoshikazu Ishii, Yuko Rush and Yutaka Ichimura.

The purpose of this book is to examine the life and fantasy films of Ishiro Honda, focusing on the original, Japanese release versions. To this effect I have decided to use the original titles for the films, a decision that will frustrate some and irritate others, as there are often multiple titles given to the films (Honda's 1953 film *The Man Who Went to Sea* is also known as *The Man Who Came to Port*); however, I have included the American release titles to help identify the films.

Ishiro Honda was a wonderful filmmaker who, by a nice coincidence, was also a wonderful person. I hope this modest tome will pay proper tribute in honoring his many achievements.

Doumo arigato gozaimasu, Honda-*san*.

Peter H. Brothers
Santa Barbara, California
October, 2009

SECTION I:
"GENTLEMAN WITH A SMILE."

A Carp on the Cutting Board

The Boar of Yamagata

A CARP ON A CUTTING BOARD

After a film is completed, directors are like carps on cutting boards, as the movie is not unlike a dish served up to an audience. Even if I tell them that it is a delicious meal with lots of nutrition, if the audience takes a bite and finds it disgusting, there isn't anything more I can do. Of course, I will be very happy if someone says it *was* delicious...or will they want to dump it into a ditch?

— From Honda's 1954 essay "The Carp on the Cutting Board," *Southern Japan Newspaper*

While Honda is best remembered today for having directed the original *Godzilla* film, there was considerably more to his career. Honda worked on 82 feature-length films, 36 as assistant director and 46 as principal director (as well as three documentary shorts, plus 29 episodes for seven different television programs). Of those 46 films, 25 were in the fantasy-film realm (or genre), making him arguably the most-prolific director of such films in the history of the cinema. The remaining 21 covered a wide-range of subjects, from adolescent escapist faire to home dramas, from light comedies to war pictures. While only seven of his first 23 films (30%) dealt with fantasy, 19 of out the remaining 23 (76%) were fantasy-related. In retrospect then it is not surprising to learn that Honda's genre films completely overshadowed his other work; yet it is frankly because of those films that he is even remembered today.

The Support Team

Typically credited as the man who made the Japanese monster films, Honda would be the first to point out that he was merely a part of a much-larger team; a collaboration of men who now are known as true "Giants of the Genre." First and foremost among the key members of Honda's support team was the man who produced not only the first 22 Godzilla films, but also each and every one of Honda's fantasy films: Toho producer Tomoyuki Tanaka (1910—1997). Tanaka had tried his hand at acting early in his career but eventually turned to production work. His greatest claim-to-fame was the incredible gamble to produce a monster film the likes of which had never been seen or attempted in Japan. *Godzilla* became a huge hit and, as a result, Tanaka produced an immediate sequel called *Godzilla's Counterattack*. Even though that particular assignment fell to another director, Tanaka entrusted Honda with many other fantasy film projects, and after several more hits, Tanaka felt confident that Honda was the best man to helm such unusual films.

Many considered Tanaka as Godzilla's true "father," shepherding as he did the series from its original dark conception to the light-hearted family fare that followed, before returning once again to its original grim tone (almost as if Godzilla itself was a living being with a robust youth, an immature middle-age and a feisty maturity). This connection between a father and a son could not have proved more aptly ironic when, 16 months after Godzilla's "official" death in *Godzilla vs. Destroyer* (1995), Tanaka passed away at the age of 86.

Without doubt, the most crucial partnership of the entire Toho fantasy film series was the one between Honda and Japan's "Father of Special Effects," Eiji Tsuburaya (1901—1970). Tsuburaya began his career in motion pictures in 1919 at the tender age of 18, working as a scenario writer, until eventually rising to the rank of cameraman. It was during this time that he introduced many innovative techniques to Japan's film industry; he was particularly fond of using smoke to simulate fog, mist and cloud effects to such an extent that he became known as "Smoke" Tsuburaya.

Tsuburaya's life changed in 1933 when he saw *King Kong* for the first time. And, as with a man who would become Tsuburaya's rival in the years to come—stop-motion animator Ray Harryhausen—seeing *Kong* channeled Tsuburaya's life in the direction of creating special effects. Unlike Harryhausen however Tsuburaya had to confront the fact that special effects was a technique frowned upon by Japanese producers, who felt that effects work "cheated" the audience in not presenting the genuine article (not surprisingly, such effects were derisively labeled as "trick effects"). Despite this prejudice, Tsuburaya persevered and eventually joined P.C.L. in 1937, and his bold deployment of convincing miniatures gained him national recognition with *Navy Bomber Squadron* (1940), a film which also earned for him the first of many "Special Visual Technique" awards.

Tsuburaya's effects work culminated with his 1942 masterpiece, *The War at Sea from Hawaii to Malaysia*, a propaganda film which recreated not only the attack on Pearl Harbor but the sinking of the English battleships *Prince of Wales* and *Repulse*. The effect sequences of the film—which included the first in Japan using optical printing—were so convincing that, to this very day, countless documentaries on the Pearl Harbor attack include Tsuburaya's shots as representations of the real thing (at their best, Tsuburaya's effects are both technical achievements and artistic accomplishments).

By the time Honda and Tsuburaya worked together on *Godzilla*, Tsuburaya's reputation had achieved legendary status; not surprising since Tsuburaya had virtually invented the special effects field in Japan (he had also been at P.C.L./Toho 14 years longer than Honda, as well as being Honda's senior by nearly ten years). Despite this, Minoru Nakano—an assistant to Tsuburaya who eventually headed the optical effects department on a number of Tsuburaya's television shows—told Stuart Galbraith IV in *Monsters Are Attacking Tokyo!* that: "Nobody ever saw them arguing, either inside the studio or out. They understood and respected one another and easily imagined how the other would interpret the script." Another of Tsuburaya's assistants, Teruyoshi Nakano, also told Galbraith "They were more alike than different and stimulated each other."

Tsuburaya's death in 1970 left a void in Honda's life that no other special effects supervisor could ever hope to replace. In fact, Honda's regard for Tsuburaya endured beyond the grave. In an essay entitled "Tsuburaya, Magician of Special Effects," written by the director shortly after Tsuburaya's death, Honda made a remarkable declaration: That he considered Eiji Tsuburaya—and *not* director Kenji Yamamoto, the man who taught him how to make movies—as his true mentor.

Classical music and film composer Akira Ifukube (1914—2006) joined the Honda-Tsuburaya team with *Godzilla*, and the music he wrote for that film set the standard for a generation of fantasy filmgoers. Honda wrote of Ifukube: "He and I worked together on 17 science-fiction and monster films during a period of 18 years, which proves that his music has been indispensable for my movies."

Not unlike Tsuburaya, Ifukube was also an independently-minded artist who struggled to make a name for himself in a profession that was not only very much in its infancy but was also frowned upon by Japanese film producers. Ifukube shared yet another trait with Tsuburaya as a man of high-principles, moral ethics and a low-tolerance for those who did not share his creative vision. Even on the very first film Ifukube worked on—1949's *The Snow Trail*—he argued with director Senkichi Taniguchi about how a certain scene should be scored. When the two men reached a stalemate, Ifukube threatened to resign; and this coming from a man who had never worked on a film before (Ifukube won the argument).

As incredible as it seems today, Ifukube normally had only four days to write a film score and two days to record it, working in a cramped studio where the size of the studio dictated the size of the orchestra (usually 40 or so players). Ifukube is known internationally as a composer of classical music, but he will be best remembered for his film work, and in particular for the movies he scored for Ishiro Honda. Ifukube composed music for over 200 films during a career that spanned nearly half a century and was awarded such honors as the Order of Culture and the Order of the Sacred Treasures. The man long acknowledged as the Maestro of Japanese Monster Film Music eventually succumbed to multiple organ failure in 2006, at the age of 91. His passing marked the departure of the last living and in many ways least-appreciated member of the greatest four-member fantasy team in the history of motion pictures.

Others who played an important role in the success of Honda's films were his longtime cinematographer Hajime Koizumi (who photographed all but eight of Honda's 25 fantasy films), art director and production designer Takeo Kita, actor/stuntman Haruo Nakajima (b. 1929) and two screenwriters who could not have been more different in personality or style: Takeshi Kimura (1912—1988) and Shinichi Sekizawa (1920—1992); between them they would script nearly all of Honda's fantasy films. Honda told author Guy Tucker, "If the story was very positive or even childish, it would go to Mr. Sekizawa. If it was negative or involved politics, it would go to Mr. Kimura. I really can't compare the two because they were so different."

Kimura was an unhappy and introverted man whose grim themes radiated throughout such films as *Radon, The First Gas Human Being, Matango, Gorath* and *Frankenstein vs. Baragon*. In all he wrote ten scripts for Honda. Sekizawa—who wrote 11 of Honda's films—was on the other hand enthusiastic and childlike. Examples of his work include *The Great War in Space, King Kong vs. Godzilla, Mothra, Submarine Warship* and *Mothra vs. Godzilla*. Perhaps not surprisingly, the films written by Kimura did not do nearly as well from a commercial standpoint as did Sekizawa's, but the fact that Honda was able to go back-and-forth between the two men's scenario's was an enormous advantage, in that the constant switching from drama to lighter subjects reenergized him.

Editing and Pacing

Honda utilized nine different film editors over the course of his 25 fantasy films—nine by Ryohei Fujii and five by Taira Kazuji—and it is generally assumed that Honda did his own editing by simply telling his editor when and where to make the cuts, which was the standard procedure for Toho's film directors. Honda's films are generally leisurely-paced affairs normally beginning with an action scene involving some crises (*Radon, The Defense Force of the Earth, Mothra*), but are never boring. As director Robert Wise once observed, "Pace is interest," and once Honda has grabbed his audience's attention he never lets it go, perhaps his greatest attribute as a filmmaker. Actor Rhodes Reason, who worked with Honda on *King Kong's Counterattack*, spoke about Honda's working methods in an interview with Brett Homenick: "It was like Hollywood in the 1930s. For instance, instead of shooting a master shot and then shooting over-the-shoulder for dialogue, they shoot one line, move the camera in the other direction for the line, and over and over." When directing a scene, Honda was always thinking of how the live-action would later be integrated with the effects footage to follow. "He almost pre-cut the movie in his head," Reason recalled, "he was very good at that."

A single "take" in a Honda film typically lasts for just a few seconds— 30 seconds was about the maximum—and his camerawork is either fluid or static, depending on the time allotted for the shooting schedule, the budget and even his own personal interest in the project. For example, in *Gorath*—which was in production for six months, had a large budget and was a project Honda was passionate about—there are 613 live-actions shots, of which 271 (nearly 44%) involving a moving camera, with pans, zooms, crane and tracking shots. However, when working on a film such as *Latitude Zero*—which had a shorter filming schedule, a tighter budget and a story Honda found ridiculous—only 262 of the 861 shots (roughly 30%) involving a moving camera.

Honda normally used camera movement to accentuate action, such as "sitting down" when an actor sits down or panning along with his actors as they move across the screen, typically kept at a minimum for greater effect (he shot in the classic style of placing the camera about five feet above the ground). In dialogue scenes, Honda kept things moving by constantly intercutting between speakers, often varying camera angles to maintain interest. To save time when the budgets became tighter, Honda filmed actors in a dialogue scene in a single shot, rather than cutting back-and-forth between them; if two actors are talking to one individual, Honda invariably films the single actor bracketed by the other two. Author Guy Tucker—in his seminal work *Age of the Gods*—has written that, "There was rarely a film made in Japan that required (and not a studio in Japan that encouraged) a great deal of coverage or repeated takes from multiple angles. Limited to a single camera and a set-in-stone budget, Honda probably used his time and film to the fullest, shooting only what was necessary, rather than many different versions of the same scene for him and the editor to puzzle over later." This process is known as "cutting in the camera."

The most-recognizable of Honda's camera techniques was his signature table-top dolly-in or tracking shot—usually filmed at waist level—which ends in a close-up of a non-speaking character to emphasize a reaction. Honda would occasionally have an actor standing up into the frame from underneath, and he filmed people's feet running past the camera for dynamic effect. The director was also fond of filling his frame in a medium or long shot with a large number of actors in a human landscape of 30 people or more, but for smaller groups, Honda normally staggered them in a triangular rows; the most-famous example was in *Godzilla* when he crowded over 200 female high school students in a gymnasium during the "Peace and Light" song.

When reminiscing about Toho's working conditions during the 1960s, American film distributor Henry G. Saperstein told John Rocco Roberto, "They had a ten-hour workday as opposed to our eight-hour day. Only a half-hour for lunch and no coffee breaks. In a Hollywood day, if you got three minutes of film out of eight hours, then it's a big day. A Toho crew would work ten hours a day, six days a week, and they really got out the footage."

The "Carp on the cutting Board" was Honda's title of an essay he wrote in 1951 after completing his first feature-length film, *The Blue Pearl*. In that essay he complained that once a director had completed filming the film then fell victim to the whims of producers, editors and others whose influence altered the finished product. This admission is an interesting one in that it indicates Honda lacked control and final approval on his films, which could explain the often-wide disparity of the cuts seen in them. For example, the editing in *Godzilla* is unique in that Honda employed a number of "wipe dissolves" between scenes, a technique he rarely employed afterwards. It seems likely that Honda was agreeable to any suggestions his editors might make on where and when to make the cuts and then simply gave them the go-ahead.

One curious element of Honda's editing was his penchant for abruptly ending crucial scenes before they came to a conclusion. When

Joji Atsumi and his police officer friend discover an alien ventilation shaft in *Defense Force*, the scene ends just as the men are starting their search, while in *MechaGodzilla's Counterattack*, Murakoshi and Ichinose are questioning a reluctant Katsura in her father's house, but the next shot shows them leaving the house. In both instances, Honda ends the scenes because the necessary information has been extrapolated: The men in *Defense Force* have found the ventilation shaft and presumably got nowhere after that, and once Katsura has made it clear she will not answer any questions, Honda ends the conversation. Another example of Honda's cutting away during a scene is in *Gorath* after Sumio suggests using atomic power to move the Earth out of the monster star's path; Dr. Tazawa agrees to the idea, so the scene ends because there is no need to continue the discussion as the crucial information has been disclosed.

Scripts and Scares

Honda rarely deviated from the shooting script which he carried with him religiously during filming because Honda—himself a screenwriter—was wary of any script changes once all had been agreed upon during preproduction (he normally worked from a screenplay's third draft). Although it was not unusual for Honda to contact a scriptwriter to advise him of any potential changes before filming began, screenwriter Sekizawa recalled that Honda was not one to force any changes into a script; but when he did wish to make a change during filming, he would contact the author and ask permission to do so. The actors usually received their scripts within two-to-four weeks before shooting started and Honda worked on many of the scripts for his films, although normally without credit, because he did not wish to take recognition away from those officially listed as the scriptwriters.

"Writers are often too literal or too abstract," the director once complained to Tucker, "I found myself constantly conferring with them since the final image was going to be left up to me." Plot-wise, there are very few surprises in a Honda film as the viewer is usually well-aware that a monster is running around, long before any of film's characters find out. As a result, a great deal of time is spent watching either pushy journalists or skeptical policemen solving a mystery already solved by the audience. There is also at least one meeting to be found; a staff summit, a military briefing, a scientific explanation or some bureaucratic conference. To be fair, these discussions—beginning with Yamane's dissertation at the Diet (home of the Japanese legislature) in 1954, to Ichinose's rationalization for a new radar system for a submarine

9

21 years later—are essential to the overall plot and serve to give the audience a respite from the frenetic action of the monster scenes.

One of Honda's favorite techniques was ending a movie with his actors lined up in a horizontal row as a kind of "curtain call," giving the film's finish a theatrical quality (*Godzilla, Radon, Baran, King Kong vs. Godzilla and Submarine Warship*); for some reason, the majority of the characters in Honda's films pointing out monsters are usually standing on the far right of a line of people. Additional examples of Honda's theatrical flair can be seen in films such as *Defense Force*, such as when a group leans forward together as an official points to a map, and a scene in *Baran* where the onlookers recoiled in unison when the monster flew away.

One of the director's fascinating—if frustrating—habits was his reluctance to scare his audience; an audience, incidentally, which *wanted* to be scared (he was no Mario Bava). It seems that Honda was the last person to abuse his position as director simply so he could shock an audience and satisfy his own ego, but this unwillingness to offend or otherwise upset the paying public resulted in films that were rarely frightening or overly-graphic. Honda was not only respectful of his audience but of his actors as well. During the filming of *Matango*, when actress Kumi Mizuno was to be transformed into a Mushroom Woman, Special Effects Assistant Teroyushi Nakano remembered: "Ishiro Honda said that since Kumi Mizuno is a good-looking lady, why not make her beautiful instead of ugly after she eats the mushrooms. Whether he did that because he was being kind or because he liked her as a person, I don't know, but we liked that idea and that's what we did. We made Ms. Mizuno beautiful instead of ugly." In this sense many of Honda's films can be described as "beautiful nightmares."

Themes and Values

> I try to express in my films things that no other art can approach. In my monster films for example, I use special effects in the same way one would use a special film stock, a special camera, and so on. Monster films permit me to use all of these elements at the same time; they are the most visual kind of film.
>
> Honda to Guy Tucker in *Age of the Gods*, Daikaiju Publishing, 1996.

Not surprisingly—given Japan's exposures to atomic fallout and Honda's own journey through the rubble of Hiroshima after the war—radiation was a recurring theme in his genre films. The first time the word "radiation" is heard in a Honda monster movie is in *Godzilla* when Dr. Tanabe announces his Geiger counter reading while examining contaminated well water (typically, Honda then cuts to a shot of disappointed villagers). 18 out of his 25 fantasy films deal with the topic either directly or indirectly: *Godzilla, Radon, Defense Force, Liquid People, The Great War in Space, Gorath, Mothra, King Kong vs. Godzilla, Matango, Mothra vs. Godzilla, Dogora, Three Giant Monsters, Frankenstein vs. Baragon, War of the Monsters, King Kong's Counterattack, All Monsters Attack, Latitude Zero* and *MechaGodzilla's Counterattack*.

Honda's own military service is reflected in many of his films, such as wartime attention to detail, as in both *Mothra* and *Matango* men are polishing their rifles. Another idea repeated in nearly all of Honda's films involved a search, be it in caves, forests, jungles, open country or city streets, in a indirect reference to Honda's numerous platoon patrols. During one such patrol, one of Honda's soldiers became separated from the main group; his men later found him—bayoneted but alive—near a stream. This could be why throughout nearly all of Honda's cinematic searches, those who are lost are eventually found (Yuriko in *Baran*, Chujo in *Mothra* and Princess Salno in *Three Giant Monsters*). Often the searches are conducted by two men and a woman (*Baran, Mothra vs. Godzilla, Frankenstein*), and it is not unusual to see a searcher being spied upon (*Abominable Snowman, Mothra vs. Godzilla, Submarine Warship, All Giant Monsters Attack*). Other repeated bits of business are ringing telephones bearing bad news, reporters being denied access in their attempts to acquire information from authorities, and natives bowing before burning alters encrusted with animal skulls.

Another carryover from the war was the concept of a character or characters being surrounded by a larger group, in what Tucker called a "swarm" (*Abominable Snowman, Defense Force, War in Space, Matango, Submarine Warship, Mothra vs. Godzilla*). Another repeated theme is "play-time is over," such as when people are enjoying some form of recreation only to have it permanently interrupted by a monstrous event (the singing sailors in *Godzilla*, the would-be skinny-dippers in *Gorath*, the teenage dancers in *Frankenstein vs. Baragon* or the hikers in *Sanda vs. Gairah*). Still another theme was having a person sacrifice themselves to atone for a sin—intentional or otherwise—such as Dr.

Serizawa in *Godzilla*, Iwamura in *War in Space*, Obata in *Giant Monsters of the South Seas* and Katsura in *MechaGodzilla's Counterattack*.

One of the more fascinating aspects of Honda's work was his often derisive treatment of native and aboriginal people worshipping ancient gods (*Snowman, Baran, King Kong vs. Godzilla*). Typically, these natives are portrayed as being either comical, ignorant, superstitious, dangerous or sometimes even deformed. Curiously, the first thing the "gods" do once they are revived, is to attack the very natives who have been worshipping them—perhaps Honda's way of "punishing" superstitious peoples for their archaic beliefs (*Godzilla, Snowman, Baran* and *Giant Monsters of the South Seas*). As it happens, when these "gods" do come to life, they are not actually the gods being worshipped, but monsters which happen to live in the area; thus, any means to placate them fail (when *Baran's* High Priest is killed by the monster, the moment was echoed 23 years later in *Dragonslayer* where a priest is killed by a dragon he considers to be Satanic. In both cases, the beasts are unaffected by the prayers because they are not supernatural horrors but living animals).

After a monster or invader has appeared, rarely are citizens shown stampeding, rioting or challenging authority in a Honda movie, as they often did in a typical Western film, such as a blind man getting trampled in *Beast from 20,000 Fathoms* (1953) or rioters clashing with military police in *War of the Worlds* (1953). Such scenes are inconceivable in a Honda film; there may be danger but never dissent, panic but never pandemonium, disarray but never disorder. Instead, Honda's evacuation scenes are unruffled and organized; there is usually ample warning of any oncoming terror, and thus there are many well-planned and coordinated escape routes, with ships docked at local harbors and buses patiently awaiting passengers. Soldiers and police happily line the streets reassuringly waving white-gloved hands while guiding the streaming populaces toward safe havens. This is because Honda felt that even during the darkest times, the focus was to be kept on the inherent decency of the human spirit to remain calm, even in the face of life-threatening emergencies.

Perhaps the director's favorite scenes were those showing people gathering together as part of an intimate gathering: The whiskey-serving in *Gorath*, the steak dinner in *King Kong vs. Godzilla*, the cooking of hamburgers in *Frankenstein vs. Baragon* or Ichiro's sukiyaki dinner in *All Monsters Attack*, all of which have a reassuring warmth to them. There is also the Honda "touch" where a person reaches out and makes a gentle physical contact with another (*Defense Force, King Kong vs. Godzilla, War of the Monsters*).

Honda stressed taking a defensive posture in fighting against any aggression, taking offensive action only when forced to and when no other option is available. Typically, it is not the military but the scientists that save the day (*Godzilla, Baran, Gorath*) as the military messes things up more (*Radon, Baran, Sanda vs. Gairah, Mothra*). By letting the scientists solve the problem—such as by inventing weapons capable of killing the beasts or disabling invaders—Honda gave them a chance to redeem themselves after inventing such terrible weapons as the atomic bomb. As it happens, many of these imaginary weapons are primarily defensive: The massive Markalites in *Defense Force*, the Toxin Tanks in *Dogora* and the A-Cycle Light Rays in *The Great Monster War* (it is an amusing concept that many of these made-to-order and untested super-weapons are conceived, designed, constructed and implemented in record time).

Sympathetic Monsters

Monsters are tragic beings. They are not evil by choice. They are born too tall, too strong, too heavy, that is their tragedy. They do not attack people because they want to, but because of their size and strength, mankind has no other choice but to defend himself. After several stories such as this, people end up having a kind of affection for the monsters, they end up caring about them.

— Honda to Roland Lethem in "Inoshiro Honda,"
Midi/Minuit Fantastique, October 1968.

The one element so unique to Honda's monster films that sets them apart from his Western contemporaries was the concept of depicting the various rampaging beasts, evil empires and offending aliens as much victims as villains. The huge monsters must die simply because they no longer belong in the modern world, although many have interpreted Honda's monsters as being warnings and admonitions of what may come if mankind continues to tamper with the natural world. In some cases, the monsters' deaths are caused not by men, but by natural forces as if the gods themselves have felt obliged to take action and rectify a wrong humanity had created, such as an erupting volcano (*Radon, Sanda vs. Gairah, Giant Monsters of the South Seas*).

The ending of *Radon* is a classic example of the contradictory quality comprising the ending to a Honda monster movie: After causing considerable havoc and loss-of-life, the two giant Pteranodons die a grisly, fiery death; yet the viewer takes no satisfaction in witnessing their destruction. The film's spectators watch the conflagration without any cheering, shouting or celebrating (the hero and heroine do not even embrace). Instead, all watch in stupefied self-doubt, unsure of their "victory." Honda not only sympathizes with his monsters but also respects them, feeling toward them an almost paternal responsibility and sensibility. "I don't think a monster should ever be a comical character," he remarked to Lethem, "The public is more entertained when the great King Kong strikes fear into the hearts of the little characters." The director went to great lengths to present his monsters not as terrifying creatures but as exotic animals which could actually live peacefully if left alone, as if they too have a right to their existence. Sadly, in a world run by Man, such a situation is quite impossible.

Even when undeniably evil forces attempt to conquer the world, Honda manages to evoke sympathy for the invaders, specifically in their final moments of defeat. At the conclusion of *Submarine Warship*, the Empress of Mu jumps into a boiling sea to die with her people, leaving us feeling sorry not only for her, but for the destruction of an entire civilization despite its efforts to subjugate the Earth. When the dastardly Mysterians fail in their attempts to conquer Japan, Honda shows us their sad and decomposing faces and flying saucers struggling to escape, and when the Xians are suffering from the effects of the "A-Cycle Light Ray," we feel their fear and dread. These ambivalent endings give Honda's fantasy films a unique depth of feeling and carry a question of hollow victories for Humanity; even after the dreaded and destructive Godzilla has been reduced to atoms, it seems unlikely the Japanese would ever think to mark the occasion by declaring a national holiday.

The Big Picture and the Little Man

How can we make a special effects scene impressive? Needless to say, special effects shooting is trick photography, not reality. In order to make the unreal look real, the director himself has to make believe that he is part of the scene. Let's assume that suddenly, there is Godzilla—as tall as 50 meters—in front of you; you actually need to have this feeling of shock. A film that records events as they occur is called a documentary.

A special effects film is fundamentally the same as a documentary.

— from Honda's essay "The Pleasure of Making
Special Effects Movies," published in *MechaGodzilla's
Counterattack* movie brochure in March 1975.

Honda always considered all of his films to be documentaries, and his style has been compared to that of a documentary filmmaker, but what exactly does that mean? By definition, a documentary filmmaker is one who objectively records events as they happen in order to educate an audience, but this was not always the case with Honda; even though he usually employed an objective narrative in his films and never stressed, influenced or otherwise forced his audience to take the side of any one individual, his films could more accurately be considered as "semi-documentaries" or "natural dramas." He nevertheless encourages empathy for innocent people whose homes have been destroyed and whose lives have been disrupted by monsters.

The Westerns of John Ford demonstrated a love for the individual over groups of people to resolve a crises, but Honda's genre work stressed the opposing viewpoint: That individuals are essentially ineffectual when battling monsters; only when humanity unites is there a chance for survival (when Detective Sakata charges a Liquid Human, only to be absorbed by it, in *The Beauty and the Liquid People*, Honda stresses that such acts of reckless bravado are of little use. It is only when the scientists and the military work together are the Liquid People defeated).

The director often filmed his leading characters from a distant and objective "third-person" viewpoint—unlike Alfred Hitchcock, who usually had his audiences identifying with a leading character—although there were rare examples such as the leading characters in *Matango* and *All Giant Monsters Attack* (Honda employed a subjective camera for brief "spectator as audience" shots so as to gain empathy for a certain character or to increase audience involvement). As a result, it is difficult to identify with any one character in a Honda film even if that person is being featured at the beginning; in any event, the character in question will be shunted into the background as soon as the monsters arrive. For Honda, this was a frustrating development—although he must have realized it was unavoidable—that, by the end of his film, the human-interest story had become inconsequential, swallowed up by the special effects climax. It was a strange irony that Honda helmed films in a genre that in many ways worked against his desires as a director.

Another aspect of Honda's "documentary-style" approach was his inclination to shoot on location, one of the director's greatest assets; indeed, the many images of the beautiful Japanese cities and countryside give his films the look and feel of mini-travelogues. As Honda once told Tucker:

> On location I'm always conscious of the scene's context. I had to be conscious of consistency in case the next shot would be an effects shot. So, I tried to avoid the difference in texture between the live-action and the effects; shooting on location, I always kept in mind that such a shot might be coming right after the one I was doing. If I wasn't sure how they would match, I didn't take a chance, so I used very modest compositions. For example, I sometimes had to avoid shots which would include the sky.

Other documentary-like aspects of Honda's films were realistic reactions from actors and extras when they encountered monsters, and the absence of music for much of the film. One other rather unique facet to Honda's films was that he often filmed non-actors as opposed to studio extras as background characters in rural or panic scenes; even the soldiers called-in to repel the beasts were authentic army troops stationed nearby, with the natives and citizens being shown to safety actually living in that area (the director filmed real miners standing-in for their cinematic roll call in *Radon* and utilized actual native villagers from the Shima Peninsula for the panic scenes during Godzilla's appearance on Odo Island, he also hired dancers from a local Shinto shrine to perform the authentic purification ceremony seen in the film). More than once the director commented that he considered all of his films to be essentially documentaries, once telling his son Ryuji that, "Nothing remains the same when time passes . . .everything is a documentary. See that sunset? That will exist only today."

Honda stressed the suffering of citizens caught in the wrong place at the wrong time as victims of unnatural forces they cannot control or understand; in many a Western monster film the viewer is rarely concerned with what happens to the average citizen. Yet for Honda, what happens to these people is of paramount concern, and their distresses must be accounted for. In *Radon*, the army has decided to shell a volcano where two large pteranodons are hibernating, but a spokesman for the local village expresses concern that military action could cause the volcano to erupt and thus endanger the village, while in *Godzilla*, Honda emphasized the suffering of the sailors' families in their unsuccessful attempts to acquire any information about their missing loved ones. Most directors would consider such scenes inconsequential to the plot, but to Honda, they were a necessary human ingredient (Honda would no doubt prefer his job description to read, not as a director of monster movies, but as a director of movies that had monsters in them).

Another element Honda stressed in his monster films was individual loss. In *Star Wars* (1977) Princess Leia says, "We have no time for sorrows," but in Honda's world, there is always time for sorrows, whether it is the inconsolable Shinsuke in *Abominable Snowman*, the hysterically-sobbing mothers in *Radon* and *Baran* or the grieving space pilot captain in *War in Space*; grieving over the loss of a loved one was of great importance to Honda. Honda's films are also peppered with scenes stressing deep emotions, such as Makoto's rejection of her father in *Submarine Warship*, Ichiro complaining about his absent parents in *All Giant Monsters Attack* and Emiko's shame in *Godzilla*.

Honda used the medium of motion pictures to issue statements on matters he considered to be of paramount importance; another element that distinguishes his films from his Western contemporaries. *Godzilla* has long been acknowledged as a treatise on the atomic bomb, but other Honda films have made statements as well: *Radon* stressed devotion to a loved one, *Mothra vs. Godzilla* commented on government bureaucracy, *Submarine Warship* was a treatise on Japan's militarism, *Matango* on moral decay, *King Kong vs. Godzilla* on commercialism and *All Monsters Attack* on latchkey kids.

Hopes, Hearts and Heroes

The Heroes in Honda's films rarely follow the pattern of those starring in a typical Western monster movie; they are often cowardly, weak and susceptible to injury. They rarely succeed, and when they do, the consequences are hardly worth the price (*Godzilla*, *Gas Human* and *Matango*). They usually lack the swaggering confidence of the villains they encounter, and when monsters appear, they are shunted into the background, impotently watching from the sidelines, unable to influence the outcome.

Of Orson Welles (born May 6, one day before Honda), Simon

Callow has written that "...his work...was designed to appeal to the brain rather than the heart." The exact opposite can be said when defining the greater-part of Honda's cinematic output. Perhaps the one theme closest to his heart involved his hope that the nations of the world would discard their differences and unify in order to defeat a common foe, a idea found in all three of Honda's science fiction films: *Defense Force*, *War in Space* and *Gorath*. The human heart also beats very strongly in Honda's cinema, even in a minor effort such as *South Seas*, when Obata is possessed by aliens intending to use him as their instrument against mankind. Despite this control however, Obata—who is by no means a model citizen—struggles against his oppressors and eventually overcomes them in an act that will end his life, but save his soul.

In *Godzilla*, the love-triangle between Ogata-Emiko-Serizawa is handled with great subtlety, as Emiko is forced to make a choice between her obligation to marry Serizawa and her heart's true calling for Ogata; in *Radon*, the love Kio feels for Shigeru obligates her to remain with him despite imminent danger. Love can not only cause conflicts but cause tragedy as well, such as the passion between Mizuno and his *inamorata* in *The First Gas Human Being*; a passion which will literally consume them both. In *MechaGodzilla's Counterattack*, Katsura is so devoted to her father, that she is willing to overlook his cooperating with aliens intending to conquer the Earth. One idea used more than once involved the love a human man has for a female robot: Astronaut Glenn's love for Miss Namikawa in *War of the Monsters* and Ichinose's love for the cyborg Katsura in *MechaGodzilla's Counterattack*; both love affairs end tragically.

Reassurance was also a vital element in Honda's movies, and it is interesting to speculate if he was making a personal statement regarding his own doubts as to his capabilities and the support he sought from his wife: Emiko guarantees her love for Ogata in *Godzilla*, while in *The Great War in Space*, Ichrio comforts Etsuko by guaranteeing his undying love for her; there is also a moment in *Gorath* when Kiyo bolsters Dr. Tazawa's crumbling morale. Camaraderie among male professionals was another issue Honda was fond of examining, be it the friendly rivalry between "Diamond G-Man" Mark Jackson and detective Kommei in *Dogora*, or the astronauts Glenn and Fuji in *War of the Monsters* (one appealing aspect of Honda's films is the exuberant celebration of teamwork following a victory, such as in *War in Space*, *Gorath* and *MechaGodzilla's Counterattack*).

Sex was one topic rarely explored in a Honda film—possibly due to the tenure of the times and censorship concerns—nevertheless, there is an element of sensuality in his work, ironically most prevalent in his horror films, be it the fleshy, sultry dancers in *Liquid People*, *Vapor Man's* gorgeous Fujichiyo or the opposite pulls of the virginal Miki and the seductive Mami in *Matango*; yet, when Maki seduces Fumio in *Matango*, the moment is more exotic than erotic (two kissing scenes in Honda's fantasy films are goodbye kisses: Glen to Namikawa in *War of the Monsters* and Dr. Masson to Dr. Barton in *Latitude Zero*). As it happens, women are often employed as man bait: Nightclub singer Chikako attracts diligent policemen, respectable professors and dangerous gangsters in *Liquid People*, while Hamako in *Dogora* pretends to fall for Mark Jackson in order to grab his diamonds, while both police and assassins risk their lives over Princess Selina Salno in *Three Giant Monsters*.

However, if sex was sometimes presented in a less-than-flattering light, it looked positively sanguine when compared to Honda's handling of religion. In *Defense Force*, the *Bon Odori* Buddhist festival (a dancing ceremony meant to console the spirits of the dead) is interrupted by a forest fire started by aliens, in *Gorath*, a *tsunami* inundates a religious shrine. In *Mothra*, the Junichiro character makes an awkward attempt at genuflecting during a critical moment, and *tori* gates—the entrances to a shrine's inner grounds—are routinely destroyed in Honda's films (*Defense Force*, *Three Giant Monsters*). The Shinto ceremony in *Godzilla* fails to mollify the monster, and when a Shinto priest attempts to ward off evil sprits in *Mothra vs. Godzilla*, he acts and looks ridiculous. It was as if Honda was stating that old religious beliefs were irrelevant in the modern age; perhaps this is why—despite having been raised in a Buddhist household—the image of Buddha is never once seen in a Honda film with one possible exception; during the early part of *Baran* when two Japanese enter a native village and glance at a stone indicating Baran's territory, the image of a Buddha-like figure carved into the side of a mountain can briefly be seen.

The treatment of women underwent a drastic transformation in Honda's work. In his early films such as *Godzilla*, *Radon*, *Defense Force*, *Baran*, *Space War* and *King Kong vs. Godzilla*, women were weepy and helpless screamers, fragile flowers who had to be rescued by the heroic males. As time went on however, women became professionals working alongside their male counterparts: Astronauts Kyoko and Sylvia in *War in Space*, photographers Michi in *Mothra* and Junko in *Mothra vs. Godzilla*, and journalists Yuriko in *Baran* and Kyoko in *Gas Human*.

On the negative side, women were often subjugated to physical abuse: The slaps Chikako receives from the gangster in *Liquid People* and Hamako from her boss in *Dogora*, the beatings given to Chika by the village patriarch in *Abominable Snowman*, the throttling Noako gets from her brother in *Three Giant Monsters*, the shootings of Madame Piranha in *King Kong's Counterattack* and Kyoko having her earrings ripped-out by her brother in *All Monsters Attack*. While Honda's heroines were often helpless, their male counterparts faired little better and often needed assistance themselves; both Shigeru in *Radon* and Tatsuo in *Gorath* suffer from amnesia and cower in the face of danger.

Villains and Violence

> I could never make a gangster film or write a film about wicked people because I don't believe that wicked people exist in this world. Sometimes, people find themselves in an environment where it is unavoidable to act badly, but I would never want to make a film that is only about evil.
>
> — Honda to his wife Mimi as related in an interview Mimi gave to Shiro Kimijima in *The Complete Works of Ishiro Honda*, Sonorama, Asahi, 2000.

Honda cared deeply about the characters in his films, depicting them as either heroes to be praised or villains to be punished—sometimes, severely. Aliens usually arrive under the guise of peaceful intentions (the Mysterians and Xians) or to improving their surroundings (the Kilaaks and the aliens from the Third Planet in the Black Hole). In many cases Man himself is responsible for initiating the disasters that befall him, be it tampering with technology (*Godzilla, Gas Human, Mothra*) or meddling with nature (*Abominable Snowman, Radon, Baran*).

Human villains are usually portrayed as either inept thugs or megalomaniacal geniuses. In depicting criminals as being stupid, however, Honda lent them a comedic touch, such as the diamond smugglers in *Dogora*, the assassins in *Three Giant Monsters* or the bank robbers in *All Giant Monsters Attack*. Intelligent villains are much-more flamboyant and even dress the part: *King Kong Counterattack's* Dr. Huu and *Latitude Zero's* Malic spring immediately to mind. Perhaps due to their arrogance, Honda granted his villains spectacular and stylized deaths scenes: Malmess in *Three Giant Monsters*, the diamond smugglers in *Dogora* and Clark Nelson's pirouette of death in *Mothra*. Oddly, the villains are normally killed not by the heroes, but by the monsters—and even then, by accident (*Dogora, Three Giant Monsters* and *Latitude Zero*).

Working With Actors

> Honda was a perfect guy to work with. Very, very smooth guy to work with. He wasn't as meticulous as some of the other directors in Japan...He would speak a little bit of English when there were other (non-Japanese) actors and sometimes I would be called over to help him out when he'd say 'I can't get it through this guy's thick head what I want him to do!'... Honda knew what he wanted and if he got it on film, that was it. A lot of times you would do a scene 10 or 12 times, and other times you'd do it on the first take.

> — Robert Dunham to Kip Doto in "Toho's Favorite Foreigner," *Markalite* No. 2, Winter 1991.

Candid photos of Honda on a set show him closely coaching his actors while holding onto a rolled copy of the script which he carried around with him religiously during filming. The director was particularly keen on dictating the physicality of his actors' movements and gestures to a precise degree, walking them through their scenes, showing them how he wanted them to move, how to react and even which buttons to push on a console. This technique—while putting a director's personal stamp on his films—tends to rob actors of their creative freedom of movement, leading them to essentially mimic the director's gestures. It is not surprising then to learn that any improvisation from an actor on a Honda set was very rare (in fact, if an actor had trouble saying a certain word or line of dialogue, Honda would change or even delete it). Also rare on a set was any tension, as Honda went out of his way to ensure that things ran smoothly and that everyone was comfortable doing their jobs.

If an actor's physical business was specifically dictated by Honda, the actors' interpretations of their characters was normally left up to them. When working with the highly-skilled actors employed at Toho this did not normally present a problem; on the other hand, when Honda was dealing with either foreign actors or Japanese actors not terribly interested in their parts, the results were less-than satisfactory. It seems strange that a man who once commanded men on the battlefield was helpless in the face of incompetent actors, two glaring examples being Yumi Shirakawa in *Liquid People* and Russ Tamblyn in *Sanda vs. Gairah*. In such cases, Honda simply sat back and filmed whatever came across and hoped for the best, a possible indication of a man more concerned about meeting a deadline than in making a movie to his precise specifications.

Honda was never above taking suggestions from his actors; indeed, it seems he hardly ever said no to them. Perhaps he believed that a suggestion coming from an actor indicated he cared enough about his part to think about it, and so by agreeing to the suggestion, Honda in a sense rewarded the actor for his interest. Yoshio Tsuchiya was a particularly keen actor who loved playing offbeat parts: In *Defense Force* he played the leader of the Mysterians and suggested to Honda he be allowed to adlib a line regarding buying up parcels of the Moon, and while playing the Controller of Planet X in *War of the Monsters*, Tsuchiya wished to create his own Xian language; in both cases, Honda agreed (when Akiko Wakabashi suggested to Honda she play the mesmerized princess/prophetess in *Three Giant Monsters* as if she were sleepwalking, Honda gave her the go-ahead).

Actor Akira Kubo recalled that Honda would sometimes sit in his chair and have an assistant communicate what he wanted, but occasionally he himself would talk directly to his cast. Tsuchiya remembered that off the set Honda was very gracious with his time, but during the actual shoot, was involved with the general business of filmmaking and very much into his own world; in other words, Honda directed his films and not his actors.

Honda was well-aware that not all of the actors he worked with appreciated genre work, but he eventually cast those who did, because to him these actors were very versatile. For these actors, working on a monster movie was little different than working on any other kind of film and was an assignment to be taken seriously. Honda had his own stock company from which he often personally cast his films, and the result of this creative bonding fostered a sense of teamwork whose unity and rapport translated onto the screen. Honda—who did not speak fluent English—usually enlisted Toho staffer Heihachiro "Henry" Okawa as an interpreter when giving instructions to non-Japanese actors. Okawa occasionally appeared in bit parts for Honda in such films as *Three Giant Monsters*, *All Monsters Attack*, *Sanda vs. Gaira*, and in *Defense Force* where he played, appropriately enough, an interpreter.

The pool of actors from which Honda could tap had spent years developing their talents at Toho, and during those heady times kept quite busy (Yu Fujiki made 24 films in one year alone). The atmosphere on a Honda set was friendly, laid-back and informal—any tension under such conditions was inconceivable—and actors and technicians went about their business quickly, quietly and efficiently. Honda would typically walk around the set wearing his trademark battered fishing hat that in itself lent a casual air to the proceedings, although for official Toho publicity photos he would don a snappier-looking cap. As actress Kumi Mizuno recalled, Honda truly enjoyed working with his actors and never bullied or intimidated them, instead softly guiding them with quiet reassurance and gentle encouragement, and was particularly courteous to his actresses.

Mizuno's benevolent impression of Honda was returned in equal proportion as Honda stated years later he considered her to be his favorite actor to work with: "She was a very genuine actress," Honda told *Cult Movies* writer David Milner, "It was as if she just stepped into the film and became a part of it" (another Honda favorite was American Nick Adams, who was twice-paired with Mizuno in Honda movies). Honda enjoyed the company of his actors and crew away from the set as well, as Kimi remembered in *Monsters Are Attacking Tokyo!*: "He often would bring ten or twenty members of his staff to our house. He didn't go out drinking with them; he instead invited them to his home because he preferred being there. He'd say, 'Why don't you come over to my place?' a lot. The actors always came by to visit and they really loved him."

Yosuke Natsuki—who played a detective in both *Dogora* and *Three Giant Monsters*—agreed, telling Galbraith that, "All of us, the actors and the crew, went to his house near the studio and drank beer or had barbecues with his family after work. He was a gentleman with a smile, both at work and at home." Many performers recalled their experiences on a Honda set with pleasure, and Mie Hama—who acted in both of Honda's Kong films—paid him the highest-complement of all when she called him an "actor's director."

Frustrated Fantasies

I have never been completely satisfied with my movies. Techniques and special effects always play a huge part and these are difficult to perfect. I always imagine how some of the shots will look prior to filming, but making them look real is very difficult and never what I had imagined. After watching one of my movies I always think that, with a bigger budget, the film would have been better. I would like to make science-fiction films that take place in the future. Also, I would like to make documentaries without any monsters, and monster movies with big budgets!

— Honda to Roland Lethem in "Inoshiro Honda,"
Midi/Minuit Fantastique, October 1968.

Honda rarely attended movie premieres, preferring instead to watch them—and the audiences' reaction—as an ordinary paying customer. In fact, when Honda first joined P.C.L., executives believed that his outward temperament (which included singing traditional Japanese folk songs on his birthday) made him ideally suited to make movies about women. "He was a romantic person," his wife remembered, "and feminine in some ways." Kensho Yamashita, one of Honda's assistant directors, remembered that Honda first impressed him as a stern and introverted deep-thinker, but after a time discovered him to be approachable and generous. Honda's easygoing personality and positive outlook on life became an integral part of even his grimmest films; one watches them as if being told a scary story by a kindly uncle.

If Honda found a particular project he was working on to be a stimulating one (such as *Liquid People*), the result was a film imbued with a great deal of style and verve; however, if a project came along that did not interest him (such as *Dogora*), the result could be lackluster and even careless. Honda became increasingly frustrated as the quality of the scripts given to him declined over the years; while finding the early projects fascinating diversions, by the mid-sixties, Honda had grown frustrated and tired of making movies that had become increasingly juvenile and less genuine, more ridiculous than real.

Although he insisted he refused directing a script unless it met with his total approval, Honda helmed more than his fair share of disappointing films, although why he took on such projects—knowing full-well what he was getting into—is a matter of some conjecture; perhaps he felt that he might make be able to make something out of nothing, or he may have taken on the assignment simply because he was a loyal company man and his job was to direct films regardless of their content or how he personally felt about them.

One issue that was of particular annoyance to Honda was not the lack of a decent budget—although that certainly was a main concern on more than one occasion—but the lack of *time* he was given to make a movie. He was comfortable directing one or two films a year (typically Honda had four-to-six months to make a movie), but by the early sixties, this leisurely pace had come to an end, as producer Tanaka sped up the process: *Mothra vs. Godzilla* was made in four months, *Submarine Warship* in three and *Dogora* in just two—and all this was expected to be accomplished from a director who did not liked being rushed (Kimi agreed that her husband did not do his best work when given a short shooting schedule).

Tanaka's decision to induce the films with humor for a younger audience played havoc with Honda's initial conception of how his films should be received. Kenji Sahara felt that Toho's altering of the series violated Honda's original conception and Honda could not have agreed more, but admitted in later years that he could never really oppose Toho's change in the Godzilla character. "Once you made a film," he told Lethem, "it becomes the property of the studio. There's a great deal of discussion during the writing of a script, but once the shooting starts, the discussions end. Once I became part of Toho, I no longer had any reason to complain to my employer; one may have objections before joining a company, but once you are on the inside, you really can't. That's my opinion." Nevertheless, by the mid-sixties, Honda felt it was time to let someone else guide the series and as the decade came to an end, the mature tone that once was the hallmark of the Toho fantasy films Honda had cut his cinematic teeth on was over and done with, and the decline of the films' artistic merits dragged Honda's career down along with them.

The director—an avowed romantic sentimentalist—longed to make movies that explored other avenues besides monsters destroying cities and was particularly keen on making films concerning everyday life in Japan in the face of changing times. Occasionally, Honda was able to weave subliminal messages into his films, but he was continuously thwarted in this regard by Tanaka, a man interested in giving his paying public the visceral thrill of seeing big beasts in action for big box-office revenues (Honda once wrote a film treatment dealing with young Okinawan fishermen who decide to give up their trade for the big-city life in Tokyo, but Toho wasn't interested). Many of Honda's former colleagues felt that the vast majority of the films Honda directed were done not be choice but by assignment.

In *Godzilla and My Movie Life*, Honda stated that "The only one who says "cut" is the *director*—so once I say "cut" I wash my hands of the production; otherwise I get too nervous about the little things that are no longer important, the opportunity for new or different ideas and the time for improvement or progress on the story has been lost." Honda always felt that Toho's decision to let him make *Godzilla* was not a risky one; after all, if the film failed, there would be many other opportunities for additional special effects films, but what Honda failed to take into consideration was that *had* the film been a failure, there would have been very little chance of any further big-budgeted effects fantasy films being produced for him—or anyone else for that matter—in the foreseeable future. In the final analysis, Toho Studios owes an entire genre and years of profitably to the films directed by Ishiro Honda.

THE BOAR OF YAMAGATA

Ishiro Honda, the man who told many fantastic tales through the medium of motion pictures, did not consider himself to be much of a storyteller. However, there was one story he was fond of telling on more than one occasion, and it was one rooted not in fantasy, but fact:

> "There was once a two-year-old child who found himself all alone near a village. It was a hot summer day and the sun beat down on him fiercely. The child could feel the heat of the ground through the straw slippers on his feet and hear the loud sound of a nearby stream— and, he was crying. Before long, a young man came up to the child and asked him why he was so sad, but the boy was just too upset to answer him. That's when the youth realized that the child had wandered too far from his village and was lost. So, he picked the boy up and brought him back to his home, which was only 100 meters away.

> "That child," Honda said, ending his story with a wink, "was *me!*"

Childhood Memories

The prefecture of Yamagata, Japan, is located in the Higashitagawa County district of Shimekake (formally Ootsuna), approximately 300km north of Tokyo. There, located in the middle of a natural wonderland of mountains and rivers at the foot of Mount Yuden, is a small village called Asahimura.

Yamagata has four distinct seasons. In the Spring, the melting of winter snows bring fresh greenery to the trees, while cherry blossoms bloom in abundance, and it was on the Spring day of May 7th, 1911, that Ishiro Honda was born as the last of five children to Yoshihiro and Miyo Honda. Three brothers and a sister had preceded him, and since Ishiro had been born in the Chinese year of the boar, he was named "Ishiro;" the "I" coming from the Japanese word *ino* ("boar") and *shiro*

27

which designated him as the fourth son. Because his parents used only the letter *i* from the *kanji* letter character from the word *ino*, it led many people over the years to misspell Honda's first name as "Inoshiro."

Honda's descendants had been priests and farmers, and Ishiro's father was the chief priest of the temple on Mount Yuden. To make a living, Yoshihiro sold talismans in the various provinces during the summer, while his wife made a modest income working as an assistant to a charcoal burner. The land the Honda's lived on was used to grow chestnuts and rice, and during the snow season the boys helped to harvest potatoes, radishes and carrots as well as making *miso* soup and soy sauce at their home.

Life in Shimekake was simple and unpretentious and was comprised of some 30 families who cropped rice and participated in that rare trade once known as "sericulture," the breeding of silkworms for their threads. The factory that housed the silk-making operation was staffed by nearly all of the young people living in the district.

Honda's earliest memory was of playing with his friends, making dams in the Mogami River and swimming in the reservoir during the summer and sleighing down snow-covered hillsides in the winter. Honda's mother was 42 years old when she gave birth to him, and Honda remembered her as a being a very kind and patient person. As for his father, Honda recalled that people were always telling him his dad acted just like the real Buddha. Honda's general memories of those early days were of a hard but happy experience.

Growing up, Honda listened to stories of local legends that were told during the wintertime in order to ward-off boredom. The boy rarely attended temple services—only going during the festivals—nor were any of his brothers particularly devout, even though they did go to temple to study for the priesthood. Nonetheless, Honda and his brothers began questioning the need to visit temples for learning and none of them ever seriously considered becoming priests because they were much more interested in science.

Eventually, Honda's eldest brother graduated from medical school to become a medical officer in the army. Stressing to his youngest brother the need for study, he sent Ishiro a number of youth-oriented magazines on contemporary subjects as well as scientific journals. Honda looked forward to receiving the magazines, which he not only read eagerly, but submitted articles and even an occasional poem for publication; amusingly, though none of Honda's essays were ever printed, his poetry often was. In any event, Honda continued to submit articles due mainly to the fact that he enjoyed writing them.

The Move To Tokyo

In 1921, the Honda family moved to the Tokyo suburb of Takaido where Yoshihiro would work at the Iou Temple. There were additional considerations for the move as well as by that time, the population in the village had been steadily decreasing and Honda's oldest brother had been thinking about opening a clinic in Tokyo. When Honda was in the third grade, he was transferred to the Takaido Elementary School; a rare move because many families were not allowed to move there unless they had business in the city.

When Honda was asked years later how he felt about moving to Tokyo, he answered that he essentially had no choice but to accept the change. He never felt the need to ever go back to Yamagata and his mother was happy that they had moved to Tokyo. Honda had no worries about transferring to a new school, but due to his strong country accent, he often suffered ridicule at the hands of his classmates whenever he spoke; however, this did not bother him because he knew the way he spoke sounded strange to the city kids. He recalled that though there were lots of mean kids, fortunately he was never picked-on or bullied.

It was while in elementary school that Honda witnessed something that would change his life forever: A "Movie Night" held on the school's playground, for it was there and then that he saw his very first film. Honda was stunned and amazed as no one had even heard of motion pictures in Yamagata, nor was anything about them ever written about them; he was fascinated seeing how a machine could show a moving picture on a screen. Duly impressed, Honda's appetite was whetted and he wanted to see more of them (Honda recalled the film was a silent American "Bluebird" Western from the 1920s, regarding a young girl who was kidnapped and raised by Native American Indians as one of their own. She eventually learns how to ride a horse and fight like an Indian, and considered her own natural brother to be her enemy. The girl ultimately is shocked when she learns the truth about herself after becoming an adult; interestingly, many of Honda's future films dealt with natives in conflict with outsiders).

When Honda was in the sixth grade, his father became the head priest at a temple in Kanagawa, so the family once again relocated and Honda was enrolled in the Tachibana Elementary School. There was a movie theater in Sangenjyaya and Honda went there often because he liked movies and it was also very close to his home. They showed different kinds of movies which Honda saw many times. Honda preferred movies dealing with history—finding contemporary films somewhat boring—as well as famous films and films made with large budgets. Because Yoshihiro's religion prevented him from seeing movies, Honda would see them alone before returning home to tell the film's story to his father. Honda's father enjoyed hearing these stories so much that he overlooked the fact that, technically speaking, it was illegal for a kid Honda's age to go into a theater without an adult. So, even at an early age, Honda was already becoming a storyteller of films.

The screenings of the silent films were accompanied by a live narrator called a *benshi*, and Honda discovered that the narrator's commentary was sometimes more entertaining and enlightening than the film itself. On one occasion, Honda went with an older brother to see a movie that would have a profound effect on him: F. W. Murnau's *The Last Laugh* (1926), narrated by Musei Tokunaga. The story involved an old door attendant in a luxury hotel who made a minor mistake and was demoted to a janitor. The man tried to keep this a secret from his family, still returning home everyday wearing his door-attendant costume, until it was discovered that he was actually a janitor.

Tokunaga then turned to the audience and said that since such an ending would have been too sad, the director instead ended the film another way; whereupon they then watched as the old man inherited millions of dollars and became rich. Afterwards, Honda remembered the he had previously believed that movies were made by the actors, but after hearing Tokunaga's commentary, he realized the movie was really made by the director. Although Honda didn't exactly know what kind of work directors did, it seemed to him that they were the ones in charge of making a movie.

In 1928, Honda attended Kougyokusya Middle School as an Art Major. An apt pupil, Honda became an honor student on more than one occasion, studying such diverse subjects as Japanese Culture, Geography and History (his interest in Geography and History never left him). Unfortunately, Honda discovered that the required courses now included such classes as Physics and Chemistry, and as a result, his grades suffered. Honda took note of the fact that for the first time, "Film" was now considered an art form; albeit one that ranked dead-last out of the eight defined "Classes of Art," behind literature, music, painting, theatre, architecture, sculpture and dancing.

Film as a Career

After graduating from Kougyokusya in 1931, Honda entered the newly-built Japan University (*Nihonn Daigaku*) and was the eighth student to enroll in the new Film major, along with future film directors Senkichi Taniguchi and Fumio Kamei. However, the class was a bit of a disappointment, as Honda later recalled: "The university had a Film Department," he told Galbraith, "but it was a Film Department in name only as it didn't have any facilities, any equipment or any books; I think I saw a camera twice in my entire time there. We didn't have many classes teaching us about movies. Most of the instructors were from the film industry and told us it was impossible to teach film in a classroom, so they usually cancelled classes. As a result, I went to the movies more often and took notes."

In 1932, while in his second year in college, Honda became friendly with the professor teaching the Film class: 33-year-old Iwao Mori, then an executive at Photo Chemical Laboratories (P.C.L.) Studios, established that same year. Mori had created a cinema group that met once a week called "The Friday Club," and it was through this organization that he hoped to interest young people in working at P.C.L. Although there were close to 100 graduates in Honda's class, very few made it into the movie industry; instead, many found jobs as tour guides in museums.

It was standard procedure for graduates to enter P.C.L. by passing an entrance exam (as did future director Akira Kurosawa), but Honda discovered that taking the exam would not be an obstacle, as Mori personally recruited the 22-year-old Honda to join the Production Department at P.C.L. after he graduated in August of 1933. Honda believed the reason for the personal invitation was due to his association with a music critic named Hiro Nakane, telling Shingo Yamamoto: "I would visit his home quite often because I believed that music would one day play an important part in films. Well, Mr. Nakane was a friend of Mr. Mori's and he must have mentioned me to him."

In the film industry in Japan in those days, it was a tradition one began his career as an assistant director for a long time before becoming a director; which would certainly prove to be the case with Honda, who would spend the next 18 years of his life (on and off) as an assistant director. Six graduate students entered P.C.L., working in various departments such as Management, Scriptwriting and Directing. Taniguchi, Kamei and Honda all became "Fourth Assistant Directors;" essentially *fait touts* doing everything from lugging around equipment to running errands. Eventually, they would develop close working relationships with their mentors, learning how to write scripts, edit films, deciding which lenses to use and working as scripters responsible for maintaining continuity; all were all excellent introductions to the methods of filmmaking.

Toward the end of 1933, Honda received his first official movie credit as an assistant director to Sotoji Kimura on a film called *Just an Average Kid*, but the following year would see two momentous events occur in his life. The first was meeting the man who he would assistant-direct on many occasions: 31-year-old Director/Writer/Producer Kajiro Yamamoto, then filming the first in a series of movies starring the popular comedian Enoken (Kenichi Enomoto) in *Enoken's Adolescence*; the second was the passing of the mandatory military entrance exam. That same year, Honda assisted Shigeo Yagura on *The Old Silk Shoes* and Mikio Narise on *The Three Sisters with Maiden Hearts*.

Honda still went to see other films as well, and was particularly awed by Robert J. Flaherty's 1934 *Man of Aran*. Honda—who had a profound love for the ocean—wrote about the experience in an essay printed in *Tokushinbunka* magazine 18 years later:

> The movie depicts man's severe battle against nature on a small island of Ireland surrounded by the rough sea. On this island, people made vegetables on rocks covered by seaweed in substitution for soil. Salty scent permeated the dwellers' skin and even the walls and floors of their homes. Watching the heavy seas crushing against the high cliffs on the screen, I felt I had never seen the ocean so close before.

Then, in January of 1935—one year after passing the entrance exam—Honda joined an infantry regiment and in less than a month was involved in one of the seminal events in Japanese history.

The War Intrudes

In an attempt to destroy the influence of industrialists and politicians advising Emperor Hirohito, on February 26, 1936, fanatical army officers assassinated two key advisers; assisted by other army insurgents, they surrounded the Japanese Foreign Office and essentially held the greater part of Tokyo hostage for three days. Honda's first military action was to accompany his garrison to secure the area and encircle the radicals. The plot to overthrow the government failed when the Army's High Command decided not to support the insurgents; as a result, the leaders of the mutiny were persuaded to commit suicide rather than face a trial that would put the Army in a bad light.

His first assignment over, Honda was then sent to Manchuria in

May, and it was while stationed there—on December 13, 1937—that the Chinese city of Nanking fell to the Imperial Japanese Army (on the heels of the surrender occurred one of history's most-notorious atrocities: "The Rape of Nanking," when Japanese army troops routinely committed countless crimes on anywhere from several hundred to a quarter million Chinese civilians; the figures are still hotly debated). Although soldiering in the Imperial Japanese Army at the time of the Nanking Incident, Honda was not involved as he was at that time stationed in the Manchuria province, which by then had been relatively stabilized and secured by Japanese forces.

It was during his time in Manchuria that Honda experienced his first test of fire in a running gun battle with Chinese troops. Although initially terrified of being killed, Honda realized that such chances were slim; as it happened, Honda's skill with a rifle was so proficient that he eventually was awarded a special medal for marksmanship. In Honda's mind there was never any question of his surviving the war, telling Shingo Yamamoto years later:

> I told myself that I would not be killed by a bullet, because I had to return home and work in the movie industry; otherwise, there would have been no meaning to my life. I was against the war but I never gave up my training; I actually enjoyed target practice and worked hard to be the best—which is why I received a medal for it. I never received any beatings from my superiors and also never beat-up any of my men. When I was shining my shoes, I tried to focus on finding a way to finish it as fast as possible, using the minimal amount of oil. I tried to find interest in what I had to do; otherwise, army life could be overwhelming.

Honda was discharged from his first tour of duty in March of 1937; five months later, P.C.L.—along with several other studios—merged to become the Toho Motion Picture Company, located in the Sijo-Gakuen suburb of Setagaya, Tokyo. Honda was soon back at work there, assisting Yamamoto for the first time on *A Husband's Chastity*, and it was then that the 26-year-old Honda met another eager assistant director and a man who would become his closest friend and a legend in worldwide cinema: 27-year-old Akira Kurosawa. Kurosawa had joined P.C.L. shortly after Honda did, but due to Kurosawa's obvious talents and ambition, he was soon promoted to First Assistant Director while Honda remained Second Assistant Director.

One responsibility belonging to the Second Assistant Director was overseeing set preparations prior to filming. During one particularly hectic day, Honda assisted the set builders by layering a grainy texture over paint so as to represent wood, a job that earned Honda the nickname "Keeper of the Grain." Honda tried to predict what the directors would want and made every effort to see what needed to be done, then do it before he was told; although sometimes, they just wanted him to wait for instructions. Nevertheless, Honda always tried to take care of things by himself, rather than asking someone else to do it, such as changing or preparing the set. As a result, the other staff members would get embarrassed and put in a similar effort.

In 1934, Honda's efforts were rewarded with additional assignments for Yamamoto, including *The Beautiful Hawk* and two Enoken pictures, *Momma, the Hat - The Nice Way (Part I)* and *Returning is Scary But the Weather Will Clear if You Wait (Part II)*, followed by Mikio Narise's *Avalanche* and Sadao Yamanaka's acclaimed antiwar film, *Humanity and Paper Balloons*. Honda's assistant duties continued to gain momentum and, in 1938, he worked with Kurosawa for the first time on Eisuke Takizawa's *Geothermal*. Honda then assisted Mansaku Itami on *Legend of the Giant* and again with Narise on *Tsuruhashi Tsurujiro*, plus another Yamamoto film, *Toujiro's Love*.

Kimi

There was another "love" Honda was to encounter and it was in the form of a script girl named Kimi Yamazaki. Born in Suigaido, Ibaraki, Japan in 1917, Kimi's family were wealthy landowners, and being the youngest of her family, Kimi was sheltered and spoiled, which contributed to her being in relatively poor health during most of her adolescence. As a result, she was forced to stay home a great deal, so a teacher recommended she read a number of books, the majority being of a liberal nature. When her teacher suggested Kimi write an article for a local magazine, she wrote about the exploitation of a local farm, an article that created such an uproar that her father begged her never to become a writer.

Despite this discouragement, Kimi's interest in writing continued to grow. Unfortunately, when she was 19, her family went bankrupt so she left home to seek an independent life, a rarity for Japanese women in those days; as it was, the majority of jobs available to women involved mainly clerical work. One day Kimi came across a classified ad for a motion picture company called United Movies, and after passing a written test, was hired and was soon writing copy for the studio's newsreels. Unfortunately, United Movies was a small operation and soon ran out of funds, whereupon the company's president recommended that Kimi apply to Toho Studios for employment, where she was soon hired. After Honda had returned from his first war tour, he stopped by to pay a social call to the editing department, and it was there and then that he and Kimi met for the first time.

Ishiro claimed he was attracted to Kimi due to character traits that he himself lacked, "Not," she later stressed to Hiroshi Takeuchi, "because I so was beautiful or cute!" For her part, Kimi was drawn to Honda by his kindness and open-minded attitude. On thing about Honda that struck Kimi as odd, was his desire to become a movie director. "Being a gentle man like that," she explained, "I never thought that he would become a movie director, since the movie industry was extremely competitive. I thought he just liked movies and that he was happy as long as he was involved in the business one way or another."

As Kimi remembered to Takeuchi, Honda's proposal to her was brief and to the point; returning together from a day at the studio, Honda turned to her and causally asked, "Well, shall we get married?"

Kimi's response was equally frank, but tinged with memories of her family's bankruptcy. "That's fine with me," she replied, "but I never want to be poor." Although Honda assured her that they would never be penniless, Kimi later good-naturedly told Takeuchi, "As it turned out, we were poor until the day he died. He was a liar!"

Strangely, Honda received little support for his marriage to Kimi from his friend Kurosawa, who felt that due to their "oil and water" temperaments they would never make a good couple. Kurosawa was not the only one who had doubts about the union, as Kimi's parents also disapproved of the match, particularly her father, who felt the movie industry—as yet not widely accepted as a respectable profession—was no guarantee of a steady income. It seemed to Kimi that people were just trying to break up the union except for Kenji Yamamoto, who always supported the idea, telling Kimi that if she really loved Honda then she should marry him regardless of how others felt.

And so, in March of 1939, the 28-year-old Ishiro and 22-year-old Kimi were married. As Kimi told Shinsuke Nakajima years later, "Our newly-wedded life was just like in the famous folk song *Kandagawa* (a sentimental song that looked back fondly on college days). We walked to the only public bath in town holding onto one little soapbox. Every time I hear that song, I cry, because it reminds me of that day" (during those times many people lived where there were no private baths, so they instead went to a public bath called a *sento*, where they were charged a modest fee in order to use the facilities. Obviously the newlyweds were on a very tight budget, but the marriage by all accounts was a good one, lasting until Ishiro's death 54 years later).

Returning to the War

Mimi regretfully retired from Toho to become a homemaker and future housewife, while Honda worked for directors Takeshi Sato on *Virgin Sara*, Hideo Koguni on *Roppa Goes to the City of Music* and Yamamoto on *Enoken's Messy Hair Cut*. In December, Honda was assisting Yamamoto on an epic semi-documentary called *The Horse* but was forced to resign from the assignment due to notification of reinstatement into military service (as it turned out, *Horse* would be three years in the making; Honda finally caught up with it during a servicemen's film night while he was stationed in China). Eventually, Honda became the only employee at Toho ever to be away from the company for such a long period of time due to wartime service; he later joked he was in-and-out every two or three movies. As a result, people who had entered the company after Honda did were now in a higher position than he had been when he returned.

Honda's second call to duty came during the last month of Kimi's pregnancy with their first child; he left soon after she gave birth to a girl named Takako in January of 1940. As Kimi recounted in an interview published in *The Complete Works of Ishiro Honda*:

> You could never understand unless you had actually lived back then and knew of those days, but going to war was a duty, and there was no way out of it. When Ishiro received his second call-up papers, I thought about hiding them under the floor as long as I could; however, that would not have been acceptable. When he left, I saw him off in Akasaka with my father and my baby. Every time he was called up, he always told me that he would come back, so I just had to believe him and wait. There were times when I would look up at the night sky, see a shooting star and wonder, 'Did he just die?'"

It would be nearly two years before Kimi would see her husband again.

Honda learned about Japan's December 1941 attack on Pearl Harbor while stationed in a small village called Dangyang near the upper-basin of the Yangzi River in Central China. Just before being discharged for the second time in 1942, Honda saw a film called *The War at Sea from Hawaii to Malaysia* featuring the astonishing special effects work of Eiji Tsuburaya. After returning home from the service a second time, Honda was promoted to First Assistant Director where he worked for the first time with Tsuburaya on Yamamoto's *Colonel Kato's Falcon Squadron.*

As with many great partnerships, the one between Honda and Tsuburaya got-off on the wrong foot. In an essay Honda wrote for *Bungeisyunju* magazine, he recalled how he was intrigued as to what sort of new techniques Tsuburaya was going to use for the *Kato* film, and asked him many questions. "At the time," Honda wrote, "Tsuburaya was working on a scene where a formation of more than a dozen Hayabusa fighter planes came flying over clouds with Commander Kato's plane in the lead. The clouds were made of white cotton fiber and piled up on a baseboard, while the airplane models were hung from a long stick manipulated by thin wires."

From where he was standing, Honda could see the wires; an observation he tactlessly reported to Tsuburaya, who responded with understandable irritation: "I *know* that, I'm going to fix it *right now!*" Once looking through the camera's viewfinder however, Honda could not help but be impressed by how Tsuburaya made the whole scene look so convincing. To Honda, it seemed that Tsuburaya was not unlike an inventor or a physicist trying to discover something new through his experiments. *Kato* would not be completed until March of 1944 when the 32-year-old Honda was called back into service for a third time, this time reporting for duty in Kokan, China (located between Shanghai and Nankeen). During this period, Honda's second child, a son named Ryuji (Takashi) was born.

By this time, Honda was a platoon sergeant, whose duties included searching for Chinese "insurgent" guerillas as well as being in charge of uniforms, weapons and the training of new soldiers, teaching them that obeying orders was vital in order to survive and to keep physically fit at all times. "When you're surrounded by crossfire," he warned them, " the *worst* thing you can do is retreat. There's no better target than a back. You can only escape by advancing." Whenever Honda was expecting fresh troops to arrive, he laid out new uniforms and made sure all the name tags were on them. On occasions when he had to cook meals, he tried to find the most economical way to prepare them, even buying the vegetables himself from Chinese merchants (unlike his contemporaries, Honda always treated the Chinese as human beings, being friendly to the point of even speaking some rudimentary Chinese).

Just as Honda had learned about his nation's entrance into World War II while in the armed forces, so he also learned of Japan's defeat on August 14th while stationed at Kokan four and a-half years later. A short time later he was among thousands of Japanese troops surrendering *en masse* to American Marines in Soshu (north of Shanghai) on September 7th before ironically being transferred to one of the infamous Japanese-run Prison-of-War camps, located along the coastal region of the Yangzi River in Central China. It would be another six months before Honda was transferred to Shanghai, where he was finally repatriated in March of 1946.

It is not known if Kimi had any idea whether her husband had survived the war or not; as it was, she knew very little about her husband's wartime service, just knowing he was far away fighting in a foreign land. On his way home, Honda passed through the rubble of what had once been the thriving city of Hiroshima, decimated in the wake of an atomic bombing the previous August.

In *Godzilla and My Move Life*, Honda reminisced about his wartime service:

> My generation was the last one where officer candidates were volunteers; everyone else was required to take officer training after they graduated from school. It wasn't a requirement for me, so I didn't volunteer. I knew that if I didn't volunteer, I could go back home after serving a year and a-half in the military, because— if you became an officer candidate—you were required to be on-call for two weeks every year and I didn't want to do that. I didn't want the military to interrupt my work, so that's why I never volunteered to be an officer candidate. I was simply drafted every time...I was very angry about the situation and that made me eager to stay alive. I often told other soldiers that I wouldn't die, even if Japan lost the war, until I saw my wife and kids. I was willing to run to the top of the Himalayas if I was ever chased by the enemy, *that's* how much I simply ouldn't accept dying in the war.

Honda served three separate tours of duty, the first from January 1935 to March 1937 and the second (and longest) from December 1939 through December of 1942; the third tour lasted from March of 1944 through August of 1945 before Honda spent six months as a POW. Honda's time-off between his first tour lasted from March of 1937 through December of 1939 and December of 1942 through March of 1944 during his second reprieve. In total, Honda spent more than seven years serving in Japan's Imperial Army.

Kimi was naturally delighted to have her husband home again but was shocked by his appearance, as Honda had not only lost a considerable amount of weight, but his hair had turned completely gray; he was also very ill. The family's financial condition was precarious and Yamamoto thoughtfully suggested to his faithful subordinate that he take a corporate position at Toho, where the work was less-physical and the money considerably better. But Honda—frustrated by his long absence and eager to return to work—insisted on remaining on the directorial staff. Although Kimi appreciated her husband's resolve she regretted his decision, telling Takeuchi years later:

> That was his choice, so I had to go along. When he came back from the war, I felt badly that all of his friends had already become directors; I thought he would feel pressured about having to catch up with them, but he never seemed to let it bother him. He told me, 'They have their own lives to lead, as I have mine.' He was never in a hurry to become a director.

Honda's first assignment in 1947 found him assisting no less than three different directors—Tadashi Imai, Hideo Sakikawa and Kiyoshi Kusuda—on *24 Hours in the Underground*, followed by two of Yamamoto's Enoken films, *The New Age of Fools Part I* and *The New Age of Fools Part II*, followed by *The Spring Feast*. Honda did not have an official credit listed in 1948, but in 1949 he officially directed his first film called *Ise Island*, essentially a promotional film aimed at increasing tourism to the island's famous shrine. Honda not only produced, directed and wrote the majority of the screenplay, but also helped design an underwater camera used to film women pearl divers diving to the bottom of the sea— an innovative technique utilized to considerable effectiveness. Honda later considered the film one of his most memorable and cherished accomplishments, and after completing the 30-minute film (which took nearly eight months to complete), Honda then assisted Yamamoto on *Child of the Wind* and *Spring Fun*.

In 1949, Honda worked as an assistant-director on Kurosawa's *Stray Dog*, scouting and filming locations, as well as directing his first scene in a major motion picture of star Toshio Mifune walking through a crowd. Honda himself appeared on celluloid for the first time, doubling for the villain as he ran away from the camera (the villain's name—although never mentioned in the film—is billed as "Honda" in the credits). Honda then produced and directed an educational movie called *The Story of a Consumer Cooperative* in 1950 and in 1951, worked with Yamamoto for the last time on *Erejii*.

Those were heady years for Japan's motion-picture companies as there were no less than six major film corporations—each with its own distinct method of making movies—with some studios churning out two major releases every week (these studios released 370 feature films in 1954 alone, shown in some 7,000 theaters and grossing some ¥20 billion—$55 million—overall).

The First Films

Years later, Honda was asked if he felt his low-key personality was the reason why Toho took such a long time before finally giving him the opportunity to direct his own films. "That's possible," he admitted in an interview with Singo Yamamoto, "The company probably didn't see me as someone who would become a director right away and I didn't have the ability to write a great script in one or two weeks. I was also shy and retiring." In any event—at the age of 40—Honda was assigned to direct his first full-length feature film for general release, a semi-documentary on the everyday life of women pearl divers, *The Blue Pearl*. Honda wanted to reuse the underwater camera he had built for *Ise Shima*, so he was looking for new material involving women abalone divers when he discovered a novel written by Katsuro Yamada called *The Deserted Undersea World*. In his 1952 essay entitled "Movies With Ocean Themes," Honda wrote:

> Ever since they were 15 or 16—almost everyday—they have gone under the water and have earned 80% of their living expenses by catching beard clams, *wakame* (seaweed native to the coasts of Japan) and agar. They go 15 to 20 meters under the sea and hunt prey hidden between rocks. What could be more cinematic? It

cannot be depicted in writing and your imagination
will never come close to the reality. Seeing the divers
wriggling like mermaids under the sea...I was impressed
with the severity of their lives and the beauty of their
professionalism. That's when I realized the power of the
image. If only I could have filmed it in color!

Honda was determined not merely to show the lives of the divers
above the water but depict their underwater world as well—a dangerous
environment the divers casually contended with on a daily basis. After
the film was completed, Honda arranged a private screening for the
divers' spouses, friends and relatives and was moved by their reactions,
later writing: "The movie showed what the divers did every day of their
lives, but that cannot be depicted in writing and your imagination will
never come close to the reality. The husbands had never seen their wives
swimming underwater—only watching them from a boat—so they were
very moved by the sight of their wives diving to the bottom.

Honda did not outwardly show his emotions at finally making a film
he could call his own, but Yamamoto was overjoyed, telling him, "Your
hard work has finally paid off!" However, Honda had his first experience
with what he later called being a "Carp on a Cutting Board" during the
scene where the main character died. The moment was supposed to
have been longer than the one seen in the final print, but the editorial
supervisor told Honda that his ending was much too long. Honda
emphasized that the scene was crucial and would not have the same
impact if it was shortened, but was told to shorten it anyway. Years later
Honda still remembered how upset he was about the incident.

Honda's second film—made in 1952—was *The Skin of the South*,
followed by *The Man Who Went to Sea. Skin of the South* took place
on the Satsuma Peninsula of Kago Island near the volcanic region of
Southern Kyushu on the Shirasu Plateau, areas known for having soft
soil where whole crops are washed away during the heavy rains. The
story involved a college researcher who tries to figure out a way to
prevent the flooding (as with *The Blue Pearl* and many a Honda film to
follow, the movie's theme dealt with man versus the environment).

Honda's script involved a researcher who fell in love with a girl
who lived in the local village. After doing his research, the man was
ultimately able to devise a way to successfully prevent the flooding.
After completing the script, Honda went to visit a professor at Kago
Island University for technical advice on matters concerning flooding
and was shocked to learn there was no way to actually prevent a flood

from happening! Nonplussed, Honda reworked the script, leaving the story's ending open to interpretation while stressing that man must prepare for natural disasters.

The Man Who Went to Sea was a documentary-style story about gunners on a whale-hunter boat and was a significant film in Honda's career, for not only did he share his first "official" screenplay credit with Masashige Narusawa and Shinzo Kajino, it marked the first time he worked with both Tsuburaya *and* producer Tomoyuki Tanaka (while not necessarily a special effects film, the movie utilized a great many process shots that depended on Tsuburaya's expertise).

The following year, Honda directed two films at opposite ends of the spectrum, the first was a love story called *Adolescence Part II* which dealt with the issue of coeducation and the relationships between young people in postwar Japan (the first *Adolescence* had been directed by Seiji Maruyama the year before and had been a great success). *Eagle of the Pacific* was quite another matter, a big-budgeted war picture with an all-star cast.

The film dramatized Japan's entry into World War II, with emphasis given on the involvement of the revered Admiral of the Imperial Japanese Navy, Isoruku Yamamoto. Honda considered the film to be his genuine *debut* as a director of significant feature-length films, and the fact that Tanaka (who co-produced with Sojiro Motoki) trusted Honda with such an important project indicated a growing confidence in the young director's abilities and potential.

Initially, Honda had written a script called *Kamikaze Attack Troops*, but Mori—now head of production at Toho—felt it was too close to the war's end to produce such a project. In any event, Honda considered Shinobu Hashimoto's screenplay a masterpiece and the experience of working closely with Tsuburaya as they developed the storyboards together as unforgettable. Honda directed a crucial moment in the film when Yamamoto (brilliantly portrayed by Denjiro Okochi) pleaded with Prime Minister Konoe to avoid a military conflict with America by diplomatic means. Honda considered this scene to be the most gratifying of his career.

During another scene, a Zero fighter pilot and his plane were to catch fire. The man who volunteered to perform the dangerous stunt was 24-year-old Haruo Nakajima, whose courage, stamina, good humor and work ethics Honda would later recall when casting the unprecedented part of a 50-meter monster the following year.

The Eagle of the Pacific was a resounding success, earning more than ¥100,000,00, but 1954 found Honda involved in a war film of a different type, that of a love story between the leader of a Japanese fighter squadron and a head nurse, both stationed in the South Pacific called *Farewell Rabaul*. Nine years after the end of World War II, there was a feeling for many Japanese to regard the past event with a certain nostalgia; there even a popular song called "The Rabaul Song." Honda tried to show the evil of war through the lives of people who were involved in it against their wills and of the sadness of civilians trapped by the war; Honda had many nice memories about making the movie and considered it to be one of his personal favorites.

Honda was now a hot property and Kimi did what she could to provide an environment where he could concentrate on his movie-making work. For example, Honda hated noise, so Kimi made certain he was in a quiet environment; she also took over all the troublesome issues that Honda didn't like, such as going to the bank or tax office (she later remembered that the only time he went to the post office was to drop off a postcard in the mail box). "When it came time for him to renew his contract with Toho," she told Shinsuke Nakajima years later, "the studio called *me* instead of *him* to take care of the paperwork! He even died without knowing how much he was actually being paid! He was only doing what he wanted to do, and that made me happy for him."

Honda's next film would be a "Lucky Seventh" and a project that was not only unique and unusual in the extreme but one that—had another not been cancelled—might never have been made at all.

Making "Radiation Visible"

When a proposed co-international project with Indonesia fell through at the last minute, producer Tanaka was left with a shooting schedule, a budget, a release date but no film. While browsing through a cinematic trade journal, he read about the phenomenal success of an American monster film released the previous year called *The Beast From 20,000 Fathoms* (1953), in which a prehistoric monster was revived from an atomic test and a film itself which came about due to the great success of the re-release of RKO's immortal *King Kong* in 1952. Finding the prospect of cashing-in on the new trend of monster movies tantalizing, Tanaka took the idea to Mori, who agreed to green light the project if Tsuburaya could handle the special effects.

Tanaka was taking a huge risk as nothing like a "credible" monster movie had ever been made in Japan—prior films involving monsters were usually explained away as either being ghost stories or dreams. In

43

his memoirs published in 1983, Tanaka remembered how he met with Tsuburaya, stressing the need for a scary monster to credibly appear in a serious film, "Otherwise," he told his special effects master, "I don't see how we can pull this off." For Tsuburaya, the project was a dream-come-true, as he had always wanted to make a monster film along the lines of *King Kong*. Now, 21 years later, he was being given the chance to do exactly that.

Tanaka's next step was to contact the director of the cancelled Indonesian project, Senkichi Taniguchi (at that point, the monster was conceived as a giant octopus attacking Japanese shipping in the Indian Ocean). Taniguchi passed on the project, finding the entire concept ludicrous. Tanaka now found himself without a director before choosing Honda, who had already helmed a number of films dealing with oceanic themes and whose star was undeniably on the rise.

As it happened, Honda was not terribly enthusiastic about directing a monster film either and brooded about it at home. "I think he was a little stressed at the time," Kimi told Yoshihiko Shibata years later. "When he came home, he didn't play with the children like he usually did, but instead stayed in his office and never really talked to me about it. Nevertheless, I heard a lot of rumors about the film; people were saying that it was a huge-scaled monster movie and they had never seen a movie like that before, but I didn't really ask him about it and just left him alone."

When various staff members and actors came to the house, Honda told them not to be embarrassed about making the movie, telling everyone that he was making the movie to make audiences think about what humans would do if something like a huge monster really appeared due to the effect of the atomic bomb. He stressed that—if they thought the idea of a monster film seemed silly—to resign from the project. For his part, Honda had every intention on making the movie with a serious tone.

As it happened, a real-life horror triggered Honda's total involvement with the film, telling Galbraith that: "The real inspiration (for the movie) was the nuclear incident." On March 1st, 1954, the United States Navy exploded the most powerful nuclear device ever created over the Bikini Atoll, containing an explosive power equal to 20 million tons of TNT—more than 1,000 times the destructive power of the atomic bomb dropped on Hiroshima—over the Bikini Atoll near the Marshall Islands. Eighty miles east of the explosion, a 140-ton Japanese tuna trawler ironically named *The Lucky Dragon No. 5* and its 23-member crew was covered in nuclear ash from the explosion. After several of the crewmembers became desperately ill, the captain ordered the ship to return to port, where shortly thereafter a crewmember died from radiation poisoning.

A huge public outcry followed as "*The Lucky Dragon* Incident" was considered by the Japanese as their third unwilling baptism by the Bomb. Inspired, Honda realized he could now make his monster movie while indirectly commenting on "*The Lucky Dragon* Incident" as well as making a statement on the evils of nuclear weapons and Japan's own civilian wartime experience. In the meantime, Tanaka changed the monster from an octopus to a huge reptile, a concept which delighted Honda. The monster would represent the American atomic bomb in what Honda called an attempt to make "radiation visible" (to reinforce this concept, Honda insisted the creature breath a ray infused with radiation).

Honda carefully avoided a direct reference to "*The Lucky Dragon* Incident," only hinting at it in the first scene when a fishing boat is wiped out by a symbolic representation of the Hiroshima explosion. Honda disclosed afterward that elucidating or moralizing in his movies was not his bag; the key was always to entertain the audience. If certain members were perceptive enough to get the symbolism of the nuclear connection, then great; if not, they could simply sit-back and enjoy themselves with the rest of the crowd.

Honda's unique approach resulted in a film that succeeded both as entertainment and as social commentary, and while not all viewers grasped the atomic bomb connection, they still found the compelling human drama and spectacular effects engaging enough to thoroughly enjoy the experience, one that was unique in the annals of Japanese filmmaking. The movie, eventually named Godzilla (*Gojira*), was a resounding success—over 33,000 people saw it when it opened in Toho's four major theatre on November 3rd, setting a premiere attendance record—and finished as one of the top ten moneymakers of 1954.

The Golden Years

With three hits in a row to his credit, Honda was now one of Japan's hottest directors, but after helming two intense war films and the somber *Godzilla*, he was given a change of pace, directing a light-comedy called *Love Makeup*, released in January of 1955. He then worked briefly on the story development of *The Invisible Man*, a horror film eventually directed by Motoyoshi Oda; in fact, Oda was given the assignment to direct Tanaka's hurriedly-conceived sequel to *Godzilla* released only five months later, *Godzilla's Counterattack*.

Meanwhile, the director of the first Godzilla film was on location in the Japan Alps, working on *Abominable Snowman*, a superb monster movie whose grim tone rivaled that of *Godzilla's*. Honda then switched gears again, directing another light comedy called *Crybaby*, released in June (*Snowman* premiered in August to modest business, falling far short of *Godzilla's* revenue).

Honda's first film in 1956 was *Young Tree* in January, followed by an independently-produced short film, *Night School*, released in April while *Goodbye to the People of Tokyo*—a short 61-minute film—was a June release. In August, an Americanized version of *Godzilla* entitled *Godzilla, King of the Monsters!* became the first film of Japanese origin to play in mainstream movie houses around-the-world to tremendous business, becoming the first of many Honda films to play outside of Japan. Honda's final film of 1956 was also his first in color, the remarkable *Radon: The Giant Monster From the Sky*, released in December.

Continuing to direct diverse subject matter was becoming commonplace for Honda, who had his busiest year in 1957 as he directed no-less than five feature-length films: *Good Luck to These Two* (February), *A Tea Picker's Song of Goodbye* (July), *A Rainbow Plays in My Heart* (August) and *A Person I Call My Sister* (September). In May of that year, an unusual picture played in Japanese theaters, one that had originally been produced by Toho and directed by Honda, now returning in an altered form from America with deleted scenes plus new footage starring an American actor named Raymond Burr. The film was the Americanized *Godzilla*, now playing in Japan under the title of *Godzilla, the Monster King*. Honda reportedly saw the film and enjoyed the experience (meanwhile, RKO Pictures distributed *Radon* in America as *Rodan! The Flying Monster*). Honda's final film assignment for the year was his first science-fiction film and his first made in the widescreen (1.33:1) format, the vibrant *The Defense Force of the Earth;* released in December, playing to over three and a-half million people.

By 1958, Honda's fantasy films were beginning to outstrip his human-interest stories and comedies. *A Song for a Bride* premiered in February, followed by Honda's first horror film, *The Beauty and the Liquid People*, released in June and playing to less than half a-million people. *Baran, the Giant Monster* was next; an odd film which utilized stock footage from earlier Godzilla films compressed to fit the widescreen format. The film looked every bit the convoluted product that it was and was released in October as a run-of-the-mill monster movie and it was not a great success. December would bring more bad news for Honda although he probably never knew about it, as his brilliantly-conceived *Abominable Snowman* was effectively hacked in-half by Distributors Corporation of America for the U.S. version called *Half-Human*.

Honda maintained his busy shooting schedule throughout 1959; after working briefly on a story treatment for *The Telegraphed Man* (later filmed by Jun Fukuda), Honda helmed three comedies: *An Echo Calls You* in January, *Inao—the Story of an Iron Arm* in March and *Seniors, Juniors, Co-Workers* in September (in May, *Defense Force* had found American distribution through RKO as *The Mysterians*). The director ended the decade with a splashy science-fiction epic called *The Great War in Space*, released in December, and although attendance was modest—with just over half-a-million viewers—five months later the film found its American release through Columbia Pictures as *Battle in Outer Space*.

In 1960 Honda directed two films, the first being *Sanbo, the Magic Waterwheel* (a Russian-Finnish production released in June where he supervised the Japanese actors dubbing the film), and the second the haunting *The First Gas Human Being*, released in December. However, while *Gas Human* played to only 250,000 people, Honda's next film would be his biggest success since *Godzilla*.

Turning 50 in 1961, Honda next directed the marvelous *Mothra*. Released in July, it was one of the director's signature works and another huge hit, with nine million people going to see it (*The Scarlet Man* was Honda's only other directorial effort that year, released just two months later). From that point on and for the next five years, Honda would exclusively be directing fantasy films.

Gorath, the Mysterious Star was a March release in 1962 and one of the finest science-fiction films ever made, as well as being a personal favorite of Honda's who considered Tsuburaya's effects-work to be the finest of his career, a sentiment shared by Tsuburaya's assistant on the film, Teruyoshi Nakano. However, business was relatively unspectacular, with only half-a-million people going to see it (nonetheless, Honda was glad to hear years later that the movie was highly regarded by audiences outside of Japan). Another Honda film that was highly regarded outside of Japan was *Mothra*, released to great American business through Columbia Pictures in May; yet another great international success was in the making in August, a comedy starring the cinema's two most colossal monsters and with a colossal budget of ¥5,000,000.

Released with great fanfare as Toho's 30th anniversary film, *King Kong vs. Godzilla* would be Honda's most-successfully financial film, grossing ¥350,000,000 during its initial run (it would be re-released a number of times—always playing to large audiences—author Guy Tucker estimated the film eventually made a profit of $1.5 *billion* worldwide). Over 11 million people went to see the film when it was first released, a record that still stands as the most-attendance ever for a Godzilla film. While location shooting around Mount Fuji, Honda took a bad step and fell, resulting in a broken arm and a strained neck. After staying at a hospital just long enough to be patched up, he was back at work on the set, directing with his arm in a sling.

In December of 1962, *Baran* found its American release four years after it had been made through Crown International as *Varan the Unbelievable*. In the meantime, dissatisfied with the lack of state-of-the-art effects equipment available at Toho, Tsuburaya visited Disney Studios. After given a tour of the facilities and introduced to a mechanical marvel called the Oxberry 1900 Optical Printer, Tsuburaya persuaded the Fuji TV Company to purchase one for his use; with it, the quality of Tsuburaya's composites improved dramatically. It would mark a significant beginning, for in April of 1963, Tsuburaya formed his own television company called "Tsuburaya Special Techniques Productions," which would develop and produce fantasy and science fiction television shows. In June, Universal Pictures distributed *King Kong vs. Godzilla* worldwide to tremendous business.

Honda's next three films were among the greatest of his career, beginning with his finest horror film, the morbid *Matango*, released in August. The film did not do brisk business in Japan, playing to only half-a-million attendees and sadly was never released theatrically in America. The film was not highly-regarded by Japanese critics—Honda half-jokingly commenting to editor Shinsuke Nakajima years later that the reason for the film's commercial failure was due to the lack of critical appreciation. "Unless your film is caught in the critics' net," he told Nakajima, "it will be washed away into history."

Matango was followed by Honda's finest fantasy film, *Submarine Warship*, released in December, where it was the hit of the Christmas season. This triumphant trio of films was completed in April of 1964 with the release of what many consider to be the high-water mark of the Godzilla series: *Mothra vs. Godzilla*. Playing to over three and a-half million people, it was undeniably an acceptable figure but still a huge drop from the enormous revenues earned by the comedic *King Kong vs. Godzilla*. In America in May, Brenco Pictures distributed *Gas Human Being* as *The Human Vapor*, while Columbia Pictures released *Gorath, the Mysterious Star* as simply *Gorath*.

The Production Line

Following *Mothra vs. Godzilla*, Honda directed a film about an impersonal alien monster called *Dogora, the Space Monster*, an August release. In September, American International Pictures (AIP) distributed *Mothra vs. Godzilla* in America as *Godzilla vs. the Thing*, one of the last Honda films to premiere in first-run American movie houses. Honda completed his directorial assignments for 1964 with *Three Giant Monsters—The Greatest Battle on Earth*, a film that would mark a severe shift in the Godzilla series, as well as introducing a dynamic new monster: King Ghidorah (Ghidrah). The film—with its intentional moments of monster humor—did slightly better business than had *Mothra vs. Godzilla*, with over 4,320,000 people going to see it; an indication to Tanaka that meant comedy and frenetic monster footage would set the future tone of the series.

In March of 1965, AIP distributed *Submarine Warship* in America as *Atragon*, while in September, Continental Distributing issued *Three Giant Monsters* as *Ghidrah, the Three-Headed Monster*. At the same time, pressure was being put on Toho by other Japanese studios producing their own monster films—particularly the Daiei Company—when it released a film about a monster turtle called *The Monster Gamera* in November of 1965. The film did tremendous business, but of greater significance to Tanaka was the fact that the monster was seen as a champion of children. After writing an essay called "The Fascination of Make-Believe Movies" for the February issue of *Toho Movies*, Honda directed the first Toho monster movie ever to be made in collaboration with an American production company (AIP), with the August release of the impressive *Frankenstein vs. Baragon, the Subterranean Monster*.

The concept of aliens taking over the Earth was now being melded into the Godzilla series with the December release of *The Great Monster War* which did fine business, playing to 3,780,000 moviegoers; however, as with *Three Giant Monsters*, a number of scenes in *Monster War* were specifically tailored for a juvenile audience.

Parting Company

In 1965, frustrated at both the direction his career and the Godzilla series were taking—and with no other work being offered to him—Honda asked to be released from his contractual obligations with Toho. From that point on he essentially freelanced, although he would only direct movies for Toho. The break was apparently an amiable one sanctioned by Tanaka, who was becoming concerned with having but one director exclusively helming the Godzilla films (there could have been other reasons, such as the steadily-dwindling profits and perhaps a desire on the producer's part to have a director with new ideas and a greater enthusiasm for the series).

Although leaving his beloved Toho was a difficult decision for Honda to make after so many years, he stated later that he was actually happy to get away: "Frankly," he told David Milner, "I was having a hard time humanizing Godzilla the way Toho wanted...I was even hesitant to let Mothra act as a mediator between Godzilla and Rodan in *The Greatest Giant Monster Battle on Earth*; it certainly would have been difficult for me to direct *Son of Godzilla*." As it happened, the next two Godzilla films were directed by Jun Fukuda, taking a different tone than had Honda's; more-lively, less-serious and playing to better houses: *Godzilla, Ebirah, Mothra—Big Duel in the South Seas* was released in December of 1966 and was seen by over four million attendees, while *Monster Island's Decisive Battle: Son of Godzilla* was released in December of 1967, playing to just over three million people.

Honda did direct two films in 1966, the entertaining but emotionally-hollow *Frankenstein's Monsters: Sanda vs. Gairah*, then—after helming ten consecutive monster films—Honda was assigned his 40th film, a sentimental comedy called *Will You Marry Me?* A low-budget affair, it nonetheless guaranteed a good profit, since it starred the then popular duo of Yuzo Kayama and Yoko Naito (Kayama had appeared in a series of enormously popular "Young Guy" films, always playing his trademark guitar; although, in *Marry Me*, he was *sans* guitar). Released in October, it would be the last non-fantasy film Honda would ever direct.

In 1966, Honda wrote an essay on the interesting topic of "How to Comfort Women" for the April issue of *Movie Art*. That June, an interview between Honda and actress Kumi Mizuno was published in *Toho Movies*, while in July, *Frankenstein vs. Baragon, the Subterranean Monster*, was released in America as *Frankenstein Conquers the World*. That year also saw the debut of "Ultra Q" by Tsuburaya Productions, a 28-episode TV series that ran from January 2nd through July 3rd, followed by the July 17, 1966 premiere about a superhero named "Ultraman." This television show would become Tsuburaya Productions' most-enduring legacy, running on Japanese television for many years and spawning numerous television sequels and films.

During this period, Tsuburaya dropped by Honda's home to ask if the director would join him at Tsuburaya Productions as a management executive. The request put Honda in a difficult position; while he respected Tsuburaya immensely and treasured their partnership, he still felt obligated to the studio that had given him the opportunity to earn a living. There was one other issue as well, as Honda still wanted to make movies and knew he could not effectively balance being both a movie maker and a production executive.

As a result, Honda consequently declined Tsuburaya's invitation. It was an awkward and uncomfortable decision; Tsuburaya was obviously disappointed in Honda's decision, but for Honda, it was a tremulous turning-point: In failing to join his friend's courageous example, he had failed himself. As a result, the relationship took a hit, and although the greatest directorial team of live-action and special effects in the history of the cinema would continue to work together, it would never be the same between them.

Toho's 35th Anniversary film, *King Kong's Counterattack*, was released in July of 1967 and marked yet another departure of a treasured association for Honda, as he parted company with his cinematographer Hajime Koizumi, who had filmed Honda's genre movies since *Defense Force* over ten years earlier (Honda never elaborated on his decision not to use Koizumi for his future films, but intimated that Toho pressured him to work with a newer team of technicians). With some reluctance, Honda began his association with the medium of television that year, directing two episodes of a show called "The Newly Weds." Honda found the small screen format not to his liking—but the alternative was becoming less-than desirable.

June of 1968 saw the American release of *King Kong's Counterattack* through Universal Pictures as *King Kong Escapes*, while in July, Honda wrote an essay called "Making the Man of the Future" for *Toho Movies*. "I think I'm making too many monster movies," Honda glumly told a French film interviewer that same year, "but that's because of the direction Toho Studios is taking." As it happened, Honda directed only one film in 1968 and it was—naturally—another monster movie: *All Monsters Attack*, an all-out, all-star monster epic released in August, playing to over two and a-half million people (Aip premiered the film in America the following May as *Destroy All Monsters!*).

End of an Era

In July of 1969, the loony *Latitude Zero: Big Military Operation* was released to good business, a film marking the second collaboration between Honda and his new special effects supervisor—Tsuburaya's longtime cinematographer, Teisho (Sadamasa) Arikawa. Honda considered the project to have been mentally taxing; one possible reason for this was that Eiji Tsuburaya had not only been Honda's favorite effects man, but he was also a trusted friend, a revered partner and a source of inspiration (this despite the fact they were polar opposites as personalities: Honda was a modest company man while Tsuburaya had an enormous ego and an independent nature). For anyone hoping to step into the *maestro's* shoes and replicate his effects work was one thing, but expecting him to work on the same personal and professional level with Honda was too much to ask for.

As it turned out, the contemporary combination of Honda/ Arikawa did not click nearly as well as the Honda/Tsuburaya one had (Teruyoshi Nakano—who would soon replace Arikawa as effects director—explained that Tsuburaya was an artist, while Arikawa merely a technician). This could have explained why Honda personally directed the special effects sequences on his next film, *Godzilla, Minya, Gabara: All Giant Monsters Attack*, an odd film where the monster scenes took place entirely in a boy's imagination. The film premiered in December of 1969 and played to less-than one and a-half million people, the lowest-attended film in the series up to that point. To keep busy, Honda continued to direct television shows, helming episodes 5 and 12 of a series called "Be Strong, Men and Husbands!"

Considering just how busy Tsuburaya had been with his television productions and Honda's earlier rejection of the invitation to leave Toho, it was a surprised Honda who received an unexpected visit from his former special effects supervisor during one November afternoon in 1969. Tsuburaya wished to go over details for his upcoming Mitsubishi Pavilion to be displayed at the World Exposition (Expo 1970) held in Osaka, an exhibit requiring nothing less than a storm and an erupting volcano. Tsuburaya was heading the project team which included future Godzilla film director Yoshimitsu Banno.

In his poignant 1970 essay "The Magician of Special Effects," Honda wrote of Tsuburaya:

> He sat down on a big stool besides the TV in the living room and said, with his usual genial countenance, "You know, the work for the Expo's Museum of the Future is finally getting underway. In March, you and I can talk about our next film project." He then he told me about a dream he had when he was a boy. "Let's make a film about airplanes! It will be a film that will give children a

chance to dream *big*, something amusing and fantastic and not just about monsters destroying buildings." I was all for it. "The movie business is now a difficult one," Tsuburaya sighed, "But, we'll do our best." His words still linger in my ears.

What Tsuburaya neglected to mention was that he had earlier asked director Taniguichi to helm the project, which was to be a Japanese version of the English film, *Those Magnificent Men in Their flying Machines* from 1965. It was only after Taniguichi declined the offer that Tsuburaya decided to call on Honda. The two men parted, never realizing it was their final meeting. In August, Tsuburaya's health declined and he was hospitalized; nevertheless, three months later, his company had commenced production on a new, one-hour, 13-part TV series called "Mighty Jack." Honda never visited Tsuburaya in the hospital, feeling that if he saw him, they would both be talking bitterly about their serious concerns over Japan's film industry. Even when Tsuburaya was relocated shortly thereafter to his county home in Ito, Izu, Honda was not overly-concerned over his health, having been told that he was on the mend and looking forward to working with him in March.

It thus came as a great shock to all concerned when the New Year of 1970 began on a disastrous note, that Eiji Tsuburaya—known with great affection by his staff as *Oyaji* ("Pop") when not within earshot—died from complications of pneumonia at his home on January 25th at the age of 68. Honda (who would himself turn 60 just four months later) learned about Tsuburaya's death while at home the next day and hurried over to the studio to confirm the terrible news. Although Tsuburaya's death was not entirely unexpected—after all, he was up in years, kept up a demanding work schedule and was a chain-smoking diabetic—it nonetheless devastated moral at the studio.

Honda could not believe it himself, but found comfort in the fact that Tsuburaya had died peacefully in his sleep, no doubt while dreaming about his next project. "He should have lived longer," Honda lamented in his essay. "Our teamwork is over. It's like there is a big void that no one else can fill. It will take a lot of time and effort for these talented successors who were trained by him to be able to fill this gap...We've lost the irreplaceable man."

In May of that year, AIP released *The Giant Monster War* as *Monster Zero* (co-billed with *Sanda Against Gairah*, now called *War of the Gargantuas*) to American audiences. Apparently, Honda still had issues dealing with the passing of his longtime associate, as he wrote a memorial essay for the March issue of the *Houen* magazine, as well as another article entitled "Tsuburaya, the Magician of Special Effects," printed in the April issue of *Syunju Liberal Arts* magazine. Honda's next film, *Gezora, Ganime, Kameba: Decisive Battle! Giant Monsters of the South Seas*, was released in August of 1970 and was a straightforward monster film literally carried by the actors; it also marked the last time that Arikawa—who never completely won over Honda's confidence—would ever supervise the effects work for a Toho film. Arikawa's departure was followed by yet another, when Toho declined to offer Honda any further film assignments.

For Honda, it was a mixed blessing, as he later estimated he lost ten pounds on every film he had been working on of late. In December, one of these films—*Latitude Zero: Big Military Operation*—was released in America as *Latitude Zero*.

Anticlimax

In May of 1971, Honda turned 60 years of age. If there was no longer any work to be found directing feature films, there was always television. As if to somehow make amends to his departed friend—and perhaps aware of his own mortality—Honda became actively involved with Tsuburaya Productions, directing no-less than four episodes of the TV fantasy series "Ultra Man Returns," as well as the first two episodes of "Mirror Man."

During the Spring of that year, Honda received an unexpected phone call from of all people, Tomoyuki Tanaka; not to direct a film, but to inspect one as the latest film in the Godzilla series, *Godzilla vs. Hedorah*, was nearing post-production. Tanaka was recuperating in a hospital from a recent illness and was asking Honda to check on the progress being made by *Hedorah's* director, Yoshimitsu Banno. The film's grim theme revolved around industrial pollution and was a transitional film from the lighthearted fare that had preceded it in recent years. Banno was also a new hand at directing and Tanaka requested Honda view the film's rough-cut in case he felt any scenes needed to be re-shot.

After viewing some of Banno's footage, Honda contacted Tanaka and suggested doing retakes for a number of scenes, but Tanaka replied that he preferred Honda direct new footage rather than re-shoot footage already in the can; Banno also balked at the idea of re-shooting any of his scenes and instead requested Honda simply tell Tanaka that only one or two new scenes would be added (it is not known which scenes were directed by Honda or which he felt should be redone; however, it seems plausible that Honda may have directed the scene where men playing mahjong are inundated by the Smog Monster's lethal slime, keeping with Honda's recurrent theme of "playtime is over." Additional footage, such as a boy reacting in horror at the remains of Hedorah's onslaught and a women's' aerobic class suddenly taken ill by Hedorah's passing, seem likely to have been filmed by Honda, who typically stressed the impact monsters had on ordinary citizens).

Caught in the middle, Honda duly reported to a satisfied Tanaka, who assumed the matter had been resolved until weeks later when he saw the finished film, which involved drugs, reckless youths and even a scene where Godzilla flew in the air. Horrified, Tanaka not only banned Banno from directing any future Godzilla films but felt the entire *debacle* could have been avoided if Honda had only been more stringent in his supervision.

Honda continued to direct television shows, helming the 51st and final episode of "Ultraman Returns," as well as four episodes of "Emergency Commandment 10-4, 10-10," plus five shows for the "Thundermask" series. In March, the Honda-directed premier episode of "Mirror Man" was released in theatres as part of a "Toho Champion Film Festival," while in December, Maron Films issued the stateside release of *All Giant Monsters Attack*—re-titled *Godzilla's Revenge*—paired on a double-bill with an English horror film called *Island of the Burning Damned*. Not long after, Honda was shocked to learn that his friend Akira Kurosawa—who had been suffering from ill health, exhaustion, disappointment and depression—had attempted suicide.

After *Hedorah's* release, Tanaka handed the directorial reigns of the Godzilla series back into the safe hands of Jun Fukuda, but by the time of 1972's *Godzilla vs. Gigan*, the days of large profits were coming to a close. Budgets were being slashed and additional cost-cutting programs were initiated as Haruo Nakajima—who would soon hang up his Godzilla costume—told Ed Godziszewski: "Toho Film Company had 280 actors around the time of *Godzilla vs. Gigan* and the company policy then suddenly changed; they fired all 280 actors." To make matters worse, audience attendance was continuing to dwindle due to television.

In 1973, Toho released *The Submersion of Japan*—with the special effects unit now under the official supervision of Teruyoshi Nakano—and was a huge hit, but neither it nor its sequel, *Catastrophe 1999* (released the following year), were offered to Honda. That same year, "Zone, the Meteor Man" became Honda's final foray into television as he directed episodes three and four (which featured guest appearances by Godzilla), 12, 13, 18, 19, 23 and 24. During this time, Honda wrote an essay called "Memories of Godzilla" for the book "Eiji Tsuburaya, A Legend in the Japanese Film Industry." Then, on September 21st, Kajiro Yamamoto, the director of 57 films who taught Honda the directorial ropes and his senior by nine years, passed away at the age of 71 from cirrhosis of the liver.

Swansong

By the middle of the 1970s, the Godzilla film series had reached its *nadir*. After directing *Gigan*, Jun Fukuda helmed *Godzilla vs. Megalon* (1973) and *Godzilla vs. MechaGodzilla* (1974), films that fell far-short of the high standards previously set by Honda and Tsuburaya. Admittedly, the team of Fukuda/Nakano had to make do with far-less than had the earlier team, as in addition to budget cuts were other cost-cutting factors such as filming effects footage in landscaped-miniatures to save money by not having to build elaborate miniature cities, as well as hiring no-name actors and using a substantial amount of stock footage from earlier films.

Perhaps this was why that—four and-a-half years after having been put out to pasture—Honda was asked to return to the director's chair to helm 1975's *MechaGodzilla's Counterattack*. Despite giving the series a certain *panache* it had been lacking for so long as well as having the "tragic hope" and "doomed optimism" that is woven through so much of Honda's work, *MechaGodzilla's Counterattack*, released in March of 1975, was a dismal failure, playing to less than one million people; the lowest-attendance ever for a Godzilla film (directed by the same man who had earlier helmed the series' biggest success, *King Kong vs. Godzilla*). It was the last full-length feature film Honda would ever direct and an inglorious end to an often-exceptional film career.

After *Counterattack*, Tanaka finally felt the time had come to part ways with Honda—which to Honda meant only one thing—if he would not be directing films for Toho, he would not be directing films for anyone else, telling Galbraith years later that: "Toho stopped bringing me any new projects. You see, I generally didn't develop projects myself, so when *Counterattack* was completed, that was it for me." The ending of his association with Toho was, while not a total surprise, no-less bitter for a man who had hoped to be making movies until the end of his life, instead witnessing the end of his career.

Even so, Honda's love and fascination for the fantasy film genre was still very evident, as that same year he wrote an article called "The Fun of Special Effects" for a pamphlet promoting *Counterattack*, as well as participating in a roundtable discussion held at the Second Japan Special Effects Show in Setagaya. In December of 1977, Tanaka—inspired by George Lucas' *Star Wars*—produced a wild-and-wooly space fantasy called *Planet Warfare* (*The War in Space*), and although tailor-made for the talents of the man who had directed *The Great War in Space* and *War of the Monsters*, Tanaka assigned the project to Fukuda.

In the summer of 1978, Bob Conn Enterprises distributed the last Honda film ever to play theatrically in America: *MechaGodzilla's Counterattack*, now called *Terror of MechaGodzilla*. Later that year, Honda wrote an article entitled "Godzilla's Surroundings" for the book *Godzilla, the Star of Special Effects*, as well as editing a research book titled, "Super Special Effects." May 14, 1979, saw the death of the man who recommended Honda join P.C.L. Studios: Iwao Mori; he was joined in death less than four months later by Honda's longtime art director, Takeo Kita.

That same year, Honda and Mimi moved out of their large home in Tokyo to a modest two-story dwelling in Seijo, conveniently located within walking distance of a golf course. There, Honda spent most of his free time golfing with his new neighbor—Akira Kurosawa—and it was during one of those golf sessions the two men decided to work together again for the first time in over three decades, beginning with Honda working as Chief of Production on Kurosawa's *Kagemusya*, released in 1980. When a French film writer asked Honda why a director of Godzilla films was working with Akira Kurosawa, Honda bristled a bit before answering: "I don't *have* to work with him if I don't *want* to, but Mr. Kurosawa prefers to work with me. I also feel good about working with him and will help him in any way I can."

It was also in 1980 that a film directed by Honda 17 years earlier was making the rounds: *Mothra vs. Godzilla*, drawing in nearly three million people, the most attendance for a Godzilla film since *Son of Godzilla* (the attendance figure was filed away by Tanaka for further reference). In the meantime, Honda submitted to Toho an idea for a film on the subject of the 10th Century Japanese folktale Princess Kaguya called *Princess of the Moon*; the picture was eventually made five years later but without Honda's involvement. Honda also told writer Milner about another proposed project called *The Fishermen*: "I wrote a synopsis and it was going to be a semi-documentary drama. It was mainly about the younger generation wanting to leave Okinawa for life in the big city." Toho cancelled the project after the synopsis had been submitted, but the picture was eventually made by another studio as a straightforward documentary.

After turning 70 years old in 1981, Honda appeared with one of his favorite actors, Akihiko Hirata (then 54), on a talk show filmed at the Amateur Special Effects Festival in Nakano, Tokyo. The following year, Honda returned to the festival as presenter and judge for an independent film contest. On February 11, 1982, another of Honda's favorite actors, Takeshi Shimura, died at the age of 77.

In 1983, Honda contributed an article entitled "Special Effects and Me" for the book *Toho Special Effects Encyclopedia*, as well as a recommendation introduction for the book *Monster Godzilla*, written by Shigeru Kayamoa. On August 5th, actor Hirata hosted a premiere recording of Akira Ifukube's "Special Effect Symphonies in Hibiya," with Honda appearing to make a brief speech (sadly, Hirata died less than one year later of lung cancer). The following day, on August 6th—the 38th anniversary of the Hiroshima bombing—*Godzilla* and *War of the Monsters* were reissued to theaters as part of another Toho Monster Film Festival, followed by the August 11th re-release of *Three Giant Monsters*.

Meanwhile, former Honda assistant director Kohji Hashimoto—who previously had cut his cinematic teeth assisting Honda on *King Kong vs. Godzilla*—made his directorial debut on Toho's big-budgeted science-fiction film, *Sayonara Jupiter*, released in October; the film was a commercial failure, another fact noted by Tanaka. In November, Toho continued to rake in profits due in greater part to the efforts of those long-since departed or cast adrift, when three of Honda's greatest films: *Godzilla*, *Radon* and *Mothra* were released as part of yet another film festival. In December, Honda wrote an essay called "Young Fans are Hoping for the Next Japanese Special Effects Film;" as it happened, one was in the making at that very moment.

Twilight

After a nine-year absence from the Big Screen, Tanaka decided it was time to revitalize the Godzilla series and actually contacted Honda regarding the possibility of returning to direct what would eventually be known as *The Return of Godzilla (Godzilla 1984)*; but Honda by this time had had enough and politely declined the invitation. Tanaka then reluctantly went back to Hashimoto, who then visited Honda for a moral-boosting pep talk. Whatever the two men discussed did the trick, for when *Return of Godzilla* was released in December of 1984, over three million people went to see it; the movie grossed $11 million, the most for a Godzilla film since *King Kong vs. Godzilla*. To Tanaka, this meant that the Godzilla series could continue without Honda's involvement; as it was, Honda was already occupied, working for Kurosawa as First Assistant Director on *Ran*, released in 1985.

In 1984, Honda organized and produced the release of the 11th in a series of video tapes called "Toho Monsters, Special Effects Encyclopedia," in which he was interviewed at length by Toshio Sakai; the interview then appeared in print form for *Spaceship* magazine, covering Volumes 18 through 22. In 1985, another in-depth interview with Honda appeared in Volumes 2 thru 5 of the magazine, *Toho Special Effects Films*, while in December, Honda edited Toshio Sakai's book, *The Godzilla Collection*. Honda then returned to the screen as an actor for the first time since doubling for Mifune in *Stray Dog* when he appeared in his first credited role in a surprise cameo near the end of a 1987 comedy called *Come Back Hero*, directed by Yarutokya Yaruze.

The year of 1998 began with tragic news for Honda as his most-profound screenwriter, Takeshi Kimura, suffocated to death alone and helpless from an obstruction in his throat at the age of 76. Two years later, Honda contributed an essay called "Adolescent Restraint" for Vol. Two of the *Akira Kurosawa Album*, while that same year made another cameo appearance in the film, *Summer with the Foreigners*. On May 22nd, Honda participated in a roundtable discussion called "Monster Movies and the Atomic Bomb" presented by the Akira Kurosawa Research Group, the contents of which were published in the group's magazine on June 31, 1992.

Honda then wrote an article called "Godzilla, Sold to America for $25,000," for the February 1989 issue of *Bungei Shunju* magazine, as well as writing a preface for Yuji Kaita's portfolio, *Monster Caricature*. November was marked by yet another significant passing, that of Honda's most-commercially successful screenwriter, Shinichi Sekizawa, who died at the age of 72. In December came the release of the latest Godzilla film, *Godzilla vs. Biollante*, which played to mixed reviews and poor business (Honda did not think much of the film himself, believing that Koichi Kawakita—now helming the special effects—had missed several opportunities).

Before the year was over, Honda assisted Kurosawa on *Dreams*, released in 1990, both directing and writing "The Tunnel" and "Mount Fuji in Red" sequences. In the "Tunnel" sequence, Honda finally put on film a dream he had had for a number of years, that of a platoon commander facing the ghosts of those who had served under him, wiped-out on his careless orders (Mimi remembered being incredibly impressed when she saw the segment). "Mount Fuji in Red" would be Honda's last cinematic treatise on the dangers of radiation in a sequence involving an accident at a nuclear power plant as a man attempts to rescue a family before it is too late—significantly, the family consisted of a mother and her children, reminiscent of the doomed family that cowered under the flying embers in *Godzilla*.

In 1990, Honda assisted Kurosawa on *Rhapsody in August*, released in 1991, writing the script and filming the location work with his typically-understated brilliance. The segment which involved a lingering crane shot showing ants crawling up a tree reemphasized Honda's love and respect of the natural world and was fittingly his final directorial effort, capping off a cinematic career that had begun over half-a-century earlier. Honda then wrote the first of eight essays called "Why Movies," for a community film magazine called *Gomoku Movie Emails*.

Turning 80 in 1991, Honda wrote yet another essay for the March issue of *Novel Club* magazine; that same year he was interviewed by Youji Yamamoto for the June issue of *Cinematography Weekly*. Honda once again sat in as an audience member watching the latest Godzilla film, *Godzilla vs. King Ghidorah*, which opened to theaters in December. The film was far-better received than *Biollante*, but Honda was once again unimpressed; this time with what he saw as a lack of integrity in the performances of the younger actors.

Despite his advanced age, Honda answered yet another invitation to give a lecture, this time for the "Furuyu Movie Festival" in Fuji Town, Saga. Honda's seemingly boundless energy and love of film was again brought to Tanaka's attention, who again considered hiring Honda to direct the next Godzilla film—then in preproduction—*Godzilla vs. MechaGodzilla*.

In 1992, Honda assisted Kurosawa for the last time on the director's 30th film, *Madadayo*, released in 1993. Honda was responsible for helming the second-unit location shots of Post-War Japan (filmed in Gotemba, west of Tokyo); the sets were specially-constructed to show the aftereffects of the devastating fire raids brought about by the American Air Force, another theme Honda had expounded upon in his *Godzilla* 38 years earlier (the film's title is a response given by a professor in answer to a toast that asked—since he was nearing the end of his career—if he was now ready to die. The response translates as "Not yet," a belief that Kurosawa and Honda both obviously shared). Honda was then interviewed by Hisashi Inoue for the February issue of *Reading Stories* and was the subject of a research book published in September written by Naofumi Higuchi.

In December of 1992, David Milner visited Honda at his home for an interview for *Cult Movies* magazine. "What first struck me about Honda," Milner wrote many years later for a website created about the director in 2008, "was that instead of the elderly and perhaps somewhat frail man I was expecting meet...I was being introduced to a very energetic individual dressed in a sweat suit who seemed like he was ready to go jogging and could have run circles around me!" That same month, the newest Godzilla film, *Godzilla vs. Mothra*, was an enormous hit, making more money than any Godzilla film ever had before (over four million people went to see it, but whether or not Honda was among them is unknown).

The year ended with an "official rumor" that Tanaka was seriously considering having Honda return to the director's chair for the next film in the series, eventually released in 1993, as *Godzilla vs. MechaGodzilla*. The rumor came as a surprise to many—especially Honda, flattered that he was even being considered for the project; however, whether or not the 81-year-old director would have had the stamina to direct his first full-length feature film in nearly 18 years would become a mute point two months later. Honda gave another interview, published in Volume Seven of the "Godzilla vs. Mothra" issue of the *Toho Special Effect Movie Series* magazine, published in January. It would be the last interview Honda would ever give.

An "Uncrowned King"

For the past several years, Honda had been suffering from respiratory problems—not surprisingly as he had been an inveterate cigarette smoker for most of his adult life—a difficulty he typically-endured without much complaint. However, the problem had now become so severe that Honda finally checked himself into a hospital late one Tuesday evening on February 28th. Shortly after being admitted, the attendant nurse was so alarmed by Honda's condition that she immediately confined him to a bed before leaving to get an oxygen tank; but, by the time she returned, it was too late. Ishiro Honda had died of respiratory failure, typically without making a fuss.

The following day, Japanese newspapers reported his passing, and on March 6th Honda's nondenominational funeral—organized by Toho—was held in the Setagaya Temple. The first to pay his respects was Honda's longtime cinematographer Hajime Koizumi, but the vast majority of attendees were actors, which would have delighted Honda. Among those speaking in tribute was Akira Kurosawa, who also wrote an accurate dedication on Honda's tombstone: "In memory of a man who loved motion pictures all his life."

On March 11th, Asahi Television aired a memorial program on "M10," and on April 17th the last film Honda ever worked on—*Madadayo*—was released to theaters. The following May, *Stray Dog* was released on Video Laser Disc; the notes Honda wrote for the jacket cover became his posthumous manuscript. In a touching testimonial, director Nobuhiko Obayashi used a photograph of Honda to represent a departed grandfather for his film *Samurai Kids*, released that summer. In December, a memorial message written by Teruyoshi Nakano and Tomoharu Kajida appeared in Vol. 8 of the *Toho Special Effect Movie Series* called "Godzilla vs. MechaGodzilla," while a previously-unreleased interview with the director appeared in the "MechaGodzilla" issue of the *Godzilla Encyclopedia* magazine.

In 1994, a special film called *Japanese Movie Directors, Vol. 17, Ishiro Honda, Parts I through III* was shown in Sangenjyaya City, the same city where Honda had spent many happy hours as a youth watching movies. In December, a collection of various interviews done with Honda were published in the book *Godzilla and My Movie Life*. In the book, Mimi Honda had this to say about the man she called an "uncrowned king," telling Shiro Kimijima:

> It's very strange—only after my husband passed away did I realize the impact of his work. Godzilla was the first Japanese film to earn a lot of money overseas, he never mentioned that kind of stuff to me! He left me with a lot of memories and I am happy to see that so many people still remember him. After his death, many people have called and visited me and others have sent me many books and magazines about him from overseas; foreign television stations and publishers have come to interview me as well. So many people were inspired by his *Godzilla* and then entered the film industry because of it. My husband led a very fulfilling life.

SECTION II: "THE TRUTH IS THE TRUTH!"

GODZILLA (1954)
(GODZILLA, KING OF THE MONSTERS!)

ABOMINABLE SNOWMAN (1955)
(HALF-HUMAN)

GODZILLA (1954)
(GOJIRA)
GODZILLA, KING OF THE MONSTERS!

Cast & Credits

Film Register No. 1450
Release Date: November 3, 1954
Running Time: 97 minutes

Staff: Producer: Tomoyuki Tanaka; Director, Ishiro Honda; Original Story: Shigeru Kayama; Screenplay: Takeo Murata, Ishiro Honda; Director of Photography: Masao Tamai; Art Director: Takeo Kita; Set Design: Satoshi Chuko; Sound Recording: Hishashi Shimonaga; Lighting: Choshiro Ishii; Music: Akira Ifukube; Assistant Director: Koji Kajita; Editor: Yasnuobu Taira; Sound Arrangement: Ichiro Minawa; Processing: Toho Laboratory; Technical Assistance: Maritime Safety Bureau; Production Manager: Teruo Maki; Planner: Iwao Mori; Still Photographer: Issei Tanaka; Processing: Kinuta Laboratory, Ltd.; Special Effects Techniques: Director: Eiji Tsuburaya; Matte Processing: Hiroshi Mukoyama; Art: Akira Watanabe; Lighting: Kuichiro Kishida.

Cast: Akira Takarada (Hideto Ogata); Momoko Kochi (Emiko Yamane); Akihiko Hirata (Dr. Daisuke Serizawa); Takashi Shimura (Dr. Kyohei Yamane); Fuyuki Murakami (Dr. Tanabe); Sachio Sakai (Reporter Hagiwara); Toranosuke Ogawa (President of Nankai Shipping Company); Ren Yamamoto (Masaji); Miki (Kan) Hayashi (Diet Committee Chairman); Seijiro Onda (Diet Member Mr. Oyama); Takeo Oikawa (JSDF Chief); Keiji Sakakida (Oto Island Mayor Inada); Toyoaki Suzuki (Shinkichi); Kokuten Kodo (Elderly Oto Island Fisherman); Kin Sugai (Diet Member Ms. Ozawa); Tamae Sengo (Young Mother); Shizuko Azuma (Woman on Train); Tsuruko Mano (Shinkichi's Mother); Tadashi Okabe (Dr. Tanabe's Assistant); Kiyoshi Kanda (Man on Train); Ren Imaizumi (NSC Radio Section Chief); Masaaki Tachibana (Announcer on Tower); Ichiro Tai (TV Announcer); Yasuhisa Tsutsumi (Oto Island Villager); Jiro Suzukawa (Oto Island Villager); Saburo Iketani (Newscaster on Boat); Katsumi Tezuka (Newspaper Editor/Godzilla); Haruo Nakajima (Newspaper Staff/Power Substation Engineer/Godzilla).

The Film

No single chapter in any one book can fully cover the story of the making of *Godzilla*—a subject worthy of a book in itself—and whose circumstances surrounding its creation as fascinating as the film itself. Working from an original story by Shigeru Kayama and co-writing the screenplay with Takeo Murata, Honda wove a brilliantly-crafted tale focusing more on a scientist tortured by his horrific invention than on the monster itself (indeed; the film could be more-accurately be titled, *The Betrayal of Dr. Serizawa*).

Parallels to the movie's inspiration can be seen early-on, most-notably in a direct reference to *The Lucky Dragon No. 5* as a life-preserver on the *Eiko-Maru's* railing reads: *"Eiko-Maru No. 5."* And although all of the ship's crew will perish, Honda places particular emphasis on the plight of the radio operator, as it was *Lucky Dragon's* radio operator Aikichi Kuboyama who died from radiation poisoning on September 23, six months after the Bikini detonation and less than two months before the film's premiere.

Yet, even though the film's title character wreaks havoc and kills thousands, Honda insisted the monster be construed as an innocent and tragic creature inadvertently created by man's impetuous use of atomic power. To lend it realism, the creature reacts realistically to stimuli as any animal would: To the sounds of a fire-engine siren, the sight of birds in an aviary and to the various violent barricades it encounters, destroying only when attacked or threatened (Honda suggested that the creature's roar sound like an air-raid siren to emphasize its connection to the fire raids that devastated Japan near the end of the war).

Kayama's original story contained odd and eccentric characters, but Murata and Honda took Kayama's story and fleshed-out the characters by giving them purpose and meaning, filling the frames with breakdowns, conflicts, contrasts, flashbacks and ironies woven throughout; as we leave one thread of the plot we pick up another to follow. While certain character elements were borrowed from *Beast From 20,000 Fathoms* (such as having an elder paleontologist and his young female assistant) and special effects sequences directly inspired from *King Kong* (the monster breaks through a barrier, destroys a commuter train and dies tragically in a fall), *Godzilla* is a highly-original work without precedent and not an easy film to define: Part documentary, part social commentary, part allegory and part monster movie (when a young woman mocks Odo (Oto) Island's patriarch of the Godzilla legend, the old man—in a moment repeated in many a Honda film—warns the young disbeliever not to mock the ancient beliefs..

Looking back, it seems clear that Tsuburaya's entire career was at stake with *Godzilla*; after all, he had for years been trying to raise the quality of Japanese cinema's special effects level to as close as possible with the West—now came the time to prove that he could. *Godzilla* was indeed a dream assignment come true, but had Tsuburaya failed there may well have been another suicide connected with the film—and it wouldn't have been on-screen.

The proof in Tsuburaya's pudding was the monster's second, apocalyptic attack on Tokyo—a virtual recreation of the Tokyo fire-raid that took place on March 9, 1945 that killed over 100,000 people—in a complicated effects sequence lasting nearly 15 minutes and incorporating 242 separate shots for an average of one every four seconds. 160 of these shots— more than half the total—are effects shots. Even the inconsistencies of the effects work—shaky mattes, overexposures, the variations in the monster's appearance and its atomic ray (sometimes live-action steam, sometimes animated as either a fine stream or a broad pattern)—actually helped to portray a world where reality gives way to a nightmare filmed in its entirety.

Godzilla's 877 shots and 97 minutes are comprised of shadows and silence, hope and despair, destruction and panic, but ultimately of a human sacrifice so noble as to define definition. Yasnuobu Taira's editing is not only seamless but extremely creative, utilizing a "wipe" transition as if we were turning the pages of a frightening fairy tale; when Godzilla approaches the high-tension towers, Honda intercut shots of the monster's approach with guns being trained on it, and when the beast reaches the towers, Honda cut the music in a heart-stopping moment before showing a close-up of a hand (his, as a matter-of-fact) throwing a power switch electrifying the towers.

After the rescue ship has been destroyed, and Hagiwara is phoning in his report from the steamship office, the camera tracks to the right in a medium shot showing anxious relatives, but Honda interrupts the shot by inserting the face of a screaming woman in a jarring and unsettling close-up, stressing her personal grief. After Ogata warns Emiko that the ship taking them to Odo Island may be sunk at any moment, Emiko looks nervously down at the water which dissolves nicely from the "peaks" of the waves to the "peaks" of Odo Island. When Emiko leaves her father to brood alone in his dark study, the shot beautifully dissolves to an opposing one of neon lights shining and people bustling about, peppered with the sounds of happy car horns and music.

The two-minute scene showing Godzilla rising behind Mount Hachiba is a montage of terror comprised of 29 shots; again, one every four seconds (as Emiko stumbles as she tries to run away, she looks up and screams as she sees the monster coming closer, a moment to be echoed in future Honda monster films). The editing of Masaji's death is also brilliantly-staged with effective close-ups, 180-degree flips and a particularly-inventive reverse-tracking shot of Masaji running toward the camera, only to stop at a window when he hears Shinkichi calling out his name as a bolt of lightening illuminates his destiny (arguably the greatest "money shot" in Honda's fantasy film career); Honda then cuts to a close-up of a prostrate Shinkichi screaming into the camera lens.

Mirroring the on-screen dangers were real ones encountered during filming, particularly with the underwater scenes, which Honda later recalled as being his greatest challenge. A thorough search revealed that the clearest waters in Japan were on the east side of Tokyo Bay between the Mie and Wakayama borders. It was a lot of work producing and testing the waterproof equipment, as well as training the diving crews; although even after extensive preparation a near-tragedy was avoided when a member of the salvage company helping to run the oxygen line, made a mistake while operating the air pump, resulting in the near-drowning of cameraman Jo Aizawa.

Nor was Honda immune to the dangers as he was so preoccupied with filming that he neglected to sufficiently shield himself from an all-day session under a hot summer sun; the results were severe blisters and second-degree burns (as he revealed to friends years afterwards: "My back is still full of freckles!").

Masao Tamai's detached photography records the events with understated objectivity—just as Honda intended he should—painting a documentary-like picture of a twilight netherworld of claustrophobic and predestined doom, with expert compositions, dramatic lighting and *mise en scene* (visual impressions created by the surroundings). This impression is very apparent in the scene where Emiko and Serizawa walk down the brick-walled stairs to his lab as if descending into Hell; the very walls seem to impend. The film's opening shot taken from the rear of a ship will end with a similar shot, as Honda used this technique in his early films to give them a cyclical quality.

The air is constantly choked with dust and smoke and there is darkness everywhere with faint, almost expressionist lighting designed and executed by Choshiro Ishii. Diagonal shadows on background walls are repeatedly seen in the film, inferring a battle between the forces of light and darkness, with the outcome very much in doubt. When

Serizawa is recounting to Emiko the story of the Oxygen Destroyer in Emiko's flashback, Tamai tilts his camera to emphasize an unnatural situation, followed by a lovely shot of Emiko sitting in front an aquarium. When Emiko visits Serizawa near the end of the film, we see Ogata's shadow rising into view on the extreme left as Serizawa walks toward the camera. During the "Prayer For Peace" song, diffused light coming from elevated windows—combined with the girls' angelical singing (females being a cinematically time-honored symbol of rebirth)—gives the scene an ethereal quality in what may have been the first cinematic plea for nuclear disarmament.

At the dock when the sightseers are wishing Yamane's group a happy farewell, Honda shows Emiko, Ogata and Yamane standing at the rail with Ogata in the middle, hinting that Ogata will soon "come between" the father and his daughter. The scratchy sequence showing actual wartime footage of a depth-bomb training mission will be in sharp contrast to freshly-filmed scenes of military preparedness to follow in subsequent films. In the film's crucial moment—when Serizawa asks Emiko if she would like to see his newest invention—Honda gives us an intense close-up of Emiko nodding in silent agreement.

Akira Ifukube's score for *Godzilla* has become legendary; his driving, urgent overture—a three-note *motif* that seems to repeatedly call out the name, "Go-Ji-Ra, Go-Ji-Ra"—gives the impression of a relentless, inexorable force of immense power coming ever nearer (as the monster rises from Tokyo Bay, it splashes about angrily, Ifukube coloring the moment with pounding piano keys and muted brass in slowly rising registers, mirroring the monster's ascending rage). Ifukube uses musical *motifs* (musical themes identifying a character or moment) such as when the rescue boat goes down in "*Bingo-Maru* Sinking:" As the bubbles rise to the surface of the water, we hear a tingling of piano keys; then, as the boat explodes and begins to sink, shimmering violin strings and an oboe play in sequentially lower octaves (this is essentially the "panic" music used for the film, a portion of which is heard during Godzilla's appearance during the "Storm on Odo Island," and when "Godzilla Comes Ashore" during the creature's first appearance in Tokyo).

When Serizawa tells Emiko about the "Oxygen Destroyer," the composer cleverly and subtly implies an internal conflict with a mournful cello solo (representing the Oxygen Destroyer), accompanied by a single, repeating piano key note (Godzilla). His somber and affecting hospital score in "Devastated Tokyo"—scored mainly for strings playing in long, drawn-out measures describing devastation and loss, punctuated by a reed flute hinting at hope—returns in a more-elaborate form in "Godzilla

Under the Sea," one of the composer's greatest cues and the longest in the film, timing in at just under six and a-half minutes. It is a reflective and melancholy piece which indicates not only somber reassurance but a regretful death (two, as a matter-of-fact). Even Ifukube's incidental music—such as the sailors' song heard at the beginning of the film ("Ship Music") and the ceremonial music on Odo Island ("Odo Temple Festival")—have a lilting sadness to them.

The acting is excellent, with Honda coaxing the very best out of his four leading players: Akira Takarada as Ogata (then barely out of his teens), Momoko Kochi as Emiko and Takeshi Shimura as Yamane (Shimura was appearing in his fourth out of the director's first seven films; after Serizawa's suicide, the Shimura manages to convey Yamane's admiration, grief and regret all while uttering the name, "Serizawa"). Particularly effective is Akihiko Hirata as Dr. Serizawa in what became the defining role of his career; as Serizawa watches the beast writhing in agony as a result of the Oxygen Destroyer, Hirata—"handicapped" as it were with the use of only one eye to express emotion—nevertheless shows in successive cuts: awe, fascination and contentment (when Serizawa reaches the breaking point after watching the televised "Prayer For Peace," he turns away only to look up again with a firm resolve, a lovely piece of acting).

More than any single element that makes this extraordinary film succeed as believable fiction is Honda's taut and understated direction; the glue that holds it all together. Compelling, convincing, involving and realistic; just one minute into the film, Honda immediately grabs the viewer's attention with a catastrophic event, marking an opening sequence setting the course for a generation of filmmaking. The close-up of a ringing telephone soon answered by Ogata set a trend as the next several films involved scenes with phone messages bearing bad news; other trends are initiated, such as the scene in the darkened Yamane household when Yamane, Emiko, Ogata and Shinkichi are gathered in the living room before all Hell breaks loose (the calm before the storm), Western diplomats attending a briefing (Honda's first modest scene showing international cooperation) and shots of civilians being safely evacuated from the danger area.

Many shots are inventive and show attention to detail, such as when the radioman is desperately trying to send a distress call, Honda creatively showing fires through a background porthole. Honda accentuates the pandemonium in the Nankai Steamship Company with an off-screen agitated announcer and loud, radio-teletype signals, and when Yamane first approaches the podium in the Diet, he tucks his tie inside his jacket in a realistic moment (when Yamane later gives a briefing to explain the monster's origins, Honda colors the scene with skeptical cackles of laughter from the audience).

Godzilla is filled with more overt use of symbolism than any Honda film to follow: After the sailors on the *Eiko-Maru No. 5* are blinded by an explosion (a recreation of the *pikadon* or "flash-boom" of the Hiroshima blast), a table upon which a Mahjong game had been played is overturned, a guitar and chains are shown on the deck, implying the sailors are prisoners to their fate. In the film's most direct reference to the war, people run under the Kachidoki Bridge carrying their belongings; smoke billows about and ambulances rush to the scene as one hears the distant "thump" of the creature's footsteps (like exploding bombs growing ever nearer) while searchlights scan the night sky as they did during the war. After Ogata's failed attempt to gain Yamane's approval for marrying his daughter, Honda brilliantly cuts to a shot a shot of two canaries chirping in a cage in a visual metaphor of Ogata and Emiko's "trapped" situation, and when the jets gain the upper hand against the monster, Honda has the watching crowd cheering as spectators would at a baseball game (a concept repeated on a more modest scale in his final film, *MechaGodzilla's Counterattack*).

The film's finest sequence is the "Prayer For Peace" which deliberately replicates the anguish and suffering of the Hiroshima and Nagasaki survivors with scarred and wounded citizens being cared for on the hospital floor (when the American version played in America with this scene intact, *Cue* magazine's film critic Alta Maloney noted of the shots: "They look suspiciously like actual films taken after the dropping of the atom bombs in Japan. They are uncomfortable views," thus paying Honda a tremendous complement).

As the sequence continues, victims are brought into the hospital while nurses explain to some injured children what is happening around them. A heartrending tracking shot follows showing wounded lying on the hospital floor being tenderly cared for by relatives, and people are seen praying around a radio. The sequence culminates with an impressive shot of 200 female high school students arranged in diagonal rows singing in a gymnasium (when they first come into view, Ifukube's music swells in a highly-effective moment). As originally storyboarded (Shot No. 194), initially only a small group of girls were to be singing around a piano, but Honda enhanced the sequence considerably to increase its dramatic impact (Ifukube personally conducted the live-recording).

In what would become a trademark climax to his films, Honda ends the movie with both joy at what has been gained, but sadness at what has been lost (as Ogata relates Serizawa's last words to Emiko, the choir music swells on the soundtrack as Yamane wonders aloud— almost speaking directly to the viewer—that, unless nuclear testing is curtailed, other Godzillas may well appear to threaten mankind). Then, in another characteristic ending for the director, Honda's actors line-up along the ship's railing in a "curtain call" as they bow and salute a man who surrendered both his life and principles for the common good. We then are shown a horizon shot of a peaceful sea under scattered clouds with the sun's rays glistening off the water. It is a tranquil, almost romantic image, but Honda undercuts it with Ifukube's mournful music, reminding us of a sad sacrifice, leaving the viewer with a feeling of emptiness and a tear in the eye; not only from grief but from witnessing a beautiful work of art.

Godzilla would become Honda's most-famous film and his greatest achievement in the fantasy field, initiating one of the longest-running film series in history—as well as an entire genre—yet, Japanese critics were not appreciative of the film's bold concept, apparently unaware of the warning Honda intended it to be, calling it "strange" or "weird" (Honda's fantasy films were generally given the same biased critical treatment in Japan as they did overseas. Characteristically, Honda felt badly more for his actors' feelings than for his own).

Producer Tanaka would have been justified in being apprehensive as to just how Japanese audiences would react to the film; how would they feel watching recreated horrors from less-than ten years earlier? As it happened, *Godzilla* drew in nearly 10 million Japanese—one out of every nine people living in Japan at the time went to see it—Japanese who were now able to deal with such horrific images of their not-so-distant past; indeed, the film's apparent cathartic effect was best described by horror film historian Carlos Clarens as "...an exorcistic reenactment of the catastrophe of Hiroshima" (when Diet member Ms. Ozawa shouts out "The truth is the truth!" it may have been Honda's way of reminding his movie audience of their nation's wartime accountability).

Two years later, *Godzilla* would become the first Japanese film released in major theaters around the world when America's Embassy Pictures distributed the film, now called *Godzilla, King of the Monsters!*, in a altered form. For many people it was their first exposure to Japanese filmmaking, and although the new version downplayed the atomic bomb connection (intentionally or otherwise), the newly-inserted footage directed and edited by Terry Morse nonetheless paid Honda's film an immense compliment by treating it with respect, maintaining the spirit if not the letter of the original film (for example, all of Ifukube's marvelous music remained intact).

Before *Godzilla* was made, Japanese films were an indigenous product made by Japanese filmmakers for Japanese audiences; however, because the monster could be seen as a global threat—and because alienation, loss and suffering are relevant human issues—*Godzilla* enjoyed great international success overseas. As a result and quite by accident, Ishiro Honda had directed the most-famous Japanese film ever made.

The impact of the film's success would alter Honda's career in a manner he never could have anticipated at the time, but for now he could afford to modestly bask its glory, which included seeing *Godzilla* finishing as one of the top-ten money-making films of the year. But there was even a greater reward and tribute when the director received a phone call from Toho's President and Founder, Ichizo Kobayashi, personally calling to congratulate him on his success.

For Honda, it was the ultimate accolade.

ABOMINABLE SNOWMAN (1955)
(YUJIN YUKIOTAKO)
HALF HUMAN

Cast & Credits

Film Register No. 1685
Release Date: August 14, 1955
Running Time: 95 minutes, ten seconds

Staff: Producer: Tomoyuki Tanaka; Original Story: Shigeru Kayama; Director: Ishiro Honda; Story: Shigeru Kayama, Takeshi Kimura; Screenplay: Takeo Murata; Cinematography: Tadashi Iimura; Art Director: Takeo Kita; Sound Recording: Yoshio Nishikawa; Lighting: Soichi Yokoi; Music: Masaru Sato; Assistant Director: Kihachi Okamoto; Special Effects: Eiji Tsuburaya, Akira Watanabe, Hiroshi Mukoyama and Masao Shirota; Editor: Shuichi Ambara; Sound Arrangement: Ichiro Minawa; Developing: Toho Laboratory; Production Manager: Tatsuo Kuroda; Still Photos: Goichi Araki.

Cast: Akira Takarada (Tadashi Iijima); Akemi Negishi (Chika); Momoko Kochi (MachikoTakeno); Nobuo Nakamura (Prof. Shigeki Koizumi); Sachio Sakai (Nakata); Kokuten Kodo (Village Chief); Yoshio Kosugi (Ohba aka "Oba," "Ohaba"); Akira Tani (Matsui); Kenji Kasahara (Shinsuke Takeno); Senkichi Omura (One-Eyed Villager); Koji Suzuki (Kurihara); Ren Yamamoto (Shinagawa); Akira Sera (Hotel Manager Matsui); Yasuhisa Tsutsumi (Newspaper Reporter Kodama); Tadashi Okabe (Kiyoshi Takeno); Etsuro Saijo (Roku-san); Kamayuki Tsubono (Guide); Akira Yamada (Kaji); Yasuo Onishi, Yutaka Nakayama, Koichi Sato, Kazuo Fukada (Circus Members); Ichiro Chiba (Chief of Search Party); Jiro Kumagai (Policeman); Akio Kusama, Shigeo Kato, Akira Kitchoji, Keiichiro Katsumoto (Villagers); Rinsaku Ogata (Guide); Hiroshi Akitsu (Railroad Stationmaster); Noriko Kosawa (Village Woman); Sanshiro Sukenaga (Snowman); Tadashi Ito (Snowman's Son).

The Film

When Tanaka was considering what monster would follow Godzilla in 1955, it came as no surprise—with photographs taken by British explorer Eric Shipton allegedly showing footprints belonging to an Abominable Snowman (more accurately called a "yeti") buzzing the scientific community—he decided his next monster movie would feature such a creature. The sequel to *Godzilla, Godzilla's Counterattack,* was already in production when the yeti assignment fell to Honda and would be helmed by Motoyoshi Oda as part of Toho's policy of assigning films to new directors.

Honda's team was essentially the same that assisted him on *Godzilla*: Kayama wrote the original story, while Murata assisted Honda in writing the screenplay. Honda then went on location to the snow country of Hakuba (a famous ski resort in the Nagano prefecture), with on-site technical assistance coming from the University of Rikkyo's expert mountain-climbing club.

Abominable Snowman is every bit as compelling as *Godzilla,* and the film echoes elements found in *King Kong,* such as that of a primitive creature doomed by its coming into contact with civilization. The tribe worshipping the beast is barbaric, superstitious and suffers physical deformities due to inbreeding, and their treatment of women is deplorable; it is obvious that any contact with the outside world is to be severely punished. While appeasement and offerings of food and prayer to the beast presumably grant the natives' immunity from attack (as it did with Kong); it seems obvious that—without any Snowwomen around—the species is ultimately doomed to extinction.

One wonders why the creature killed the men in the cabin, although the phone call does gives us a clue: First, we hear a scream over the phone, then the sound of a gunshot, implying the Snowman came into the cabin seeking shelter from the blizzard and thus alarming the two men, one of whom (Gen-San) picked up a gun and shot at the animal, frightening it to such an extant that it turned deadly). Michiko's unconscious state lasts long enough to make us believe she may be in a coma, and while Professor Koizumi's expedition has to travel many miles through treacherous terrain in order to find the Snowman, circus owner Ohba and his team have discovered a convenient mountain road leading right to the Snowman's lair.

The final shots of the magnificently-structured sequence of the Snowman and Chika hurtling to their doom into the bubbling pit, followed by close-ups of the team members staring in shock while eerie, primitive choir music swells on the soundtrack, is one of the most-chilling endings to any Honda film; or at least the film *should* have ended there, but instead a more upbeat ending was tacked on which takes us back to the train depot (where a remarkably casual reporter thanks the group for their incredible story) as a ticket agent cheerily announces their train is approaching (no doubt on time). By this time, the rain that had been pelting down at the beginning of the film at night has now stopped, and it is now daylight. The group then exits the station as a brief reprise of the hiking music—this time on an upbeat note with a full orchestra—accompanies a dissolve to the film's final image of a panoramic shot of the beautiful snow-covered mountains, dotted with luscious pine trees shining under a bright sun, which is not quite enough to leave the viewer with a sense of reassurance.

Eiji Tsuburaya's work in *Snowman* was scaled-down considerably from *Godzilla*, but it was no less audacious or innovative, with numerous elaborate glass matte shots beautifully integrated with the live scenery footage. The scenes of the trucks carrying the Snowman down the mountain road were shot on an open set using natural lighting, while the mountain itself was recreated based on photographs of the actual topography, a technique Tsuburaya had been using for many years (one amazingly bold effects shot utilizing a traveling matte showed the Snowman picking up Ohba before launching him into the bottom of the ravine, inexplicably cut from the American version). The interior of the Snowman's lair was convincingly realized as a conical-shaped hill enclosed under a dome-like ceiling in a superb matte shot done in the camera by the legendary Hiroshi Mukaiya.

According to an original Toho press release for the film, a talent search was held to discover who would play the Snowman by auditioning tall people, the tallest one getting the part! This was in all probability a promotional gimmick, as it seems highly unlikely that casting such an important role would be given to someone based merely on their height. Instead, in a unique situation, the man who designed the costume (Toshinori Oohasi) wore it as well (billed as actor Sanshiro Sagara; both curiously without official screen credit).

Oohasi is now considered to be the Father of Japanese Monster Suits, going all the way back to 1938 when he designed a King Kong costume for a long-lost period parody film called *King Kong Appears in Edo* (1938). The first Japanese makeup man to use latex in the base of his unique creations, Oohasi assisted Teizo Toshimitsu in the construction of the original Godzilla costume by utilizing lightweight materials, eventually working his way up as an assistant to Tsuburaya.

Oohasi's methods of building his suits formed the foundation for the creation of the costumes used in the *Ultra Q* TV series in 1965; while as an actor, Sagara worked on a number of films for Daiei Studios, as well as performing in many a Kurosawa picture, usually playing a samurai warrior. Oohasi worked outside of Japan as well, as in the early fifties he was hired by Walt Disney as a technical advisor for the construction of the original Disneyland, he also worked on *Planet of the Apes* (1968) where his unaccredited contribution was to develop the foam latex and other rubber appendages used in the film.

A special effects master, a suit-maker, an actor, a stuntman, a make-up designer and a director, Oohasi is an unheralded figure in the fantasy film realm (working as the Snowman was never easy, but it carried its own unique risks off-screen as well. While staying at a ski resort during the filming in Hakuba, Sagara decided to try-out his Snowman creation on a maid who worked at the hotel, who quite naturally screamed her head off at the sight of it. This attracted the attention of an adjacent tenant who happened to be a kendo master and he came to the rescue by beating-up the Abominable Snowman).

As related years later by Tsuburaya, an attempt was made to make the Snowman look as authentic as possible by utilizing eyewitness accounts of the animal, as well as research information on the prehistoric pithecanthropus and the mythical "Peking Man." The first sketches of the Snowman were begun in late 1954, with the clay prototype design not approved until nearly six months later. The original designs for the Snowman were as a ten-foot-high monster with a savage face, evil eyes and sharp, craggily teeth; a truly terrifying apparition. Possibly at Honda's request however, the monster' appearance was toned-down to that of a more benevolent-looking beast with distinctively warm features, aided by Oohasi's own gentle eyes.

The costume was an unqualified triumph, even more so when one considers the limited materials and resources available at the time. To this day, it is the best depiction of a "yeti" ever seen on film, but perhaps Oohasi's greatest accomplishment was in the design of the Snowman's face, which had to be flexible and lifelike. Oohasi built a mold out of his own face, then used that in the final design. Various molds of the face were created to match the Snowman's appropriate mood; the mask had a movable jaw and the range of expressions was remarkable, particularly in the final scene in the cave, where the beast displays looks of defiance, weakness and even lust.

Abominable Snowman is a beautifully photographed film due in no small part to the superb work of Tadashi Iimura. Particularly memorable are shots of the Snowman's footprints in the snow outside the cabin, the moon-lit shadow of the Snowman on Machiko's tent, an elevated crane shot of the native village, Chika's ring rolling to a stop on the floor of her hut, Michiko looking out from inside the inn during the snowstorm, the innkeeper sounding the alarm bell in the blizzard and an extremely effective reverse tracking shot of the Snowman walking toward the camera. Photographing on location is never easy, yet Iimura's camera is constantly on the move with tracking shots and pans. Several weeks of filming were involved working in snow-covered terrain over rough ground and at altitude with the principal actors and with heavy camera equipment.

Honda filmed the scene between Chika and Ohba and his assistant with the girl speaking directly into the camera, creating a "spectator-as-character" perspective technique Honda was fond of using on rare occasions in order to gain sympathy for the speaker (what is curious and unsettling about this particular point-of-view shot is that the character Honda is forcing us to become is the loathsome Ohba). The cave sequences are spine-tingling, with Iimura's camera tracking along with the expedition with God knows what waiting to jump out of the shadows (another shot was quite inventive as just before Ohba's net is dropped on the Snowman, we see it hanging above the beast in a low-angle shot—an idea that resurfaced in *20 Million Miles to Earth* two years later).

Composer Masaru Sato's atmospheric music is woven throughout the film and is subtle yet terrifyingly effective. His "Main Title" score soars above a howling wind blowing on the soundtrack which segues into a sad harmonica rendition of a German hiking song known in Japan as "Mushiden" (and in America as "The Wooden Heart"). The music continues with staccato flutes and rolling timpani until finally reaching a crescendo of horns holding a sustained note as the credit of "Ishiro Honda" as Director comes into view as if heralding a bold, new talent.

A key musical moment occurs during "The Abominable Snowman Appears" when the music heard on the soundtrack is a softly played piano; an important point as Honda preferred his audience not to be frightened by the Snowman, but be fascinated by it; as a result, the viewer is more curious than scared and wishes to learn more about it. Sato uses soft drums to color the moment when the creature's footprints are first discovered outside the cabin ("What Was Left Behind") and ancient *Noh* music and native chanting are employed for the unnamed tribe ("The Prayer")."

The scene when Chika is confronted by Ohba and Matsui in "The

Cliff of Death" is eerily scored by a repeated two-note combination on piano (very similar to a portion of the music heralding Kobayashi's death-dive in *Godzilla's Counterattack* which was also scored by Sato and released that same year), giving the moment an eerie and unsettling quality. In "The Son's Final Moments," Sato's music sounds a *vibrato* of ascending violins reflecting the Snowman's rising fury and craving for revenge, and a mournful oboe reflecting the grief he feels over his slain son.

Akira Takarada, fresh from his sensitive performance as Ogata in *Godzilla*, is a typical Honda hero as he plays the brave but helpless Takashi (the actor's reaction upon hearing the screams of his friends over the telephone is beautifully done). Momoko Kochi does a good job, although as was typical of many a Honda heroine she does little else but cry and be scared.

Nobu Nakamura played the gruff and unsympathetic Dr. Koizumi and was one of Japan's finest actors. Thoroughly despicable in their roles as the leaders of the circus team were Akira Tani as the Hitler-mustached Matsui and Yoshio Kosugi as Ohba (Honda occasionally has Kosugi making "monkey-faces" during critical moments in the film, as if to imply he is even less-human than the Snowman).

Most alluring was the sensual Chika, performed by 21-year-old Akemi Negishi. Honda had used her the previous year as a seductive, dancing native girl in *Farewell Rabaul*, and she would become the first of many alluring female characters who leads men to their destruction in Honda's genre films. Chika is far being an innocent female despite the constant beatings she receives from the village patriarch; indeed, her impetuousness will doom both her and her tribe. Although she demonstrates compassion in helping the wounded Takashi, her revealing to the circus people the whereabouts of the Snowman will prove a sacrilege that brings devastation and destruction to all. The final image of Chika hurtling downward into the pit in the dying Snowman's grasp is, in Guy Tucker's words, an "indelible" image whose "consequences are unthinkable."

Honda's documentary-style manner of filmmaking is in evidence as he focuses on both the travails of the human participants as well as the Snowman's habits and natural surroundings; almost as if there is a hidden camera in the cave filming their lifestyle. His skillful direction draws the audience deeper into the machinations of the plot just as the expedition progresses deeper into the Snowman's domain. Honda builds suspense beautifully, particularly during the scene in the cabin as a snowstorm rages outside (all shot on a thoroughly convincing soundstage).

Honda evokes sympathy for the "monsters" while at the same time evoking dread of the vast majority of the film's human characters. Toward the end of the film we hope the Snowman will never be found to simply be left alone in peace, but Honda dictates that any contact with man bodes ill for nature (even if the Snowman were to survive, it would most-likely be as part of a circus act with his son). Honda's direction of the monster's rampage through the village is tinged with a poignant remorse, as if the beast is not fully-responsible for its actions. Indeed, the Abominable Snowman proves to be anything but abominable; it is compassionate, intelligent and even resourceful.

Abominable Snowman is unquestionably Honda's grimmest film; while not matching the body count of *Godzilla* or the grim ending of *Matango*, the film is unceasingly severe in its scenes of brutality, gore and the intense suffering inflicted upon its characters (it also has its share of natural disasters: Lightening, rainstorms, blizzards, avalanches, landslides and a firestorm). Michiko looses two of her three brothers, leaving the third traumatized for life, the Snowman species is now extinct, the native villagers have been wiped out, the circus people have been erased from the face of the earth, and the expedition has not only suffered its own devastating losses, but ultimately proves nothing about the existence of the Snowman.

One extremely-affecting scene occurs when the villagers confront the circus people, the two monstrous groups facing-off against each other until (in an idea Honda would use later in *King Kong Escapes*) the armed invader guns down a defenseless native. The mortally-wounded Oji is then surrounded by his tribe, who looks up at Ohba in confusion and dread in an extremely moving moment. Even more depressing is when Ohba shoots the Snowboy who then falls limply into the arms of his father in what is easily the most heartbreaking moment in all of Honda's fantasy films.

Abominable Snowman is the only one of Honda's genre films never to receive a video release from Toho (although it did come close in the early 1980s when a video master *was* produced in preparation for distribution; however, at the last minute, it was recalled) ostensibly due to its depiction of the unnamed and fictitious tribe pictured in the film, seen by some as being disrespectful of all aboriginal peoples living in Japan, particularly the Ainu and the Buraku who are still subject to intense discrimination. Recent attempts to contact the studio have revealed that Toho has no comment to make on the matter, apparently believing that if they ignore the film and pretend it never existed, it will somehow go away.

Undeservedly obscure (it was never reissued), the film was not a great commercial success; it's unremittingly harsh tone affording it few followers. With all this, the film is unquestionably the finest ever done on the subject of a yeti, far surpassing contemporary efforts such as *The Snow Creature* (1954), *Man Beast* (1956) and *The Abominable Snowman of the Himalayas* (1957). By 1964, however, the creature was no longer being taken seriously, reduced to a couple of comical cameos in *The 7 Faces of Dr. Lao*. Nevertheless, it is hoped that Toho will one day come to its collective and corporate senses and release *Abominable Snowman* on video. Grand and grim, *Abominable Snowman* was Honda's most-uncompromising film and an unforgettable triumph which should be seen by the worldwide audience it so richly deserves.

SECTION III:
"THE MAGIC BEGINS . . ."

RADON, THE MONSTER FROM THE SKY (1956)
(RODAN! THE FLYING MONSTER)

THE DEFENSE FORCE OF THE EARTH (1957)
(THE MYSTERIANS)

THE BEAUTY AND THE LIQUID PEOPLE (1958)
(THE H-MAN)

BARAN, THE GIANT MONSTER (1958)
(VARAN THE UNBELIEVABLE)

THE GREAT WAR IN SPACE (1959)
(BATTLE IN OUTER SPACE)

THE FIRST GAS HUMAN BEING (1960)
(THE HUMAN VAPOR)

RADON, THE MONSTER FROM THE SKY (1956)
(SORA NO DAIKAIJU RADON)
RODAN! THE FLYING MONSTER

Cast & Credits

Film Register No. 2404
Release Date: Dec. 26, 1956
Running Time: 82 minutes, 9 seconds

Staff: Producer: Tomoyuki Tanaka; Director: Ishiro Honda; Original Story: Takashi [Ken] Kuronuma; Screenplay: Takeo Murata and Takeshi Kimura; Cinematography: Isamu Ashida; Art Director: Tatsuo Kita; Recording: Masanobu Miyazaki; Lighting: Shigeru Mori; Music: Akira Ifukube; Assistant Director: Jun Fukuda; Editor: Hiroichi Iwashita; Sound Effects: Ichiro Minawa; Special Effects Techniques: Director: Eiji Tsuburaya; Art Director: Akira Watanabe; Lighting: Masao Shiroda; Optical Photography: Hiroshi Mukoyama; Developing: Toyo Laboratory; Production Manager: Teruo Maki; Still Photos: Jiro Tsuchiya.

Cast: Kenji Sahara (Shigeru Kawamura); Yumi Shirakawa (Kiyo); Akio Kobori (Police Inspector Nishimura); Akihiko Hirata (Professor Hisaichiro Kashiwagi); Fuyuki Murakami (Physicist Minami); Yasuko Nakata (Girl at Volcano); Minosuke Yamada (Mining Company Manager Osaki); Yoshibumi Tajima (Reporter Iseki); Kyomi Mizunoya (Otami); Fumindo Matsuo (Assistant Professor Hayama); Jiro Suzukawa (Yoshi); Rinsaku Ogata (Goro); Kanta Kisaragi, Ichiro Nakaya, Keiji Sakakida, Shin Yoshida, Yasuhri Shigenobu, Hideo Unagami, Ko Narita, Koji Suzuki, Haruya Sakamoto, Yasuo Onishi (Miners); Akio Kusama (Chief Engineer Suda); Katao Kawasaki (Mining Crew Chief); Kiyoshi Takagi (Hospital Physician Mizukami); Hideo Mihara (Air Defense Commander); Ren Imaizumi (Seismologist Sunakawa); Seiji Onaka (Young Man at Volcano); Jiro Kumagai (Police Officer Tashiro); Ichiro Chiba (Policeman); Junichiro Mukai (JSDF Official); Mitsuo Tsuda (Air Defense Official).

The Film

Radon was both Honda and Toho's first Japanese fantasy film made in color and a rare bird, one of only 32 of the 514 Japanese features produced that year in color. The movie brought together much of the creative talent from *Godzilla*; along with Tanaka, Tsuburaya, Honda, Murata (assisted by on this occasion by Takeshi Kimura and Ken Kuronuma), there was composer Akira Ifukube, optical photographer Hiroshi Mukoyama, art director Akira Watanabe, suit-maker Toishi Toshimitsu and actor Naruo Nakajima as the monster.

The reason for the fight between Yoshi and Goro at the beginning of the film is never explained, other than to make Goro a prime suspect in Yoshi's subsequent killing (perhaps Yoshi was upset with Goro's daughter Kiyo being in love with Shigeru). Whereas Dr. Yamane's explanation of Godzilla's existence was met with skepticism, Kashiwagi's briefing only two years later meets no such resistance.

The script's treatment of white-color professionals is biting: The doctor brought in to explain the murders has no idea how or what is killing the men in the mine, nor can any doctor cure Shigeru of his amnesia. When Izeki first arrives while Kashawagi is explaining the Meganurons, the big-city reporter nudges a local reporter out of the way. The local police chief is not terribly concerned with the Radons after the Meganurons have been dispatched, and even seems amused as he examines the photos taken by the missing newlyweds. To make matters worse, his group of armed men not only fail to kill the Meganurons, their shooting only results in further deaths and creates a cave-in that buries Shigeru.

Honda's screenwriting contributions seem evident near the beginning and end of the film: When Shigeru's boss jokingly remarks that after having taken eight million tons of ore, the hills have almost nothing left to give—a comment that seems to suggest severe consequences await man due to his ruthless ravaging of the Earth. The scene where Shigeru expresses his gratitude to Kiyo for her wanting to remain with him despite the danger was almost certainly written by Honda, who often included such tender and reassuring scenes in his films.

Tsuburaya's effects are typically innovative and imaginative, including brilliant miniatures, superb mattes and audacious puppet work; the destruction of the jeep by the flying Radon one of his most memorable shots (at one point, miniature jets trailing miniature exhaust fly through miniature clouds). The film's opening shot is actually a glass-matte painting showing Mount Aso, the dominant feature in the coal-mining town of Kyushu (the film will also end with a shot of the same mountain, although under far-less tranquil circumstances); the camera then pans to the left, where a light pole ingeniously separates the two film elements as the actual town comes into view in an ingenious 220-degree pan to the left. The Meganurons are a marvelous creation and brutally-realized, and during Radon's attack on the city, people can be seen dashing to safety inside a building with rubble falling in front of it; the execution of which almost defies description.

The confrontation between Radon and the military's tanks and rocket-launchers at Fukuoka was brilliantly executed, showing Tsuburaya at the top of his game. The miniature city itself was built to 1/20th scale and cost 8 million yen; nevertheless, Tsuburaya was displeased with the original version of the city and had it dismantled and rebuilt. Smoke and debris helped to conceal the wires supporting the Radons and jets, including "dullcoate" which was sprayed on them so as to not reflect light and thereby be noticed—although this did not always achieve the desired effect. Tsuburaya's incredible attention to detail (such as the curtains seen in the windows of the Nikkatsu Theatre) and timing (after the tanks fire at Radon, their projectiles fall short) is aided admirably by low-angle photography, a Tsuburaya hallmark (Honda would recall with amusement years later how people would walk up to him and ask where Toho rented all of the military equipment seen in the film, some of which—such as the large, "Honest John" ramp rockets and multi-missile launchers—were completely fictitious).

Director of Photography Isamu Ashida's camera work is one of *Radon's* highpoints; the natural on-location settings of green windswept grasses, cobalt blue skies and black coal hills provide a startling visual counterpoint to the blood-red human drama being played out. The camera moves as do the Radons, with many tracks and pans (Honda often has his actors crowding into the frame to emphasize a claustrophobic quality). Ashida often has the hills lurking in the background as a constant on-screen presence, and his compositions are always well lit and often arresting, such as when Shigeru and Kiyo meet in front of the hospital, the shot of men scrambling down the coal hill kicking up dust as they go, Kiyo and Shigeru running into army headquarters as long shadows are silhouetted on the ground outside, and a particularly-effective shot taken from inside the mine entrance where Shigeru and the police chief await the oncoming soldiers.

Koichi Iwashita's editing is also brilliant; there is a clever dissolve near the film's beginning after Goro and Yoshi have taken their trams into the mine; the camera travels along the shaft from right-to-left before nicely dissolving into a shot traveling from left-to-right showing Shigeru's blueprints. One of the finest transitional scenes in all of

Honda's films occurs at the clinic where Shigeru is recuperating: He is first seen sketching mineshafts which brilliantly suggest the pieces of his forgotten past; then, after Kiyo shows him two canary eggs in their nest, one of the shells begins to break open, triggering Shigeru's memory and forcing him to recall what happened to him after the cave-in in an outstanding flashback sequence (Honda later recalled working in the huge cave set as one of his happiest filmmaking experiences). Tatsuo Kita's set designs are thoroughly convincing, matching perfectly Tsuburaya's miniature recreations.

Akira Ifukube's score for *Radon*—as with so many of his scores for Honda—is highly-original and vastly underrated, described by Japanese musicologist Lawrence Tuczynski as "dark and foreboding (while) other cues are intensely emotional" and nothing at all like his score for *Godzilla* two years earlier. In 1956 alone Ifukube composed 14 film scores, *Radon* being his final assignment for the year (it is difficult to shake the feeling that, after writing pieces for more conventional films, the composer could hardly-wait to let loose and write bellicose music for a monster movie—one can almost sense his elation).

His "Main Title" music was more intricate than the one he wrote for *Godzilla*, beginning with a pounding piano as low brass clues us to underground depths, with shimmering strings anticipating the Meganurons and blaring horns alerting us to aerial adventures. Ifukube uses low brass and woodwinds in order to give the film an earthy, subterranean quality, while at the same time writing thrilling chase music when the planes are pursuing Radon.

"Radon Attacks Fukuoka II" is filled with unique orchestrations such as woodwinds fluttering in their upper registers, conveying a bizarre "chirping" effect emphasizing the monsters' bird-like qualities. Ifukube's music seems to be actually rooting for the Radons, such as when they are being chased by the jets (the cue is titled, "Radon, Get 'em!"). This music is very exciting, but the cue called "Amnesia" is very emotive, the music slowly spiraling downward as if to signify the descent of Shigeru's mind into forgetfulness.

"The Natural Beauty of Aso"—the moment when Kiyo declares her love for Shigeru near the film's end—is score with longing violins, gentle harp and somber cellos, creating a subtle and wistful effect suggesting a proper choice and an inevitable destiny. Ifukube does not score the army bombardment of the volcano, but waits until the volcano erupts and the lava flows for his "Ending" music, one of his finest pieces. Filled with sorrow, the score focuses not on the army's triumph, but on the Radons' almost mystical death, giving them a farewell that is both poignant and respectful.

Shigeru was played by the likeable 24-year-old Kenji Sahara. Two years earlier, he had been auditioning as a Toho "New Face" and, after a period of training, appeared briefly in two scenes in *Godzilla* (*Radon* would be his first starring role). Even when replaced by younger leading men in the sixties, the actor displayed great versatility as he played quirky, offbeat and evil characters in films such as *Submarine Warship*, *Mothra vs. Godzilla* and *Matango*.

Sahara's role of Shigeru was hardly that of a typical Western leading man; as with other Honda heroes, he is not a particularly strong-willed or resourceful. In fact, he is rather ineffectual and the victim of events happening around him rather than in being in control of them (some viewers find odd his rather composed reaction when the Meganuron bursts into Kiyo's home, but the actor recounted how Honda stressed "natural" reactions when facing monsters to lend the film realism). Eventually Shigeru does redeem himself somewhat as he leads the coalminers and scientists to a fragment of the Radon eggshell; a plot element which becomes a mute point as Radons will soon fill the sky. From that point on, Shigeru merely becomes a spectator to the efforts of others.

Yumi Shirakawa played the part of Kiyo, but was given little else to do but constantly cry over her situation (she breaks down half-a-dozen times during the course of the movie). With no significant dialogue to speak of, one gets the impression she was simply window dressing and little-else, but perhaps the film's most interesting character is Kashawagi, played with haughty coldness by Akihiko Hirata. An unremarkable paleontologist (and a poor one at that, his estimate of when the Cretaceous period ended is off by some 68 million years), he suddenly finds himself the "man of the hour" when he is called in to explain the monstrosities that have appeared out of nowhere. Snuggling up to the authorities, he displays a smug superiority over his fellow scientists and even sides with the military against the villagers during the army's plan to bombard the volcano.

Radon contains little in the way of subtext while still containing many of the themes Honda was fond of exploring, combined with images of almost unimaginable violence and graphic death. Yet, amongst the explicit terrors are admirable human qualities of hope, love and devotion, as well as Honda's own love and respect for the untainted beauty of the natural world. In *Godzilla*, mankind was faced with the consequences of run-away technology—"future shock" in atomic terms—whereas *Radon* was the result of man's interference with nature. But whereas *Godzilla* had a complex human drama at its core, *Radon* is simply the military vs. the monsters; even so, Honda ends the film ambivalently, switching back-and-forth from the human spectators (lined up in their "curtain call") to the flaming Radons, essentially keeping the viewer in the middle. As a result, we side with neither faction and remain objective witnesses to the Radons' grisly death.

Honda's confidence in his abilities is reflected in the film's high-tension and drama, and his camera work is creative, dramatic and effective. The grim tone established in *Godzilla* and *Abominable Snowman* continues with *Radon*, such as when Shigeru's team discovers Yoshi's dead body floating facedown over a submerged, upturned light as Ifukube supplies strummed, amplified piano strings. This is followed by an even more disturbing shot of Yoshi's corpse being lifted right before our eyes moments before it is placed into a hospital tub. While Shigeru and a doctor are discussing the man's death, the screams of his widow are heard from the outside corridor. After she is refused her hysterical request to see her dead husband, she collapses in grief as the now-fatherless child she is carrying on her back screams it's lungs out (recorded live and not post-dubbed as were the child's cries in the hospital scene in *Godzilla*). Later, after a pilot is killed in his confrontation with Radon, we are shown a close-up of his bloody helmet—found by some lucky individual—yet, there are no words of sorrow for the deceased pilot but only a "What a fool!" declaration from his superior officer, a announcement which manages to startle even the cynical Izeki.

Human grief and suffering are accentuated with the crying Kiyo, the shrieking policemen and the wailing widow; still, Honda takes time to emphasize compassion, such as when Kiyo is suffering her first breakdown with Shigeru outside the hospital as three women approaching them take a different path out of respect, and the sorrow we feel for the widow as she is led sobbing away from Kiyo's home. The film is laced with brutality and bloodshed, with the dead as much mocked as mourned. The scene when the policeman and the miners are dragged underwater to their deaths is one of Honda's more-horrific moments; after the lone survivor scrambles away from the scene, the shadows of huge claws can be seen on a background wall, and—as the miner tries to call for help—he turns and screams at the unseen monster coming toward him, a monster that is not seen but heard by the sound of something scampering in to attack him just before the screen turns black. As he screams in agony the screen goes black, followed by a shot of three more mangled bodies being brought into the hospital.

Teruyoshi Nakano was quoted in *Monsters Are Attacking Tokyo!* that both Honda and Tsuburaya "...believed that nature was the strongest force on Earth and that nobody could resist nature's will," and *Radon* adroitly summarizes this sentiment; indeed, all of the monsters in

Honda's movies can be seen as living and breathing natural disasters. As with *Abominable Snowman, Radon* demonstrates Honda's belief that when man and nature come into contact, neither side will win. The film's "cock-of-the-walk" confidence is very much in evidence from its creative team of filmmakers with moments of terror, tragedy, suspense, horror and spectacular effects, it is as finely-constructed and effective a monster film as any ever made. Uncompromising in its approach and daring in its execution, audiences either love the film or hate it (an admirable quality in any work of art), and an appropriate response toward a picture which itself does not tow the line.

Beginning with a brawl and ending with a volcanic eruption, *Radon* is a no-holds-barred, "in-your-face" monster movie that throws logic and caution to the winds created by giant, flying Pteranodons and is unconcerned about it. It is as if the team of Honda/Tsuburaya/Ifukube—having gained confidence from their earlier efforts—was ready and willing to slug-it-out with the American-made monster movies in a genre where the Japanese themselves had raised the bar to unprecedented heights (*Godzilla's* American release had occurred three months prior to the Japanese release of *Radon*). *Godzilla* had been the starting start, but *Radon* was the flying leap that catapulted Japanese monster movies into critically-admired mainstream international cinema.

To be sure, there are differences between the two films and they are significant. Both Godzilla and Radon are huge animals that innocently create havoc wherever they go, and both are brought to life by atomic testing; however, unlike Godzilla, Radon does not spread radiation poisoning everywhere *it* goes. In other words, *Radon* was very much in the tradition of a typical Western monster film, where the Bomb is employed merely to unleash the beast; other than that, there is no subtext regarding the dangers of radiation. The problems of the past were giving way to the fictions of the future.

The film's conclusion brilliantly encapsulates the classic Honda monster movies at their best, as one Radon decides to burn in death with its mate, rather than survive by itself. Accompanied by Ifukube's eloquent music, Tsuburaya's poetic effects and Arikawa's radiant photography, the ending conveys not only an unavoidable tragedy, but a regret that it all had to end this way. By *any* definition of the word, *Radon* was and is a remarkable achievement.

THE DEFENSE FORCE OF THE EARTH (1957)
(CHIKYU BOEIGUN)
THE MYSTERIANS

Cast & Credits

Film Register: No. 10267
Release Date: Dec. 28, 1957
Running Time: 88 minutes, 11 seconds

Staff: Producer: Tomoyuki Tanaka; Director: Ishiro Honda ; Original Story: Jojiro Okami; Adaptation: Shigeru Kayama; Screenplay: Takeshi Kimura; Cinematography: Hajime Koizumi; Art Director: Teruaki Abe; Sound Recording: Masanobu Miyazaki; Lighting: Kuichiro Kishida; Music: Akira Ifukube; Assistant Director: Koji Kajita; Sound Arrangement: Ichiro Minawa; Editor: Hiroichi Iwashita; Production Manager: Yasuaki Sakamoto; Special Effects Techniques: Director: Eiji Tsuburaya; Cinematography: Hidezaburo Araki and Teisho (Sadamasa) Arikawa; Art Director: Akira Watanabe; Lighting: Masao Shiroda; Matte Photography: Hiroshi Mukoyama.

Cast: Kenji Sahara (Joji Atsumi); Yumi Shirakawa (Etsuko Shiraishi); Momoko Kochi (Hiroko Iwamoto); Akihiko Hirata (Ryoichi Shiraishi); Takashi Shimura (Prof. Kenjiro Adachi); Susumu Fujita (Defense Commander Morita); Hisaya Ito (Captain Seki); Yoshio Kosugi (Air Defense Commander Sugimoto); Fuyuki Murakami (Dr. Nobuo Kawanami); Yoshio Tsuchiya (Mysterian Leader); Minosuke Yamada (Hamamoto); Tetsu Nakamura (Prof. Tabotobu Koda); Heihachiro Okawa (Interpreter); Takeo Oikawa. (Saburo Nozawa); Haruya Kato (Senzo); Senkichi Omura (Kenkichi); Yutaka Sada (Police Inspector Miyamoto); Hideo Mihara (Commander Emoto); Rikie Sanjo (Etsuko's mother); Soji Ubakata (Prof. Masao Noda); Mitsuo Tsuda (National Diet Member); Ren Imaizumi (Hayama); Shin Otomo (Officer Kawata); Jiro Kumagai (Colonel Ito); Akio Kusama (Police Chief Togawa).

The Film

Defense Force's story was written by a mystery writer and former military pilot named Jojiro Okami before it was developed further by Shigeru Kayama; Takeshi Kimura then pieced-together the final screenplay. While the novelty of an alien invasion determined to subjugate the Earth was already a well-worn concept by 1957, *Defense Force* was not without its intriguing points: Rather than routinely open-fire once landing on Earth, the Mysterians tried deception by offering an olive branch, while the idea of aliens capturing Earth women for the purposes of crossbreeding to further their race was a bold concept, even by today's standards.

The plot itself has many lapses of logic: It is never made clear how the Mysterians managed to land on the Earth and dig themselves into its soil undetected or how or when Shiraishi was first contacted by them; it also seems hard to believe that the scientist would be so heartless as to lend both his sister and fiancé to the aliens "for the sake of science." Shiraishi's famed report is known to both sides, yet the Mysterians do not object to the astrophysicist openly listing their weaknesses, and even the details of their Underground Fortress (when Shiraishi is told of the Fortress' true purpose, he seems shocked, even though he wrote about it in his report). Atsumi happens upon an entrance to the Mysterians' Dome—not by any deliberate inspection on his part but by stumbling upon it accidentally—and never bothers to inform the military about his discovery. For that matter, the Mysterians do not patrol or otherwise monitor these vulnerable entrances to their Dome; although, judging by the effectiveness of their sentries, it wouldn't have made much difference (when Atsumi sneaks past two sentries on his mission of sabotage, it bears an uncanny resemblance to a similar moment in *Star Wars* 20 years later).

The scene showing the flags of many nations waving in the wind had great significance for the Japanese, as the year before they had been permitted to join the United Nations, and thus become an official member of the world community. The Cold War tensions of the time are noted in a shot where General Morita is talking to the press; behind him are a row of flags with Japan's flag symbolically sandwiched-in between the Russian and American flags. On this occasion however, despite their differences, the nations of the world will unite to fight against the Mysterians; even the *Alpha* and *Beta* crafts fly for the "World Air Force" with the emblems of the United Nations visible on their vertical stabilizers.

The original story had no monster in it but producer Tanaka loved giant monsters in his movies as they were good box office and insisted the writers put one in. The result was Mogera (aka Moguerra), initially to have been a living creature, but changed to a robot to stress the aliens' technical abilities. Designed under the supervision of Akira Watanabe and utilizing elements that bring to mind both Godzilla and Radon, the appealing if bizarre-looking robot makes a grand entrance from the side of a hill, and its nine-minute rampage through the village is very-well handled, but serves no other purpose other than as an interesting visual diversion. *Defense Force* was the first of Honda's genre films to be effects rather than story-driven, and to that end it was one of Tsuburaya's more elaborate films up to that time, filled with all manner of optical animation (although at times the film seems scratchy during some of the optical work due to excessive handling during the printing process).

Some of the shots are eye-pooping, such as a daring matte shot showing the miniature *Alpha* lifting off from an actual airfield, and a particularly audacious moment when a soldier tries to leap clear of his sinking tank in a bold bit of puppet work. Tsuburaya's usual attention to detail is typically meticulous, such as the miniature landscape seen during Mogera 's rampage, brilliantly recreated down to a stone-built train tunnel complete with railroad tracks. Tsuburaya cleverly uses live-action mattes of streams of fire hose water when the firefighters attempt to extinguish the flames started by Mogera's attack and—in an endearing moment typical of Tsuburaya's work—as the giant robot reaches the bridge, it pauses to look down into the gulley. Tsuburaya had two reasons to be proud of *Defense Force*—his efforts not only earned him his second Special Techniques Award (*Godzilla* being the first), but his "Special Technique Section of the Production Department" ("Special Effects Department") was now officially recognized by the studio.

Defense Force was Honda's first widescreen film and the director took to the new format with zeal and attention to framing and composition, fully embracing its possibilities. Working with Honda for the first time was cinematographer Hajime Koizumi, who did such an outstanding job that Honda would utilize him exclusively for his genre work over the next decade. Many of the film's key outdoor sequences—such as the village ceremony and the Mysterians' departure—were filmed as "day-for-night" for mood effect, and the film itself is one of Honda's most lushly-photographed; the single-strip Eastman Color process radiantly capturing the gorgeous location scenery, the colorful lanterns of the festival, the orange hues of the forest fire and even the colorful neon tubes buzzing in the Mysterians' Dome (Teruaki Abe's interiors of the Mysterian's Dome were acceptable enough as being of alien origin, but his interior set of the home Ryoichi and Hiroko are being sheltered in is abysmal).

The director had many fine actors in the film, including Takeshi Shimura as Tanjiro Adachi (who shows his skill as a "thinking actor" when he pounds his shoulder to indicate the muscle cramps endured from many hours spent gazing at the heavens), and Akihiko Hirata was excellent as the conceited Ryoichi Shiraishi. Momoko Kochi (Hiroko) and Yumi Shirakawa (Etsuko) essentially played frightened females, but particularly pleasing was Kenji Sahara as Joji Atsumi in his second straight leading role in a Honda fantasy film, lending the part his typically jovial nature tinged with urgency and vulnerability (the shots of Atsumi shooting a Mysterian ray gun, looking dapper and determined in his jacket and fedora, is one of the more-unsung images of 1950's science-fiction films).

Yoshio Tsuchiya portrayed the Leader of the Mysterians. Initially cast as Joji, Tsuchiya found playing the Mysterian Leader irresistible and implored Honda to give him the part, and although Honda tried to persuade the actor to change his mind and retain his original billing—after all, it was the leading role—Tsuchiya insisted and Honda, touched by the actor's sincerity, relented. At the time of filming, Tsuchiya coincidentally belonged to a group called The Space Traveler's Association. "Then," Tsuchiya recalled in an interview years later with Steve Ryfle, "I learned that this organization really was crooked and wanted to divide up the Moon and sell it as real estate! I was so outraged that, in the movie, when the Earth scientists balk at giving the Mysterians the land they want, I ad-libbed, 'But *you're* trying to divide up the Moon and sell it!'"

Tsuchiya remembered the experience of working on *Defense Force* as anything but easy: "The lighting was intense. My costume was made out of vinyl implanted with fiberglass and my skin couldn't breathe... When my costume was lit, the fibers kind of sparkled in the studio and they were flying all over in the air. I couldn't help breathing them and it was bad, but I was young then and didn't mind much. Wearing the helmet was hot too, so I didn't put it on until right before shooting started. When I talked inside of it, it echoed like hell and gave me a headache, but the people outside couldn't hear me. So, when I finished my line, I signaled 'OK' to the people outside." To give the alien an "extraterrestrial" feel, Tsuchiya utilized stylized body and head movements; the aliens walk about stiffly and shake their bodies when they laugh. To simulate the mumbling voice of the Mysterian tongue heard faintly under the Japanese language, Tsuchiya's voice was heavily distorted with multi-layering, a task so arduous and time-consuming it was never again repeated in a Toho film.

Akira Ifukube's music for *Defense Force* resulted in one of the composer's most admired and beloved scores. Ifukube shied away from what had been the trend in science-fiction scores up to that time—electronic effects, theremins and the like—and instead utilized a conventional orchestra, with brass as a prominent element, aided by violins, flutes and a subtle but effectively-used vibraphone to give the picture an "outer-space" feel. Embroidered throughout the film is a memorable theme comprised of urgent horns, rapidly-pounding pianos, a furious flute and bellicose brass ("The First Round of Battle, "The Mysterians Retaliate" and "Furious Electron Cannon Assault"). A snippet of this music can be heard at the beginning of the "Main Title," followed by shimmering violins, brass and fluttering clarinets and ending with a dual stroke of the vibraphone predicting an uncertain future (this exciting music is heard continuously through the film, yet is so striking, it never becomes boring.)

Ifukube scores the devastated village in "The Collapse" with slow brass, fluttering clarinets and quivering violin strings stressing a disaster, while coloring a background portion of the "Mogera Attacks" segment with two ascending and recurring notes on woodwinds, cleverly stressing its gyroscopic mechanisms. His exciting music propels the film along, as in the case of "Shelter," heard during the evacuation scene, with rapid and repeating bowstrings, shrill whistles and urgent brass. The score is not only unique but unpredictable: When "The *Alpha* and the *Beta*" circle about and prepare to attack the Dome, Ifukube raises the tension with strumming strings and pounding piano. Ifukube's use of amplified piano wires and low, heavy brass during "The Kidnapping" is hardly subtle considering the supposedly clandestine nature of the operation (Ifukube does not supply any music until one of the relatives opens a door and spots the girl rising upward so as to emphasize his shock, while Honda adds a gust of wind). And, while another composer might have given an event such as the landing of the Makalites a certain vitality, in "Markalite FAHP," Ifukube gives the moment earth-shaking significance with trilling flues, a timpani roll and a blast of trumpets shrieking in their highest registers.

As the citizens seek "Shelter," Ifukube's music gives the moment a sense of exigency with rapid bow strings, shrieking trumpets and trilling flutes. A brief, 24-second cue entitled *The Mysterians Depart*—a redolent, paranormal piece orchestrated with violins and vibraphone—was regrettably deleted, but fortunately, Ifukube's "Ending" music was retained, an evocative and reflective selection played on tinkling piano keys, as if mimicking an interstellar code ordering the saucers to retreat (with the Mysterians no doubt crying "96 Tears"). This is augmented with a tentative vibraphone, longing violins with reassuring trumpets and flutes playing a sustained note, hinting at an uneasy triumph that so appropriately sums up the ending to a Honda fantasy film.

Defense Force was the first in a series of films where Honda expounded upon his favorite theme of international cooperation for the sake of world peace. Despite its occasional human heroics, *Defense Force* is ultimately a film about machines and not men, and while the effects are undeniably impressive, they are ultimately all sizzle and no steak. Even under such circumstances the director manages little human touches; in the first scene in the film during the ceremonial dance, Honda slowly tracks his camera back from the main platform and dancers so as to allow us to leisurely take-in the proceedings as if we are actually there. There is another moment when an anxious and overwhelmed policeman hands his phone over with much relief to his superior, and an odd bit of business during Mogera's attack when firefighters improbably—and fatally—take the time to repack their fire hose equipment.

The scene when Mogera is attacked by the military showcases the combined talents of Honda, Tsuburaya and Ifukube at their fullest: The scene is fast-paced, exciting and beautifully filmed (Honda pulls frames out-of the bazooka-firing sequence to speed up the action). When a grim-faced soldier opens fire with his flamethrower (a dangerous stunt filmed in open country), his flame superbly matches the miniature flame shooting at the robot and the effect—aided with seamless cuts and rapid panning—is breathtaking and utterly convincing. When the robot heads towards the camera with fires framing the shot, it is one of the most-exhilarating moments in all of Tsuburaya's work, and when the bridge is blown-up—with Honda cutting the music at the time of the explosion—it is extremely well-done.

After Atsumi tells the officials in the Diet that the monstrous mechanism was manufactured out of unknown elements, Honda punctuates the announcement by having two members of the audience stand up in astonishment. When the military holds a press conference stating that no deals will be made with the Mysterians, Honda fills the screen with no less than 50 actors. Honda ends some scenes by cutting on actor's movements, such as when Etsuko sadly turns her head after hearing the news of her fiancé's disappearance, and again when Joji fearfully looks up at Adachi after the military announces they will launch an attack on the Mysterians. Honda continues to emphasize human loss and suffering, such as the moment after the Mysterian's "plea for peace" (which conveniently sidesteps the intergalactic-breeding issue) when a devastated platoon sergeant informs General Morita that his entire regiment was wiped out and when Commander Sugimoto lowers his mike with disgust after the *Alpha* is destroyed.

Honda stresses the suffering of the aliens as well, showing how the rapidly-dropping temperature is affecting their central nervous systems—one Mysterian, backed up against a background wall, seems to be having uncontrollable muscle spasms—while close-ups of the dead, dying and decaying Mysterians leave an indelible memory in the mind of the viewer (one of Honda's most "touching" moments occurs during the evacuation scene, as mothers and their children are being escorted toward waiting ships; a soldier is waving the evacuees along when he stops, reaches out and gently touches the shoulder of a little girl as she passes by). Another key moment occurs when the bathing Atsumi watches Mogera stride by her window, a scene which caused Nakano to observe: "*That* illustrates Honda's basic approach to filmmaking. Even if the movie was about something as unrealistic as monsters, he wanted to show how they would affect people's lives."

From the design and execution of its super weapons (including the *Alpha* and *Beta* crafts, which could hardly be expected to fly given their inherently-unstable aerodynamics) to the peculiar moment when Shiraishi hands Atsumi his completed report on the Mysterians with time running out, *Defense Force* may have more *chutzpah* on a grander scale than any science-fiction film before or since; even so, it was one of Honda's favorite movies. "I like the way the film looks," he told Milner in an interview shortly before his death in 1993. "I remembered it as being an attempt to portray a very new and surprising world, using never-before-seen gadgets such as transparent plastics and neon tubes."

The moment when Adachi and his associate see the saucers through their telescope appearing from behind the Moon perfectly showcases the Golden Age of Toho's fantasy films; it is dramatic, uniquely-scored and poetic to the point of having sunlight reflect off the saucer leading the procession. In the end, the film succeeded then as now as it was intended to succeed, as purely uncomplicated escapist fare, due in no small part to the *joy de vive* brought to the fore by its filmmakers. Flamboyant if flawed, what *The Defense Force of the Earth* lacks in emotion, it more than makes up with enthusiasm. Over 50 years later, that enthusiasm is still contagious.

THE BEAUTY AND THE LIQUID PEOPLE (1958)
(BIJO TO EKATAI-NINGEN)
THE H-MAN

Cast & Credits

Film Register No. 10577
Release Date: June 24, 1958
Running Time: 87 minutes

Staff: Producer: Tomoyuki Tanaka; Director: Ishiro Honda; Original Story: Hideo Unagami; Screenplay: Takeshi Kimura; Cinematography: Hajime Koizumi; Production Design: Takeo Kita; Recording: Choshiro Mikami and Masanobu Miyazaki; Lighting: Tsuruzo Nishikawa; Music: Masaru Sato; Assistant Director: Koji Kajita; Editor: Ichiji Taira; Production Manager: Teruo Maki; Still Photos: Matsuo Yoshizaki; Special Effects Techniques: Director: Eiji Tsuburaya; Optical Cinematography: Hidezaburo Araki and Sadamasa (Teisho) Arikawa; Art Director: Akira Watanabe; Lighting: Masao Shiroda; Matte Work: Hiroshi Mukoyama.

Cast: Yumi Shirakawa (Chikako Arai); Kenji Sahara (Dr. Masada); Akihiko Hirata (Detective Tominaga); Eitaro Ozawa (Inspector Miyashita); Koreya Senda (Dr. Maki); Makoto Sato (Uchida); Hisaya Ito (Misaki); Machiko Kitagawa (Hanae); Yoshio Tsuchiya (Detective Taguchi); Naomi Shiraishi (Mineko); Ko Mishima (Gangster Kishi); Yoshibumi Tajima (Detective Sakata); Tetsu Nakamura (Chen); Haruya Kato (Sailor Who Gets Slimed); Senkichi Omura (Dai-Chan); Ayumi Sonoda (Emi); Kan Hayashi, Soji Ubakata, Mitsuo Tsuda, Yutaka Oka, Akio Kusama (Policemen); Minosuke Yamada (Chief Kusuda); Jun Fujio (Nishiyama); Ren Yamamoto (Saeki); Akira Sera (Horita); Tadao Nakamaru (Detective Seki); Yosuke Natsuki (Man on Date); Keiko Yakata (Girl on Date); Yasuhiro Shigenobu (Yasukichi); Akira Yamada (Officer Wakasugi); Nadao Kirino (Shimazaki, the Waiter); Yutaka Sada (Taxi Driver); Shin Otomo (Hamano); Yutaka Nakayama (An-Chan); Kamayuki Tsubono (Detective Ogawa).

The Film

An actor named Hideo Unagami wrote the original story for *The Beauty and the Liquid People*, but the screenplay was almost entirely the work of Takeshi Kimura, whose script typically portrays the figures in authority (the police in particular) as gruff, unreceptive and unsympathetic. As with his script for *The First Gas Human Being* two years later, *Liquid People* is more along the lines of a crime-drama dotted with horrific elements, than as a straightforward horror film. *Liquid People* begins with stock footage of a nighttime atomic bomb detonation, followed by newspaper headlines announcing that the bomb may have been responsible for the disappearance of the *Ryujim Maru II*—bringing to mind the real-life *Fukuryu-maru* ("Lucky Dragon") incident which inspired *Godzilla*.

In a moment that would have an echo in *Dogora* six years later, an individual sitting in a car arrests the attention of a local patrol officer. Much of the dialogue is memorable, such as when an exasperated Tominaga tells Masada that "Scientists should stay in their labs and experiment!" It is also a cute notion that Masada is so insistent on proving his "Ash of Death" theory to the point of entering Tominaga's squad car and telling the driver to drive to the docks; not surprisingly, Tominaga then immediately bars Masada from entering police headquarters.

The crux of the film is not the horror of the Liquid People, but the conflict between Masada and his policeman pal, Tominaga. The two are constantly at odds, only resolving their differences near the end of the film. Also—for the first time in a segment that would be repeated in films to follow—the media is denied entrance in their efforts to obtain information, in this case from the "Emergency Countermeasures Conference." Unfortunately, although the film does contains many suspenseful scenes, the film itself is not terribly suspenseful, nor does it build up any momentum toward the climax. The scary scenes—effective as they are—are constantly being interrupted by expository sequences that are not nearly as gripping (a criticism many have made about all of Honda's fantasy films).

The film's central character, Misaki, is mentioned continuously throughout the film, but except for a brief glimpse of him in the opening scene, he is never seen again—and even then we do not know who he is or his significance to the story. Kimura dishes out moral judgment in the film as characters live and die by certain rules: Emi, the sultry cabaret dancer, is not necessarily a bad person, but her tawdry profession condemns her to a horrific death (her final expression of transfixed terror is one of many chilling moments in the film). For his part, Honda choreographs Emi's signature dance number by having her reacting to a spotlight shining on her from above by squinting and squirming, as if she were some lower form of life; she then writhes about on the floor while up-tempo music and a myriad of lights flurry about. Her interpretive dance suggests running from the police and firing a machine gun.

In Toho's press release for the film, Tsuburaya wrote, "For the creation of the liquid people we decided to use gelatin and cellophane, which we crumpled then flattened into a solid mass. We also used organic glass which is more transparent and colorless than gelatin. We could have used whatever we had thought would do the job, but finally we decided to avoid using things that audiences might recognize, although we did want the forms of the things to look somewhat human." To create the effect of a breathing liquid man, water was added to a small amount of organic glass, then inserted between two pieces of transparent glass; the glasses were then repeatedly pulled apart and put back together, resulting in a jelly-like substance. Perhaps the finest shot in the picture however occurs near the end of the film when a jeep crosses a bridge over a river of fire.

Optical printing, traveling mattes, superimposition, animation, double exposure and reverse footage were among the many techniques employed to simulate the movement of the slime (one particularly-effective moment has the slime creeping up and into the girl's dressing room, done as a traveling matte). In the scene where Sakata is changed into a liquid person, a fully clothed, life-size balloon figure in human form was gradually deflated; when the air was let out, the arms, legs and head disappeared into the clothes. The final confrontation with the Liquid People in the sewers involved miniatures of the monsters made of celluloid before they were burned with gasoline. Effects cinematographer Arikawa had a number of disagreements with Tsuburaya over the filming of scenes taking place in extreme darkness as Arikawa could not film what he could not see. Nevertheless, in eccentric Tsuburaya fashion, the Master of Special Effects liked the idea of the audience having trouble seeing what was happening on the screen because he felt it added to the mysterious atmosphere.

Honda and cinematographer Koizumi were beginning to establish a good rapport—perhaps the most-important alliance for any filmmaking team—and Koizumi's work on *Liquid People* is perhaps the film's greatest asset, as it establishes a mood of ambient decay hovering over the entire story (Koizumi effectively heightens the terror in the ship-boarding sequence by lighting the sailors' faces from underneath with their lanterns). The cameraman effectively and effortlessly glides his camera through the nightclub with stylish flair, brilliantly establishing its sleazy atmosphere.

We are first introduced to what the detectives consider a "seedy joint" when the scantily-clad Emi—moving seductively about as she occasionally casts flirtatious glances at the camera—sings and sways to a *samba* beat as tuxedo-clad saxophones blare, drums roll and piano keys pound while an ensemble of modestly-clothed and talented dancers cavort under a red spotlight. Chikako is given a stylish introduction as the "Homura Club's" main attraction, singing "The Magic Begins" as a shadow of a woman playing *maracas* appears on the wall behind her adding a visual flair. She looks stunning in a form-fitting white dress and gloves as she sings a 40's-style ballad while *sashaying* down the stairs, before stopping to sing in front of three saxophonists (her second entrance later in the film is not bad either, as she wears an outfit with middle arm-length black gloves and a gorgeous, low-cut, full-length, two-toned black-and-white dress accentuating her generous bosom).

Kazuji Taira's editing is clever and inventive, particularly during the sequence in the nightclub when Shimazaki is trying to find a way out for Uchida, intercut with shots of the watching and waiting police, the dancers, the musicians and the gangsters being apprehended—five events happening simultaneously (Honda apparently appreciated Taira's work as he hired him to edit his next four fantasy films). Examples of Taira's tight editing can be seen when Tominaga and his colleagues discuss Mr. Kin; the next shot shows the man being escorted into the interrogation room, and when the police first go to Chikako's apartment, a woman suddenly enters from an opposite room before the next shot shows a detective rushing in to shut her up. When the sailors reach the captain's quarters on the abandoned ship, a sign first indicates the cabin followed by the men entering the room, and after Masada is asked to remove his life preserver from the police department, the next shot shows it being laid down on the floor of Dr. Maki's lab.

Certain incidents were referred to rather than directly shown— such as having Uchuda's death implied by the reactions of horrified witnesses—and the so-called "chase-scene" has been criticized as being unexciting, but Honda and Taira did what they could with what they were given as Toho was not about to section-off off whole city blocks of traffic for a high-speed pursuit (although it could be interpreted that the gangster deliberately did not speed so as not to attract attention). Instead, in an effort to add action and tension to the chase, Honda utilized a number of close-ups of a smirking Misaki, a determined Masada and a worried Chikako, with quick edits, black-and-photography and unusual camera angles to suggest the rear-end collision.

Masaru Sato's score for *Liquid People* is comprised of brief cues which seem rather incongruous when compared to the visuals. The "Opening" music is very effective, orchestrated with low horns and cymbals followed by a series of high-pitched, strident notes on trumpets (quivering strings enter as the nuclear bomb test footage is shown). As the credits roll over shots of a derelict ship on a moonlit sea, Sato supplies an up-tempo theme comprised of crashing cymbals, blaring trumpets and trilling flutes when this music—more appropriate for a marching band than for a dark and moody horror film—comes to an abrupt stop.

"The Man Who Vanished in the Rain"—used during the film's initial sequence of events—is typical of much of the score, comprised of a "pinging" sound effect achieved by plucking a piano string, then doubling the sound with woodwinds. One of the composer's best pieces is "Detectives in Pursuit of Uchida," heard when the police enter the wine cellar, scored with cymbals, strings and horns. "Pursuit," used during the car-chase scene, uses rapid-paced brass with tinkling piano and xylophone to lend an air of excitement to a scene desperately in need of it. Another nice moment has a bluesy, four-note motif on saxophone accompanying the image of a stranded Chikako wandering exhausted and alone through the sewers (when Chikako is preparing to leave her apartment prior to her kidnapping, the saxophone music recalls her cabaret connection).

"The Liquid Man Meets His End" is used during the final confrontation between the Liquid People and the Inferno Squad, and is both unique and memorable. Scored with ascending/descending strings and frenetic, *staccato* trumpets, it perfectly complements the bizarre, unreal action on the screen before reassuring strings enter as Chikako is finally rescued, while the "Ending" piece has the triumphant sound of rapid bowstrings and confident brass. Sato seems more at ease when scoring the source music used in the nightclub (essentially improvisational jazz), which was an effective counterpoint to the scenes of Uchida trying to escape, the police closing in on the nightclub and the invading slime. He also did a nice job orchestrating Chikako's two pleasant singing numbers (the actress was dubbed by an English-speaking singer): "The Magic Begins" and "So Deep in My Love," with lyrics written by an unidentified member of the British Embassy who was living in Japan during the time of filming.

Akihiko Hirata played Inspector Tominaga as a man under duress from his superiors, as well as having his own skepticism as he and Kenji Sahara (playing the apologetic, pesky and very young college professor, Masada) effectively convey the increasing tension developing between them which tests their friendship to the limit (to Honda, the bonding of a deep, personal and professional relationship was of paramount importance). Not nearly as convincing was the lackluster acting from the film's star, Yumi Shirakawa, who simply looked uncomfortable as Chikako. Shirakawa was certainly a capable actress, but she seemed ill-suited for genre work—rarely discussing it in later years—and perhaps appreciated more "realistic" storylines; as a result, her withdrawn performance hurts the film.

The film is filled with scenes of shocking brutality, particularly after Chikako turns the lamp on in her apartment: Honda cuts to a close-up of her face wincing in pain as a black glove suddenly comes into frame and seizes her by the throat (after she is thrown down on her bed and told to keep still, the unknown assailant assures her that "I don't want to hurt you" before slapping her four times in the face). When the police discover Nishiyama's dead body in the house at the harbor, a close-up of the man's pale skin, dead open eyes and bloodstained shirt give grim testimony to a violent end.

Liquid People is a unique film in the Honda *oeuvre*. Lacking the power and intensity of his previous monster films, *Liquid People* was instead terrifying subtle; scenes such as the derelict ship sequence and the slime people invading the dressing room are eerily disturbing and unsettling, and the scenes of the frogs bubbling away as they dissolve slightly sickening. There are a number of nice directorial touches: When Masada arrives to take a radiation reading of what is left of Detective Sakata, Chikako screams off-screen as she threatened by the slime. Waiter Shirakawa makes his second appearance in the film revealing his face by lowering his tray as an off-screen musician grunts and a saxophone bellows, punctuating the moment. When the slime claims its first sailor victim onboard the derelict ship, we first hear the man scream, see the reaction of the sailors, *then* see a close-up of the man's agonized face before it sinks out-of-frame.

Undeniably, the flashback sequence aboard the *Ryujim Maru II* was the most frightening of all the Honda/Tsuburaya collaborations, creepily scored, acted and photographed, with the shots of the sailor' bodies decomposing into slime disturbing and heightened by off-screen gasps and moans (the idea of a slime man absorbing his living brother is a disturbing notion).

The Beauty and the Liquid People is Honda's most stylish film and ironically his most underappreciated. The idea of blob-like substances absorbing people would be done elsewhere—most notably in *The Blob* (1958) and *Caltiki* (1960)—but neither effort contains the verve, artistic flair, creative cutting and gorgeous photography found in *Liquid People*. The first of Honda's three "horror/transformation films," *Liquid People* is nonetheless hampered by drawn-out debates between the police and the scientists, Sato's uneven score and Shirikawa's catatonic performance (the events taking place during film's final reel—beginning with Chikako's kidnapping and ending with her rescue—are very predictable).

Honda had now directed five genre films in five years, each one as remarkable as it was unique, presenting him with tremendously exciting and rewarding challenges. The low-key approach of *Liquid People*, with its elements of mob violence, lurid sex, steamy jazz, radiation poisoning and *film noir* elements was as radically different from any Honda film before or after. As it happened however, his next venture returned him to by-now all-too-familiar ground.

BARAN, THE GIANT MONSTER (1958)
(DAIKAIJU BARAN)
VARAN THE UNBELIEVABLE

Cast & Credits

Film Register No. 10792
Release Date: October 14, 1958
Running Time: 87 minutes, 9 seconds

Staff: Producer: Tomoyuki Tanaka; Director: Ishiro Honda; Original Story: Takashi (Ken) Kuronuma; Screenplay: Shinichi Sekizawa; Cinematography: Hajime Koizumi; Art Director: Kiyoshi Shimizu; Lighting: Mitsuo Kaneko; Recording: Wataru Onuma and Masanobu Miyazaki; Music: Akira Ifukube; Assistant Director: Koji Kajita; Sound Effects: Ichiro Minawa; Editor: Ichiji (Kazuji) Taira; Production Manager: Shotaro Kawagami; Special Effects Techniques: Director: Eiji Tsuburaya; Cinematography: Hidezaburo Araki and Sadamasa (Teisho) Arikawa; Art Director: Akira Watanabe; Lighting: Kuichiro Kishida; Matte Processing: Hiroshi Mukoyama.

Cast: Kozo Nomura (Kenji Uozaki); Ayumi Sonoda (Yuriko Shindo); Koreya Senda (Dr. Sugimoto); Akihiko Hirata (Dr. Fujimura); Fuyuki Murakami (Dr. Majima); Yoshio Tsuchiya (Lt. Katsumoto); Minosuke Yamada (Defense Commander); Hisaya Ito (Ichiro Shindo); Yoshibumi Tajima (Captain of Battleship *Uranami*); Nadao Kirino (Yutaka Wada); Akira Sera (Village Priest); Akio Kusama (First Officer Kusama); Fumiko Motoma (Gen's "Ken's" mother); Takashi Ito (Gen "Ken"); Fumindo Matsuo (Nitto Press Cameraman Motohiko Horiuchi); Soji Ubakata (Police Officer); Toku Ihara (Villager/Soldier); Mitsuo Tsuda, Jiro Kumagai, Keisuke Yamada, Haruya Sakamoto (Defense Officials); Shoichi Hirose, Koji Suzuki (Fishermen); Hideo Shibuya, Sen Hayamizu, Tokio Okawa (Camermen); Hiroko Terasawa (Camerawoman); Masaki Shinohara (Villager/Fisherman); Mitsuo Matsumoto, Yasuo Onishi (Reporters).

The Film

Sometime during 1958, Toho was commissioned by the American Broadcasting Corporation to produce the special effects for an American television monster movie, with financial backing coming from the network's motion picture division, AB-PT Productions; AB-PT was initially formed to produce a package of 20 or so movies in the late fifties and early sixties and had originally planned to finance a US-altered version of *Godzilla Raids Again* in 1957 (in retrospect, it seems odd that an American television studio would wish to co-produce either a TV series or a movie originating in Japan, as international films made for television were a rarity, particularly in the wide-screen format. It is uncertain how much money exchanged hands or how much of the movie was completed before the deal collapsed).

The film was originally shot in 1:33 Academy Aspect Ratio for television broadcasting, but when the project was cancelled, Toho decided to crop what they had filmed down to 2:35 TohoScope, before filming the remainder in 2:35 so as to match the previously shot footage in 1:33; this dreadful comprise even had a name: "Toho Pan Scope" (again, it is uncertain which new sections of the film were cropped and which sections were shot in 2:35 in order to complete the picture). When the proposed film fell through for reasons unknown, Toho decided to complete and distribute the film for its domestic audiences and wrote in a hurriedly-constructed storyline. *Baran* was a curious film in another respect, as Toho's recent genre entries were in lavish color, but *Baran* was released in moody black-and-white, a fantasy film format Honda had not shot in since *Abominable Snowman* three years earlier.

Baran is roughly divided into three parts: The island sequences, Baran at sea and the attack on the airport. The best sequence is undoubtedly the atmospheric first, while the second sequence profited from some excellent miniature work, to say nothing of Ifukube's stirring score. The third and final sequence *should* have been the most-exciting as it involved the attack on the airport and the monster's death, but instead was tedious and unremarkable (as it happens, the film's true hero is neither the male lead, the scientists or the military, but an anonymous helicopter pilot). Another significant aspect of *Baran* was its screenplay by Shinichi Sekizawa, whose name would become an integral part for many of Toho's most successful fantasy films. Two themes close to the scriptwriter's heart were forest and/or jungle settings and comedy relief, and both are prevalent in *Baran* (the differing approaches between screenwriters Sekizawa and Kimura can be seen in their treatment of journalists; in Kimura's films, they are usually arrogant and insensitive; in Sekizawa's films, they are typically comic relief).

Due to the limited time allowed for writing the script, most of the dialogue consists of endless military briefings, defeatist scientists and philosophical gibberish. The film itself gets off to a dubious start with an unexplained missile launching punctuated with a cryptic narration regarding rockets being launched into space which will have nothing to do with the plot, followed by a boring lecture and a search for rare butterflies; not exactly on the same level as searching for an Abominable Snowman. Dr. Uozaki's cursory explanation of the monster's origins is merely a condensed version of similar scenes in *Godzilla* and *Radon*, and the village patriarch refusing to be saved harkens back to *Abominable Snowman.*

The script contains many elements that were either unoriginal or would return in later Honda films, such as problems with a jeep (*Defense Force*), the sounds of a fish splashing in the lake scaring a photographer (*Submarine Warship*), an aircraft getting swatted down by a monster (*Sanda vs. Gairah*), observers on a ship ducking down when a supposedly-killed monster rises from the sea (*King Kong vs. Godzilla*) and fisherman having difficulty catching fish (*Godzilla*). In addition, the interference of outsiders bringing to a halt natives worshiping their god, their intrusion onto Holy Ground and the trapping of a female under a tree is right out of *King Kong.*

In a scene possibly inspired by *Creature From the Black Lagoon* (1954), poison is deposited into a lake to try and raise the monster; moments such as this suggest the film's main premise is about the despoiling of the environment, however nothing further is done with the notion as the point of the movie is simply about a giant monster that must be stopped.

Unlike the hideously-deformed natives who populated the *Abominable Snowman*, Baran's natives are relatively normal-looking and only one of them—their fanatical priest—will be killed rather than the entire tribe. There is a key moment when Kenji and Horiguchi implore the natives to aid them in their search of Ken and Yuriko, and forget about their "imaginary" demon, thus leaving the world of superstition behind and entering into the real world, a premise reflected in a brief shot of Gen's demon-mask lying face-up on the ground (oddly, despite the fact the natives had worshipped Baran for generations, it takes only a few words from the outsiders to convince them to shed their religious beliefs). At the end of the film, after the monster submerges, a huge explosion indicates Baran's presumed off-screen death, a sorry finish for any monster.

Tsuburaya's work on *Baran* has touches that are absolutely spellbinding—such as a miniature soldier standing up in a stalled rocket-launcher pointing out Baran's approach, and a pilot's POV shot as he dives on Baran while going through a cloud of smoke—but these are compromised by shots that have a harried, slipshod quality to them. There is a decided absence of low-level shots and wires are often visible. During the monster's assault on the airport, miniature rocket launchers career wildly down the roads while miniature tanks jerk around unrealistically, some impossibly firing off double-rounds at the beast.

There is a preponderance of close-ups of the puppet-head monster (easier and quicker to set up and film) but Baran's habitat is beautifully realized with wonderful detail, with real pumice stones used to simulate boulders shown cascading down from the craggy peaks. Some shots are quite clever, such as one of a jeep motoring past parked planes at the Haneda Airport—actually an unmoving stationary full-size jeep shot against a back-projected ground-level pan of a portion of the airport's elaborate miniature diorama. During the scene when Baran destroys the village, sharp eyes can spot the reflection of a television camera filming the action as the monster stirs up dust and dirt. The reflection occurred because the scene was shot from behind a glass plate (a portion of the painted landscape can be seen in the lower left-and-right foregrounds), making it possible to see the camera. On the plus side are three superb aerial shots of Baran swimming in the sea, accomplished with a miniature Baran towed in the open ocean.

The Haneda Airport set which Baran destroys had been intricately constructed in miniature, based on photographs of the actual airport, but Tanaka—ever concerned with rising costs—was concerned as to why Tsuburaya's effects department was spending so much time and money constructing an elaborate miniature set which was eventually going to be demolished. Tsuburaya explained that sets of this nature *had* to be overly-elaborate in case of a miscue with the live-action, stressing that having more than might be needed allowed for better coverage and was a necessary evil in order to cover one's losses.

Hajime Koizumi, who had done such a splendid job photographing *Liquid People* four months earlier, seemed to have been little interested in Baran as his work is generally flat and uninspired; there is one notable shot late in the film when the shadows of soldiers can be seen silhouetted atop a building. Another nice shot shows a disappointed

Kenji and Horiguchi returning to the gate with shafts of light streaming in from behind (Honda's black-and-white exterior sets were always very convincing, whereas his color exterior sets tended to look somewhat artificial).

The acting is not particularly memorable, with the showiest part going to Akira Sera, playing the High Priest and Keeper of the Lake Path with wonderful intensity, earning a spectacular death scene. Playing Gen's hysterical mother was Fumiko Motoma—who earned a living playing hysterical women—and whose screams can be heard in *Seven Samurai*, *Godzilla*, *Radon* and many other Toho films. Kozo Nomura (Dr. Kenji Uozaki) and Ayumi Sonoda (Yuriko) were adequate in their roles, with Fumito Matsuo supplying comedic relief as the photographer Horiguchi. Koreya Senda was unremarkable as Dr. Sugimoto, playing his part with mild consternation, but much more welcome were Yoshio Tsuchiya as a military officer and Akihiko Hirata as "Special Dynamite Inventor" Dr. Fujimura, although their talents were not given much of a chance to shine in their bland roles.

Lawrence Tuczynski has noted, "...the best part of this movie is the outstanding score," which would not be the last time this would happen in a Ishiro Honda monster film scored by Akira Ifukube. *Baran* begins extremely well, due in no small part to Ifukube's "Main Title" music, with quivering violins providing an undercurrent to an oboe playing in an ascending-descending 13-note motif which would become one of the composer's most identifiable pieces of music, followed by pounding piano keys and a male chorus chanting over an image of a spooky statue.

Ifukube's music possesses an enormous vitality that drives the picture onward, not unlike the military marches heard throughout the film. Many have argued that the maestro's orchestrations lacked the full-orchestral color of his contemporaries, but the point must be made that few if any composers were able to convey the kind of prideful power the monsters musically merit. For example, when the beast goes on the rampage, trumpets blare out "Ba-ra-dagi—Ba-ra-dagi" ("God Baran") as a musical phrase, accentuating its awesome presence.

The music creates the only suspense in "Cannon Shots at the Lake," scored with low woodwinds, quivering violins and tapping piano, returning again in "Self Defense Force Tanks Attack" in a more-ebullient manner. Ifukube's music reaches ethereal heights with blaring trumpets and pounding timpani as the monster disappears into a cloud in "Baran Flies," while "Fishing Boat Disaster" begins with the monster's appearance heralded by rapid cello strings (17 years before *Jaws*), then trumpets go berserk as the fishermen are sent to the briny deep by the monster. Since the movie is about the conflict between the military and the monster, the score has no tender or reflective themes, so Ifukube let his musical imagination run wild with his unbridled score (what is even more remarkable is that Ifukube wrote additionally outstanding tracks for the proposed US TV-movie). As it is, Akira Ifukube's score for *Baran* was his finest for a Honda monster film.

After having great artistic success with his earlier five fantasy films, Honda stumbled badly with *Baran*. During the scene when Kenji manages to locate the injured Yuriko in the forest, Honda went way-beyond the level of credibility when Kenji manages to lift a 50-foot spruce tree off Yuriko's leg, and after Fujimura reluctantly agrees to give his new explosive device a try, he awkwardly crosses in front of the camera during a medium shot of the conference. In a regrettable and ill-timed comedic bit, two Laurel and Hardy-type truck drivers beat a hasty retreat when an army officer informs them they must drive their truck of explosives near the monster, and when a pilot is told to confine Baran to the airport, his reply is laced with boredom (to make matters worse, his oxygen mask tilts at a comical angle when he turns his head); at another point, a helicopter's roterblades reach their takeoff RPM in the blink of an eye.

Admittedly, Honda was not given a great deal to work with on a human level, and as a result, his lack of enthusiasm translates into dull and lifeless scenes. The director began repeating himself and to lesser effect; as with *Godzilla* and *Abominable Snowman*, Japanese intruders run into trouble when they investigate unfriendly natives worshiping a god. With little else to do plot-wise, Honda harkened back to his army life, spending a considerable amount of screen time showing scenes of the military preparing to attack Baran; documenting the proper assembling, dispersing, loading and firing of various weapons and evacuation techniques (Honda shows a commander double-checking his men's progress as they gather up their equipment for a hasty retreat).

Baran is by no means a total loss; for example, the scene when the monster destroys the village is up to Tsuburaya's best standards, and the moment when the beast flies into the sky (a moment incredibly missing from the American version) is awe-inspiring. Nevertheless, it became easily the least-memorable of all the monster films directed by Honda; in fact, so quickly did *Baran* fade from popular memory that when the monster reappeared in a cameo in *All Monsters Attack* ten years later, most movie audiences did not recognize it.

Given its hurried nature, it is not surprising then to learn that

Baran failed at the box office; as a result, it Tanaka began to rethink about filming any future monster movies, and when he did—three years later in *Mothra*—the monster and the manner in which it was presented were of a different type entirely: The monster was attractive, colorful, dynamic and sympathetic with no scientific briefing explaining its origins, with the movie itself possessing stylish direction, memorable characters, remarkable special effects and an involving story by Sekizawa. Still, it could have been otherwise. Filmed in color, with a better story and more compelling performances—but with that same magnificent score—*Baran* might today be remembered as one of the perennial monster movies of the 1950's (certainly Ifukube knew what he had, as various selections of his *Baran* score popped-up in numerous Honda films in the coming years).

Baran was not only a derivative movie but an influential as well, and is today best-remembered as the second of only two black-and-white monster films made by the team of Honda/Ifukube/Tanaka/Tsuburaya who once made a film called, *Godzilla*. As a result, this 1958 "remake" (as some have called it) survives as a pleasant shadow of that earlier masterpiece, and is not without its own modest merits: A serious tone, atmospheric vistas and the design of the monster itself, with built-in muscles and lightweight materials that would influence future designs. The film—as contrived and convoluted as its creation—nevertheless reflects a boldness and risk-taking absent from many of the more-refined efforts that followed. Fortunately, Honda's next film would be on a far-grander scale, where the boundaries of mankind's resourcefulness, initiate and drive were limited only by the confines of space itself.

THE GREAT WAR IN SPACE (1959)
(UCHI DAISENSO)
BATTLE IN OUTER SPACE

Cast & Credits

Film Register No. 11339
Release Date: December 26, 1959
Running Time: 91 minutes, 7 seconds

Staff: Producer: Tomoyuki Tanaka; Director: Ishiro Honda; Original Story: Jojiro Okami; Screenplay: Shinichi Sekizawa; Cinematography: Hajime Koizumi; Art Director: Teruaki Abe; Recording: Rokuro Ishikawa; Sound: Masanobu Miyazaki and Choshiro Mikami; Music: Akira Ifukube; Assistant Director: Koji Kajita; Editor: Kazuji Taira; Developing: Toyo Laboratory; Production Manager: Yasuaki Sakamoto; Still Photos: Issei Tanaka; Special Effects Techniques: Eiji Tsuburaya; Optical Cinematography: Hidezaburo Araki; Cinematography: (Teisho) Sadamasa Arikawa; Art Director: Akira Watanabe; Lighting: Kuichiro Kishida; Matte Work: Hiroshi Mukoyama.

Cast: Ryo Ikebe (Ichiro Katsumiya); Kyoko Anzai (Etsuko Shiraishi); Minoru Takada (Defense Commander); Koreya Senda (Dr. Adachi); Len Stanford (Dr. Roger Richardson; U.S. Representative); Harold Conway (Dr. Immerman); George Whyman (Prof. Ahmed, Iranian Representative); Elise Richter (Sylvia); Hisaya Ito (Engineer Kogure); Yoshio Tsuchiya (Koichi Iwamura); Nadao Kirino (Crewman Okada); Kozo Nomura (Rocket Captain); Fuyuki Murakami (Inspector Ariake); Ikio Sawamura (Tokaido Railroad Track Inspector); Jiro Kumagai, Mitsuo Tsuda (Defense Officials); Katsumi Tezuka (Naval Official); Tadashi Okabe (Vice Officer); Osman Yusef , Heinz Bodmer, Koichi Sato, Rinsaku Ogata, Yutaka Oka (SPIP No. 2 Crewmen); Malcolm Pearce (Lt. Pearce/Captain of Rocket 1); Leonard Walsh, Yasuo Araki (Rocket No. 1 Crewmen); Dona Carlson (Mrs. Richardson); Yasuhisa Tsutsumi, Shigeo Kato (Tokaido Train Engineers); Kisao Katamochi (*JSS-3* Radio Operator).

The Film

In publicity materials for *Baran, the Giant Monster*, Eiji Tsuburaya wrote: "The Dark Side of the Moon is still a mystery and I would really like to make a film on that subject. However, the United States and the Soviet Union are doing a lot of research in this area, and if their Moon rockets get to the Moon and show us what is there through a televised broadcast, then we will know everything. Therefore, we must create it before it happens. It's as if science fiction and reality are competing in a race against each other!"

For a time, it seemed that reality held the lead. In January and September of 1959, the Soviet Union launched the first rockets able to reach the moon; less than one month later, a third rocket sent back the first-ever photos taken of the lunar surface and—although the "Space Race" had not yet officially begun—Tsuburaya and his effects team found themselves in a contest to illustrate what the Dark Side of the Moon looked like before the Russians did.

Jojiro Okami wrote the original story for *War in Space* as he had for *Defense Force*. Screenwriter Sekizawa's script lets the action sequences carry the film, which are roughly divided into three sections: The initial attacks on the Earth by the Natalians, the journey to the Moon to destroy the alien base and the battle for control of the Earth. The plot then of the entire movie is very simple, that the Earth is under attack from outer space and must forcibly defend itself in order to survive.

The film contains moments that innocently reflect the naïve attitude regarding such matters as radiation: The delegates enter a room where a row of successively distanced targets have been arranged in a tunnel stretching off into the distance for a demonstration of a new ray gun, and although radiation warnings are casually-posted outside—and since the gun fires a radioactive charge—the men are naturally garbed in protective clothing; although their hands and heads remain uncovered (in a typical Honda touch, just before the weapon is fired, Adachi coaxes the observers to step back). Katsumiya fires the gun and scores direct hits in the middle of the targets, and a close examination of Plate No. 35 shows the material has been completely dissolved by the ray; now infused with plutonium which the men casually handle with their bare hands (just how the Natalians knew about the existence of the ray gun is uncertain, but their fears about its effectiveness were justified, as the ray gun will ultimately destroy them).

Mirroring a moment in *Radon*, broadcasters around the world report the startling news of strange, unexplainable disasters taking place around the world, and when Dr. Richardson theorizes that an unknown force picked up Earth objects, it was a concept that Sekizawa would elaborate on further in *War of the Monsters*. When Katsumiya examines a sample of the particles under a microscope and determines that a miniature radio control device was somehow implanted into the man's brain—thus making him obedient to any alien commands—this was another idea Sekizawa would recycle, in *All Monsters Attack*. As usual, Sekizawa has to have his little joke, such as a having Radar Operator Okada drifting upwards not once but twice as he forgets to compensate for the lack of gravity in space.

When the respective crews are introduced to the approving delegates, it was a moment inspired by a ceremony that took place in Washington, D.C., eight months earlier when NASA introduced to the press the "Mercury Seven:" the first hand-picked American astronauts. One important improvement over *Defense Force* was in the depictions of the female characters; the women in *Defense Force* were helpless women, but in *War in Space*, Etsuko and Sylvia are professional astronauts.

Typical of the creative mode of thinking found in 1950s films dealing with voyages to other worlds, *War in Space* has more than its share of fanciful images; there are no nebulae located between the Earth and the Moon, and the various charts, maps and pencils inside the rocketships should be floating around in their weightless environment; nor are any sounds possible on the Moon (which also does not have any mist-filled valleys). However, the intention here is not to replicate reality, but create a believable fantasy world; when the charmingly toy-like Rovers take off with the aid of their air cushions, the effect, taken in the context of the dramatic situation, is accepted by the viewer out-of-hand in a victory of imagination (Honda was so impressed with the wireworks that he once walked up to supervisor Fumio Nakashiro and asked him, "How did you *do* that?").

When Apollo 11 landed on the Moon on July 20, 1969—and thus nearly ten years after Tsuburaya had already been there—human beings had finally set foot on another world. As it happened, there were no Natalians, but the lunar surface, bland and lifeless as it was, served as an affirmation to Tsuburaya that the excellent work his crew achieved on *War in Space* had been accurate. Watching the "Giant Leap for Mankind" for himself on live TV, Tsuburaya (who would die six months later), called up his old cinematographer Arikawa and told him: "Our special effects team did a good job, we were right. Now, we can hold up our heads before the public."

Koizumi's photography is not as striking as in *Liquid People*, but it is typically lush with Honda using many close-ups to accentuate individual reactions; there is one effective moment when Iwamura—his face spookily filling the frame—is climbing up the ladder in order to disable an unaware astronaut reading his console. Kazuji Taira's editing is a bit sloppy in the scene when Honda cuts from a medium shot of an ovation given by the delegates to the Rocket Commander, to a long shot of the group; the audience has stopped applauding, yet their applause is still audible on the soundtrack. Production Designer Yasuaki Sakamoto's sets also comes into question; although the interior of the rocketship is acceptable, his concept of curving the walls inward to reflect their cylindrical nature means that each crewmember must lower their heads to avoid hitting them on the walls—not a good thing to have to remember in an emergency!

Since what was at stake was nothing less than control of the Earth, composer Ifukube rises to the challenge with a high-stakes score lasting over an hour which includes everything from military marching music to atmospheric lyricism to jazz. Ifukube's music for the moon-watchers scene ("Starry Sky,") is very tender; played on piano, clarinet and strings; the song's "deceptive cadence" (a chord progression that does not resolve itself on the final measure) reflects the anxiety Etsuko feels as to whether Ichiro's love for her will last through the ages.

When Rocketship One encounters the destroyed *J-SS3*, Ifukube introduces a sad, reflective piece laced with mournful cellos, while the astronaut's exploration of the Lunar surface ("Onward!") was one of the composer's more striking instrumentations. The sequence contains neither dialogue nor sound effects and is instead filled with strange cello string bowings, flickering violins, pulsating piano, xylophones, woodwinds and the ubiquitous vibraphone. As the Rovers begin their search of the alien base in "The Exploration Vehicles Start Moving," Ifukube provides determined pianos and brass in a constant, steady rhythm, emphasizing the resolve of the crews, while alternating upper-and-lower piano keys imply the rotation of the Rovers' treads.

Arguably the finest musical moment in the film was one of Ifukube's most moving works: "Return of the S.P.I.P.s," an affecting *elegy* depicting astronaut Iwamura's gallant sacrifice. Ifukube supplies a plucking harp—normally associated with a divine task—along with somber strings and muted brass, with a particularly-poignant rising/falling six-note section on strings, heard when the rocket lifts off from the Moon and again at the end of the scene. What is so significant about this piece—worthy of a samurai's funeral—is that the composer was well-aware that it would be all but buried by the cacophony of sounds dominating the scene. The fact that he scored the scene in the manner which he did, regardless of the on-screen racket, is a testament to his artistry and dedication. Ifukube's music for *War in Space* has been unjustly overlooked; it is one of the finest scores ever written for science-fiction film.

Essentially, actors Ryo Ikebe (Ichiro Katsumiya) and Koreya Senda (Dr. Adachi) reprised roles originally played by Kenji Sahara and Takashi Shimura in *Defense Force*, with Etsuko Shiraishi (earlier played by Momoko Kochi) portrayed by the 20-year-old Kyoko Anzai. As with the majority of Honda's actors, they performed their roles with great intensity and passion; the moment when Senda grabs his chair to secure himself before his rocketship takes evasive action is done with such earnest sincerity that it is touching to watch. Ikebe is appropriately heroic, while Senda's performance was a vast improvement over his earlier ones in *Liquid People* and *Baran*, quite possibly because on this occasion his role had greater depth as one of the first seniors in space (the actor was 55).

In *Defense Force*, actor Yoshio Tsuchiya had played the minor but important role of the Mysterian Leader, imbuing it with his usual creativity. In *War in Space*, he plays the happy-go-lucky Iwamura, eventually showing the emotional and mental conflicts of a man controlled by the Natalians (when being instructed by his alien captors to free himself from his bounds, Tsuchiya shivers as if trying to resist the command). Tsuchiya also took an active interest in the directorial proceedings, suggesting at one point to Honda that the actors should move slowly on the Moon to better demonstrate the lightness of the lunar gravity.

There is an odd moment after Iwamura and Ahmed have struggled over the gun. When the delegates arrive, Iwamura looks up, giving Ahmed the opportunity to retrieve his pistol. Ahmed stands up and draws on the men but is chastised by the Inspector, so he lowers his gun and meekly hands it over to Iriake. The Inspector then begins to take Ahmed away, but they haven't walked two steps when Ahmed suddenly whirls around with the gun in a rare continuity error for Honda. Ahmed then makes a run for it with the delegates in hot pursuit, and the Iranian delegate then sets some sort of record as he manages—with a bleeding right arm—to evade no less than three MPs trying to tackle him, none of whom think of drawing his pistol.

The film elaborates further on Honda's hope for international cooperation, in particular the US/Japan alliance: After Dr. Roger Richardson's family arrives at the Space Center, the Japanese Adachi picks the American boy up and carries him into the building. In another scene, just prior to their rocketship taking off, an American crewmember turns to his Japanese counterpart and asks him if he is okay; and after the alien base has been destroyed, the American Richardson congratulates his Japanese crewman Kogure on his fighting sprit (when photos of the Moon are being displayed on a screen prior to the Moon mission, the pictures are flanked by the Japanese and American flags).

In many of the early science-fiction films such as *Destination Moon* (1950), massive G-Forces were thought to affect space travelers in their attempts to overcome the Earth's gravitational pull, showing them undergoing enormous strain (as it happened, the G-Forces subsequently encountered turned out to be not nearly so severe as first hypothesized). In some cases, this tense moment was achieved with scary sound and makeup effects, but the best that Honda and his team could come up with was a regrettable shot of two crewmembers pulling their faces back with their hands to show the strain of reaching escape velocity.

Then there are the typical Honda touches: After Katsumiya and Adachi escort the ambassadors and military leaders to view the two enormous rockets nearing their final construction phase, while Katsumiya is demonstrating the propulsion system, Adachi takes the time to point out the control panel to one of the foreign representatives. When Adachi recommends that the best defense for the Earth is armed preparedness, "Scout Ships" are then constructed, the aircraft bearing a striking similarity to North American's X-15 space research aircraft, which had just had its first rocket-powered flight a mere three months earlier. The Scout Ships themselves are built in Russia, then transported to launching sites throughout the United States (it is of course no small significance that the two countries working in tandem are the then opposing superpowers of the Cold War).

Honda also put a great deal of thought into the departure ceremony for the astronauts, giving them a full honor guard with a brass band playing a fanfare as the camera tracks along crowds of support people crying out "*Banzai!*" (the scene itself represents the growing national pride and self-confidence taking place in Japan at that time). Music plays triumphantly and there are smiles all-around; yet, in the sort of sentimental scene so dear to Honda, a number of the astronauts' relatives watch along the parade route as crewmembers are permitted to say goodbyes to their loved ones. A husband and wife are greeted by their daughter Sylvia and their son Pierce, and although the father holds out his hands to embrace his son, the young man shakes his father's hand instead, causing the older man to react with some embarrassment. The brother then leaves—oddly without saying goodbye to his mother—and after Sylvia embraces both her parents, she turns to unhappily leave them as the father waves a reluctant goodbye while his wife sadly rests her head on his shoulder.

Another touching scene occurs as the crew of Rocketship No. 1 silently pay their respects when they see the broken hulls of Space Station *J-SS3* drifting into space. Honda's handling of the moment when Etsuko is prevented from leaving the cave by a leaping Natalian is typical of his refusal to scare his audience, filming the scene as a long shot and thus lessening its shock value. As a result, the audience feels less like a participant and more like a spectator in another of Honda's "documentary-like" touches (Etsuko is then surrounded by the tiny aliens in a scene repeated almost verbatim in *From the Earth to the Moon* five years later). As Iwamura climbs up the ladder to enter Rocketship Two, Rocketship One disintegrates in an impressive explosion; Honda creatively having smoke from the explosion swirling around Iwamura.

Still another one of Honda's human touches occurs when Astronaut Pierce—Captain of the Second Wave Group—is shown seated in his Scout Ship. He turns to wave at a camera, apparently aware that it is being monitored by his sister, Sylvia. Honda tracks-in on the girl's reaction of surprise, concern, then finally of admiration of her brother's courage (it seems odd then that we never learn if Pierce survived his alien encounter). Honda also undercuts the human triumphs, reminding us of the cost of success, as no less than four Scout Ships are destroyed in the dogfight with the alien saucers. After the Mother Ship has been destroyed there is a great deal of cheering at the momentous moment, but Honda then goes to a shot of a military housing barracks previously destroyed by a falling saucer, followed shortly by a close-up of the grieving Rocket Commander.

The 1950s had established Honda as one of the most prolific and successful directors of fantasy films in worldwide cinema. In the span of just six years, he had helmed one splendid horror film (*The Beauty and the Liquid People*), a fairly-interesting monster movie (*Baran*), two outstanding sci-fi epics (*Defense Force, War in Space*), an excellent monster movie in color (*Radon*), a brilliant one in black-and-white (*Monster Snowman*) and one bonafide masterpiece (*Godzilla*). The next ten years would bring even greater successes, but by the time *that* decade had ended, both Honda's career and the genre he helped to create had reached a dead-end.

THE FIRST GAS HUMAN BEING (1960)
(GASU NINGEN DAI ICHIGO)
THE HUMAN VAPOR

Cast & Credits

Film Register No. 11865
Release Date: December 11, 1960
Running Time: 92 minutes

<u>Staff</u>: Producer: Tomoyuki Tanaka; Director: Ishiro Honda; Screenplay: Takeshi Kimura; Cinematography: Hajime Koizumi; Art Director: Kiyoshi Shimizu; Recording: Masao Fujiyoshi and Masanobu Miyazaki; Lighting: Toshio Takashima; Special Effects Techniques: Director: Eiji Tsuburaya; Optical Cinematography: Hidezaburo Araki; Effects Cinematography: Sadamasa (Teisho) Arikawa; Art Director: Akira Watanabe; Lighting: Kuichiro Kishida; Music: Kunio Miyauchi; Assistant Director: Koji Kajita; Editor: Ichiji Taira; Production Manager: Yasuaki Sakamoto; Still Photos: Masao Fukuda.

<u>Cast</u>: Tatsuya Mihashi (Detective Okamoto); Kaoru Yachigusa (Fujichiyo Kasuga); Yoshio Tsuchiya (Mizuno, the Vapor Man); Keiko Sata (Reporter Kyoko Kono); Hisaya Ito (Dr. Tamiya); Yoshibumi Tajima (Detective Tabata); Yoshio Kosugi (Detective Inao); Fuyuki Murakami (Dr. Sano); Bokuzen Hidari (Jiya, Fujichiyo's Servant); Takamaru Sasaki (Police Official); Minosuke Yamada (Hayama); Tatsuo Matsumura (Editor Ikeda); Yohiro Miyata (Bank Manager); Ko Mishima (Detective Fujita); Kozo Nomura (Reporter Kawasaki); Ren Yamamoto (Bank Robber Nishiyama); Somesho Matsumoto (Tutor); Yasuhisa Tsutsumi (Police Officer); Shoichi Hirose, Keiji Skakida (Prison Guards); Tetsu Nakamura (Editor Tobe); Toki Shiozawa (Riyo); Jiro Kumagai (Kajimoto); Kamayuki Tsubono (Detective Ozaki); Rinsaku Ogata (Police Officer Nakaya); Yutaka Oka, Koichi Sato, Tadahiko Kuroda (Thrill Seekers); Keisuke Yamada, Akio Kusama (Police Officials); Yukihiko Gondo (Detective Horita); Mitsuo Matsumoto (Kaneda).

The Film

The screenplays of Takeshi Kimura stressed the darker side of humanity, portraying a twisted netherworld of undulating blobs, giant underground insects and mushroom men; whereas Sekizawa's stories stressed action, flamboyant characters and comedic situations (it can truthfully be said that Sekizawa's scripts involved monsters who acted like people while Kimura's had people acting like monsters). However on this occasion, Kimura's script for *Gas Human* was not about vengeance, but veneration; starting as a routine crime drama, the film evolves into a deeply-moving dissertation on romantic obsession, science gone amok, insensitive conformism, sensationalistic journalists, unsympathetic science, a passion for the arts and ultimately a love so intense that its fulfillment results in death and destruction.

In Kimura's movie world there were two kinds of people: Those who wished to love and those who wished to be loved, a philosophy that runs through *Gas Human*. The story is about real people beset by tragedies and twists of fate beyond their control, and because of this, two sensitive, lonely, yet gifted people discover they have no real relevance or meaning to anyone except for each other. The scenes between Okamoto and Kyouko engaging in verbal byplay that seems less like bantering and more like baiting is a battle-of-wills that will be a microcosm of the broader battle which will take place between the press and the police. In a sardonic moment so typical of Kimura, after the police have arrived on the scene of the murder of the bank employee locked-up behind bars, they have to make awkward small talk with the mortified bank president until the replacement key is brought in.

Gas Human is Kimura's most affecting work, an uncompromising and unabashed look at how Japanese society is unsympathetic to individuals who do not fit under its umbrella of conventionality. The transformed Mizuno may be able to soar above the law—literally and figuratively—but he is still very much a mortal being. Despite his superhuman powers, he makes many errors in judgment, such as fleeing from the police only to lead them to Fujichiyo's house, thus implying a connection. He can rob banks with ease, but needlessly kills all who oppose him in a blind rage, and his impetuousness in freeing the prisoners accomplishes nothing to further his cause (as for Fujichiyo, she is a consummate artist uncomfortable with any other environment other than her beloved stage).

The script leaves several key points unexplained, such as what is the tragedy haunting Fujichiyo and what illness she is suffering from?

Although the reasons for her stay in the sanitarium are not disclosed, it seems logical to assume that since she and Mizuno met at the same clinic, they were both undergoing cancer treatments; in her case however the cancer is incurable, which would explain why she is so intent on giving one final performance, and why her life savings have been depleted in order to treat her illness (oddly, a cure for Mizuno's vapor condition is never discussed).

Another question is, who severed the wires intended to trigger the release of the gas? Although the U.S. version has Mizuno revealing in a voiceover that he cut the wires, Honda's version implies that Fujichiyo was responsible, since the police did discuss their plans with her, and—fearing they would jump the gun in turning the gas on (an assumption which proves correct) —she was determined to complete her routine without any interference. To be sure, a bit more exposition would have been helpful in clearing-up these questions, including a brief scene showing Mizuno lighting a cigarette so one does not wonder how Fujichiyo knew where to get a hold of his lighter.

One question simple to solve is why Fujichiyo decided to immolate herself and her lover. Well-aware that Mizuno will always be a hunted man and that there is no way they could ever hope to live a normal life together—added with the fact the future she faces with her incurable cancer is little better than withering away under the haze of pain medication—Fujichiyo decides that she cannot live without her significant other and therefore they must both die together.

Eiji Tsuburaya was kept quite busy on *Gas Human*, utilizing dry ice, invisible wires, optical animation, smoke, and matte photography with terrifyingly effectiveness. Reusing a technique employed in *Liquid People*, a balloon mannequin of the actor was alternately inflated, then deflated to convey the Gas Human's transformations. There are several amazing traveling mattes of swirling gas used to simulate the Gas Human's transformations and the chilling—indeed, almost unbelievable—scene of Mizuno's charred clothing crawling away from the theater was one of Tsuburaya's most superbly-realized effects (the following August, Tsuburaya was asked by *American Cinematographer* what monster would star in his next film. He replied, "Perhaps my next nightmare will give me the answer").

Hajime Koizumi's photography was again outstanding; his compositions are nicely framed and lit with vibrant color. There are a number of smoothly-executed tracking shots such as when Kyouko is attempting to interview the dancer at her home, and the cinematographer also makes effective use of shadows, such as in Fujichiyo's cell and when

Mizuno kills Sano. When Fujichiyo is rehearsing at her home, the door's buzzer sounds; Honda amusingly cuts to a close-up of the demonically-masked figure commanding her servant to answer the door. In a subsequent shot, the camera tracks-in on a close-up of the detective's spying face lit from reflected light from a pond before cutting to a close-up of Fujichiyo holding the mask up her lovely face in a creepy contrast before the screen "explodes" in a newspaper headline announcing the bank robbery.

One of Honda's favorite techniques was a quick-edit to stress a reaction; in this case, during Fujichiyo's confrontation with Inao when the gruff and disbelieving detective snorts: "So, you want us to believe you're *innocent*, huh?" as Honda cuts to a close-up of the dancer's shocked reaction. Honda tilts the camera during Mizuno's flashback sequence in Sano's lab to stress the weird circumstances, and during the crucial scene where Kyouko pleads with Fujichiyo to cancel her concert, Honda keeps the three-minute sequence moving with no-less than 22 separate edits shot from six different camera setups.

Composer Kunio Miyauchi used a four-note motif to identify the Gas Human, played on a melancholy accordion, while sad violin music is used for Fujichiyo. Much of the music is comprised of short cues used as source music, such as when Okamoto first sees Fujichiyo in jarring accompaniment to ancient *Noh* music in "The Beauty with the Devil's Mask," reinforced with a trilling flute, an off-kilter piano and queasy woodwinds, with sinister trumpets entering when the dancer removes her mask.

The composer uses brass and a jazz-influenced score of horns and strings heard during the "Dragon" restaurant scenes, stressing the bold, brassy and contemporary Kyouko. Music is absent throughout much of the film from that point on, not returning until "Solo Investigation" when the music—for the only time in the film—takes on a comic tone with oboe, horns and descending woodwinds as Okamoto walks along the dusty dirt road. When Kyouko first meets Fujichiyo in "Fujichiyo's Secret," the dancer's subdued manner gives an impression of a defeated grace which is reflected in the music, with somber clarinet, descending flutes and faint trumpets. As the scene progresses in "The Shadow" (as Kyouko and the detective pursue the dancer), the music takes on a sinister tone with rapid bow strings, softly-sustained trumpets, drum rifts and menacing flutes.

"Fujichiyo's Thoughts"—heard when the dancer declines Kyouko's on-stage offer to abandon the play—is scored with the Gas Human's motif of wavering organ, implying his influence in her decision. The conclusion of Fujichiyo's performance (the provocatively-tilted "Demon of Emotion") is heralded in "The Moment Approaches," beginning with the sad violins of Fujichiyo's theme transforming into a exultant soaring of strings which is immediately undercut with muted horns since the celebration will be brief. Then, low horns play somberly in the background as she brings out the cigarette lighter, with Honda stopping the score as the gas explodes. When the theater begins to burn during the "Ending," the music is action-oriented before segueing into a strumming of strings and somber horns when the chilling visage of Mizuno's burnt body comes into view. The music ends on a paradoxical note with flat-sounding horns and shimmering cymbals, indicating a terrible yet triumphant resolution.

It would be difficult to imagine a more perfectly-suited actor for the role of the Gas Human than Yoshio Tsuchiya. Tsuchiya had already appeared in a similar film— playing a newspaper reporter in 1953's *The Invisible Man*—and remembered envying the title character. His superbly-understated performance as the doomed librarian is highly effective as—rather than overtly playing a raving lunatic—Tsuchiya plays Mizuno as a pleasant and courteous person, giving the impression that spending an hour-or-two chatting with him would not be an altogether oppressive experience. When the transformed Mizuno takes a walk in the rain before changing back into his human form, the actor brilliantly registers shock, dismay and finally acceptance.

In discussing the film years later in an interview printed in *Japanese Giants*, Tsuchiya stated: "I remember reading the reviews of *Gas Human* when it was released, and some remarked what a great love story it was. I was proud of that, because I played my part as if the man *was* in love. Mizuno was carrying sorrow on his back and he was a victim of science run amok." When the film was released in America four years later it granted the actor immediate fame. "Once, when I was on a fishing trip in the Canadian Rockies, I visited a small town where *The Human Vapor* was showing. When I checked into the hotel there, the man at the desk wouldn't take my money, he told me I was a VIP. When I was eating dinner, people kept coming up and asking for my autograph."

At age 29, actress Kaoru Yachigusa played the enigmatic Fujichiyo in another superbly-realized piece of acting. Her sad, sweet face, gentle speech and graceful gestures belied a tormented individual (no stranger to the stage, Yachigusa was a classically-trained dancer who had headlined in Toho's *Madame Butterfly* just five years earlier). She is today perhaps best remembered as the love interest in the *Samurai* trilogy and was married to director Senkichi Taniguchi—the man who had turned down *Godzilla*. Given her outstanding performance, it comes as a surprise then to learn that years later the actress may not have necessarily appreciated *Gas Human's* weird story, telling interviewer Stuart Galbraith IV that she didn't remember being in the film at all!

One interesting piece of casting was Fuyuki Murakami as Dr. Sano. Murakami was a lingering background presence in a number of Honda's early films (*Godzilla, Defense Force, Baran, War in Space*), the director utilizing the actor possibly due to his scientific demeanor. In *Gas Human*, Murakami played the key role of the professor who conducts illegal and unsanctified experiments on ordinary citizens for the stated purpose of space exploration; although it is impossible to know what dark designs the doctor really had in mind (as with Serizawa, Sano shows evidence of facial scarring and his lab is also in his basement). Sano's previous experiments were presumably all failures because his subjects died, so when he tells Mizuno: "I didn't want to keep it a secret this time!" it was because the doctor was anxious to announce to the world that he had finally succeeded.

The First Gas Human is a well-crafted, compelling and moving film with surprising plot twists, a literate script, beautiful music and photography, wonderful dancing, brutal deaths and a shocking finale; Rosemary Lingua wrote that "The stunning climax with the star-crossed lovers...is reminiscent of a tragic Verdi opera." Honda sprinkles-in poignant moments amidst the madness, such as the grieving bank president being led away after his employee has been killed. Honda directed *Gas Human* in his typically deliberate manner, from the film's opening high-speed pursuit to its shattering finale, resulting in a cinematic work of passion brought to fulfillment by the his understated style (yet, Honda now seemed to be pulling his punches, such as when a detective slaps a robbery suspect in the face—off-screen).

Honda films Fujichiyo's recital in such a way that we watch it as would any audience member in a theater, and when the police are rummaging through her house during her rehearsal, we see two dramas occurring at once. The director did an excellent job in maintaining the film's suspenseful mood while raising tension much-more effectively than he had in *Liquid People*, with a prison riot populated with desperate criminals, overwhelmed police and the crazed media all swarming over each other like confused ants before cutting to a contrasting shot of Fujichiyo sitting quietly in her cell. Honda particularly builds the tension beautifully during the dance recital with the morally-torn Tabata poised to throw the switch before he is interrupted by a screaming Kyouko.

Unlike many of Honda's central characters, we come to know both

Mizuno and Fujichiyo and sympathize with them; feeling Fujichiyo's distress when her rehearsal is interrupted by the police and her bitter disappointment when her tutor informs her that the musicians are too scared to perform (Honda mirror's her sorrow by having it gently rain, only to counter it with a *bravura* entrance when Mizuno arrives, highlighted by a flash of lightening and a crash of thunder). As a result, we hope that she will be able to finish her concert and share Mizuno's joy; we are rooting *against* the police who, after all, are trying to prevent two people from being happy.

Some have suggested the love Mizuno feels for Fujichiyo is unrequited, but this is not the case as Fujichiyo confides to Kyouko that she is dancing for her lover only, and as Guy Tucker has noted—after she brings out Mizuno's cigarette lighter—Fujichiyo does not immediately light it, but instead, embraces him and savors the moment. Having thus been fulfilled as an artist and a woman, she then looks toward heaven and ignites the lighter.

The script and the film combined to create, as David Coleman called it, "...a distinct *noir* sensibility," while Greg Shoemaker has written that, "Threatened by the world around them, both (Fujichiyo and Mizuno) are transported to some more hopeful dimension, where their infatuation can continue . . ." Perhaps to suggest this ideal, Honda's final shot shows a large wreath of laudatory flowers falling in front of the dead Mizuno; both a posthumous wedding bouquet and flowers for a funeral.

In retrospect, there seems to have been a significant change in attitude after the film was released, as it seems Honda received word to cut-down on the violence and lower the body count, particularly with regard to policemen. As a result, individual on-screen fatalities would soon diminish while deaths on a massive scale were implied rather than shown. *The First Gas Human Being* was not a great financial success, but Honda's next film would not only become one of his biggest hits, but solidify not only the genre of Japanese Fantasy Films, but Honda's career.

SECTION IV:
"THE WORLD IS STILL FULL OF WONDERS!"

MOTHRA (1961)
(MOTHRA)

GORATH, THE MYSTERIOUS STAR (1962)
(GORATH)

KING KONG VS. GODZILLA (1962)
(KING KONG VS. GODZILLA)

MATANGO (1963)
(ATTACK OF THE MUSHROOM PEOPLE)

SUBMARINE WARSHIP (1963)
(ATRAGON)

MOTHRA VS. GODZILLA (1964)
(GODZILLA VS. THE THING)

MOTHRA (1961)
(MOSURA)

Cast & Credits

Film Register No. 11986
Release Date: July 30, 1961
Running Time: 101 minutes

Staff: Producer: Tomoyuki Tanaka; Director: Ishiro Honda; Original Story: Shinichiro Nakamura, Takehiko Fukunaga and Yoshie Hotta; Screenplay: Shinichi Sekizawa; Recording: Shoichi Fujinawa and Masanobu Miyazaki; Lighting: Toshio Takashima; Music: Yuji Koseki; Assistant Director: Samaji Nonagase; Editor: Ichiji (Kazuji) Taira; Production Manager: Shin Morita; Special Effects Techniques: Director: Eiji Tsuburaya; Cinematography: Sadamasa (Teisho) Arikawa; Art Director: Akira Watanabe; Lighting: Kuichiro Kishida; Matte Process; Hiroshi Mukoyama; Optical Cinematography: Yukio Manoda; Production Manager: Kan Narita; Still Photos: Issei Tanaka.

Cast: Frankie Sakai (Reporter Shinichiro Fukuda); Hiroshi Koizumi (Prof. Shinichi Chujo); Kyoko Kagawa (Photographer Michi Hanamura); Emi & Yumi Ito ("The Little Beauties" aka "Shobijin"); Jerry Ito (Clark Nelson); Ken Uehara (Dr. Harada); Akihiko Hirata (Nuclear Center Scientist); Kenji Sahara (Helicopter Observer); Seizaburo Kawazu (JSDF Commander); Takashi Shimura (Editor Sadamasa Amano); Yoshio Kosugi (Ship Captain); Yoshibumi Tajima (JSDF Official); Ko Mishima (Chief of the *Hayakaze*); Tetsu Nakamura, Johnny (Osman) Yuseph (Yusef), Hiroshi Takagi, Toshio Miura, Akira Wakamatsu (Nelson's Henchmen); Shoichi Hirose, Shigeo Kato (Dam Workers); Koro Sakurai (Countermeasures Headquarters Staffer); Yasuhisa Tsutsumi (Expedition Guard); Teruko Mita (Tea Shop Lady); Mitsuo Tsuda (Cruise ship Captain); Masamitsu Tayama (Shinji Chujo); Tadashi Okabe (Ship's Physician); Yutaka Nakayama (Motoma); Obel Wyatt (Captain Roth); Harold S. Conway (Rolisican Ambassador).

The Film

It was *Mothra*—more than any other film that Honda directed—which firmly established the permanency of the Japanese world of fantasy films into modern culture, raising the "suspension of disbelief" bar to a level no film of its type on had ever attempted before. Produced at a time when giant monster-movies were on-the-wane in the West, it renewed and reestablished the genre in Japan and is considered by many to be Honda's best directorial effort.

Initially, Tanaka had hired three novelists to write original stories based on the idea of a monster moth which were summarily submitted to Sekizawa, who promptly disregarded them and wrote his own original story (by a strange coincidence, *Mothra's* plot is very similar to that of the English-produced *Gorgo*, released four months earlier in March of 1961. Both films begin with ships on stormy seas followed by sensational discoveries made on remote islands (Nara Island in *Gorgo*). Unscrupulous men steal the native curiosities before putting them on display for profit, until the maternal guardians come to their rescue, creating massive destruction in the process. Both Gorgo and Mothra survive to return home).

The film takes place in three distinct locales: Tokyo, Rolisica and Infant Island. Of the three, Infant Island comes across as the purest, while Tokyo seems uninspired and Rolisica little more than superficial high-rise opulence (fortunately for mankind, it does however have churches). In typical Honda/Tsuburaya fashion, the film gets off to a fast start; first we are told about a ship caught in the center of a storm, and a moment later we are transported to that very ship. The script touches on such subjects as profit over principle, diplomatic immunity and even slavery is mentioned; however the real crux of the film is greed and the price paid by those exploiting a natural wonder for sensationalism and profit

When Junichiro and Chujo witness Harada's demonstration of the shielding material that can prevent the girls' telepathic waves from reaching Mothra, it was an idea Sekizawa would later use again in *War of the Monsters*, and when Nelson's men begin searching for Chujo's little brother, the boy has been hiding amongst them the whole time in a scene similar to one in *Defense Force*. When the Rolisican ambassador brings welcome news of a newly-constructed Atomic Ray Heat Cannon which can destroy the cocoon before it hatches, it brings to mind another moment in *Defense Force* when Dr. Immerman brought the "Good news!" about the Markalite (in both cases the messenger bearing good tidings was played by Harold S. Conway, an actor Honda often cast to represent Caucasian diplomats).

Mothra was the only monster in a Honda film worshipped by natives that was actually a legitimate god; Mothra is truly magical as unlike previous Honda monsters there is no explanation given as to how it came to be (perhaps a moth infused with radiation?). Another element making Mothra unique was that—unlike earlier Toho monsters—it does not attack Tokyo or Rolisica either by blind rage or accident, vengeance or instinct, but in a desperate attempt to rescue the Shobijin against nearly overwhelming odds. Not even a newly-designed Heat Ray can destroy the monster; indeed, it seems that all of man's military hardware is helpless in the face of a fairy tale. As a result, the monster invokes the audiences' sympathy (and an insect, at that); Mothra is not a bad but a benevolent bug and a creature not to be feared but revered.

Eiji Tsuburaya was Christian and it is tempting to interpret the "Mothra" symbol as a thinly disguised crucifix and declaration of Tsuburaya's own theology. Mothra is an eternal being, capable of resurrecting itself after having seemingly been killed and is also forgiving while at the same time capable of dishing out severe punishment. With *Mothra*, Tsuburaya's effects know no bound; Tokyo is recreated as a brilliant miniature including all of the military and emergency ground-force vehicles. Many of his shots contain the inventiveness and innovation that made him a legend, such as two interior shots as seen from inside Newkirk City department stores as cars smash into them, and another shot where a miniature 707 flies *through* a cloud.

Aerial shots of the caterpillar swimming in the sea were accomplished by towing the miniature Mothra in the Banyu River from a motorboat, with filming accomplished via aerial photography from a helicopter. Filing these shots was risky as the chopper had to fly over the surface of the water at low altitude. To film these scenes, Effects cinematographer Arikawa placed himself and his camera on a board which stuck partially outside the helicopter's door. As he later wrote in his memoirs: "I just leaned out of the helicopter with the camera and started shooting. The pilot was very surprised to see me doing that and kept asking me, 'Are you okay?' Are you all right?' I was fine, it was the *pilot* who turned pale!"

Koizumi's photography is very dramatic—such as when Honda mirrors the tense situation onboard the ship in the storm with an effective dolly-in close-up of the grim-faced captain—but is sometimes sloppy, such as a poorly-framed shot of a sign announcing the arrival of Dr. Roth's fight while cutting-off the head of a flight attendant standing beside it. When Chujo realizes what the Shobijin are, Honda has the actor sit up and stare straight into the camera, and when Chujo and Junichiro witness the girls' performance in Nelson's show and realize the word "Mothra" in an integral part of the lyrics, Honda emphasizes their discovery with intense close-ups of the pair. Kazuji Taira's editing is no-less impressive: When the girls later sing a traditional ballad called "The Infant Girl," the carriage carrying the girls is superimposed over Mothra swimming in the ocean as it comes to their rescue in a brilliant transition conceived by Honda.

Yuji Koseki's score effectively captures the film's sense of grandeur and imagination, and his unique orchestrations fall perfectively within the film's fantasy framework while at the same time evoking concern for the creature. The music continuously reinforces the purpose of an enormous animal that is not one of destruction but of desire, pulling for Mothra as it struggles to survive. The "Prelude" and "Main Title" sequences are flowery orchestrations complete with brass, harp and high-pitched strings, promising a dramatic dream about to unfold in grand, dazzling colors. As if hinting at the film's religious undercurrent, the composer utilizes a number of instruments normally associated with the church—harp, organ and choir music—and cleverly uses speeded-up organ music to simulate the girls' telepathic conversations.

Music is used sparingly for much of the film's early action and is not heard from after the shipwrecked survivors are found, until the expedition begins crossing the desolate terrain of Infant Island. When Chujo begins his exploration of the cave in "The Mysterious Little Beauty," it is scored with harp, bells, vibraphone and glockenspiel, with an oboe added for a mysterious undercurrent. When the girls are first snatched by Nelson's bodyguard, Koseki introduces the girls' future "Mothra's Song" song as an organ solo. This theme has become arguably the most-recognizable piece of music in the whole history of fantasy films, orchestrated with strings, flutes and drums cleverly reinforcing the girls' native origins, effectively connecting Nelson's flamboyant show with the primitive dance performed on Infant Island.

"The Birth of Baby Mothra" is heralded with trumpets, rolling cymbals and fluttering flutes, while "Operation 'Annihilate Mothra'" is a soaring selection scored with cymbals, emphatic violins, trumpets, flutes and the omnipresent harp. The main difference between Koseki's scoring of the battle scenes with the monster and Ifukube's customary approach is while Ifukube's music stresses the creatures' strength and the military's response, Koseki entreats the viewer's sympathy to side with the insect in a score fraught with anxiety, as if lamenting whether or not Mothra will live long enough to reach the girls in time. For example, "Baby Mothra Attacks" takes on a sense of urgency with low brass, blaring trumpets, flutes, violins and cymbals coloring the moment when the larvae first arrives on the mainland, while "Collapse of the 3rd Dam" and "Tokyo Tower and Mothra" are both scored with trumpets and flutes, with an occasional strumming of a harp to emphasize the larvae's "divine" mission, as well as creating a mood of urgency and desperation.

With "The Atomic Heat Ray Gun Attack Begins," Koseki continues to emphasize not only action but anxiety when the rays ignite the cocoon as soaring strings and brass introduce the piece with horns, flutes and cymbals coloring the action; the selection ends with somber brass and a mournful, extended note on strings, indicating a tragic resolution. "Adult Mothra in Flight" begins with harp and triumphant trumpet playing the "Mothra Theme" before being joined by trilling flutes and violins playing in a spiraling pattern emphasizing the destruction being caused by Mothra's wings. The scene where Nelson attempts to escape begins with crashing cymbals and a resolute theme flavored with violins; after the fugitive has been shot, somber strings and subdued trumpets announce that justice has finally been done. Koseki's "Ending" music reinforces Mothra's magical qualities as well as indicating the reverence held for it by its loyal subjects, beginning with shimmering violins and a choral chant supplemented with low brass; the music swelling as the girls enter to conclude their song with crashing gongs and cymbals.

The Shobijin were a unique concept to fantasy films and Honda handled all of their scenes with the outmost reverence—even the credits given to the two actresses playing them were displayed in different colors than the rest of the credits as if to stress their mystical qualities (the lyrics to "Mothra's Song" were written by an Indonesian college student who wrote the lyrics in Malaysian, which were then phonetically transferred back into Japanese syllables by Honda). Played by real-life twin sisters Emi and Yumi Ito, the two were a popular duo known as the "Peanuts." Beginning their careers as a singing team in the late fifties, they scored their first No. 1 hit in 1959, and their success eventually took them as far as "The Ed Sullivan Show." They retired in 1975.

The scope of the film's visuals and story were matched by its stellar cast. There are many familiar faces with such recognizable talents such as Kenji Sahara (the helicopter observer) and Akihiko Hirata (an intern) playing minor roles, although both were prominently billed in the movie's trailer. Two actors new to Honda's fantasy films were Frankie Sakai and Kyoto Kagawa as the two leads, joining reliable stalwarts Hiroshi

Koizumi as Chujo and Takeshi Shimura as the newspaper editor. Sakai was ideally cast in the role of "Snapping Turtle" Junichiro, possessing both adroit comic timing and an air of geniality. The journalist is a complex character and out of the mold of a typical Honda hero; on the surface he is pleasant and upbeat, yet he is also skilled at judo, resolute and capable of supreme courage.

His partner, played by the lovely Kagawa, is also likeable but has no apparent scruples in using underhanded means in order to obtain pictures for her paper (her look at Chujo as she sizes him up for her miniature camera is intimidating to say the least). As with Junichiro, she is not easily scared, even when confronted by Nelson's thugs, and was another continuing trend in Honda's genre films for strong and capable female professionals. As usual, Takeshi Shimura plays a gruff and cynical character with a heart of gold, while Ken Uehara—once a popular leading man—is the sympathetic and understanding Dr. Harada. As for Hiroshi Koizumi, his role of Professor Chujo would become his most recognizable in a long career, and he would essay the part again over 30 years later in *Godzilla—Tokyo SOS* (2003).

Perhaps the most memorable performance in *Mothra* was from Jerry Ito as the nefarious Clark Nelson, one of the most insidious villains in all of Honda's films. Given the constraints of having to play a character whose very background is shielded in obscurity, Ito manages to instill his role with complete conviction. Under instruction by Honda to play the part broadly, Ito reluctantly complied with plenty of snarls and sneers, supplemented with cackling and wicked grimacing. Years later, Honda admitted he was somewhat displeased with the New York-born actor's Japanese dialect (strangely, despite Ito's prominent role, the actor was not credited in the film's trailer).

Mothra was as fantasy film of epic proportions. It's totally-outlandish story forced Honda to use a drastically different approach than he had with his subtle handling of the powerfully poignant *Gas Human* the year before; yet, despite all the various elements making up much of *Mothra's* cinematic eccentricity (including the over-the-top performances of the villains such as when Nelson and his spokesman laugh in each other's faces over Mothra's "demise"), the film still manages to convey an element of sincere legitimacy that so typified Honda's best work.

In previous Japanese monster films it often appeared the military rarely hit their enormous targets, but in Mothra's case, they almost never miss as they mercilessly pelt the creature as it struggles to climb up the Tokyo tower (at one point Honda cuts the music so that the only sounds are the military's relentless pummeling of the Mothra larvae, accentuating the brutality of the onslaught). Although the sequence involving the countdown before the Atomic Cannons fire at the cocoon oddly lacks suspense, the scene where Nelson is gunned down in the Rolisican courtyard shows Honda at the peak of his powers; his control of the extras, the rapids cuts and dramatic camera work are brilliant (including five inserts going from screaming citizens to oblique close-ups of natives slain by Nelson), all combining to create a memorable tableau of drama magnificently concluded with Nelson's ballet-like death.

Although Honda always held firm that he never directed a "children's" film, *Mothra* came the closest, due in large part to its fairytale *accouterments*: The childlike Junichiro, the nasty Nelson, the vulnerable fairies and a magical monster; *Mothra* indeed has much to offer an adolescent audience. The scenes of violence were either stylized or deliberately toned-down, (such as the bloodless-scene when the natives are gunned down) and when a helicopter flying too close to Mothra's silk gets caught in its web; rather than go careering into the ground, the aircraft gracefully crashes to its doom.

One of Honda's more-memorable moments is Nelson's show, where the evil entrepreneur introduces the Shobijin by reminding the crowd that, "The world is still full of wonders!" in an artificial and gaudy pageant quite unlike the heart-felt native ritual taking place simultaneously on Infant Island (when the Shobijin join hands and sing their song about Mothra, it is a moment that has forever defined the genre). Another superb sequence is the dam disaster, with several events taking place at once: The cracking of the dam's wall, the flooding of the gorge, the wearing-away of the bridge's support structures, the crying infant inadvertently left behind, the screaming mother and Junichiro's spray-covered rescue (Honda ends the scene with a magnificent dolly-in shot of Junichiro, Michi and Chujo).

The scene when Junichiro, Michi and Chujo arrive in the courtyard with the girls is also excellent (Honda shows Nelson's spokesman and bodyguard cowering in a corner under gunpoint with tears in their eyes). Junichiro unzips the case to reveal the girls are still encased in their telepathic shield as a woman angrily calls out, "We've waited long enough! *Open* it now!" Also in the crowd are two priests (mirroring a brief shot of two holy men sitting in Mothra's cave during the hatching ceremony), one of whom observes that God is their only salvation. It is at this critical moment that bells in a nearby church begin to ring as the crowd bows in reverence.

Even so, while at times compelling, *Mothra*'s length (clocking in at just over 100 minutes) made it Honda's longest genre film, and the length shows, particularly after Nelson's death. Characteristically, Honda laces the film with sentimental touches; the American Dr. Roth is warmly greeted with flowers after arriving in Japan in yet another of Honda's nod to U.S./Japanese relations, and there are the little details such as when the press is refused entrance to the hospital as two nurses can be seen cowering at the top of the background stairs. And then there is Hope: Infant Island has suffered atomic testing, yet it has somehow survived with a verdant interior, a vital native population and a remedy for radiation sickness.

Brazen and beautiful, *Mothra* became the most famous fantasy film ever produced in Japan. For Honda, the film had been exhilarating and exhausting and his only one of 1961. The next year would be busier and would begin with a film even more optimistic than *Mothra*, with a story not about the survival of a monster moth, but of all mankind.

GORATH, THE MYSTERIOUS STAR (1962)
(YOSEI GORASU)
GORATH

Cast & Credits

Film Register No. 12689
Release Date: March 21, 1962
Running Time: 88 minutes

Staff: Producer: Tomoyuki Tanaka; Director: Ishiro Honda; Original Story: Jojiro Okami; Screenplay: Takeshi Kimura; Cinematography: Hajime Koizumi; Art Directors: Takeo Kita and Teruaki Abe; Recording: Toshiya Ban; Lighting: Toshio Takashima; Music: Kan Ishii; Sound Arrangement: Hisashi Shimonaga; Assistant Director: Koji Kajita; Editor: Reiko Kaneko; Production Manager: Yasuaki Sakamoto; Special Effects Techniques: Director: Eiji Tsuburaya; Cinematography: Sadamasa (Teisho) Arikawa and Sokei Tomioka; Optical Cinematography: Taka Yuki and Yukio Manoda; Art Director: Akira Watanabe; Lighting: Kuichiro Kishida; Matte Processing: Hiroshi Mukoyama.

Cast: Ryo Ikebe (Dr. Tazawa); Yumi Shirakawa (Tomoko Sonoda); Akira Kubo (Astronaut Tatsuo Kanai); Kumi Mizuno (Takiko Nomura); Hiroshi Tachikawa (Astronaut Wakabayashi); Akihiko Hirata (Captain Endo); Kenji Sahara (Vice Captain Saiki); Jun Tazaki (Captain Sonoda); Ken Uehara (Dr. Konno); Takashi Shimura (Kensuke Sonoda); Seizaburo Kawazu (Minister of Commerce Tada); Ko Mishima (Engineer Shinda); Sachio Sakai (Physician); Takamaru Sasaki (Prime Minister Seki); Ko Nishimura (Space Agency Chairman Murata); Eitaro Ozawa (Minister of Justice Kinami); Masanori Nihei (Astronaut Ito); George Furness (Dr. Hooverman); Ross Benette (Gibson); Nadao Kirino (*Hawk's* First Officer Manabe); Fumio Sakamoto (Sumio Sonoda); Ikio Sawamura (Taxi Driver); Shimpei Mitsui (Newspaper Reporter); Rinsaku Ogata, Koichi Sato, Koji Suzuki, Tadashi Okabe, Yasuhiko Saijo, (*Eagle* Crew); Akira Yamada, Wataru Omae, Yasuo Araki, Kazuo Imai (*Hawk* Crew).

The Film

Jojiro Okami—who had previously written *The Defense Force of the Earth* and *The Great War in Space*—wrote *Gorath's* original story, a story that bears more than a passing resemblance to George Pal's *When Worlds Collide* (1951), where a star named Bellus is on a collision course with the Earth. However, despite the similar premises of the two films they are exact opposites in their final resolutions; in the Pal film there is simply no hope of saving the Earth, but there is a chance that a limited number of humans can board a space ship in time to fly to Zyra, a planet traveling around Bellus. Thus, a "Space Ark" is constructed, taking off moments before the Earth is destroyed and lands on Zyra, which is capable of supporting life. *Gorath's* screenplay, written by the usually downbeat Takeshi Kimura, has the Earth being saved by the simple expedient of moving it out of the path of the monster star (Honda even researched at Tokyo University to see if such a thing was mathematically possible).

The United Nations was playing an ever-expanding role in Honda's science-fiction trilogy: In *Defense Force*, the organization was modestly represented by a creased flag hanging on a wall in a military briefing room, while *War in Space* had a convention of U.N. delegates gathered to seek a solution to the invaders. In both cases, the meetings took place in Japan, but in *Gorath*, the international discussions take place within the confines of the U.N. itself, portions of which were recreated to the smallest detail; even the mathematical equations chalked-up on the huge blackboard were authentic. Kimura's script contains basic elements found in much of his work, such as bureaucratic bickering over who was responsible for diverting the *Hawk's* mission from Saturn to Gorath and an opportunistic press, yet despite these recurring themes the film is Honda's ultimate treatise on his hope that all nations can unite to accomplish the impossible.

In a sequence filled with outstanding aerial photography and helicopter stunt work, the astronauts sing a song extolling their virtues as space pilots while making a triumphant flyover of the world's largest manmade broadcasting antenna and a source of Japanese pride, the newly-constructed Tokyo Tower. Another moment extolling Japanese virtue and ingenuity is the scene in Sonoda's study when Konno smugly observed that while other countries are building spaceships, the ones built by Japan are "the best."

However, the film literally comes to a halt when Magma is introduced, and the dialogue scene between Konno, Tazawa and Sonoda was probably written by Honda as it stresses a scientific interest in keeping the giant walrus alive (the scene is especially odd in light of the fact that the last time Tazawa and Konno met, they bitterly argued over the first rocket test. Presumably the two scientists set aside their differences in light of this new menace). The scenes with Magma accomplished little, other than giving Tsuburaya's staff more work to do. Fortunately, *Gorath* is such an exquisitely-made picture that even the intrusion of a giant walrus does not damage it beyond redemption (curiously, the notion of a giant walrus disrupting things at the Pole occurred 15 years later in *Sinbad and the Eye of the Tiger*).

Eiji Tsuburaya's special effects were the most elaborate and skillfully executed work in his career; the mattes, miniatures, wire works, animation and composites are all outstanding, and his use of forced perspective was never better. The construction of the South Pole base sequence was one of the seminal moments in his career introduced through skillful editing as the first two shots are pans showing a portion of the fleet seen from altitude, followed by a remarkable long shot showing the ships heading toward the Pole before Tsuburaya cuts to a close-up of a ship forging through the ice. Ships break through ice flows while equipment and material are being offloaded as helicopters carrying everything from personnel to pipes fill the skies (the VTOL aircraft anticipated the English-built Harrier "Jump Jet" by four years; Tsuburaya liked the Beetle so much he used it in his 1966 "Ultraman" TV series).

Trucks traverse across the landscape as massive girders rise from the ice with men working in sub-zero conditions, using welding torches to fuse towering steel girders into place, and huge cranes lift tons of equipment while tractors dig gigantic trenches into the frozen soil. The stage used to house the miniature set was huge, encompassing nearly 18,000 square feet of Sound Stage No. 8. Many of shots are taken from above and the sound of helicopters fills the soundtrack, giving added emphasis to the continuous activity revolving around the base and its immense scale of operation (a more understated, but no less ingenious, shot shows a tremendous miniature of the Tokyo skyline at dusk—complete with automobile traffic on freeway overpasses—as seen through Kiyo's living room window).

Hajimi Koizumi's camera is constantly on the move with inventive shots, including an elaborate tracking shot early-on through the *Hawk's* crew section, before elevating and tracking to where Sonoda and Manabe are sitting. When Magma first appears, a tire was suspended just below the front of the camera, then shaken violently by a technician.

When Tatuso's memory is triggered as he watches a broadcast of the monster star, his anguished face completely fills the frame while he stares directly into the camera, and after the technicians have realized the success of their operation, Tazawa is passed around to the plaudits and congratulations of his fellow team-members in an exhilarating 280-degree pan.

The sets designed for *Gorath* by Teruaki Abe and Takeo Kita were larger, both in scope and expense, than in any of Honda's previous fantasy films and showed a great attention to detail as every piece of equipment seems to have been designed for a specific function, with the various spacesuits appearing both functional and intelligently-designed. The interior of the rocketships, the Control Room of the South Pole Operation Base (even Professor Kenoke's study) looked totally authentic.

Editor Reiko Kaneko brilliantly cuts from the exploding *Hawk* to the wild celebration in a festival-filled street during the Christmas season; another clever segue occurs when the girls are stopped by a bunch of gaily-colored balloons as people cry out "Merry Christmas!" transitioning to balloons and people singing "Jingle Bells" as Kiyo walks down her neighborhood street. Another effective dissolve goes from Gorath's destruction of the Comet Carina to an aerial view of Tokyo at night, with the stars dissolving into the nightlights of the city.

Kan Ishii's "Main Title" music—accompanied by a crash of thunder against a backdrop of receding stars—immediately sets the tone for the film, with a dramatic strumming of strings before the entrance of bellicose brass evolving into a strong and driving *accelerando* pace, building in volume and intensity, to indicate a rapidly-approaching menace. The music then reaches a crescendo with strings, brass and two cymbal crashes in a superb opening theme.

"Captain Sonoda's Funeral" is an honorable a*dagio* to a hero, filled with admiration and regret (Honda handling the scene with his usual dignity and decorum, keeping it brief as if sensitive to the family's anguish). Scored with somber cellos, longing violins and punctuated with faint, trembling percussion, the piece ends with shimmering strings and an emphatic drum; while the happy-go-lucky and ebullient "We Are Space Pilots" is scored not unlike a college fight song with the musical phrases ending with resounding brass as the lyrics carry the tune with trumpets filling the gap between the vocals.

"Construction of the South Pole Base" is comprised of two separate musical phrases—one played by strings and the other on brass—establishing a determined and unwavering pace, while "Amnesia" is scored with short *staccato* notes for violins stressing shock, counterbalanced by low brass and percussion harkening an uncertain future. "The Collapse of Pipe No. 33" begins with an undulating theme scored with brass evolving into frantic cymbals and strings, capturing the drama and the panic of the cave-in.

"Magma vs. the V.T.O.L. Jet" effectively enhances the drama of the two VTOL attacks on the monster with a steady, repeated pounding of drums subsiding into fluttering clarinets and strings as the scientists land to take a closer look at the buried beast. When the animal rises from the rubble, timpani rolls and drumbeats increase in intensity, while strings play urgently and brass plays in a minor key with a fluttering of flutes as the VTOL rises and finishes off the monster. Tense bowstrings, off-set by coronets and blaring trumpets, highlights "Two Minutes to Go" as Kanai's visual encounter with Gorath triggers his memory; the sequence ending with a softly-fluttering flute. In "Did We Escape It?" sinister brass and violins are heard as the menace looms ever closer, with trombones dominating the piece when the Earth is moved into safety at the last possible moment, before playing in a subdued key as Gorath continues on, describing a menace still very much at large, but fortuitously on its way elsewhere to destroy worlds unknown.

The catalyst who brings the world together for its own survival almost without encouragement was personified in the character of Dr. Tazawa, played with firm resolve by the star of *War in Space*, Ryo Ikebe. Undoubtedly the greatest hero in all of Honda's genre work, Tazawa is a hard-working and inventive individual—modest to a fault—and a man of great internal strength and conviction who is not ashamed to show his emotions (upon entering the darkened room of the damaged jet pod and seeing the underbelly of the giant walrus, Ikebe first neglects to turn on his flashlight; however, just before pointing it upward, he switches it on, saving the "take"). Shortly after the crises of Gorath has passed, Tazawa's assistant, Gibson, voices concern that their biggest challenge lies ahead in putting the Earth back on its original course. Tazawa has thought the matter out: "Yes," he admits, "but we'll need twice the power we used before in putting the Earth back into its correct orbit." Then, with a teasing smile, he adds, "Kind of like walking on water!" Although Gibson is taken back by this glib reply, Tazawa looks confidently forward and predicts: "We'll do it." There is no doubt that he will.

Kumi Mizuno—already a blossoming goddess at 25—was acting in her first film for Honda and would eventually become the director's favorite leading lady (coincidentally, former female leading lady Yumi Shirakawa was appearing in her last film for Honda). Akira Kubo

(Astronaut Cadet Tatsuo) had first acted for Honda at the tender age of 17 in the director's *Adolescence, Part II* and *Farewell, Rabaul*. He plays Tatsuo as an initially immature and fun-loving cadet, only to later become much more earnest and mature in his approach to the situation (when Tatsuo visits Ari's apartment during his spell of forgetfulness, he looks around at his now-unfamiliar surroundings as he hears an ominous broadcast warning the world of an impending danger of which he has no knowledge).

Jun Tazaki, playing the doomed Captain Sonoda, had by that time already appeared in 50 films since 1950, and was a recognizable figure to many Japanese movie-goers; thus his early demise packed a considerable impact, and the actor's heroic, stern and tragic performance set the tone of deadly earnest (after chastising his crew to return to their places—and just after his aide Manabe exits the scene—a tear runs down Sonoda's cheek in an exquisitely-timed moment).

Gorath was one of Honda's finest directorial efforts, demonstrating that, if he found a project compelling, it showed in his work. His guidance of the film through its various stages is sure and steady; from the *Hawk's* tragedy to Sonoda's touching wake, from the Diet council's discomfort to the urgency of the U. N. meetings, from the desperation of the Earth's preparedness at the Pole to Tazawa's triumph. The culmination of Honda's space epics, *Gorath's* grand scale did not prevent him from including his human touches, such as when Tazawa's phone conversation with Kiyo is interrupted by his snooping staff, and the scene when Sumio is sitting at his dad's desk, pretending to be a great scientist; there is also a cute bit when Sonoda's instincts get the best of him after Magma surfaces from the rocks: Instead of escaping from the mammoth walrus, the fascinated scientist walks right toward it.

During the scene when Sonoda bid his crew farewell, Honda had the actor speaking almost directly into the camera, with Manabe standing silently in the background. The shot is reminiscent of Dr. Yamane's sad soliloquy at the end of *Godzilla*, where he too looked almost right into the lens with Dr. Tanabe listening behind him; perhaps this was Honda's way of downplaying any mordant sentimentality, or avoiding a preaching element into his films, by having another character present in the shot. Honda skillfully builds the tension and suspense in the scene where the rockets are fired for the first time; we can also sense the intense relief and joy of all concerned as he tracks-in on an excited newscaster shouting: "It's a success! A huge success! The South Pole Operation is a success! *Mankind has succeeded in moving the Earth!*"

Gorath was Honda's favorite film and the one he was most proud of as a director; although in other interviews he mentioned *Godzilla* as being his favorite because it was his first genre film, *Gorath* held greater relevance and meaning for the future of mankind and thus held a deeper meaning for its director. *Godzilla* was, after all, essentially a grim film with tragic overtones, predicting mankind's destruction due to his misuse of atomic power, while *Gorath* harnesses that very same power for the benefit of civilization. As Honda once told Guy Tucker:

> The intention I have embraced in directing and the angle from which I perceive these films has never changed. It has come from my own interest in science and also from a deep regret that the nations of the world cannot trust one another, even when they take each other's hand. That's why, even in my films after *Godzilla*, I have made it an established practice to have the scientists of the world gather together for the sake of cooperation and to avoid catastrophe.

As a result, *Gorath* was Honda's most emphatic cinematic statement on his basic belief of the inherent and inextinguishable goodness of humanity and his faith in the survival of the planet; indeed, the film's final lines were almost certainly written by the director himself:

> "Everyone, this is only the beginning. Together, we overcame the threat of the Mysterious Star, Gorath. If we were able to cooperate and overcome that danger, why not take this opportunity to work together for all eternity?"

Honda's next project would reunite him with the creature which had given him his greatest fame and recognition—Godzilla—this time locked in mortal combat with a monster once called "The Eight Wonder of the World" three decades earlier. As in *Gorath*, there would again be a battle for survival; only this time, the battle would not be for life, but for laughs.

KING KONG VS. GODZILLA (1962)
(KINGU KONGU TAI GOJIRA)

Cast & Credits

Film Register No. 12823
Release Date: August 11, 1962
Running Time: 98 minutes

Staff: Producer: Tomoyuki Tanaka; Director: Ishiro Honda; Original Story: Willis H. O'Brien, Shinichi Sekizawa, George Worthing Yates; Screenplay: Shinichi Sekizawa; Director of Photography: Hajime Koizumi; Art Director: Takeo Kita, Teruaki (Kimei) Abe; Recording: Masao Fujiyoshi; Lighting: Toshio Takashima; Music: Akira Ifukube; Sound Recording: Hisashi Shimonaga; Assistant Director: Koji Kajita; Editor: Reiko Kaneko; Sound Arrangement: Sadamasa Nishimoto; Production Manager: Shigeru Nakamura; Special Effects Techniques: Director: Eiji Tsuburaya; Photography: Teisho (Sadamasa) Arikawa, Sokei (Mototaka) Tomioka; Optical Photography: Takao Yuki, Yukio Manoda; Art Design: Akira Watanabe; Lighting: Kuichiro Kishida.

Cast: Tadao Takashima (Osamu Sakurai); Kenji Sahara (Kazuo Fujita); Yu Fujiki (Kinsaburo Furue); Ichiro Arishima (Mr. Tako); Jun Tazaki (General Masumi Shinzo); Akihiko Hirata (Dr. Shigezawa); Mie Hama (Fumiko Sakurai); Akiko Wakabayashi (Tamie); Akemi Negishi (Faro Island Dancer); Yoshi Kosugi (Faro Island Chief); Yoshifumi Tajima (Ship Captain); Ikio Sawamura (Faro Island Witch Doctor); Somesho Matsumoto ("Prime Minister" Dr. Oyaka); Ko Mishima (Naval Officer); Sachio Sakai (Obayashi); Tatsuo Matsumura (Dr. Makioka aka Makino); Senikichi Omura (Konno); Ren Yamamoto (JSDF Captain); Haruya Kato (PP Employee); Shin Otomo (Captain of Kong Transport Ship); Nadao Kirino, Yasuhisa Tsutsumi, Haruya Sakamoto (Soldiers); Yutaka Nakayama (Radio Operator on Ship Godzilla Sinks Off-Screen); Naoya Kusakawa (Reporter); Mitsuo Tsuda (Officer); Haruko Togo (Mrs. Sato); Kenzo Tabu (Host of "The Wonderful World Series").

The Film

King Kong vs. Godzilla had its origins going back to 1933 after the release of the classic *King Kong*. The astonishing special effects were conceived and executed by Willis O'Brien, but by 1960, his career had fallen on hard times. Taking out of mothballs a pet project called *King Kong vs. Frankenstein*—and after securing the rights from RKO to use Kong's character—he met a producer named John Beck and gave him several charcoal sketches containing conceptual art for the film. Beck stated he would try to drum up interest in the project and, after failing to find an interested party in the United States, gave Toho Studios a call.

Seeing the box-office potential of teaming up Kong against Godzilla, Tanaka convinced Beck to replace the Frankenstein character with the reptilian monster, and a deal was made whereby RKO would release the rights to Toho Studios in exchange for a percentage of the profits, with Universal Studios obtaining sole distribution rights outside of Japan and all Asian profits going to Toho. Shortly thereafter, Willis O'Brien (who had not heard from Beck since loaning him the sketches) learned that his beloved project would be filmed not only without his creative input, but not even in his own country when it was announced *King Kong vs. Godzilla* was being produced by Toho Studios.

The movie's tone is immediately established with a view of the Earth spinning rapidly amongst wispy vapors and shining stars as a deep voice warns of a possible tragedy befalling the planet before zooming in over the Solomon Islands as people scream on the soundtrack. It is an impressive beginning soon ruined when the host of a show called "The Wonderful World Series" (the planet and not baseball) steps in front of the Earth, now revealed as a mere prop (the planet Earth—the existence of which hung in the balance in the previous film—was now a sight gag).

In an already well-worn *cliché*, natives are seen bowing before a burning altar encrusted with animal skulls and horns. The comedy with the natives and their chief is in dubious taste; when Osamu switches on Konno's radio, a tinny piano and bongo drums issue forth as a highly-pitched voice sings an unflattering song about the "blacks" living on the island. The chief is nonetheless delighted with the device, prompting Osamu to take out some cigarettes and offer them to the natives— including a boy named Chiro—prompting Sakura to tell his friend, "When it rains, it pours," before giving the eight-year-old two cigarettes with a warning: "Don't tell your mother where you got them!"

There is much physical humor in the film such as when Kazuo demonstrates the strength of his wire to a horrified Osamu by the simple expedient of strapping it around himself before dangling and swinging over the side of the balcony. Some of the dialogue is amusing as well, such as during the *bon voyage* party at Pacific Pharmaceuticals when Obashi tells his boss that he did not invite the press to the event, as he was instructed to invite the media only for "important" news. Later, when Tako is moaning about how Godzilla's appearance is dominating the media, Obashi admits that "There's even a movie!"

The whole point of the film is voiced when Osamu, Kinsaburo and Tako are listening to a professor drone-on about his recent discovery of large red berries found on an island in the South Seas, adding that a portion of the island is protected by an animal the natives consider to be their god. Osamu is skeptical and asks his boss a prophetic question: "Will we be using monsters to advertise?" As author David Kalat has pointed out, *KKvG* then is a film about the dubious merits of commercialism, promotion and marketing with a dash of bureaucratic red tape (which Carl Denham never had to contend with) such as when a naval officer arrives on Tako's ship with the news that—since Kong is being brought to Japan without consent on an unauthorized ship—no permission will be granted to allow the ape to disembark on Japanese soil (in other words, the former Eighth Wonder of the World is now considered to be smuggled goods).

A deliberate attempt was made to stress the fact that *KKvG* is a sequel in the Godzilla series, when the crest of an iceberg gives-way to reveal the King of the Monsters pawing its way out of the ice, after being buried alive in '55. Prime Minister Shigezawa matter-of-factly informs the press, "After all, we couldn't expect Godzilla to remain frozen in that iceberg forever," in a reference to the monster having been entombed in an icy avalanche at the conclusion of its previous appearance in *Godzilla's Counterattack.* When the mighty ape seizes Fumiko and makes his way to the Diet, Kong—once used to the bright lights of Broadway—now shields his eyes from army searchlights before beginning a modest climb to the top of the Diet in an obvious homage to Kong's 1933 scamper up the Empire State Building (sadly, this is worlds apart).

KKvG contained some of Tsuburaya's poorest effects work at a time when he had recently done some of his finest in *Gorath* and *Mothra.* As usual, the man wearing the Godzilla costume was Haruo Nakajima (who also choreographed the fights between Kong and Godzilla) who did his usually proficient job in playing the radioactive menace with great gusto and vitality, whereas the man in the Kong costume—Shoicihi Hirose—

seemed out of his element, acting nothing like a real gorilla (Nakajima related to Michiko Imamura years later that Hirose did a very good job during rehearsals, but was "badly mediocre" once filming began. Tsuburaya was so disappointed with Hirose's acting that he called Nakajima aside and whispered: "There's no future for Mr. Hirose as a monster actor"). There was also an unthinkable moment which never again occurred in a Godzilla film when the King of the Monsters tries to run away from his opponent after Kong first grabs his tail; another uncharacteristic moment happened when Godzilla does not even think to use its radioactive breath to melt away high-tension tower lines as it had eight years earlier.

The effects were sloppy and hurried such as when Kong is first seen on his raft in a long shot filmed in real-time followed by a close-up in slow-motion. During the low-level close-up of the second pass of the commuter train, the light in the last car suddenly goes off before it fully-passes from view. The shot of Kong sliding down the hillside at Godzilla is terrific, but the next shot—showing the two monsters colliding as stiff puppets—is atrocious. Although the miniatures were up to Tsuburaya's high standards they were not always filmed from the best angles: When Godzilla attacks the polar base, the tanks are filmed from such a high-angle it belies their miniature nature. There were some fine effects however such as an overhead composite-matte of the sleeping Kong surrounded by dancing natives, Godzilla blasting a helicopter out of the sky and a scene when soldiers volley flares into a river infused with gasoline, causing it to ignite in an effects shot that is more complicated to achieve than it looks (then there is the wretched King Kong costume, but the less said about that, the better).

Koizumi's photography was again very good; one effective shot shows Fumiko running toward the getaway truck as it pulls away from her in one of the movie's few serious moments, and a shot of soldiers keeping low to the ground as Godzilla approaches the trap. An outstanding scene is in the command tent when the Army confronts Kong at the Diet; the cameraman's use of light, color and contrast convey the seriousness of the situation. In general, the production design by Takeo Kita and Teruaki Abe was acceptable, but Faro Island (aka Pharaoh or Fallow Island) was a disappointment, consisting of unremarkable matte paintings, a poorly constructed miniature wall and a large open set with sand covering the linoleum floor—Skull Mountain it isn't.

There is an interesting moment when Kazuo—enraged and helpless over his girlfriend's predicament of being held in the hand of Kong—can stand it no longer and freaks out as he screams at Kong, "Damn you, you stupid idiot! Let Fumiko go! Let her *go*! What's the *matter* with you?" Honda then cuts to a medium shot of Kazuo filmed from the side and slightly behind the actor as he shrieks his lover's name before he bends over in despair; Honda films the scene in such a manner as if giving the character a modicum of dignity during his trauma. The editing is also open to question as the film keeps switching from deadly drama to crazy comedy, although there is an effective cut from a defense official screaming after Kazuo to a shot of Godzilla's feet making short work of the commuter train.

Tadao Takashima (Osamu) and Yu Fujiki (Kinsaburo) play-off each other well as a classic straight-man/funny man comedy team, but the film's funniest performance comes from the man known as the "Japanese Chaplin," Ichiro Arishima, as Mr. Tako (although with his frock tail-coat, glasses and mustache he seems more like an Asian Groucho Marx). A fine comedian, Arishima came up with little comedic bits such as blowing kisses at Kong, taking a drink from Kinsaburo's glass during the press extravaganza and nearly falling off the cliff as he watches Kong swim away. Perhaps the actor's best moment is in the scene when Kong survives the detonation of the raft: Arishima registers delight at Kong surviving the explosion before cowering in fear when the beast roars in a perfect summation of the fascination people have with monsters: We love them because they scare us.

Jun Tazaki's portrayal of General Shinzo is the best "serious" performance in the picture, giving it its few touches of dignity, while Akihiko Hirata once again plays a bland official. Mie Hama (Fumiko) had not been particularly interested in an acting career, and her lack of appreciation for her craft—particularly fantasy film work—resulted in a general lack of enthusiasm that registered on-screen (kudos must go to her however in the scene where she has to splash through a river in what must have been a cold and uncomfortable chore for the actress).

Kenji Sahara as Kazuo is his usually appealing self—complete with his infectious smile—although he is also given a chance to express embarrassment, fear and shock when the occasion demands; when he rescues Fumiko from the sleeping Kong, his expression belies fright and uncertainty as opposed to the typically daring and confident Western hero (incredibly, after rescuing Fumiko from Kong—after having previously rescued her from Godzilla—Kazuo does not even accompany her to the hospital).

Akemi Negishi—who had played the arousing Chika in *Abominable Snowman*—is the native dancer who has a busy night; mere minutes after nearly being eaten-alive by a giant octopus, she must lead her tribe in a reverential dance to mollify King Kong. The dance itself was choreographed by Honda, who choreographed all of the native dances in his films, amazingly never repeating routines (the director also choreographed his fight scenes, which—due to the fact they were done by actors and not stuntmen—were one of the weaker elements in his films). The dance is an interesting affair, what with much flexing and gyrating, yet the natives seem curiously bored with their party as if being tired of having to constantly leap about on a moment's notice to help Kong sleep of his drunk.

Akira Ifukube's music for the film was its greatest asset. His "Main Title" music begins with a gong and rapid bowstrings, augmented by the chanting and wailing of natives in a pagan ceremonial atmosphere stressing Kong's island origins. Ifukube made much use of the electone (an electronic organ) and vibraphones joined by violins and piano with low brass to mark the *Seahawk*'s doomed voyage, while primitive drums, horns and woodwinds color the sequences on Faro Island (this music would return as the "Infant Island" theme in a more-embellished form in the subsequent Godzilla film).

In his score for the original *Godzilla*, Ifukube colored the monster's character with rapid bowstrings to give it an air of mounting panic. In *KKvG*, Ifukube introduces a new theme for Godzilla, which would become even more recognizable: A slower and more deliberate piece, scored for low brass, which gradually builds in tempo to give the impression of a creature of great, unrelenting power. One particularly interesting piece was written for the octopus; a ponderous and descending theme played on brass and counterbalanced by violins to lend the creature a slimy, undulating quality.

King Kong's theme (first heard in "Giant Octopus vs. King Kong") is colored with low, audacious brass and quivering electone, lending Kong an air of drunken bravado. Ifukube's scoring of the monsters' initial confrontation beings with an English horn playing in rapid individual notes (as if mimicking Kong's naked feet padding through the forest), later complemented by electone, trumpets and a synthesized contrabassoon. "The Plan to Transport King Kong" is a lively and likeable theme introduced with drums, violins and woodwinds joined by trombones and a bellowing tuba, with the electone supplying a nice refrain.

After an eight-year absence, *KKvG* reunited Honda with Godzilla, this time in wide-screen, color and stereophonic sound. Unlike Kong's comedic scenes, the scenes with Godzilla reestablished it as a towering terror of destruction, although the fight scenes between the two monsters were played mainly for laughs. At times, Honda's direction is a bit off and seems uncomfortable, switching back-and-forth between the comedy and drama, particularly aboard the *Seahawk* sequence, which was melodramatic and clumsy (when the scientists tumble during an underwater jolt, they fell like a row of dominoes rather than all at once). One particularly bad moment occurs when Kinsaburo whirls the lizard around; both Honda and the actor hold on the shot longer than necessary, giving away the fact the animal was a very artificial-looking prop.

In general, the film contains an impression of unrehearsed spontaneity—possibly due to its general air of improvisation—and the zany comedy scenes which did not always balance well with its more-serious moments; for example, the *Seahawk* disaster is continuously interrupted by the silliness of Pacific Pharmaceutical's *bon voyage* party (although the U.S. version simply did away with the celebration and let the saga of the *Seahawk* play without interruption), and when Kong inadvertently spills out a dozen or-so train commuters to their deaths it is hardly a comedic moment. Honda's best scene was probably when Kong struggles to free himself from the raft with the crew being jostled around convincingly on the deck, and the director adds his usual "touching" moment aboard the *Seahawk*, when the captain places his hand on his subordinate's shoulder when receiving a discouraging damage report.

KKvG was one of Honda's weaker directorial efforts—not surprising since the director always maintained that monsters should always be taken seriously. Not that the film is not without some drama, such as a wonderful panic scene showing people dashing madly about before boarding a commuter train, as Koizumi's camera tracks along with the crowd. In the confusion, Fumiko and Kazuo become separated by the train's doors and, in a poignant moment, can see but not reach other (ironically, the fact that Kazuo is unable to board the train will save his life). There is another fine shot of the passengers being jolted forward when Kong grabs onto the train.

When the two monster first meet in the great valley, Kong approaches on ground level while Godzilla arrives on a high bluff, as if symbolically looking down on his Western rival. Many have viewed the film not so much a clash of Eastern and Western monsters, but a cinematic expression of Japan's growing confidence as a world economy, now sufficiently recovered from the war to take on the country that had a generation earlier had reduced it to rubble (there was one scene with a very definite message: When the two monsters tear apart the Atami

Castle if was for a reason as the castle is not authentic but an attraction built in 1959 for the tourist trade).

The creator of the original Kong did not live to see either version of the film; three months after *KKvG* was released in Japan, Willis O'Brien suffered a massive heart attack and died on November 8, 1962. Seven months later—on June 6, 1963, and just over thirty years after the release of the original *King Kong*—*King Kong vs. Godzilla* began its American run and became an enormous success. The film made millions for Universal and Toho and did much for the reputations of Tanaka and Beck at the expense of the reputations of Honda and Tsuburaya (when Universal first received the Japanese print they were appalled to find it a comedy so they deliberately added serious footage. The resultant U.S. version gives the impression that, while the rest of the world is calmly concerned with what is happening in Japan, the Japanese dealing with the problem are juvenile and ridiculous).

The shift in the focus of the series from catastrophe to comedy was eerily-predicted in the scene when a woman and her child are evacuating after Godzilla has arrived on the mainland; the news is chilling to the adults but the boy is delighted, he wants to see Godzilla! *King Kong vs. Godzilla* remains the only intentionally-comedic Godzilla film ever made, and is a true anemology in Honda's career, sandwiched between two cinematic conceptions of what man could achieve at his best (*Gorath*) and his worst (*Matango*). Ironically, it became Honda's greatest commercial success and has been re-released in Japan several times over the years, where it always plays to large audiences. To this day people still watch it with amusement, but the last laugh will always belong to Willis H. O'Brien.

MATANGO (1963)
ATTACK OF THE MUSHROOM PEOPLE

Cast & Credits

Film Register No. 13263
Release Date: August 11, 1963
Running Time: 89 minutes

<u>Staff</u>: Producer: Tomoyuki Tanaka; Director: Ishiro Honda; Original Story: Shinichi Hoshi and Masami Fukushima, Based on "A Voice in the Darkness" by William H. Hodgson; Screenplay: Takeshi Kimura; Cinematography: Hajime Koizumi; Art Director: Shigekazu Ikuno; Recording: Fumio Yanoguchi; Lighting: Shoshichi Kojima; Music: Sadao (Beppu) Wakemiya; Sound Arrangement: Hisashi Shimonaga; Assistant Director: Koji Kajita; Editor: Reiko Kaneko; Sound Effects: Minoru Kaneyama; Production Manager: Shigeru Nakamura; Special Effects Techniques: Director: Eiji Tsuburaya; Cinematography: Sadamasa (Teisho) Arikawa and Sokei Tomioka.

<u>Cast</u>: Akira Kubo (Kenji Murai); Kumi Mizuno (Mami Sekiguchi); Hiroshi Koizumi (Naoyuki Sakuda); Kenji Sahara (Senzo Koyama); Hiroshi Tachikawa (Etsuro Yoshida); Yoshio Tsuchiya (Fumio Kasai); Miki Yashiro (Akiko Soma); Hideyo Amamoto, Keisuke Yamada, Katsumi Tezuka, Haruo Nakajima, Tokio Okawa, Koji Urugi, Masaki Shinohara, Kuniyoshi Kajima, Toku Ihara, Mitsuko Hayashi, Kakue Ichibanji (Mushroom Men); Jiro Kumagai, Akio Kusama, Yutaka Oka, Kazuo Hinata (Medical Center Doctors).

The Film

Matango was inspired by William Hope Hodgson's short story "The Voice in the Night," first published in 1907, which involved a ship at night that comes upon an unseen man floating on a small boat in the mist pleading for food for himself and for his female companion who are both marooned on an island. The man begs not to be seen, and after receiving some food, tells his incredible tale of horror and anguish. A number of key elements of Hodgson's story were incorporated into *Matango*, which was a collaboration between science-fiction editor/writer Masami Fukushima and Shinichi Hoshi (Takeshi Kimura drafted the final screenplay).

As with *Abominable Snowman*, the movie begins on an upbeat note only to quickly dissolve into a world of nightmarish terror. The film is an *expose'* on the moral decay afflicting all who reach the island; yet, had all worked together, escape would not have been impossible. As it happens, partnerships are forged then dissolved overnight, turtle eggs become a bartered item on the Black Market, lovers are used and then exchanged without a second glance and friendship and loyalty become meaningless words. Unlike the vast majority of Honda's fantasy films, *Matango* was not "effects driven" but "character driven," with the "Seven Deadly Sins" all present and accounted for, averaging out to one for each person.

Perhaps the film's main blemish is in the design and manipulation of the full-grown Mushroom People. Over 50 different designs were considered with Shigeru Komatsuzaki sketching the approved model and Teizo Toshimitsu given the task of creating the full-scale costumes. The costumes were constructed out of latex and Styrofoam coated with a reflective material called "Scotchlite" as well as fluorescent paints to reflect the studio lights and give the impression of phosphorescence. When the costumes were completed—in bright pinkish colors, raised nodules and thinly curled and gold tactile hairs—Tsuburaya laughed when he saw them.

To achieve the swelling and growing effect of the mushrooms, Tsuburaya's crew discovered a material now known as polystyrene foam which, when put into a cylinder and combined with water, rapidly expands in less than a minute. As Honda later recalled to Shingo Yamamoto: "This made the scene look very creepy. When we tested the material in the staff room, everyone burst out in applause." Plaster was mixed and formed into mushroom shapes before being added to a forming agent to accomplish the swelling effect.

Cinematographer Koizumi did his best work for Honda on *Matango*; one can almost smell the mold and air of ambient decay hovering over the film. As usual, close-ups are briefly employed, but are highly effective, and Koizumi's camera lurks around the confining corners of the derelict ship, peering into hallways and cabins as if eavesdropping on the interlopers. A number of bizarre images lasting no more than a second were interspersed throughout the film in keeping with its generally hallucinogenic nature: A close-up of a blind and stuffed turtle, the rising apparition confronting Mami and Akiko in the jungle, the "monster" in the captain's cabin, Kenji seeing his reflection in shards of broken glass and Kenji and Naoyuki's "ghostly" encounter in the ship's hallway.

During the castaways initial search of the island, Koizumi superimposes their feet over shots of the jungle foliage, emphasizing their long and difficult trek (the island itself is far from a tropical paradise, with sheer cliffs dotting the interior thick with jungle foliage, the air moist and either gut-wrenchingly hot or bone-chillingly cold, capricious fog which is everywhere obliterating the landscape and disorienting the hapless explorer; and although the sun does make brief and sporadic appearances from time-to-time, it does little to alleviate the dampness that hangs over the island like a shroud—even the sand on the beach is black).

Koizumi's work is highly creative such as when Akiko is watching her beau battle a Mushroom Man, Koizumi filming her in a close-up with the shadows of the battling figures crossing over her face (in a previous moment, Honda cut to an intense close-up of her tear-filled face looking directly into the camera after she has been backhanded by her boyfriend). The cinematographer utilized a number of hand-held shots and kept close to much of the action to stress the dramatic tension (the location photography was filmed on the poisonous snake and insect-infested islands of Oshima and Hachijyojima). The superb interior sets were designed by Shigekazu (Juichi) Ikuno and Tadashi Kioke; the three-masted schooner is aptly displayed as a wrecked ship with decaying sails, a rotted outer hull and rigging lines hanging about like so many twisted spider webs. The interior of the ship is a magnificent tribute to rust, mold and thick dust covering everything in a swath of putrefaction (a number of scenes were shot through filters with strange hues, superimposed fog and mist-filled air).

The contrast between the rotting ship and the beautiful mushroom grove are shown to brilliant advantage, and there is a wonderful dissolve during Etsuro's flashback to the nightclub when he is seen sitting next to Akiko in a two-shot; as he looks at her with lust, the fire burning between them is revealed as his signal fire. In a shot recalling a moment from *Abominable Snowman*, a monster reveals itself spying on a lovely female through an opening, and when the possessed Etsuro tells his intended prey that "I'm going to kill all of you," Honda has him looking directly into the camera, just as Mami does later when she tells Fumio that "I've waited a long time to hear you begging for help."

Film Composer Sadao Bekku's uplifting, Hawaiian-style "Sea Breeze" sung in "la-la" fashion by Mizuno, begins with a ukulele before blooming into an orchestrated score hinting at Mizuno's showbiz origins; as close as Honda ever came to directing a musical. The majority of the cues are brief, bitter and distended fragments of music such as "Dark Clouds," comprised of plucking cello strings, quivering violins and raspy coronets. Bekku clues the audience in on the terrors to come with "Changing Course," written as undulating upper-and-lower octaves played by violins and utilized later as the Mushroom People's theme, while muted, low horns return, augmented by xylophones, eerily trailing violins and rising and falling violins and flutes which signify the moment when the yacht becomes "Adrift."

"The Illusion," heard when Etsuro imagines seeing the huge ship at sea, is scored with quivering violins playing in gradually unnervingly ascending rhythms, while "An Isolated Island Shrouded in Mist" is a somber, descending two-note motif played on horns and woodwinds followed by coronets, plucking strings and shimmering cymbals when Senzo first sees the island—not exactly an auspicious introduction. Sad strings and a vibraphone's echo score the scene when Mami makes her fateful decision at Senzo's grave in "The Matango Woman," while Bekku perfectly punctuates the moment when Fumio ingests his mushroom in "A Million and One Matango," beginning with fluttering woodwinds, bells and flutes before swaying into organ music taking us into the dream sequence with its bizarre combination of vibraphone, bells, saxophone, harp, coronet and flute.

"The Two Remaining People" is a tender piece hinting at Honda's doomed optimism—scored with violins and patches of "Adrift"—as Kenji tries to encourage Akiko not to give up. In "Murai and Akiko, The Matango Attack," the music is extremely creative, with crashing gongs accentuating the moments when the Mushroom People try to reach Kenji and Akiko. As Kenji manages to sail away from the island, Bekku colors the moment with a sustained note played on strings to register the uncertainty of his voyage in "Pushed to the Extreme."

The acting in *Matango* represented the finest in all of Honda's genre

155

work as Tucker acknowledged, "And virtually all of them did the best work of their careers." At age 27, Akira Kubo (Kenji) did a tremendous job as a typically-weakly-heroic leading man, and his final scene in the sanitarium is very touching (when Kubo asked Honda what should be on his mind when searching the derelict ship, Honda suggested the actor use his sense of smell). Kubo considered the role to be the favorite of his film career.

Yoshio Tsuchiya (Fumio) had often played weak-willed characters subject to temptation, and in *Matango* he gives a compelling performance which stands in stark contrast to his self-assured Mizuno in *Gas Human* (tellingly, after Fumio succumbs to the Mushroom Men, he is never seen again; a failure as a man, he no doubt was a failure as a Mushroom Man). Hiroshi Koizumi (Naoyuki)—usually cast as an undemonstrative scientist—played his part with passion and showed a considerable range of emotions (the actor conveyed the fact that his character *must* leave the island lest he succumb to his own weaknesses).

Perhaps the movie's most memorable performances came from Kenji Sahara (Senzo) and Kumi Mizuno (Mami). Sahara was a former matinee idol but in *Matango*, he plays a lowly and rude character, even voluntarily removing a false tooth to embellish his part. Sahara later recalled the encouragement Honda gave him in allowing him play a part so very much against his type, which the actor regarded as a supreme vote of confidence in his abilities. Senzo wears his sunglasses (usually a sign in a Honda picture of a nefarious individual) throughout the entire film and is a brute but not a fool; it is his intense lecture to the group which motivates them all to search for food. He also makes a number of prophetic statements, such as how women on ships have a history of causing men to loose their heads, and another that he will probably never have the chance to spend the money Fumio gives him in exchange for the turtle eggs (after he has been shot by Etsuro, the sailor clings to a rope as he falls—a "lifeline" that eventually runs out).

Kumi Mizuno was 26 years old when she appeared in *Matango* and her memories of the filming were as warm as she revealed in an interview with Galbraith years later: "My strongest memory of Mr. Honda was when we went on location...we lived there for a month and Mr. Honda was the only one who didn't change during that time." Oddly, in Etsuro's flashback to the nightclub, Mami is seen singing in the background, but Honda did not gives her a close-up. When the possessed Mami confronts Fumio, she looks more ravishing than at any other time in her career, her glistening white skin making her appear like a shining goddess. It would become her most-memorable scene in a Honda film in her most incandescent screen performance (seductive, flirtatious yet vulnerable) as well as being the favorite role of *her* career (her passionate scene with the possessed Etsuro is the most sexually-charged moment in all of Honda—but then, consider the circumstances). Also effective was Hiroshi Tachikawa as the warped Etsuro, going from flippant to enraged, then finally to possessed as he happily holds up a mushroom like a glass of vintage port (Kimura perversely has the writer become an alcoholic and the first to succumb to the mushrooms).

The film's finest scene—and one of the finest in Honda's career—is when Mami and Fumio arrive at the Mushroom Forest where she wistfully tells him, "The rain is making the mushrooms grow big and strong with each drop." Leading him to the food, Honda tracks the camera back as Fumio looks around nervously, following her around like a wounded puppy, as Mami happily anticipates what is to come. Fumio watches with astonishment as Mami calmly picks a mushroom off a tree and eats it. "It's delicious," she sighs, "We should have eaten them sooner." The camera then tracks-in on Fumio as he takes a mushroom and samples it, while Mami watches him with immense satisfaction in a cinematic retelling of the Garden of Eden, with Mami's "Eve" tempting Fumio's "Adam" with the "Forbidden Vegetable."

After Kenji realizes that Akiko has disappeared, he heads to the only place left to look: the mushroom forest. But before he leaves, Honda holds on various close-ups of the brown, rotting and rusted interior of the ship before transitioning to the lush, green, mist-filled floor of the mushroom grove, accentuating the inducement which has doomed all. Even with all the negativity in the film, Honda had to get some optimistic words in, and probably penned the scene where Kenji and Akiko take a stroll on the beach, during which Kenji explains how desperate situations seem to bring out the worst in people: "Under trying conditions, men tend to be selfish and cruel; that's when we must act in a rational manner. We must help each other" (a sentiment echoed the following year in a crucial scene in *Mothra vs. Godzilla*).

Likewise, the moment in the clinic when Kenji suddenly turns around to reveal his mutated face was done with an uncharacteristic zoom as a light suddenly shines on his face. Although effective, it seems a bit forced, as if Honda felt the need to artificially emphasize the moment of revelation (a more subdued effect—such as having the actor slowly approaching the camera and into the light—would have been far more disquieting). There is also the odd notion that the marooned people are all able to make it ashore while still wearing their shoes and hats; Senzo even manages to bring his duffle bag along with him.

But the most frustrating moment in the film comes after a Mushroom Man gains entry into the castaways' cabin, only to suddenly vanish into thin air (Senzo's anger in the subsequent scene may well have mirrored that of many an audience member, confused and irritated by Honda's abrupt ending of a potentially exciting moment). According to Toho's synopsis of the film, the creature was supposed to be "ghost-like" and vanish into thin air. *Matango* is hardly as horrifying as it could have been, such as Kenji's confrontation with the monsters in the Mushroom Forest, as Greg Shoemaker has written: "The film fails when the mushroom monsters, provided by man-in-suit latex costumes, are shown in full view in the bright green light of the jungle forestation. They are floppy, rubber 'Pans' in their own manner, giggling in high, child-like voices, leading the survivors to their doom. Editing full-shots of the mushroom people to shorten on-screen time or their total deletion with a substitution of dark, mist bound interiors and moving shadows of hinted-at shapes would have intensified the horror."

Even showing the monsters still in their humanoid shape would have been preferable to the towering creations that—as Tsuchiya later put it—looked more appropriate for an attraction ride at Disneyland than a grim horror film. As it is, the shots of actor Kubo's head popping violently into the frame, staring wide-eyed at the camera while screaming at the top of his lungs are as likely to elicit as many giggles as gasps. As Honda told Lethem in 1968: "I have never thought about making movies in order to scare an audience and I don't think I ever will." When Lethem pressed Honda further, the annoyed director snapped, "As I *told* you, I am *not* interested in simply scaring people" (which could be why Toho never assigned Honda to direct any future horror films).

As a result, there are those who consider *Matango* to be Honda's greatest missed opportunity; however, Honda would have been the first to point out that his intention was not to stress the mutations of the Mushroom Men, but to tell about the moral decay of those under duress who are more concerned with their personal motives than in helping each other. What the director no-doubt found *most* disturbing was the scene where Fumio is surrounded by Mushroom Men, the last vestiges of his remaining human dignity leaving him as he meekly surrenders to his fate amidst the grotesque forms howling at his humiliating spectacle; as far as Honda was concerned, *that* was *real* horror.

Matango is the most-claustrophobic of Honda's films; we too begin to feel we are marooned and have no escape. Some have speculated *Matango* was meant to show the suffering of the atomic bomb survivors or as a warning to Japanese youth to stay away from drugs. Honda never admitted to either premise, commenting instead on the excessive lifestyles of foreigners visiting the Muira Peninsula (south of Yokohama in the Kanagawa-ken prefecture of Honshu in Central Japan), which then as now has a vibrant sailing community and yacht harbor located in nearby Aburatsubo Bay. In an interview printed in *Godzilla and My Movie Life*, Honda described them: "They played all kinds of games, yet had already tired of the ordinary things, hungry for some extreme, even shocking experience."

Matango's ending was unlike any Honda had ever done or would ever do again; there was no ambiguity, ambivalence or paradox this time as Kenji—a man with the best of intentions and the highest moral fiber— is cursed, halted forever in his transformation; not quite a Mushroom Man, not quite a man (presumably he ate some mushrooms he found on the yacht while attempting to sail back to Japan, which accounts for his incomplete conversion). The ending does however reinforce the director's typically objective approach: As Kenji turns to view the city, Honda does not give us a close-up of the man's tortured face so we can sense his suffering, but instead shows us the city at night as he will see it from that point onward; it's time for us to go, there is nothing we or anyone else can do.

This ending had great personal poignancy for screenwriter Kimura, who, as with Kenji in his final days, was a man disassociated from society and who would die lonely and forgotten. Whether or not Kimura would have wanted it that way is an interesting question, but regardless of Kimura's dim view of humanity, Honda respected both the man and his work to such an extent that the director invited the screenwriter to view the films' final cut, anxious at his response. As Guy Tucker wrote in *Age of the Gods*, when the film came to an end, Kimura turned to Honda and whispered: "No complaints"—an opinion audiences all over the world share to this very day.

SUBMARINE WARSHIP (1963)
KAITEI GUNKAN
ATRAGON

Cast & Credits

Film Register No. 13386
Release Date: December 22, 1963
Running Time: 94 minutes and 7 seconds

Staff: Producer: Tomoyuki Tanaka; Director: Ishiro Honda; Story Based on the novels "Undersea Battleship" by Shunro Oshikawa and "The Undersea Kingdom" by Shigeru Komatsuzaki; Screenplay: Shinichi Sekizawa; Cinematography: Hajime Koizumi; Production Design: Takeo Kita; Recording: Masanao Uehara; Lighting: Shoshichi Kojima; Music: Akira Ifukube; Sound Arrangement: Hisahsi Shimonaga; Assistant Director Koji Kajita; Editor: Ryohei Fujii; Sound Effects: Minoru Kaneyama; Developing: Tokyo Laboratory; Production Manager: Shigeru Nakamura; Special Effects Techniques: Eiji Tsuburaya; Cinematography: (Teisho) Sadamasa Arikawa and Sokei Tomioka.

Cast: Tadao Takashima (Susumu Hatanaka); Yoko Fujiyama (Makoto Jinguji); Yu Fujiki (Yoshindo Nishibe); Kenji Sahara (Gyoto Umino); Ken Uehara (Admiral Kosumi); Hiroshi Koizumi (Detective Ito); Jun Tazaki (Admiral Jinguji); Yoshibumi Tajima (Saburo Amano); Akihiko Hirata (Mu Agent 23); Hideyo Amamoto (Mu High Priest); Susumu Fujita (Defense Official); Minoru Takada (Defense Commander); Hisaya Ito (Engineer Shindo); Ikio Sawamura (Taxi Driver); Tetsuko Kobayashi (Empress of Mu); Akemi Kita (Model Rimako); Hiroshi Hasegawa (Lt. Fuji); Nadao Kirino (Engineer); Haruya Sakamoto (Atragon Soldier Yamada); Tetsu Nakamura (Cargo Ship Captain); Yutaka Nakayama (Guard on Cargo Ship); Koji Uno (Mt. Mihara Policeman); Sadako Amemiya (Memoko Photo Studio Technician); Rinsaku Ogata (Mt. Mihara Soldier); Hideo Otsuka (Marunouchi Defense Officer); Yutaka Oka, Yukihiko Gondo, Masayoshi Kawanabe (Mt. Mihara Sightseeing Bus Passengers).

The Film

Teruyoshi Nakano once told Stuart Galbraith IV, "Mr. Honda said you can't pay too much attention to the background, because if you do it won't have the impact you intended. If you want to film the ocean, and you spend time trying to find the best angle to shoot it, it's like you're trying too hard, and killing the real look of the most beautiful ocean." Honda had cherished the ocean since he was a boy, and in many ways *Submarine Warship* was Honda's *homage* to that element, as the vast majority of the film take place either near the surface of the sea, on it, near it or under it.

For *Atragon*, Sekizawa wrote what many consider to be his finest script for Honda in a happy coincidence as it followed *Matango*, which was possibly Kimura's best script for Honda. Sekizawa was stationed in the South Pacific during the war, which for the most part involved being stationed in the Solomon Islands and trying to avoid boredom and death from starvation. With little else to pass the time, rumors became *de rigur*; one in particular involved a new Japanese super-weapon under construction on a remote island. The movie's direct inspiration came from a popular novel called *The Submarine Warship* by Shunro Oshikawa, in which an iconoclastic naval commander named Captain Sakurai has set up a base of operations on a remote South Seas island in order to build a super-submarine that will establish Japan as a world naval power (further inspiration came from Shigeru Komatsuzaki's illustrated story, *The Undersea Kingdom*).

Assisting with the screenplay were Shigeru Komatsuzaki and Shunro Oshikawa (there seems to have been yet another nod to a George Pal effort, this one from two years earlier: *Atlantis, the Lost Continent*. During the scene in the Mus' Great Hall, strange crystalline braziers are glowing, calling to mind *Atlantis's* huge, crystal-based ray weapon. Sudden earthquakes, an ancient civilization capable of futuristic weapons, fantastic submarines and a craving to rule the world are other elements arguably inspired from the Pal picture). Sekizawa's script included a rare pre-title sequence involving Agent 23's kidnapping of an industrial engineer, and as usual, the writer put his little touches of humor into the film—such as comedic bits again involving a photographer and an upturned coffee pot thought to announce the arrival of a "Steaming Man"—but they do not intrude with the film's serious nature, although one gag that should have been eliminated occurs after Jinguchi has finished discussing his Zero Cannon weapon, at which point Umino sneezed. There is another anomalous bit when Admiral Kosumi receives a package sent to him in care of police headquarters; the return address identifying the sender as none other than "Agent 23 of the Mu Empire," and even though an ordinance expert suspects the package may contain an explosive and insists on opening it himself, everyone remains in the room.

The film is filled with memorable characters: The resolute Jinguchi, the bitter Makoto, the fiercely loyal Amano and so on. The core of the plot is not about Jinguchi's thirst for revenge and retribution, but the strained relationship between he and his daughter; one cannot forget the past while the other cannot forgive it. Bitter about the eventual outcome of the war, it is reasonable to expect that a career military man such as Jinguchi would not want to use his submarine for any other purpose other than to restore Japan's naval prestige, no matter how hard Kosumi begs or how bad things look for the Earth. Jinguchi is as unrelenting in his decision as his men are in their loyalty toward him.

Once Makoto is kidnapped, however, all sense of restoring national pride and avenging Japan's WW II defeat fall to the wayside, overcome by the basic and unwavering human instinct to protect one's child. It is a totally-believable premise having Makoto's abduction be the motivation for Jinguchi to change his mind and thus save mankind (ironically for the Mus, it would have made much more sense for them to have kidnapped Jinguchi's daughter and hold her as a hostage under the threat of death should her father decide to aid the Earth; in effect, had the Empire simply left Makoto alone, Jinguchi would have had no reason to change his mind).

Ito points out that—had Umino been denied permission to join them on their search for Jinguchi—the reporter would doubtless have printed the story, but apparently the notion of keeping the journalist in police custody occurs to no one. A more-serious error shows Umino tossing a homing beacon overboard to alert a Mu submarine, an unnecessary moment which alerts the audience to the fact that he is a Mu agent. It is not worth close exanimation of a number of other elements, such as how a handful of natives and Jinguchi's crew could ever build a mammoth submarine (to say nothing of a dry dock carved inside of a mountain) or why the Empress would need to activate a switch releasing Manda from solid rock, since the beast had earlier been seen swimming in the open ocean, but such lapses are forgivable in light of the film's overall excellence.

There were the usual problems to be faced and dealt with during filming, what with the inherent peculiarities and risks involved with live-action effects. During the scene when the dry dock is destroyed, the resulting concussion from the pyrotechnics caused a studio light to fall onto the miniature set where it quite naturally became part of the rubble. When the *Atragon* team begins their search-and-destroy mission running down stairs, a portion of *Atragon's* drill-section can be seen protruding through a rear wall in a brilliant matte, and when Atragon's search-and-destroy mission encounters several Mu guards, the assault team fire their Zero Rifles, freezing the guards into immobility depicted as clever dissolves from live-action into matte paintings. In one brilliant shot, after two Mu submarines have been frozen by Atragon's Zero Cannon, ice forms around them while simultaneous explosions occur in the background before they are rocked about like bowling pins.

Honda was not always satisfied with Tsuburaya's work but he usually kept such opinions to himself; only years later did he reveal his displeasure with the miniature Mu Empire, which—instead of a grandiose layout showing the undersea kingdom—Tsuburaya had used only a few brief establishing shots (this could have been at least partially due to a restricted budget and a narrow timeframe, as Assistant Effects Director Teruyoshi Nakano remembered that Tsuburaya was given less than a month to do the effects work, adding that Tsuburaya cried tears of joy once filming was successfully completed on schedule).

Cinematographer Hajime Koizumi's work in *Atragon* ranks among his best; as usual, his lighting, use of shadows, composition and color are outstanding (after the *Red Satan* is destroyed, Honda begins the next scene—the interrogation of Kosumi by his former staff—with a shot of the admiral with his back to the camera, "surrounded" as it were, by his former comrades). In the moment after Makoto is ignored by her father during their first meeting, Koizumi shows Makoto's head sadly bowed-down in the subsequent shot, and when sailors unlock a doorway hatch in order to enter the buried *Atragon's* Command Center, Koizumi's camera tracks-in behind them (as the Empress of Mu is running off to throw herself into the sea, Honda shows all five kidnapped victims of the Mu Empire in a single shot).

The evening confrontation between Jinguchi and Makoto at the lake, with sparkling blue waters framed through the green jungle foliage, is arguably the most beautifully-filmed scene in all of Honda's genre films. After the tight confines of *Matango*, Kozumi easily transitioned to *Atragon's* grander scale as his camera work during the dancing ceremony is highly-creative, with numerous set-ups, pans, tracking shots and close-ups (the most symbolic shot in the film occurs when the High Priest is discounting his agents' reports as to *Atragon's* invasion of the Mu Empire; the three characters are framed inside the open mouth of an overhead stature of Manda as if the vanquished god is swallowing them up).

Takeo Kita's production design is excellent as the interior of *Atragon*'s Command Center is crowded with all manner of levers and switches, while Kosumi's office is well-appointed (although the equipment built for the captain's bridge—as indeed for all of the ships in Kita's films—had an unfortunate tendency to wiggle). The color blue is predominant in many scenes, giving added emphasis to the film's aquatic nature, while the Mu Empire itself is an odd blend of the old and the new. If Kita's intention was to show the Mu Empire as being the "cradle of civilization," he outdid himself, as the Empire's interiors are an eclectic blend of Abyssinian "Bah Relief" sculptures, Renaissance marble columns, Babylonian furniture, Asian statues and Gothic arches, although the main influence appears to be Egyptian. The Mus are dressed in Egyptian-style clothing and, during the establishing shot of the Empress seated at her throne, two large Egyptian statues can be seen standing behind her. The Mu citizenry itself seems quite diverse; although the High Priest and Priestess are unmistakably Asian, many members of the Royal Court—as well as those manning the Mu submarine—are Caucasian (this was no accident as Honda occasionally cast American servicemen and their wives in scenes calling for an international flavor).

Akira Ifukube was scoring his first film for Honda since *King Kong vs. Godzilla* and again, the composer's bold and innovative use of instrumentation added immeasurably to the overall success of the film and its epic scale. The composer scores "The Toho Logo" introduction with pounding drums and electone (used on nearly every cue in the film), followed by a 12-note motif representing the Mu Empire. Ifukube then musically "answers" the challenge of the Empire with his "Main Title" music playing the *Atragon* theme in 4/4 time (one beat every second); an intimidating, resolute piece that begins with a gong and is dominated by brass (Jinguchi's determination) and bow strings (the mighty battleship).

In "The *Red Satan*," Ifukube begins with a cymbal crash before adding violins and low brass playing in a downward progression, mirroring the submarines' underwater pursuit, with shrieking trumpets and faint, quivering violins punctuating the atmosphere. The power and the glory of the mighty *Atragon* is represented in "Test Maneuvers of the Undersea Warship," with French horns and a rift played on a field drum, followed by triumphant trumpets and flutes playing in an *ostinato* (repeated) pattern as the mighty ship begins to move.

"Makoto's Theme" is a sad, reflective piece heard when she and her father first meet and heard again in a longer version during their argument at the lake. This extended version is introduced by a double-reeded English horn (essentially a larger version of the oboe) with vibraphones added for atmosphere brilliantly scored in a discordant manner, answered by somber strings. Ifukube cleverly ends the sequence with faint trumpets and horns representing the militarist's deflated condition. "The Prayer of the Mu Empire" is a three-minute musical extravaganza, containing hints of boastful native trappings hinting at desperation (the piece was composed before the scene was filmed and played over a loudspeaker to guarantee synchronization with the dancers' movements). Beginning with a wailing chorus, soft clarinets, piano and mellow horns, the piece evolves into a pounding, rhythmic dance scored with xylophone, mallets, tom-toms and gongs. A female chorus hums while men chant their ode to Manda, with the chants increasing in their rapidity as they near the finish with sustained notes ending as the female chorus shrieks on a quivering, final note. The introductory music for "Manda, the Guardian Dragon" is appropriately-scored with screaming trumpets and a fluttering contrabassoon to lend the creature its slithering, serpentine quality.

Kettledrums, suspended cymbals and timpani—followed by the electone and a fluttering oboe—dominate "Tokyo Bay Goes up in Flames" when the Mu submarine incinerates the ships in Tokyo Bay, followed by brass bombastically playing the Mu Empire's theme.

For the unusual sequence when the escapees make it to the sub while evading Manda ("The Rescue") Ifukube wrote an unusual score populated with bassoon, double-bassoon, bass clarinet, quivering viola, cello, flutter-tongue flutes, vibraphone, low woodwinds, violins playing in their lowest registers, pounding timpani, electone and muted trumpets playing in a "wah-wah" pattern.

"The Volunteer Corps Swing into Action" depicts the moment when the Mu Empire is attacked by the *Atragon*'s volunteers with fluttering flutes and piano answered by muted drums playing a portion of the Mus' theme, indicating the civilization's imminent demise. The piece then develops into a relentless pattern of drum riffs and violins, with clarinets playing in a circular pattern to signify the Mu's whirling machinery. The film's "Ending" piece begins not on a winning note but on a woeful one, with muted trumpet and subtle electone playing the Mu's ceremonial dance music in a minor key. Low horns and affecting strings conclude the piece with two sustained and final notes heard on horns, indicating a typically-hollow Honda victory.

Of all the actors who appeared in *Warship*, perhaps the one who had the greatest impact was Jun Tazaki, outstanding as Captain Hachiro

Jinguchi; proud and fiercely loyal but blind to his own instincts and ambitions (Jinguchi is an almost mythical character as his name is mentioned or otherwise referred to two-dozen times before he finally appears on the screen). Admiral Koisumi was played by former matinee idol Ken Uehara (in a deeply-emotive moment, as Jinguchi approaches his former commander whom he has not seen in 20 years, Uehara's utterance of "Jinguchi" is sublime).

Kenji Sahara was delightfully hammy as Umino, and Hiroshi Koizumi did his usually dependable job as an taciturn detective, while Tadao Takashima and Yu Fujiki played off each other as beautifully as they had in *King Kong vs. Godzilla*. One interesting piece of casting was Yoko Fujiyama as Makoto. A pretty if somewhat detached actress, Fujiyama's lack of emotion actually enhances her portrayal of the embittered Makoto (although no information is ever forthcoming regarding the circumstances of Makoto's birth, given the young lady's somewhat exotic features, it seems likely that her mother was probably a native girl living on Saipan when Jinguchi was stationed there). Eisei Amamoto—who only the year before had played a nameless Mushroom Man—is wonderful as the ebullient High Priest; showier parts would soon follow. For the key role of the Empress of Mu, Honda cast Tetsuko Kobayashi; the director discovering the 21-year-old one night while he was watching television. Though relatively unknown and appearing in her one and only film for Toho, she played the Empress with cocky assertiveness (sadly, she died of an undisclosed illness at the age of 54).

Honda's evident enthusiasm for the project is evident in every scene and possibly influenced by a change of pace after the macabre *Matango*. There are a number of excellent scenes: Agent 23's abortive kidnapping attempt at the beach, the pursuit of a Mu submarine by the American submarine (intriguingly named *Red Satan*), the launching and surfacing of *Atragon*, the confrontation between Makoto and her father by the lake, the ceremonial native dance in the Mu throne room, the search-and-destroy mission deep in the bowels of the Empire carried-out by *Atragon's* volunteers wearing "pure" white protective clothing, and of course the memorably-moving final scene in a classic Honda "happy/sad ending," with his actors lined up in their usual "curtain call" while they watch the destruction of the Mu Empire in stunned silence.

There are a number of splendid little touches as well, such as the exasperated look Jinguchi gives to Nishibe after the photographer asks if Atragon has finally been dug out of the rubble, the little bow Agent 23 respectfully gives to Kosumi before diving into the sea and the High Priest drooling over *Atragon's* blueprints with childlike envy

(Honda continued to tone-down the violence, such as when a Mu sentry is disabled by the *back*-end of a spear). When the captain of the ship attacked by the Mu Empire listens to a radio broadcast announcing that the United Nations Security Council has rebuked Agent 23's film as a hoax, it is the first indication in a Honda film that the U.N.—once the director's bastion for peaceful coexistence—would from now on play an ever-decreasing role.

Honda's versatility is showcased as not only did he capably capture intimate and emotional scenes but those on a far-grandeur scale, such as the magnificent ceremonial dance scene which utilized hundreds of extras. Honda's handling of the Empress's death scene (who, like many a past Japanese soldier, commits suicide rather than be captured and be shamefully taken prisoner) was characteristic of his best work; sad but not maudlin, touching but toned-down. *Atragon* was Honda's most-perfectly realized fantasy film: Fast-paced, involving, exhilarating and moving, with subtexts of revenge, repression and retribution at its core. It is a thoroughly-satisfying escapist experience—representative of the best of its type any studio has ever offered—and is one of the finest fantasy films ever made.

MOTHRA VS. GODZILLA (1963)
(MOSURA TAI GOJIRA)
GODZILLA VS. THE THING

Cast & Credits

Film Register No. 13523
Release Date: April 29, 1964
Running Time: 89 Minutes

Staff: Producers: Tomoyuki Tanaka and Sanezumi Fujimoto; Director: Ishiro Honda; Screenplay: Shinichi Sekizawa; Director of Photography: Hajime Koizumi; Art Director: Takeo Kita; Sound Recording: Fumio Yanoguchi; Lighting: Shoshichi Kojima; Original Music: Akira Ifukube; Stock Music: Hiroshi Miyagawa; Sound Effects: Hisashi Shimonaga; Assistant Director: Koji Kajita; Editor: Ryohei Fujii; Sound Arrangement: Sadamasa Nishimoto; Production Manager: Boku Morimoto; Special Effects Techniques: Director: Eiji Tsuburaya; Director of Photography: Teisho (Sadamasa) Arikawa; Sokei (Mototaka) Tomioka; Optical Photography: Yukio Manoda and Yoshiyuki Tokumasa.

Cast: Akira Takarada (Ichiro Sakai); Yuriko "Yoka" Hoshi (Junko Nakanishi); Hiroshi Koizumi (Professor Miura); Yu Fujiki (Jiro "Tanimura" Nakamura); Kenji Sahara (Shiro Torahata); Emi and Yumi Ito (Shobijin); Jun Tazaki (Newspaper Editor Maruta); Yoshifumi Tajima (Kumayama); Kenzo Tabu (Politician); Yutaka Sada (Screaming Man at Port); Akira Tani (Chief of Local Fishermen); Susumu Fujita (JDSF Commander); Ikio Sawamura (Shinto Priest); Ren Yamamoto (Captain of Small Boat); Kozo Nomura (JDSF Officer); Yasuhisa Tsutsumi (Policeman); Mitsuo Tsuda (JDSF Officer); Shim Otomo (Police Chief); Yoshio Kosugi (Infant Island Chief); Miki Yashiro (Miss Kobayashi); Terumi Oka (Waitresses); Hideo Shibuya (Reporter); Kenzo Echigo (Soldier); Tadashi Okabe, Haruya Sakamoto (JSDF Officers); Haruo Suzuki (JSDF Radio Operator); Haruo Nakajima (Godzilla).

The Film

This was Honda's third Godzilla film and although he must have been pleased with seeing the monster returning to its rampaging roots, he realized it was already beginning to loose his original vision of the beast as being the embodiment of man's tampering with nuclear power; at one point in the film, Sakai and Junko are "de-contaminated" in a casually-humorous scene many-times-removed from the serious implications of radiation poisoning from a decade earlier.

Screenwriter Sekizawa had gotten off to a bumpy beginning in the genre with *Baran*, but soon found his footing with *War in Space*, *Mothra* and *King Kong vs. Godzilla* where his blending of humor and action resulted in moneymaking films. Sekizawa's script for *Mothra vs. Godzilla* was fast-moving, well-written and involving, utilizing several socially-relevant issues and containing convincing characterizations, allowing Honda to comment freely on politics, religion, commercialism, greed and bureaucracy. *MvG* succeeds on every level.

The film's crucial scene occurs when Sakai, Junko and Miura plead with the natives to help them fight Godzilla, but when the natives—even the Shobijin—scold and deny any aid, Junko insists that the natives have a moral obligation to help them, stating that "God plays no favorites!" Sakai adds one other important point: By being connected as members of the human race, the natives must help simply because they are in a position to do so. It is at this point that Mothra chirps and the Shobijin then lead the three Japanese to follow them, where they see Mothra sitting in a sacred chamber called the "Dying Place" as a shaft of holy light illuminates its pious presence. The fairies persuade the mighty moth to fight Godzilla, knowing full well that she will not have the strength to return (in this way, Mothra reveals herself as a representation of the supreme human virtues of courage, forgiveness and self-sacrifice).

Mothra's second screen appearance was a distinct improvement over her first as it was given greater flexibility; a slight flutter at the wing tips, a twisting head and radio-controlled twitching legs, which resulted in a more convincingly-vibrant insect (the adult Mothra was flown by a Y-shaped brace that opened and closed to create the flapping of the moth's wings). The size of the giant moth was decreased from 100 meters three years earlier to 40 meters, and the wingspan down from 250 meters to 100 meters, for better contrast with the 50-meter Godzilla (the actual size of the adult Mothra prop was three meters long with a nine-meter wingspan).

In regarding Tsuburaya's effects, the key word was always

"consistency," and *MvG* represents the apex of what he could achieve as the film's effects are on a par with his stellar accomplishments in *Gorath* and *Submarine Warship*. Always an innovator, on this occasion Tsuburaya avoided the construction of elaborate city miniatures, and instead utilized real buildings in optical composites, with the matte line cut to follow the tops of the buildings and Godzilla matted-in with sky-painted backdrops (curiously, Godzilla appears somewhat fuzzy, indicating that more than one exposure was used). The short scene showing the egg being washed away from the island shows Tsuburaya's technicians at their best; the scene is achieved with such beautiful craftsmanship that the average viewer merely takes this complex effects shot for granted.

The fight between Mothra and Godzilla is the penultimate battle between Good and Evil; it has real drama and conveys a sense of urgency, heightened by the awareness of the egg's vulnerability and Mothra's own weakened condition (when Godzilla sprays Mothra in a direct hit, it is a shocking moment). It was unquestionably Tsuburaya's finest monster battle; action-packed, well-structured, suspenseful and quickly resolved as opposed to the rather protracted beast-battles yet-to-come. Mothra and Godzilla fight for possession of the egg in a sequence utilizing hand-held puppets, wind machines, stop-motion animation, intense close-ups and both low and high-speed photography.

For the first time in a Godzilla film, Tsuburaya utilized the Oxberry optical printer, resulting in the beautiful composite photography seen throughout the film (achieved by Yoichi Manoda and Hiroshi Mukoyama), including a stunning shot of the Shobijin being revealed to Torahata and Kumoyama at Happy Enterprises and an elevated shot of the egg surrounded by fisherman. Minoru Nakano's optical animation and Tsuburaya's editing is top-notch, notably in the scene when the tanks shell Godzilla as they pursue it, the scene shifting back-and-forth from the tanks to the creature in a series of rapid cuts. Tsuburaya was still allowing himself his little eccentricities, such as when Sakai, Junko and Miura arrive on Infant Island; behind them sits one of Tsuburaya's weirdest creations: A blinking and living skeleton of a large sea-turtle.

Composer Akira Ifukube gets the audiences' hearts racing immediately with an electrifying opening theme, beginning with crashing gongs and a frenzied pianoforte before segueing into belligerent brass backed-up by shimmering cymbals playing a variation of Godzilla's theme. This then transitions into a relentless string section, punctuated with a tapping piano key playing in a steadily-rising *ostinato* in a motif that will be heard throughout the film. Trumpets then enter, playing a portion of the "Mothra" theme (the trumpet notes sounding the syllables for the Japanese name of "Mo-Su-Ra"), hinting of the titanic struggle to come.

Ifukube scores "The Rainbow-Colored Object" with vibraphone, sinister strings, twirling woodwinds and grim bassoon, while "The Giant Egg in the Waters off Shizunoura" uses a fluttering organ, cymbals, impressive strings and serious woodwinds playing in ascending-descending tones (a portion of this piece—"The Giant Egg Washes Ashore"—ends with two drawn-out notes on violins, emphasizing the object's divine significance). When the Shobijin first plead with Sakai, Miura and Junko to help them return Mothra's egg, Ifukube subtly introduces a portion of his "Sacred Fountain" theme heard later in the film.

"The Little Beauty's Theme Song" is scored with a repeated tapping of two organ keys backed by tinkling piano, beautifully describing the duality and tiny nature of the girls, while trumpets play in rapid ascension heralding "Mothra on the Hilltop," which ends with a portion of "Mothra's Song." As the giant incubator is turned on, Ifukube inserts the "The Giant Egg" music in a more-sinister orchestration, implying dastardly consequences.

"Infant Island"—a hauntingly beautiful theme—is played on contrabassoon and oboe, while the "The Devil's Purification" is sinisterly scored with quivering organ, violins playing at their upper registers, and soft piano and vibraphone punctuated with a single-note on coronet. Soft, reassuring woodwinds and plucking harp color "The Sacred Fountain," a moving piece beautifully harmonized by The Peanuts, while "Mothra's Song" begins with a portion of the original song penned by Yuji Koseki, with the musical phrase ending with off-key piano notes, oboe, electone and tapping timpani, emphasizing the creature's incurable condition.

When the twin girls sing "Mothra's Song"—a cue initially heard in the original *Mothra*—it is sung *accapella*, with just a modicum of music wafting gently in the background, almost in unison with the dipping of the giant insect's wings in a perfect combination of sight and sound for one of the more-touching moments in the series. This song ends on a resolute note, with rolling timpani and reed flute, before soaring to a finale playing a portion of Ifukube's "Mothra" theme. Writer Mike Copner described the scene of the twin-Mothra hatching in "The Birth of Baby Mothra:" "...(the music's) sweeping harp and string harmonies (are) filled with dynamic emotion. We feel as a privileged witness to a monumental event and a mystical secret seldom revealed."

Ifukube's longest cue was written for the final confrontation between Godzilla and the Mothra larvae, and is essentially a reworking of the "Main Title" music heard throughout the film. Scored with blaring horns, strident strings, shimmering cymbals, pounding timpani, tinkling piano, quavering organ and crashing gongs, the music was so impressive that the studio musicians applauded at the end of the session. Because of Emi and Yumi Ito's narrow vocal range (they typically sang popular tunes), Ifukube found it difficult to compose music for the pair; as a result, "The Holy Fountain" was a challenging assignment. As for "Mahala Mothra," Ifukube obtained permission to use a bit of the original *Mothra* theme, then re-scored the background music for the fairies to communicate a primeval impression.

During "Baby Mothra vs. Godzilla," Ifukube's trumpets blare out a musically-unresolved four-note chord as Godzilla arrives on shore with the two caterpillars following behind it, until one of them grabs the monster's tail; Ifukube then uses discordant piano keys to mark the critical moment. As Godzilla whirls madly about in a moment of panic and confusion, discordant piano keys are pounded indicating the uncertainly of the situation, until the caterpillars begin spraying Godzilla with their silken webs, the composer cleverly coloring the web-shootings with organ keys playing a different note for each caterpillar, supplemented with tinkling piano.

There was one unpleasant memory for Ifukube during the filming and it happened in the scene when Godzilla's head rises from behind a hill. The composer did not score the appearance of the monster so Honda suggested that Ifukube put in the opening of "The Appearance of Godzilla" theme for greater impact. Ifukube stated that no music was called for since the sight of Godzilla was stirring in its own right. Honda concurred and the matter seemed closed until Ifukube viewed the final print at a staff meeting, when he heard the music right where he did not want it to be, as Honda had inserted the track without the composer's permission. The following confrontation perfectly summed up both men's personalities to a tee: As Ifukube glared at the director, Honda shrugged his shoulders and softly offered an apology.

Honda directs his actors with his usually-quiet efficiency, resulting in a movie that flows well without any sluggish scenes (Honda never "forces" action onto his viewers so as to give his movies vitality, but lets the story and characters lead the way and set the tone). Akira Takarada plays Sakai as a short-tempered yet ultimately compassionate person in what would be his last decent role in a Honda film. As author Kalat has written, "... Takarada gives one of his best performances. When

Mothra's egg hatches two giant larvae, he registers a look on his face that conveys simultaneous relief and horrified apprehension." Yuriko Hoshi's portrayal of Junko was that of another spunky and professional woman who is both inquisitive and courageous. Hiroshi Koizumi competently plays a cynical scientist while Yu Fujiki—appearing without his perennial sidekick Tadao Takashima—supplies comedic relief as the egg-eater without ever becoming an intrusion. Returning for their second appearance are Emi and Yumi Ito as the Shobijin; the pair would appear in a total of eight films over a seven-year period. *MvG* gave them more to do than they had in *Mothra*, as on this occasion they show joy, anger and fear while still speaking and acting in unison.

The films most-memorable performances however are Kenji Sahara as the slimy, sinister and smirking Torahata (a man whose greed costs him the ultimate price) and Yoshibumi Tajima as Torahatta's public "hatchet man," the nasty yet vulnerable and somehow likeable "Great Entrepreneur" Kumayama. Kumayama blows cigarette smoke directly into Junko's camera lens (and our faces), and as he makes his pitch to buy the Shobijin, he tosses a glance at the fairies that can best be described as diabolical. Playing his part with relish and stealing every scene he's in, Tajima (whose first name is spelled as both Yoshibumi and Yoshifumi) creates a fascinating characterization. Normally regulated to secondary supporting parts to which he would shortly return, Tajima was an example of how even a minor-parts player could rise to the occasion when given a substantial role, a tribute to Honda's ability and confidence in casting actors in important parts, regardless of their box-office stature.

Mothra vs. Godzilla was the beginning of the end for Toho's serious approach to the Godzilla film series as—coming as it did on the heels of the enormously successful *King Kong vs. Godzilla*—*MvG* brought in considerably-less revenue. Remembering how *KKvG's* lighthearted approach brought in audiences by the millions, Tanaka recommended that Sekizawa and Tsuburaya add more elements of humor to the Godzilla series; the consequences would ultimately snowball the series into plots that were successively-more unnatural, characters more contrived and situations that stretched the audiences' suspension of disbelief beyond reasonable limits.

With *MvG* Honda had more themes to touch-on on than he could ever wish for: Government inefficiency, transgression, forgiveness, political posturing, Divine Intervention, unrestrained capitalism, government corruption, threats to the eco-system, journalistic ethics, military inefficiency and nuclear testing. And yet, even with all these elements, Honda still creates an entertaining and highly-enjoyable monster film which never preaches or becomes heavy-handed; the emphasis stays on the story and its compelling characters; even the humorous touches are acceptable and do not affect the movie's resolute tone. Although Honda always maintained that he never made films "exclusively" for children, in discussing the film years later in *Godzilla and My Movie Life*, he said:

> By that time, children were becoming the target audience, but I didn't want to frighten them. For me, it is important for children to enjoy themselves, so I tried to appeal to both adults and children and create something which would entertain both groups. As an adult, I produce films with adult intentions while still hoping to make them accessible to children, even those children who might not find such ideas entertaining. It is a world made by the adults for the children.

As an example of this philosophy, Honda softens the blow of Mothra's death by immediately following it with a sight gag as Nakamura inadvertently hitches a ride on an army jeep.

The director's handling of the Infant Island sequences is affectingly powerful, Honda stressing the uncertainty during the drink-purification scene and we can almost feel the shame and embarrassment of the Japanese visitors who have come begging for mercy. After Kumayama wrestles Torahata to the floor, he delivers a series of punches which result in a bloodied nose in an uncharacteristically-graphic scene for a Honda film (a ingenious touch follows when the camera blurs before coming into focus as Torahata regains his senses to see Godzilla approaching the hotel).

Such is Honda's skill that even after the two title monsters have fought and one has killed the other (normally a monster movie's highpoint), he still manages to keep the audiences' interest stirring for the remaining 24 minutes of the movie. His handling of the scene when the spectators are fleeing for their lives after Godzilla rises from the mud is brilliant, and in the film's final scene—as Jiro wonders aloud how they could ever thank the girls for their help—Sakai confidentially answers that "The only way to thank them is to make a better world;" in other words, Mankind will be saved on this occasion but it must always prove itself worthy and there is always room for improvement. The final image of the four main characters waving goodbye to the Shobijin contained great significance for Honda, as it was not only a farewell to a magnificent era but to the heights of the director's career as well; both had reached a *crescendo*.

It had been a remarkable run, but every film series reaches a high-water mark with nowhere else to go but downward. Satisfactory films would follow, but the vast majority of these were adequate at best and mediocre at worst. From this point on there would be no more *Mothras*, *Goraths* or *Godzillas*, no films with the sweeping scale of *War in Space* or *Submarine Warship*, nor any examining the human condition as in *Gas Human* or *Matango*; Honda's films would be churned out like so much butter, grist for the run of the Toho factory mill. *Mothra vs. Godzilla* had set a standard of fantasy filmmaking excellence that none of the subsequent Godzilla films would ever top, let alone equal.

It was Honda's last great film.

SECTION V:
"STILL A YOUNG SOLDIER."

Dogora, the Space Monster (1964)
(Dagora, the Space Monster)

Three Giant Monsters — The Greatest
Battle on Earth (1964)
(Ghidrah, the Three-Headed Monster)

Frankenstein vs. Baragon, the
Subterranean Monster (1965)
(Frankenstein Conquers the World)

The War of the Monsters (1965)
(Monster Zero)

Frankenstein's Monsters: Sanda vs. Gairah (1966)
(War of the Gargantuas)

DOGORA, THE SPACE MONSTER (1964)
(UCHU DAIKAIJU DOGORA)
DAGORA, THE SPACE MONSTER

Cast & Credits

Film Register No. 13636
Released Date: August 11, 1964
Running Time: 81 minutes, six seconds

Staff: Producers: Tomoyuki Tanaka and Hiroyoshi Tamichi; Director: Ishiro Honda; Original Story: Jojiro Okami; Screenplay: Shinichi Sekizawa; Cinematography: Hajime Koizumi; Production Design: Takeo Kita; Recording: Fumio Yanoguchi; Lighting: Shoshichi Kojima; Music: Akira Ifukube; Sound: Hisashi Shimonaga; Assistant Director: Ken Sano; Editor: Ryohei Fujii; Sound Effects: Osamu Chiku; Production Manager: Shigeru Nakamura; Special Effects: Director: Eiji Tsuburaya; Cinematography: Sadamasa (Teisho) Arikawa and Sokei Tomioka; Optical Cinematography: Yukio Manoda and Yoshiyuki Tokumasa; Art Director: Akira Watanabe; Lighting: Kuichiro Kishida.

Cast: Yosuke Natsuki (Detective Komai); Yoko Fujiyama (Masaya Kirino); Hiroshi Koizumi (Space Wave Laboratory Chief Kirino); Akiko Wakabayashi (Diamond Thief Hamako); Nobuo Nakamura (Prof. Munakata); Seizaburo Kawazu (Diamond Thief Group Leader); Dan Yuma (Mark Jackson); Susumu Fujita (Kyushu District Defense Commander Iwasa); Jun Tazaki (Chief of Detectives); Yoshibumi Tajima (Diamond Thief Tada); Hideyo Amamoto (Diamond Thief Maki); Nadao Kirino, Akira Wakamatsu, Haruya Kato (Additional Diamond Thieves); Jun Funato (Detective Shinda); Yasuhisa Tsutsumi, Tadashi Okabe (Ginza Policemen); Koji Iwamoto (Prof. Munakata's Assistant); Mitsuo Tsuda, Takuzo Kumagai (Defense Officials); Chotaro Togin (Coal Truck Driver); Shoichi Hirose (Tempodo Night Watchman/Coal Field Man); Yutaka Nakayama (Coal Truck Assistant).

The Film

As had been the custom of late, Shinichi Sekizawa fashioned a screenplay after Jojiro Okami's original story submission. *Dogora* was a unique monster (the most abstractly-impersonal of Tsuburaya's creations) and the film's premise—a giant space creature sucking-up coal before presumably ingesting human beings—is not without merit. The script writer was heavily-influenced by the popular James Bond movie series and *Dogora* contains a number of plot elements worthy of any spy flick: Outer-space gadgetry, secret panels, beautiful women, a Caucasian secret agent armed with international "credentials," snappily-dressed villains, futuristic machines and karate chops (in a bit lifted from *Goldfinger* released in Japan a few months earlier, Hamako switches the license plates on her car). Other contrived bits of spy business are repeated, such as Jackson and Kommei decoying each other by leaving their shoes partially-hidden under a curtain, and at one point Jackson knocks out Kommei with a karate-chop with Kommei later tossing Jackson over his shoulder with a judo move!

One curious moment occurs in Jackson's hotel room after the broker makes two drinks moments before requesting the detective be on his way: As Kommei takes a sip, Jackson opens the top shelf of a chest of drawers which arouses Kommei's suspicions. Kommei then gets up and stops the broker just as he is grabbing a pistol and informs him, "You're coming with me to the police station." Jackson seems quite agreeable to the suggestion until he suddenly bolts for the door, causing Kommei to fire a warning shot into the air without regard for the safety of any guests staying on the upper floors. No harm is done however as the "gun" is merely a party-favor that shoots streamers about the room. Jackson then leaves, somehow managing to lock the door behind him leaving the detective trapped in the room (the scene brings up an intriguing question: Does Jackson always keep a party-gun handy for just such emergencies?).

At the movie's final scene at the airport, Jackson is about to board his 707 flight when Kommei stops him, wondering if there were ever any real diamonds. Jackson admits that there never were any as "That was our plan all along" (if so, then why not inform the Japanese authorities about the ruse?). Nor it is never revealed how the diamonds on the transport truck were switched to sugar cubes or how Hamako knew about the decoy. The armored truck is transporting the diamonds at nighttime—incredibly, considering the recent rash of diamond heists, without an escort—before coming upon the sight of Hamako's seemingly lifeless body lying in the road ahead, but the impact is lessened as we had earlier seen the jewel thieves setting this up. Later, when Kommei and Jackson are tied-up in Jackson's hotel room, one of the thieves barges in sputtering that the girl got away from him; again, this is no surprise, as we already knew of her intentions.

Tsuburaya's effects are minimal and not nearly as spectacular as they had been in his previous efforts as the destruction caused by Dogora is confined to a limited area. The monster itself is not terribly frightening or interesting, constructed out of plastic and suspended upside-down in a water tank to give it a buoyant effect while wires manipulated the tentacles. The majority of the effect scenes showing Dogora's attacks on the coalfields were accomplished via reverse photography, while a number of process shots were grimy and scratchy, well-below Tsuburaya's usually-high standards. To make matters worse, the lighting of the live action and the back-projected images often did not match; nevertheless, Japan's Master of Special Effects still had a trick or two up his sleeve that could make a viewer blink in awe, such as the final effects shot showing five miniature jets flying in formation.

For the first time in a Honda film, Koizumi's camera work was found lacking, with actors and diamonds often out-of-focus (one particularly embarrassing shot occurs after members of the press are leaving the briefing room; as actor Tazaki turns to watch them, he gives the audience a view of his hairpiece). In a shot of the villains waiting it out in the Kyushu Hotel lobby, Koizumi creatively utilizes a portion of a sculpture of modern art to frame their faces, and after the thieves have their bag of explosives detonated by Kommei, the cops run out of the smoke. As inconsistent as Koizumi's camera work was however, it looked positively immaculate when compared to Takeo Kita's shabby sets; the layout of Munakata's lab has no rhyme or reason to it and the interiors of the hotel rooms look as if they had been made out of cardboard.

Akira Ifukube's score was another disappointment as cues for the monster are repeated incessantly whenever it appears. Beginning with fluctuating trombones and screaming trumpets, violins soon take over with a tremulous theremin (a zitherlike instrument used effectively in such films as Bernard Herrmann's 1951 score for *The Day the Earth Stood Still*) to give the beast its otherworld identity. Outside of that, what *is* remarkable about the score is how little of it there is, particularly in scenes that normally cry out for the kind of support only music can give, such as the scene in the hotel when Kommei and Jackson are tied-up with fuses burning toward sticks of dynamite, and the chase scene on the beach which only has music when the boulders start dropping from the sky; and even then it was again the monster's motif.

Ifukube made his musical presence known mainly during the scenes when the toxin is being replicated and transported via truck convoys to the army in "Dogora's Natural Enemy," an up-tempo theme initiated with a piano solo, followed by strumming violins urgently moving the scene along. A lone horn chimes in reflectively until additional horns join in as the music ultimately swells to Ifukube's characteristic military-style cadence (only Ifukube could make a scene with trucks moving along a dusty dirt road exciting). The final battle with the monster, "The Air Corps Launches an Offensive," is a rousing piece scored with drums, horns and rapidly strumming bowstrings accompanied by strident trombones; mid-way through the piece, the intense bowstrings are accompanied by triumphant trumpets as the first towering Chemical Unit arrives in an effective moment.

Akiko Wakabayashi played Hamako with alluring mystery, although it was never made clear why she wanted to double-cross her comrades (Wakabayashi's connection to the Bond films became further cemented when she appeared in *You Only Live Twice* three years later). The director mainly seemed to take a personal interest regarding Wakabayashi's scenes as she is given many a fine close-up including an effective close-up of her agonized face when she is struck by a bullet in the back (in the scene where she gets slapped to the ground by the Boss, Honda films it in an elevated long shot to lessen the brutality of the moment).

The film's other leading actress was Yoko Fujiyama as Masayo. While in *Submarine Warship* her passive aloofness well-suited her character of the bitter and withdrawn Makoto, this coldness did not translate as effectively in *Dogora*, as she was incapable of radiating any on-screen warmth. Once again, Hiroshi Koizumi plays a bland scientist in a part which seems to have been written in order to give him something to do, as his character is not terribly essential to the plot.

Nobuo Nakamura, unseen in a Honda fantasy film since *Abominable Snowman*, played another gruff professor as Dr. Munakata, underplaying his role with considerable skill and *panache*. Nakamura portrayed the doctor as an sour intellect with a doleful sense of humor, and a man so completely preoccupied with his work, that when Kommei is showing him pictures of the jewelry heist in the police station, the doctor rarely makes eye contact. General Iwasa is played by Susumu Fujita, and Fujita and Nakamura played off each of other very well; indeed, their on-again-off-again rapport is the most-interesting aspect of the film. When Iwasa calls Nakamura a "deaf old man" before recognizing him, the professor identifies himself as "still a young soldier," getting his revenge when he openly doubts the general's initial attempt at subduing Dogora.

Robert Dunham essayed the role of the enigmatic Mark Jackson in a role clearly pattered after James Bond; when Jackson is brought in to the thieves' hideout, he is not the least bit intimated by the threatening surroundings, even though there are no less than four guns drawn on him (Dunham was actually billed as "Dan Yuma" because his real name proved difficult for the average Japanese to pronounce, although he soon discovered that when pronounced quickly, "Dan Yuma" sounded like "*tane uma*"—the Japanese term for "stud horse"). Possessing that rare combination of a Caucasian actor who spoke excellent Japanese speech and fine acting skills to boot, Dunham is marvelous as the "Diamond G-Man." Yosuke Natsuki plays the lead role of Police Inspector Kommei, and while a capable if uncharismatic actor, Natsuki is appropriately stern but not terribly interesting to watch and a bit of a letdown when recalling the more-versatile Tatsuya Mihashi's portrayal of Detective Okamoto in *Gas Human*. As far as the actors playing the principal jewel thieves are concerned they all gleefully chew their scenery, with Seizaburo Kawazu as the Boss, his suave number-two man (Yoshibumi Tajima), safecracker Maki (Eisei Amamoto) and the whiny pipsqueak, Sabu (Haruya Kato).

Honda took an overt step in portraying the jewel thieves as stupid to such a degree that it is impossible to take them seriously (which may well have been his intention). The thieves are basically bungling fools that essentially accomplish nothing; it's a wonder they can use a blowtorch without burning their fingers off. As a result, many viewers have interpreted *Dogora* as a comedy, which it is not. *Dogora* shows Honda and his crew starting to slip on minute details in a possible indication of a bored director longing for more worthwhile projects (in the scene where the Boss receives instructions to contact headquarters, the half-hour chime of an unseen grandfather clock is heard, but the following shot shows a desk clock well past the half-hour).

As Mark Jackson starts to get up off the floor after being thrown down by Kommei, he is first seen rubbing his neck, then his back in the following shot as he stands up. Even more revealing is the scene when the thieves have tied-up Jackson and Kommei; finding the pendant with the locker number on it, the Boss tosses it over to Hamako who unsuccessfully tries to twirl it around her wrist. A moment later, the Boss lights his cigarillo, but not all the way around the foot, leaving it half-lit. It could be that these mildly-clumsy moments were left-in to show the jewel thieves as incompetent idiots, although a more plausible explanation could be that the director either didn't notice them or didn't feel the need to re-shoot them.

The chase scene on the beach lasts for nearly three minutes, but despite all the running-around, it is only marginally interesting; gunshots are exchanged and explosives are hurled back-and-forth between the two opposing factions, but no one is injured (at one point, when Kommei retrieves an explosive tossed at him, he implausibly takes the time to glance at it before tossing it back). Honda's worst scene was when Jackson and Kommei are tied up in the hotel room. It is not the least bit suspenseful, and when the sticks of dynamite are hurled through the pane glass windows, they merely emit harmless puffs of smoke. Honda was no doubt more interested in the inter-personal conflicts between Munakata/Iwasa and Kommei/Jackson, and he also made yet another stab at U.S./Japanese relations: When Jackson is checking in at the Okura Hotel, an American family of four is happily walking through the lobby, eager to tour Japan.

In the film's final scene at the airport, when Kommei good-naturedly tells Jackson, "You were a pain in the neck," Jackson rests his hand on Kommei's shoulder in another typical Honda "touch." Masayo and Kirino then arrive to see Dr. Munakata off, as the scientist has been invited to give a talk on the Space Cells at the United Nations—the only time the organization had been mentioned in the entire movie. When Jackson offers to carry the professor's bag, Munakata insists that he is "still a young soldier" and there are smiles and waves all around—rarely did a Honda fantasy film have such a completely happy ending.

Not only were the deaths decreasing and the laughs increasing in Honda's monster films, Honda was well-aware that his human stories were beginning to be overshadowed by Tsuburaya's monsters; it was beginning to look as though the "Honda/Tsuburaya" films were in reality "Tsuburaya/Honda" films. *Mothra vs. Godzilla* had made considerably less money than *King Kong vs. Godzilla*, and *Dogora* was a financial disappointment as well; perhaps because of this, *Dogora* was the last of Honda's monster movies starring only one monster.

It seems logical to assume that the orders had come down from Tanaka to lighten the mood; thus, the groundwork was laid for the following film, whose very structure was similar to *Dogora's*, a confusing cornucopia of detectives and assassins, royalty and espionage, stargazers and shooting stars. Godzilla would be back as so would Mothra and Radon, and even the twin fairies of Infant Island. There would once again be another monster from space; only this time, one which was a vast improvement over Dogora and one that would momentarily instill the series with renewed vigor to such an extent that its popularity would rival even the King of the Monsters.

THREE GIANT MONSTERS —
THE GREATEST BATTLE ON EARTH (1964)
(SAN DAIKAIJU — CHIKYU SAIDAI NO KESSEN)
GHIDRAH, THE THREE-HEADED MONSTER

Cast & Credits

Film Register No. 13572
Release Date: December 20, 1964
Running Time: 93 Minutes

Staff: Producer: Tomoyuki Tanaka; Director: Ishiro Honda; Screenplay: Shinichi Sekizawa; Director of Photography: Hajime Koizumi; Art Director: Takeo Kita; Sound Recording: Fumio Yanoguchi; Lighting: Shoshichi Kojima; Music: Akira Ifukube; Sound: Hisashi Shimonaga; Assistant Director: Ken Sano; Editor: Ryohei Fujii; Sound Effects: Osamu Chiku; Production Manager: Shigeru Nakamura; Special Effects: Director: Eiji Tsuburaya; Photography: Teisho (Sadamasa) Arikawa; Sokei (Mototaka) Tomioka; Optical Photography: Yukio Manoda, Yoshiyuki Tokumasa; Art Director: Akira Watanabe.

Cast: Yosuke Natsuki (Detective Shindo); Yuriko Hoshi (Naoko Shindo); Hiroshi Koizumi (Professor Murai); Takashi Shimura (Dr. Tsukamoto); Emi and Yumi Ito (Shobijin); Akiko Wakabayashi (Princess Dorina "Selena" Salno); Hisaya Ito (Assassin Malmes "Malness"); Susumu Kurobe (Mustached Assassin); Toru Ibuki (Short Assassin); Kazuo Suzuki (Lock Picker Assassin); Akihiko Hirata (Chief Detective Okita); Kenji Sahara (Editor-in-Chief Kanamaki); Yoshifumi Tajima (Ship Captain); Eisei Amamoto (Servant Wu); Yoshio Kosugi (Village Policeman); Minoru Takada (Conference Chairman); Yuriko Hanabusa (Mrs. Shindo); Haruya Kato (Komaki, Noako's Assistant); Ikio Sawamura (Fisherman); Nakajiro Tomita (Minister of Defense); Shigeki Ishida, Junichiro Mukai, Takuzo (Jiro) Kumagai (Conference Members); Shin Otomo (Malmes' Boss); Yutaka Nakayama (Man Who Looses Hat); Tamami Urayama (Wife of Man Who Looses Hat); Senkichi Omura (Man Who Retrieves Hat).

The Film

Dogora had been a fairly uninteresting affair, but Senichi Sekizawa's script for *Three Giant Monsters* was more complicated and contained more exotic characters, while at the same time still retaining elements from the previous film, such as criminals on the loose from the law. The difference with *Three Giant Monsters* was in its multitude of plot elements: Meteorites, monsters, Flying Saucer People, a princess, a prophetess, hired guns, the Shobijin and several monsters. As a result, the viewer's focus is pulled in many different directions; with each storyline battling to be the star attraction, this tug-of-war becomes tiring after a while. Had the story been simply about the Princess and the assassins—with Shindo trying to offer her protection while his sister is trying to get a scoop for her paper—it might have made for an interesting and more focused film. Instead, the monsters seem like less than a necessity and more of a interruption to the overall story. The movie is almost a sequel to *Dogora* if not an outright remake, only this time with a duchess instead of diamonds being the center of attention, and again bad guys running around end-up being killed by boulders falling from the sky.

The script is scattered throughout with remarkable coincidences: Naoko and her brother run into each other in the middle of Shibuya, while Malmess and his men have not only managed to check into the same hotel as Naoko and the prophetess, but even have opposite rooms on the same floor! Malmess is somehow able to locate the princess in the middle of open country—not a novel idea for a Sekizawa script as he had used it before in *Baran*—and is on the receiving end of not one but *two* landslides created by King Ghidorah, the second of which finally kills him (as in *Dogora*, all the criminals are killed not deliberately by the authorities but unintentionally by the monsters). The low-point in the picture occurs in the silly scene where the Shobijin decipher the dialogue between the demons (with Mothra's help) as it turns out that both Godzilla and Radon's hatred of humanity dissuades them from teaming-up and saving the Earth by fighting the Space Monster. Godzilla in particular seems to have a specific grudge against mankind, turning its head in wounded vanity before petulantly pointing out that, "Humans are always bullying me around!"

After having relatively little to do effects-wise with *Dogora*, Tsuburaya and his team went-to-town on *Three Giant Monsters*. The film contains many of Tsuburaya's finest moments, showing refinements from earlier techniques, such as an excellent glass matte shot of Infant Island and a terrific shot of the Shobijin appearing from behind Naoko's lifted purse. The miniatures are also up to Tsuburaya's superb standards, particularly in regard to the natural landscapes. Shots of Ghidorah flying through the sky are awesome and there is a nice shot where Godzilla knocks over a tower as a car in the foreground speeds away. The composite work of the Shobijin in their container interacting with the actors is flawless, and the landslide that buries the assassins' car is thoroughly-convincing (Ghidorah also destroys a *tori* gate in a shot that is nothing short of sensational).

Effects Cinematographer Arikawa's camera takes full advantage of the wide-screen format: When Radon flies toward Godzilla in their first confrontation, dust can be seen rising from the ground beneath the tips of both wings (although the camera started filming a bit too soon as the puppet is stationary for a split-second). In a stunning optical shot, Ghidorah hovers in the distant sky as men point to it, followed by a low-angle shot of a magnificent model of the Matsumoto Castle before the Space Monster passes over it, scattering shingles by the hundreds. There are some misfires, such as when Radon first appears (its beak flapping unnaturally in a moment thankfully cut from the US print), and the meteorite's landing in the gorge is spoiled by a faintly-blurred matte line.

In the scene when Radon knocks Godzilla down into the lake, a painted glass shot of marsh grass moves due to the effects camera panning to capture the action—but there were still some terrific moments as well, such as with Ghidorah itself, magnificently realized (even more so when one considers the difficulties of working with multiple heads, tails and wings all fluttering about and supported by multiple wires; how Tsuburaya and his optical staff where able to match the movements of the monsters heads with the optical lightening bolts emanating from their mouths is a marvel). Ghidorah's design may have been inspired by a flying dragon from a remarkable 1956 Russian fantasy film called *Ilya Moromets* (released in as *The Sword and the Dragon*). In that film, the dragon—named Gorynych—flies rather slowly and breathes fire only after it lands, where it was essentially immobile and dispatched with relative ease.

There is nothing slow or immobile about Ghidorah, wonderfully-realized on film as a full-blown hyperkinetic space-berserker capable of spitting out rays of enormous power from a monster containing more destructive power than Godzilla and Radon combined (even Mothra—the supreme monster emissary—never once tries to communicate with it). The dragon's three heads functioned independently of each other, and composer Ifukube brilliantly reinforces this concept by identifying each head with a different note played on an electone (n a key moment often overlooked, when Godzilla first charges Ghidorah, the Space Monster zaps Godzilla, forcing the King of the Monsters back for a moment until it renews its attack. This commitment to fight and never retreat—regardless of the odds—would become the monster's most-enduring legacy. Incredibly, in the film Godzilla never once uses its atomic ray against Ghidorah).

Three Giant Monsters was one of Honda's most-beautifully photographed films; Koizumi's photography is typically radiant and effectively captures the beautiful Fall location scenery (as he did nine years earlier for *Abominable Snowman*, Honda takes his actors and crew on location in Japan's Northern Alps). Koizumi superimposes images of the Shobijins singing to Mothra to reinforce the bond between them, and when the fisherman identifies the princess from the photographs shown to him, he looks directly into the camera in an intense close-up to signify the moment. The cinematographer did a better job of keeping his actors in focus than he had in *Dogora*, yet several shots—such as close-ups of the princess during the assassination attempt in the hotel—were still somewhat fuzzy (after Radon first appears, Honda cuts to an effective zoom of the prophetess backlit by a huge white cloud). However, Takeo Kita's sets again looked cheap and flimsy (his hotel room set was again abysmal), and while the villains are as sharply dressed as they had been in *Dogora*, the neck frills worn by the citizens of Sergina was an unfortunate costume choice.

Akira Ifukube's score for *Ghidorah* was an improvement over his earlier *Dogora*; his "Main Title" music begins with a five-note theme played on an English horn before exploding into brass and cymbals, bringing to mind the Godzilla theme from *King Kong vs. Godzilla*. The music then segues into a *motif* Ifukube initially used for *Baran, the Giant Monster*—now Radon's theme—with harp music indicating the Infant Island connection. The composer scores the "Princess Salno" scenes with music suggesting an ancient Asian culture: Woodwinds, vibraphone, flutes, oboe and xylophone, while a reed-flute plays a portion of the "Infant Island" music from *Mothra vs. Godzilla*.

When the princess receives the warning on her plane in "The Flash," a high-pitched theremin enters—supplemented with a piano playing a six-note theme that will later be identified with the Space Monster—connecting the girl and Ghidorah from the outset. The music used during the "Kurobe Valley Theme" scenes is dominated by horns playing a sustained note to indicate a vast valley, joined by softly-playing high-pitched trumpets with additional horns playing in slower tempos to mark the explorers' long and arduous trek. In "Discovery of the Meteor," Ifukube again predicts Ghidorah's arrival by repeating the six-note theme, this time on a blaring trumpet, accompanied by a theremin to reinforce the outer-space relationship.

Music associated with Mothra is laced with emotional violins and cellos answering in a lower key before being augmented by a raspy trumpet (an effect achieved by the player gurgling his throat), mirroring the caterpillar's dangerous situation. When Mothra first uses its silk against Godzilla, Ifukube cleverly scores the moment with the shrieking, raspy trumpet emphasizing the worm's growing impatience with Godzilla and Radon's dispute. The "Ending" song begins with a sad clarinet, a strumming harp and yearning strings, while a softly-tapping drum is joined by regretful horns as Shindo watches Selina fly out of his life forever. Then, reassuring brass and strings enter as the fairies offer their goodbyes, with harp strings and trumpets blaring loudly at the film's climax. Much of Ifukube's music is repeated throughout the film (particularly during the battle scenes); what is perhaps most-surprising is not the repetition of the music but the lack of it, under 40 minutes, or less than-half of the film's running time. Even more remarkable are the key scenes left unscored: Malmess first spotting the princess in the hotel, the prophetess telling the terrifying tale of King Ghidorah and all three assassination attempts.

As they had in *Dogora*, Yosuke Natsuki (Detective Shindo) and Akiko Wakabayashi (Princess Salno) play key roles and gave better performances than they had in *Three Giant Monsters*—not surprising as their parts gave them much more to do. Natsuki was able to display different emotions—even uncertainty and fear—and was fond of swift, sudden gestures such as when pointing out to Okita that only one man could explain how the princess survived the airplane explosion. Wakabayashi plays two roles: The princess and the prophetess. She was particularly good during her confrontation with Malmess and his gang as she alternately shows confidence, fear and recollection, while at the same time registering uncertainty as to her real identity.

Yuriko Hoshi (Naoko) and Hiroshi Koizumi (Murai) essentially reprieve their roles from *Mothra vs. Godzilla*, with Hoshi playing her part with spunk and spirit, although unfortunately tinged now with petulance and immaturity. As before, Koizumi has little to show in the way of emotion, as his lackluster scientist character does little more than make observations—which could explain the actor's obviously bored and disinterested expression during the farewell scene in the airport lobby. Koizumi was one of Honda's favorite actors and had appeared in a number of the director's films—doing stellar work in both *Mothra* and

Matango—but the lack of challenging character parts annoyed him and he never again appeared in any of Honda's films.

Takashi Shimura (Dr. Tsukamoto) and Akihiko Hirata (Okita) returned to the series and made their usually-welcome appearances. Shimura plays Tsukamoto with sympathy and understanding, while at the same time barking impatiently at his staff as he tries to evacuate the princess. Hirata had less to do in his role as an impartial police chief, although he did lend it the appropriate amount of skepticism (not unlike his chief detective role in *Liquid People*). Hisaya Ito played Chief Assassin Malmess with appropriate coldness, while Kenji Sahara infused his part with his usual energy in a brief cameo as the Editor-in-Chief of Naoko's newspaper (playing the minor role of Selna's servant Wu was Eisei Amamoto, who later would essay the major role of the evil Dr. Huu in *King Kong's Counterattack*, thus playing both a Wu and a Huu!).

Emi and Yumi Ito reprise their Shobijin roles for the last time, playing their parts with great sincerity and compassion (Honda also handled their scenes with the utmost reverence). They are first introduced on the "What Are They Doing Now?" show as curtains part to reveal a tawdry miniature landscape set with rainbow colors flashing about, as a modestly-talented studio orchestra plays a raucous fanfare. From Stage Left, a spotlight illuminates a tiny wiggling carpet upon which the Shobijin arrive, dressed in native garb as they curtsy to the crowd which greets them with but a token of the excited shrieking when Clark Nelson first introduced them to the world. It seems somehow unsuitable to see the noble Shobijin—whose prayers to Mothra had saved the world on two previous occasions—appearing on a cheap variety show. They sing a song called "Let's Try to be Happy," a song that is later completely reprised when the Shobijin call upon Mothra, at which point it becomes a bit tiresome.

Honda's managing of the assassins was done more seriously than he had directed the buffoons in *Dogora*, although they were still failures as much as the jewel thieves had been. Honda reinforces the assassins' solidarity during the moment when Malmess is threatening to kill the princess in her hotel room by having the three background accomplices slowly advancing from behind her. When Okita informs Shindo of a possible assassination attempt on the princess, Honda slowly tracks-in on his chief to stress the importance of the information, and when Murai suggests using Mothra as a weapon against Ghidorah in the Diet, Honda has spectators audibly murmuring in the background.

The director punctuated violent on-screen action with intense close-ups of a spectator's reaction—such as after Mothra is hurled about by

Ghidorah's rays—and he did an especially good job of directing the panic scene in the Diet when Ghidorah arrives, with gale force winds blowing from outside the glass doors as guards frantically try to secure them and everyone looking around in terror. Another outstanding moment was when the Venusian tells her scary story of King Ghidorah; Honda holds on two sustained and intense close-ups of the girl as she looks around with staring eyes; even the normally upbeat Shobijin are alarmed (as she does so, she looks in three distinct directions, uncannily suggesting the three heads of King Ghidorah). Honda again shows the destruction wrought upon innocent people by the monsters as he pans over a line up of peasantry watching the destruction of their homes, and there are the little Honda touches such as when Naoko expresses her cynicism of aliens to the scientists on the roof, Honda having two technicians standing up in astonishment.

However, Honda's direction of the farewell scene at the airport is a boring and stagnant affair, coming as it does near the end of a 100-minute film. When Miura enters the Tsukamoto clinic during the gun battle, he hits one of the thugs on the head with a wrench before availing himself of the assassins' silencer, then—in a silly bit of business—he compares the two weapons before choosing the gun. Even worse is an error Honda makes in the film's very first scene: When Naoko is interviewing the president of the U.F.O.-watchers, Honda switches back-and-forth between them in over-the-shoulders shots, unaware that an actor named Hiroshi Akitsu (a man with a large nose, a stern expression and broad-rimmed glasses) is in the background in *both* shots. How the normally-meticulous Honda could have been so careless is difficult to understand.

In many ways, *Three Giant Monsters* was the most-significant film in the entire Godzilla series, drastically altering the beast from high-anxiety to high-camp for a considerable number of years, growing sillier as the years progressed. The movies would continue to stress outrageous visuals that would overwhelm whatever attempts Honda made with his human story, and while such infusions of monster humor in the battle scenes was expected in a deliberate comedy such as *King Kong vs. Godzilla*, *Three Giant Monsters* was supposed to be a film with a serious tone; as a result, the film is impossible to take seriously, only dramatically "taking off" when King Ghidorah does. The film's biggest blunder was in Sekizawa and Tsuburaya's humanizing of the monsters—the very concept of having Godzilla doing something as human as tossing rocks or sitting down was appalling—Honda had always envisioned his monsters as casualties and not clowns.

There was also the matter of going beyond a reasonable amount of what could be expected from an audience to accept. It was one thing to ask them to believe in monsters and tiny twin fairies, but having monsters arguing amongst themselves while a huge caterpillar's lecture is translated by fairies saying "Godzilla, what terrible language!" was going too far; the acceptable limit of suspension of disbelief had finally been exceeded. Despite this, Honda claimed years later that he enjoyed working on *Three Giant Monsters*, and was no doubt intrigued to learn about his next project; a more-serious—though no less outlandish—affair starring yet another monster, this time, the most famous one of all.

FRANKENSTEIN VS. BARAGON, THE SUBTERRANEAN MONSTER (1965)

(FURANKENSHUTAIN TAI CHITEI KAIJU BARAGON)
FRANKENSTEIN CONQUERS THE WORLD

Cast & Credits

Film Register No. 13999
Released Date: Aug. 8, 1965
Running Time: 90 minutes, seven seconds

Staff: Producer: Tomoyuki Tanaka; Director: Ishiro Honda; Screenplay: Kaoru Mabuchi (Takeshi Kimura); Cinematography: Hajime Koizumi; Art Director: Takeo Kita; Recording: Wataru Konuma; Lighting: Shoshichi Kojima; Music: Akira Ifukube; Sound: Hisashi Shimonaga; Assistant Director: Koji Kajita; Editor: Ryohei Fujii; Sound Effects: Sadamasa Nishimoto; Production Manager: Yorihiko Yamada; Special Effects: Director: Eiji Tsuburaya; Cinematography: Sadamasa (Teisho) Arikawa and Sokei Tomioka; Optical Cinematography: Yukio Manoda and Yoshiyuki Tokumasa; Art Director: Akira Watanabe; Lighting: Kuichiro Kishida; Matte Processing: Hiroshi Mukoyama.

Cast: Tadao Takashima (Dr. Kenichiro Kawaji); Nick Adams (Dr. James Bowen); Kumi Mizuno (Dr. Sueko Togami); Yoshio Tsuchiya (Kawai); Koji Furuhata (Frankenstein); Jun Tazaki (Okayama Police Chief Hideo Nishi); Susumu Fujita, Hisaya Ito (Osaka Police Officials); Takashi Shimura (Hiroshima Army Doctor); Nobuo Nakamura (Museum Curator Dr. Suga); Kenji Sahara (Okayama Police Officer Tadokoro); Yoshifumi Tajima (Submarine Commander Captain Murata); Akiji (Kozo) Nomura, Hiroto Kimura, Masaaki Tachibana, Tadashi Okabe (Reporters); Haruya Kato (TTV director); Ikio Sawamura (Man With Leash); Noriaki Inoue (Boy at Shirane Hospital); Keiko Sawai (Tazuko Toi); Noriko Takahashi (Girl at Shirane Hospital); Peter Mann (Dr. Reisendorf); Ren Yamamoto (Motoki); Yutaka Sada (Hiroshima Hospital Administrator); Kenzo Tabu (Newspaper Editor); Shigeki Ishida (University Professor); Haruo Nakajima (Baragon/Helicopter Pilot).

The Film

Frankenstein vs. Baragon was based on a story by Reuben Bercovitch, and while various people contributed to the screenplay, the final version was almost entirely the work of Takeshi Kimura (working with Honda for the first time since their brilliant *Matango*). The movie's beginning seems to have been at least partially inspired by a real event: During World War II, a German-Japanese plot was hatched to turn much of the United States into a radioactive wasteland. A Japanese submarine (the *I-52*) was returning to Japan with the lethal ingredients for an atomic bomb, when it was sunk by Navy warplanes on June 24, 1944.

For Honda, this new project would be a welcome change in that the title monster had the potential of engendering a certain modicum of sympathy; the Frankenstein monster is not an outright menace but an innocent victim, a human being suffering from the effects of the Hiroshima bombing. He is fed and called out of his hiding by a woman's kindness, and it is this kindness which shelters and cares for him; but when he sees and hears a primal, urgent scream, it kindles involuntary rage and violence. However, even this rage is overcome when a bright light reflecting from a necklace is shined in his face; his fears are basic, his pleasures simple. Nonetheless, due to a combination of misunderstanding, persecution, rejection and sorrow—ultimately stripped of his humanity by the primal instinct of self-preservation— Frankenstein must resort to becoming a monster, killing simply in order to live.

When the Hiroshima hospital staff is preparing to work on the Frankenstein heart, a lone B-29 is flying above the city; the clock on the hospital wall confirms the time as 8:15. It will soon be revealed that the date is August 6, 1945, as a moment later the city is suddenly obliterated in a blinding flash of fire (ironically, the film was released to Japanese theatres on August 8, 1965, nearly 25 years to the day of the actual bombing). Later at the hospital, when the boy is having a meal in front of members of the press, he has the distinctive built-up brow that Universal Studio's Jack Pierce designed in 1931—by then well-associated with Frankenstein—but no one in the room makes the connection. The film is tinged with Kimura's signature cynicism: When Bowman admits to Sueko about his remorseful feelings for having participated in the development of the Hiroshima bomb—and his decision to put things right by returning to America and "starting all over again"—an unseen voice calls out "Idiot!" as if mocking Bowman's apologetic declaration of his guilt. Kimura's script again makes use of his favorite themes: A lack of sympathy from authorities, a lack of empathy from the media and a lack of mercy from the military.

Eiji Tsuburaya was many things: A courageous genius, an independent thinker, a daring innovator, a risk-taker, a visionary rebel and a temperamental man with the heart of a child; in short, he was everything Honda was not and could be seen as the director's alter-ego, which could be one reason why they made such a great team. He was also eccentric and *Frankenstein* contains a number of scenes giving an indication that Tsuburaya's idiosyncrasies were beginning to get the worst of him. On the whole, the effects work in *Frankenstein* is exceptional and Tsuburaya's best since *Gorath*; the optical work, the composites, the superimpositions and the wire works are first-rate (one unique shot shows Frankenstein surfacing in the lake as Tsuburaya mattes-in a live-action plate—complete with windows—showing the bridge crew looking out at Frankenstein; the view gives us a sense of perspective as if we too are on the bridge). Tsuburaya supplies other eye-popping moments such as when a tree tossed by Frankenstein lands onto a house in a superb optical effect. However, while the mobility of Frankenstein's severed hand offered many spine-tingling possibilities, Tsuburaya simply utilized a battery-run prop hand which only slightly undulated, lacked in detail and was not terribly realistic.

Honda's use of symbolism occurs early on in the film as a number of shots were filmed through bars or panes of glass, suggesting that the principal characters are prisoners of their fate. Shadows are also used to considerable effect such as when Frankenstein moves toward the camera from the darkened rear-portion of his cell into the lit foreground, resulting in a disturbing close-up (Honda films a number of unsettling close-ups of the imprisoned Frankenstein looking at the camera to evoke audience sympathy, although whether he succeeded is questionable). When the boy is struck by the cab, cameraman Koizumi cleverly first shows the driver's reaction to what he sees as the object is hidden from our view, creating a suspenseful moment. Koizumi and Honda did a fine job filming the mist-filled forest sequence, and after Sueko looks into her microscope at the radiated tissue in the lab, Honda cuts to a close-up of the boy hiding in the bushes, cementing their connection. When Bowman walks on out Sueko, she turns and faces the camera in a shot meant to create empathy for her; Honda would use this technique again in the scene after Madame Piranha gets shot by Dr. Huu in *King Kong's Counterattack* two years later.

When the boy's hand disappears from the container, Koizumi utilizes a hand-held camera in a POV shot as we also look through the lab for it (early on in the film, as Bowman makes his rounds, the camera becomes subjective as it closes in on the ailing Kazuko). When the boy is cornered in the cave, Kozumi makes splendid use it's horizontal opening which fits perfectly into the wide-screen format, and after Bowman and Sueko have been escorted by soldiers to the top of a hill in order to gaze down at the destroyed chateau, a Honda "human landscape" fills the frame with some 20 actors (another favorite technique was a quick-cut reaction, here dramatically done when Bowman calls out to Sueko after Frankenstein has thrown the television through the window).

One of Koizumi's best moments occurs when Frankenstein is flushed out of the powder magazine cave: As Bowman and Sueko flee the scene, the monster's huge silhouette can be seen looming menacingly on a background wall in a splendid application of light and shadow. Ryohei Fujii's editing and continuity are also excellent, and Riki Konna's makeup for Frankenstein is appropriately ghastly—almost too much so—whereas the makeup for the aged Dr. Liesendorf left much to be desired as the lining of his skullcap is all-too visible.

The general air of enthusiasm that permeated the *Frankenstein* project is also evident in Akira Ifukube's sensational score; just as Tsuburaya recycled *Baran's* roar for Baragon, Ifukube reused a number of cues he had initially composed for *Baran* for his *Frankenstein* score, such as the scenes with the subs and when Frankenstein is spying on the soldiers. Ifukube also recycled his octopus music from *King Kong vs. Godzilla* during Frankenstein's battle with the octopus (an alternate ending filmed but never shown to Japanese audiences) and even wrote three brief rock-n-roll tunes.

Ifukube's "Main Title" music eerily begins with the plucking of a "prepared" (modified) piano—which will later be associated with Frankenstein's hand—followed by a single note tapped on a vibraphone, which transforms into an ominous flurry of brass which will later become Frankenstein's theme. From this, Ifukube introduces a bass flute, followed by the subtle tapping of a gong, then a screeching of violin strings, electone organ music, alto saxophone and softly-sinister bass clarinets. "Hiroshima" begins with a mournful chord on brass, timpani and a pounding of off-key piano notes to lend the scene a disquieting quality, before ingeniously repeating the phrase with woodwinds to indicate the tragic event now in the past. When Frankenstein first peers through the bushes in "The Vanishing Shadow," Ifukube introduces the boy with a haunting theme played on alto flute, accompanied by piano and a muted trumpet, before violins and organ bridge the music, returning to the moody flutes heard at the beginning of the cue.

Gentle flutes and tinkling piano music comprise "Miyajima" as Bowman and Sueko pay their respects at the shrine and graveyard; Ifukube then introducing an English horn to give the piece a sad, reflective, yet hopeful impression which nonetheless ends on an unresolved coda. Ifukube scores the moment when "Sueko's Pendant" arrests the attention of Frankenstein by introducing shimmering violins for suspense, before adding horns for danger, then swelling into full-blown brass as the tension rises when Bowman hits the boy with a chair. Then, an *ocarina* (Japanese flute) enters indicating the weird turn of events, accompanied by a tinkling piano cleverly mimicking the swaying pendant. When the hand is first seen crawling across the floor in "Discovery of the Wrist," Ifukube goes wild with tinkling piano, organ, low woodwinds and a screeching electone. "The Whereabouts of the Wrist"(heard when the lab personnel are frantically searching for the boy's desiccated hand) begins with a rapidly strumming violin supplemented by organ, vibraphone, piano and a muffled trumpet.

Ifukube augments the spooky mood necessary for the forest exploration magnificently in "Search in the Fog," beginning with four notes on a English horn joined by a strange, "whistling teapot" sound created by violin bows playing on metal strings. Trumpets playing in their lowest registers are supplemented by menacing clarinets and a tapping cymbal marking the explorers' treacherous trek through the woods, until shrill whistles and strings are interrupted by pounding drums and heavy horns joined by a tentative flute; it is one of Ifukube's most-suspenseful pieces of film music.

Actor Nick Adams brought to his portrayal of Dr. Bowen an intensity lacking in Honda's recent films up to that time. The actor enjoyed working on *Frankenstein* and had great respect for Honda, referring to the director as a "gentleman" (he also reportedly took to his co-star, the beautiful Kumi Mizuno as well). Adams' enthusiasm became infectious—particularly with Honda—who appreciated his drive and professionalism. Adams plays Bowman as a tortured man who nonetheless makes a sincere effort to fit in to the Japanese culture: When Bowman arrives at Sueko's apartment carrying birthday flowers he is dressed in the traditional kimono robe, and when he and Sueko take a drive around Miayashima and visit the local shrine, Sueko prays to her ancestors with Bowman sensitively following her example. The actor infuses the character with a great deal of his own intense personality, impatiently charging through crowds and angrily slamming his fist down when he learns the Frankenstein hand is missing (in still another nod to Japanese/American cooperation, as Kawai prepares to return home with the scientists bidding him farewell, the Japanese Sueko bows while Bowman does an American "catch ya later" gesture).

Kumi Mizuno brought her own brand of charm to her role of the sympathetic Sueko Togami. Although close professionally, Sueko and Bowman are not really romantically linked. In any event, the onscreen chemistry between the two is unmistakable—Honda, who was also very fond of Mizuno, must have sensed the mutual attraction between them—and rumors suggesting an intimate relationship between Adams and Mizuno have circulated for years (in the scene when the three scientists are heading into the forest to find Frankenstein, Adam's takes Mizuno's hand, making one wonder if the gesture was Adam's idea or Honda's).

Tadao Takashima plays Yuzo Kawaji as a scientist who—as with so many in the history of horror films—is ultimately seduced by his fascination with Frankenstein; yet he is visibly disturbed when Dr. Liesendorf pontificates about the regeneration of Frankenstein's body parts, nervous to the point of taking a drink before performing his amputation of the boy's hand and childlike when he finally gets his hands on Frankenstein's severed hand; all of which show a believable and gradual transformation from a reasonable and compassionate man to one driven and determined to study Frankenstein, no matter what the cost. Yoshio Tsuchiya (Kawai) had his unique on-screen presence and his brief if not essential scenes add an interesting and welcome spice to the grim brew (appearing for the last time in a Honda film was the great Takeshi Shimura, playing the brief role of the Hiroshima doctor who intends to study the heart).

Frankenstein was played by Koji Furuhata in his one-and-only film role, Honda discovering him while the young man was working as a clerk in a grocery store! Due to the actor's inexperience, Honda took greater pains than usual in carefully coaching him to develop his character as an artificially-created human being, and because Furuhata was not a trained actor, his natural sincerity translated agreeably onto the screen (the role was a demanding as well in that it also required Furuhata to perform stunts when he wrestled with Baragon). However, Furuhata's lack of acting experience proved to be an impediment in a role that would have not been an easy one even for a professional actor, particularly when trying to invoke compassion for what is essentially a freak-of-nature (the post-dubbed grunts and ugly makeup were of little help in this regard). The audience never really gets to know or understand Frankenstein, and his lack of articulation stresses this deficiency, making him almost an alien presence. While certainly portraying the monster as an oppressed and misunderstood outsider, Furuhata was never able to achieve as much sympathy as pity.

Working with a script that appealed to him, plus the charismatic acting from his leading players, seemed to reinvigorate Honda as his direction was confident, incisive and his best since *Mothra vs. Godzilla*; the earthquake, the monster's escape from the lab and the search in the mist-filled forest rank among the director's finest moments. In fact, the film's *virtuoso* opening two-minute sequence—complete with a mad scientist, Nazis, exaggerated sound effects (and no dialogue)—is dramatic, humorous, ironic and tragic. When Kawaji is engaged in a heated *contratan* with the manager of the clinic regarding Frankenstein's lodging, it turns into a rare shouting match for a Honda film.

One of Honda's best scenes has Bowman arriving at the clinic to find that pandemonium has broken loose, urging fire extinguishers be used to blind the boy who is at that moment sitting happily in his cell, snacking on food and blissfully unaware of the bodies of two dead TV crewmen lying before him; their vacant eyes gazing upward while he chuckles off-screen in the movie's most disturbing moment (particularly effective was the moment when—after hearing the sounds of gunshots—Bowman goes berserk, screaming: "Don't kill him! Don't kill him!" to such an extent that he has to be physically restrained).

When Frankenstein makes a threatening advance on Sueko, Bowman smacks him with a chair, Honda having the actor swinging the chair at the camera in a close-up, thus placing us momentarily in Frankenstein's place as he receives the blow. The integration between the live-action and effects work is as usual flawless, particularly in the scene when Frankenstein escapes from the lab and when Baragon appears near the *chateau*. As the young people run in terror from Baragon, Honda shoots several inserts of their running feet, and when the police sergeant is receiving information on Frankenstein on a phone in the clinic, Honda has two female technicians fearfully listening in the background.

At the conclusion of the film Bowman says of the Frankenstein monster: "He couldn't live in this world," which was of course the basis for all of Honda's monster films. Honda himself observed that "Frankenstein is not a monster. He is a giant human, and what was needed to be shown was how difficult that was for him. This production was not a simple monster movie but a tragic story of science gone wrong...it was a massive effort requiring all of my passion for perfection." The movie comes close to being a classic—in fact the first half is just tremendous—but the "heart" of the picture leaves when Frankenstein leaves Sueko's apartment, which from that moment on becomes just another "monster-on-the-loose" movie (towards the end of the film the viewer feels the same exhausted detachment as do the witnesses watching the final battle between the monsters—a fact that Honda was by then well-aware of. "I like the beginning of the film," he told Shinsuke Nakajima, "but the story changed when the fight between Frankenstein and Baragon began").

In essence, the human story was simply not strong enough to withstand a 12-minute monster fight, the longest in Tsuburaya's career (three minutes longer than the "Battle of the Century" between Kong and Godzilla). Also, the decision to have Frankenstein grow even uglier as the film progressed was an unfortunate decision, in that it drained him of what little humanity he possessed; near the end of the film it's a toss-up as to which monster is uglier. Had Frankenstein not turned *quite* so ugly at the end of the film, perhaps fighting Baragon to the death before dying from his own wounds, a definite pathos might well have been achieved.

In any event, Honda had taken to the filming of *Frankenstein* with gusto and found it to be a gratifying if exhausting experience; this was just as well for his next film would be more-outrageous still, reuniting not only Godzilla, Radon and King Ghidorah, but Nick Adams and Kumi Mizuno. The result was one of the Honda's most beloved movies.

THE WAR OF THE MONSTERS (1965)
(KAIJU DAISENSO)
MONSTER ZERO

Cast & Credits

Film Register No. 14151
Release Date: December 19, 1965
Running Time: 94 Minutes

<u>Staff</u>: Executive Producer: Henry G. Saperstein; Producer: Tomoyuki Tanaka; Director: Ishiro Honda; Director of Photography: Hajime Koizumi; Art Director: Takeo Kita; Sound Recording: Wataru Konuma; Lighting: Shoshichi Kojima; Music: Akira Ifukube; Sound Arrangement: Hisashi Shimonaga; Assistant Director: Koji Kajita; Editor: Ryohei Fujii; Sound Effects: Sadamasa Nishimoto; Matte Processing: Hiroshi Mukoyama; Gaffer: Shoichi Kojima; Production Mangers: Masao Suzuki, Tadashi Koike, Issei Tanaka; Special Effects: Director: Eiji Tsuburaya; Director of Photography: Teisho (Sadamasa) Arikawa, Sokei (Mototaka) Tomioka; Optical Photography: Yukio Manoda, Sadao Iizuka.

<u>Cast</u>: Akira Takarada (Astronaut Kazuo Fuji); Nick Adams (Astronaut F. Glenn); Kumi Mizuno (Miss Namikawa); Keiko Sawai (Haruno Fuji); Jun Tazaki (Dr. Sakurai); Yoshio Tsuchiya (Controller of Planet X); Akira Kubo (Tatsuo Torii "Teri"); Takamaru Sasaki (Council Chairman); Fuyuki Murakami (Medical Representative); Yoshifumi Tajima (JDSF Mobil Commander); Kenzo Tabu (President of World Education Corporation); Noriko Sengoku (Tatsuo's Mother); Somesho Matsumoto (Religious Representative); Gen Shimizu (JDSF Representative); Toru Ibuki, Kazuo Suzuki, Koji Uno (WEC Employees); Toki Shiozawa (Women's Group Representative); Mitsuo Tsuda, Takuzo (Jiro) Kumagai (JDSF Officers); Masaaki Tachibana, Tadashi Okabe, Haruo Suzuki (WSA Technicians); Kamayuki Tsubono, Minoru Ito (Reporters); Haruo Nakajimi (Godzilla); Masaki Shinohara (Radon); Shoichi Hirose (King Ghidorah).

The Film

Honda's 17th fantasy film returned him to the world of outer space with all of its *accoutrements*: Aliens, ray guns, rocket ships, interplanetary travel, journeys to new worlds, flying saucers and advanced-technology. To this cosmic stew was added a theft-warning device (invented for one of the world's safest cities) and three manic monsters; just a few of the ingredients making up this highly-entertaining film. Sekizawa's script is brisk and lively and does not stand up to close scrutiny: The Xians' scheme to take over the Earth is elaborately-planned as they go to great lengths to use a fictitious business called "World Education Corporation" as a front, then take the trouble to buy the rights to Teri's invention to get it away from him; when a much simpler solution would have been to simply kill Teri, then destroy his blueprints.

The original idea was to have dozens of Namikawas on Planet X, but time and budget constraints made this impossible. Both astronauts have guns blown out of their hands and individuals are always sneaking about; the Xians hide three saucers in Lake Myojin without "permission," and Glenn and Fuji take an unauthorized stroll through the Xian complex. The concept of the Xians giving the citizens of the Earth 24 hours to make up their mind to surrender makes little sense other than giving them the time needed to come up with a solution.

There are other conundrums, such as how the aliens managed to steal the *P-1* and store it underground, and at one point Fuji hands Dr. Sakurai a note, describing it as "Some more trouble," but we never learn what the trouble is, just as we never learn how the Xians' computers clued them into trouble brewing on Earth—and are the containers the Namikawa doubles are seen carrying in the Gold Room recordings of threats to other worlds? The Xians do not actually "control" the monsters in the sense of ordering them around and telling them what to do, but can subdue them at will; once released, the monsters then go about their destructive business (this idea of an alien power depositing a monster anywhere in the world was recycled by Sekizawa in *All Monsters Attack* three years later, and 36 years after that in *Godzilla: Final Wars*).

Sharing his soundproofed cell with Glenn, Teri realizes that the Xians bought his invention due to the loud sound it makes—and by a fortunate coincidence, he happens to have one in his coat pocket! After initially overcoming the guards (which shows how effective the alien cell's soundproofing is), Teri then inexplicably turns off his alarm (perhaps to save the batteries) as the men attempt to escape through the front door. Finding a Xian guard blocking their escape, Glenn is able to overpower one alien, but another Xian guard is so enraged at seeing Teri that he forgets all about using his space gun and instead tries to strangle the inventor!

Glenn and Teri overcome the Xians guarding the boat and send the ship off to be blasted into splinters by the Controller; but how all this was accomplished, and how Glenn and Teri knew this would happen, is never explained. In the Controller's saucer, "Computer Five shows a discrepancy" as red lights flash all around, although the reason for the disturbance is unclear. And when the sound of Teri's device is sent through the skies, one wonders how high the sound waves could actually travel, or why the Xians simply didn't fly out of range; but perhaps the most-incredible moment occurs after Dr. Sakurai informs Fuji that the Controller foolishly revealed that the monsters were being controlled by magnetic waves. Fuji asks: "Is that *significant?*"

Tsuburaya's staff did very well on *War of the Monsters*; the outer space sequences are convincingly beautiful, with the matte painting of Jupiter particularly outstanding (overall the matte and optical work is very good, although the wire works are occasionally visible). Godzilla and Radon look basically unchanged since *Three Giant Monsters*, but the comedic antics were now an integral part of the battle scenes. The effects were a hit-and-miss affair (the overhead shot of Ghidorah rising from the water at the end of the film is extremely well done); when the entangled monsters tumbled over a hillside, the effect is fine, but when they hit the water they look as flat as a pancake, and although the destruction of the house on Makura Island is terrific, the shot of another house being washed away by a tidal wave was not very unconvincing.

Ghidorah seems to have slowed down a bit since his initial appearance, as it does gentle glides as opposed to the frenzied flying it had done just a year earlier; although the Space Monster's initial entrance is very effective (coming into view from a cloud while flying straight at the camera), for some reason the yellow-and-green-colored bolts the creature spat out earlier were now simplified to mere scratches; gold on Planet X, white on Planet Earth). Arikawa's camera work has some nice moments, such as a shot seen from inside the alien's entrance chamber as two saucers approach the camera, and there were a number of effective ground-level shots of Godzilla's feet and tail destroying various buildings.

One word that best describes Hajime Koizumi's camerawork in *War of the Monsters* is "routine," evidence of a rapid shooting schedule and a bored director. Creatively there is very little of the dynamic camera work seen in *Frankenstein*, although Koizumi does tilt his camera during the tense moments aboard the Controller's saucer, filming it through red filters. One of the more cinematic moments in the movie occurs during the teahouse sequence: As written, the two-minute scene afforded little in terms of dynamism, so Honda and Koizumi utilized nine edits filmed from eight separate set-ups, for an average of one shot every 13 seconds, lending flow and interest to what otherwise would have been a stagnant scene. One interesting bit of location filming takes place on the road to Lake Myojin, when Glenn and Fuji are discussing Glenn's "dream;" filmed at dusk with natural lighting, Koizumi strangely opted to film the actors through the car's windshield, rather than remove it for a clearer image. To compensate for the occasional blurry faces, Koizumi used two camera setups, always keeping the speaker in focus.

Again, Takeo Kita's sets left something to be desired; it's hard to tell if the Star Flower Club has a roof or not, and the teahouse set is oddly dressed with hanging lamps, stuffed birds in cages and large, crude caricatures of people's faces looming on background walls. World Space Authority's Control Center is acceptable enough, but there is a lack of attention to detail: When Sakurai is trying to reassure Haruno about his "well-trained" astronauts, the reel-to-reel computer tapes in the background are seen to be turning inward *toward* each other, rather than in the same direction. The Xian base looked appropriately alien—if sparsely appointed—with one intriguing touch of *decor*: When the Controller is in his Control Room on Planet X, he is sitting in an overstuff golden chair in front of a star-studded black globe covered with strings of lights, suggesting not only the Xians' fascination with gold, but of a solar system in bondage.

Ryohei Fujii's editing maintains a quick pace throughout the film; when Fuji leaves the scene of the alien footprints to return to the *P-1*, the next shot shows him at the deserted landing site, and when Glenn and Fuji raise their hands in surrender after being captured in the Gold Room, the next shot shows them being held at space gun-point with the guns popping-out at them from the shadows. In a beautifully-timed moment, when the Controller lowers his head admitting his planet's failure in defeating King Ghidorah, the screen behind him displaying the monsters' battle shows smoke billowing up, as if to accentuate his defeat.

Akira Ifukube's score for *War of the Monsters* borrows heavily from themes used in previous films such as the "Main Title" music—a rousing theme written for drums, trumpets, strident strings and cymbals, that had been used in the original *Godzilla* during the depth-bomb sequence. Themes earlier associated with Godzilla, Radon and

Ghidorah were used during the battle scenes in *War of the Monsters*, and a recycled portion of the music heard during the explorer's search for the meteor in *Three Giant Monsters* is utilized when the astronauts leave the monsters behind on Planet X and again at the film's *finale*.

Ifukube did manage some softly suspenseful moments in his music for Planet X, comprised of haunting woodwinds, quivering violins, tinkling piano, xylophone, theremin and organ. "The Three Monsters on Planet X" was basically a reworking of Ghidorah's original theme with organ, cymbal, drums and horns augmented by a screaming trumpet. A French horn, rapid bow strings, drum riffs and trumpets color "Washigasawa and Lake Myojin," while pounding piano and brass end with a sustained note on organ for a sinister march-like melody in "The Earth in Utter Chaos," heard during the worldwide riots.

One impressive musical moment takes place when the saucers surface from the lake; the piece begins with a fluttering English horn and sinister piano, joined by plucking bass strings and trembling violin, before exploding into cymbal and brass as the saucers rise from the water. Four notes on shrieking trumpets then take over, counterbalanced by a three-note motif on lower brass with cymbals and rolling timpani, topped-off by quivering strings and theremin. Ifukube composed original music for both restaurant scenes; "The Star Flower Club" is purposely-scored with pretentious piano and violin, which takes on a lilting quality when Miss Namikawa enters (during the moment when Haruno and Teri are arguing over the merits of his invention, the violin plays in an agitated manner).

Yoshio Tsuchiya was beginning to make a career out of playing extraterrestrials, having asked for and receiving the part of the alien leader in *Defense Force*. An eccentric man by nature with a quirky sense of humor, Tsuchiya appreciated and relished the chance to play such offbeat roles, endowing the Controller with a serious and suspicious nature, as well as being short-tempered and condescendingly superior. His voice was not as heavily-distorted as when he played the Mysterian leader, and more of his facial features are visible; but unlike the slow, deliberate movements of the Leader, Tsuchiya' Controller employs swift and short gestures punctuated with strange hand signals (during moments of humility, the Controller places his hand over the red dot on his uniform where the human heart is usually presumed to be located, which begs a question: Do the Xians really have their hearts in the same place as human beings or is the gesture simply a token one?).

Akira Takarada plays astronaut Fuji as a petulant and scornful man disdainful of his daughter's intentions to marry the nebbish Teri, before eventually (and with apparent regret) relenting. For Akira Kubo, his role as the nerdy inventor Tetsuo Teri was as far-removed from his tragically-heroic Kenji in *Matango* as could be imagined, yet the actor's characterization of Teri was impressive in its own right and no less-convincing. Keiko Sawai did an acceptable job as Teri's love-interest Haruno, but her part gives her little to do other than be constantly concerned (in an attempt to give the actress's part more of an impact, Honda varies her hairstyles throughout the film). As Dr. Sakurai, Jun Tazaki was his usually officious self, but the actor appears fatigued, lending his scenes little vitality; one moment possibly indicating his exhaustion was when he involuntarily twitched his head while discussing the merits of the A-Cycle Light Ray.

As the enigmatic Miss Namikawa, Kumi Mizuno created yet another unforgettable character, and the role was a tricky one, as she played an emotionless alien robot which has somehow fallen in love with a mortal being. Mizuno endows her part with an air of both sensuality and mystery; when Glenn asks what's bothering her before he leaves for Planet X, Mizuno's pained expression conveys an internal conflict (in Honda's world, even a machine cannot deny the yearning of the human spirit). As for Nick Adams, his part of Astronaut Glenn was a definite comedown from his earlier Dr. Bowman in *Frankenstein*, but not due from any lack of interest or skill on the actor's part, but from the limitations of the *clichéd* role of Astronaut Glenn.

In *Frankenstein*, Adams played a guilt-ridden scientist, but in *War of the Monsters*, he was more of a space cowboy. There is very little complexity to Glenn's character, yet Adams manages to color the role with his own unique brand of cocky machismo and bravado; so much so that even an alien robot cannot help but fall in love with him (a favorite moment for fans of the actor takes place when he bids goodbye to Namikawa, nudging her chin before saying "I'll marry you when I get back," nicely punctuated by the actor's grin of confidence as he walks toward the camera). When Glenn sees Namikawa's doubles on Planet X, he registers both confusion and distress, but in the main he spends most of his time being annoyed and antagonistic (towards the end of the scene during the briefing in the Diet discussing the merits of the Xians, the actor slumps in his chair and folds his hands in apparent boredom).

The chemistry between Mizuno and Adams on display in *Frankenstein* is reexibited with greater definiteness in *War of the Monsters*, and this chemistry was best exhibited in their longest and last scene together, the film's highpoint and the second of only two dialogue scenes between them. Adams registers anger, disappointment, frustration and finally tenderness; yet strangely, when Namikawa declares her love for him—effectively sealing her doom—the astronaut does not return the sentiment. Sadly, *War of the Monsters* was Adams' final film for Honda as the actor soon returned to America in a vain attempt to revive his sagging box-office appeal. Outside of an occasional television appearance however he was out of mainstream movie casting, and a little more than three years after *War of the Monsters* was released, on February 7, 1968, Nick Adams—who almost certainly would have played leading roles in future Honda films—died of an apparent suicide at the age of 37.

One interesting directorial moment occurs when the crowd watches Glenn, Fuji and Sakurai board the alien vessel for Planet X; all are smiles as they first wave goodbye, becoming worried frowns a moment later as they lower their arms. Honda commits a rare gaffe when Haruno spots Glenn getting into a car from his elevated floor in the tea room, identifying the driver as Miss Namikawa; a sighting impossible to perform from such a steep angle. The director did not approve of Godzilla's jig on Planet X ("That had no business being in the movie" he told Guy Tucker), but his reluctance to remove it reflected not only an unwillingness to challenge a respected and long-time collaborator in Tsuburaya, but also a feeling that it was simply no longer worth the effort; indicating the temperament of a man rapidly losing interest in the movies he was making (as when he surrendered at war's end, could it be Honda felt that giving up was a preferable option rather than entering into a confrontation when the game was already lost?).

The most memorable moment in *War of the Monsters* was the confrontation between Glenn and Namikawa. Despite the rudimentary dialogue, Honda's sincere approach to the scene—complemented by the earnestly-sincere performances of Adams and Mizuno (the entire sequence consisting almost entirely of close-ups)—made it one of Honda's signature scenes. Honda manages a significant "touch" moments after the final saucer has been destroyed, when Teri exclaims, "We did it!" before clutching Haruno's hand as Glenn reaches over and places his hand over theirs, reinforcing a shared American-Japanese triumph (Honda also has both Glenn and Teri handle Namikawa's note to Glenn, indicating their shared interest in her).

A rapidly-paced and visual treat painted in lavish, gaudy colors and sprinkled with memorable dialogue, *War of the Monsters* was meant from the get-go to be a harmless diversion; yet, while admittedly being fun to watch, it is fluff without form and style without substance (when the Controller's saucer enters its hidden cavern—an elaborate affair complete with a large combination dial, sequential lightening and crystals fluctuating in dazzling rainbow patterns—it is all very pretty, but without explanation or purpose, it is meaningless).

War of the Monsters was Honda's fifth Godzilla film and his fourth in as many years, and although the director enjoyed directing Godzilla films (he had always liked the character), he had grown tired of the direction the series was taking. The frustration must have reached critical mass, for Honda finally made his displeasure known to the producer. Tanaka listened and removed Honda from directing any future Godzilla films for the time being; however, if Honda believed this meant he was going to be granted an immediate and permanent departure from the genre which he had helped to create, he was in for a bitter disappointment.

FRANKENSTEIN'S MONSTERS:
SANDA VS. GAIRAH (1966)
(FURANKENSHUTAIN NO KAIju: SANDA TAI GAIRAH
WAR OF THE GARGANTUAS

Cast & Credits

Film Register No. 14525
Release Date: July 31, 1966
Running Time: 88 minutes, 7 seconds

Staff: Producers: Tomoyuki Tanaka and Kenichiro Tsunoda; Director: Ishiro Honda; Screenplay: Kaoru Mabuchi and Ishiro Honda; Cinematography: Hajime Koizumi; Art Director: Takeo Kita; Recording: Norio (Tone) Tokon; Lighting: Toshio Takashima; Music: Akira Ifukube; Sound Arrangement: Hisashi Shimonaga; Assistant Director: Koji Kajita; Editor: Ryohei Fujii; Sound Effects: Sadamasa Nishimoto; Production Manager: Shoichi Koga; Special Effects Techniques: Director: Eiji Tsuburaya; Cinematography: Sadamasa (Teisho) Arikawa and Sokei Tomioka; Optical Cinematography: Yoshiyuki Tokumasa.; Art Director: Yasuyuki Inoue; Lighting: Kuichiro Kishida

Cast: Kenji Sahara (Dr. Yuzo Mamiya); Kumi Mizuno (Akemi Togawa); Russ Tamblyn (Dr. Paul Stewart); Jun Tazaki (JSDF General Hashimoto); Kipp Hamilton (Nightclub Singer); Yoshibumi Tajima (Maritime Safety Official); Nobuo Nakamura (Toto University Professor Kita); Hisaya Ito (Maritime Safety Chief Izumida); Nadao Kirino (General's Aide Kazuma); Yasuhisa Tutsumi, Haruya Sakamoto, Koji Urugi, Kamayuki Tsubono, Rinsaku Ogata, Mitsuo Tsuda (JSDF Soldiers); Henry Okawa (Yokosuka Hospital Physician); Shoichi Hirose (Mountain Guide); Ikio Sawamura (Elderly Fisherman); Ren Yamamoto (Sailor Saburo Kameda); Noriaki Inoue (Mountain Guide); Yasuhiko Saijo (Man Who Won't Leave Car); Wataru Omae (Haneda Airport Air-Traffic Controller); Kyoko Mori (Yokosuka Hospital Nurse); Hiroko Minami (Girlfriend of Man Who Won't Leave Car); Tadashi Okabe, Yoshio Katsube, Masaaki Tachibana, Hideo Shibuya, Yutaka Oka (Reporters).

The Film

The financial success of *Frankenstein vs. Baragon* was enough of an incentive for Tanaka to produce a sequel; not really a problem, as the film's ending in the original Japanese version simply had Frankenstein swallowed up by the Earth. Takeshi Kimura wrote the screenplay based on a story treatment by Reuben Bercovitch with an assist from Honda (receiving his first official screenwriting credit since *Godzilla*). With Honda's added involvement it would seem that *Frankenstein's Monsters: Sanda vs. Gairah* couldn't miss, but unfortunately it turned out to be one of the director's more ineffectual efforts.

For reasons unknown—although *Sanda vs. Gairah* was made only one year after *Frankenstein*—the events occurring in *Sanda vs. Gairah* take place five years later. Also changed were the names of all three doctors: Bowman was now Stewart, Sueko was switched to Akemi and Kawaji became Majida. The movie was basically about the gargantuas with the first half of the film dedicated to Gairah, and the second to both beasts, before leading up to their colossal confrontation in Tokyo. When the reporters question Akemi as to her memories of Frankenstein, she flashes back to when she was feeding him as a small boy (hairier than we remember him and now sounding like a chimpanzee); she also recounts that Frankenstein came to her apartment before he disappeared, which is indeed what had happened in the previous film.

As in *Frankenstein*, the media speculates that mysterious deaths have been caused by the Frankenstein monster, apparently remembering little from their previously false accusations. Stewart and Akemi hike up a hill with local students in Yamata until they reach a peak where they see a trail of huge footprints, recalling similar moments from *Godzilla* and *Abominable Snowman*. Whatever contributions Honda may have made to the script are open to conjecture, but they may have involved the numerous scenes (one lasting 20 minutes) comprised almost entirely of military preparedness with the green gargantua on the move and the military preparing to do battle with it, the dialogue being purely of a military nature.

One moment unmistakably Honda's was when Stewart offers a pretty posy to the wounded Akemi—considering Honda's intense fondness for the actress this would not be surprising—he even has Mizuno looking right into the camera (strangely missing from the Japanese version but included in the American print, Akemi mourns, "I prayed so that I could save his life"). Kimura's input was undoubtedly the scenes involving the aggressive press and unsympathetic military, particularly during the scene when marine officers grill an obviously-ailing seaman while a helpless hospital staff looks on (Stewart's cynical attitude was almost certainly a Kimura contribution).

Not since *Baran* had there been a Honda monster film with so little subtext; while *Sanda vs. Gairah* was an improvement *Baran* with its widescreen color, intense action and vivid special effects, *Baran* at least had a story while *Sanda vs. Gairah* has barely a plot. Despite the picture's terrific opening sequence with the octopus—filmed in *gran guinol* style and another example of the Honda/Tsuburaya/Ifukube partnership at its best (imagine the idea of a sailor getting a glimpse of the monster trying to consume him)—it bogs down immediately with the following scenes concerning the maritime safety bureau trying to figure out what has happened; hardly essential since we already know.

Compared to the exciting and involving *Frankenstein, Sanda vs. Gairah* was a definite disappointment, right down to its hackneyed ending where a volcano comes out of nowhere to consume the brawling beasts; an ending scene similar to *Radon's* but lacking the earlier film's artistic embellishment and poignancy (while Frankenstein's demise in the first film could be attributed to Divine Intervention, *Sanda vs. Gairah's* ending can only be interpreted for what it is: a silly gimmick to end the picture). Nevertheless, *Sanda vs. Gairah* contains many terrific "set-piece" effect sequences, including a brilliant shot of Gairah trying to catch miniature sailors swimming away from it, as well as a scene utilizing "Maser Cannons" mowing down tall timbers like so many weeds—one can even see the barks of the trees after they have been cut down (sharp eyes can spot a small spotlight employed to guide the post-optical animation work for the Maser rays, so as to be in-sync with the live-action pyrotechnics). Tsuburaya's miniature landscapes—complete with forests, rivers, lakes and magnificently painted backdrops—were the most accomplished of his career.

Again, Hajime Koizumi's *blasé* photography matches Honda's lackadaisical direction; his camera simply records the mediocre live-action scenes (much-more gratifying are Teisho Arikawa and Sokei Tomioka's splendid effects photography and Shoichi Koga's art direction). Ryohei Fujii's editing lacks the crispness of his *War of the Monsters* from a year earlier, although it was at its best during the scenes cutting back-and-forth between Gairah and the military (there is one distinctive Honda/Fujii touch: After Gairah has thrown a jeep away it burst into flames, Honda then cuts from the flaming jeep to a shot of the general's adjunct screaming into his microphone).

By now, Akira Ifukube had scored everyone of Honda' genre films since *Mothra vs. Godzilla* for a total of six films in only two years, and while many of these scores are outstanding, the same could not be said for *Sanda vs. Gairah*. The film's "Main Title" music is very good, beginning as it does with the ubiquitous theremin and short bowstrings followed by low brass, pounding drums and trilling trumpets, and his "Giant Octopus: The "Devil of the Sea" is a weird and wonderful piece opening with theremin, clarinet and strange whistling sounds. Ifukube then introduces drawn-out bowstrings and piano before adding pompous brass, gong and quivering organ, as trombones play a protracted, descending note with trumpet, drums and rapid bowstrings emphasizing the bizarre situation.

A gentler piece is "Akemi's Memories," heard when the woman is with the young Frankenstein; tinkling piano and soft flutes stress the creature's childlike qualities, while forlorn violins predict his inevitable fate (the piece ends with a nine-note motif already associated with Frankenstein from the previous film). Ifukube colors "Footprints in the Snow-Covered Valley" in a manner similar to his music for the mountain-climbing expedition in *Three Giant Monsters*, with horns giving a sense of vastness and scale, augmented by clarinet, muted trumpet and ending with piano, quivering violins and low woodwinds when Sanda's footprints are spotted.

"Feel in My Heart"—Ifukube's title for the song more widely known as "The Words Get Stuck in My Throat"—was scored in typical "Swinging Sixties" pop-tune fashion, with Kipp Hamilton as a kind-of Petulia Clark, who she slightly resembled. Driven by twangy electrical guitar, steady percussion and blaring trumpet, some of the song's lyrics ("microphone," "amplify" and "turn the power on") sound more like a commercial for a Sony speaker system than for a love song, and while not exactly "Downtown," it is a nice little number.

The cue used during the eruption of the volcano arguably contains one the longest title in Ifukube's itinerary: "Battle to the Death at the Volcano on the Ocean Floor." Beginning with a suspenseful drum, low woodwinds and trembling violins, a blaring solo trumpet enters at the moment of eruption, playing a mournful melody comprised of ascending and descending notes. This use of the trumpet (normally associated with "Taps" and other military melodies) serves as a sort of salute and tribute to the spirited struggle between the two monsters now coming to an end. Although occasionally interesting, Ifukube's score for *Sanda vs. Gairah* was one of his least-substantial efforts, suffering as it did from the inclusion of themes regularly repeated as well as cues heard in earlier films.

Nick Adams was unfortunately unavailable to reprise his role of the doctor, so co-producer Henry Saperstein rustled up another American actor: Russ Tamblyn, who had appeared in two of George Pal's fantasy films, *Tom Thumb* (1958) and *The Wonderful World of the Brothers' Grimm* (1962). Honda was well-aware that certain actors did not mind appearing in genre films, while others did not care for them at all; Russ Tamblyn regrettably belonged to the latter category. Tamblyn's portrayal of Dr. Paul Stewart has been met with considerable criticism over the years and it is widely considered as one of the worst performances in a Honda fantasy films and with good reason; the actor sleepwalks through his role, never varying his expression, seldom making eye contact with his fellow actors and rarely reacts to what others are saying around him.

Certainly as written, the role of Stewart has little of the dynamism of Bowen and is not exactly a man-of-action: When Akemi is surrounded by the press crowding in on her, Stewart hardly lifts a finger to help her, although one can easily picture Nick Adams charging through the crowd to rescue her. Upon hearing the sounds of air-raid sirens sweeping throughout the city, instead of bolting out-of-bed, Stewart tries to blot out the noise by pulling his pillow over his head. Even when Akemi is hanging onto a branch for dear life, Tamblyn seems at best mildly concerned.

It all makes one wonders why Nick Adams did not appear in the film; as it happened, the actor actually was in Japan at the time working on a film called *The Killing Bottle*. Adams and Mizuno had first met during the Spring of 1965 while filming *Frankenstein*, and it was most likely during their second film together (*War of the Monsters*, filmed in the Fall of 1965) that the two began a serious relationship, during which time Adams divorced his wife back in the States before proposing to Mizuno. Mizuno turned his offer down as she was already engaged, and as a result, Adams would have been less-than-eager to work with her again, thus leaving Honda to deal with the disinterred Tamblyn. It was a more than a great pity, for Adams would have injected the part with his charismatic intensity, to say nothing of the on-screen chemistry between him and Mizuno.

Tamblyn was bored but he wasn't angry; Kenji Sahara was both. Brooding over his brief and insignificant cameo in *Frankenstein*, Sahara was deeply disappointed with the thankless role of Dr. Yuzo Majida and understandably so. It wasn't that the part was small (it wasn't) or because the billing was bad (it wasn't, he received third billing and was actually listed first in the movie's trailer), but because the part was so poorly written as to be an embarrassment for any actor assigned to play it. In the film, Majida is simply a moron, constantly coming up with ideas that don't hold water; indeed, nobody in the film seems to take him seriously, least of all his scientific colleagues. When asked by the marine officers if the flesh sample he took off the boat proves Frankenstein was the culprit, all he can do is say he isn't certain (reminiscent of the apologetic scientists he played in both *Defense Force* and *Liquid People*). With some embarrassment, Majida duly takes the sample to Dr. Kita, who immediately makes a positive identification and promptly disregards him. Sahara's disinterest in his role comes across as plainly as did Tamblyn's, particularly in their first scene when he is sitting next to Tamblyn during the briefing with the press—as Stewart suggests the reporters question the sailor once again, Sahara is wearing a stern expression and is looking off to the side—an indication that though he was in the shot, he wasn't "in the scene" at all.

Caught between two unhappy male leads was Kumi Mizuno as Akemi, giving her role a sincerity and passion lacking from nearly everyone else's performance in the film. Even the silly plot and stilted dialogue does not faze her; when she tells Stewart that she alone can save Frankenstein and then subsequently dashes off to find him, her look of total conviction—and the longing in her voice—makes us believe she means what she says. Akemi is a woman of courage and vulnerability, boldly confronting a general in an attempt to make him believe that Sanda is harmless (while her two cohorts say nothing to support her) and her scene with the baby gargantua is genuinely affecting. Mizuno's incandescent sexually, her luminescent presence and her wonderful acting skills are the movie's three high points; otherwise *Sanda vs. Gairah* would be unbearable to watch. She literally carries the film.

Honda considered *Sanda vs. Gairah* to be one of his least-favorite films. "I found this one a little boring," he told Tucker, "I am glad people like it, but that film didn't really have much heart. I was mainly interested in the idea of cloning, which is a social issue now; you could make a great scientific drama about that." Honda's displeasure was twofold. Never a "hands-on" director (his easygoing nature prohibited him from interfering with his actors' unsatisfactory interpretations of their roles), Honda essentially left the acting portion of the picture to his actors in the same manner he that left the movie's set designs to his set designers, and the special effects to the effects people and so on. In other words, he trusted his associates to perform their tasks as ardently and efficiently as possible, giving them little in the way of advice or guidance.

When directing topflight actors such as Takeshi Shimura or

Akihiko Hirata, there was very little need for micro-direction, as such talented people were accomplished professionals willing to sincerely apply themselves to whatever project was being offered them. As such, whatever blame one imparts on Tamblyn for his dissatisfactory acting job must also be applied to Honda, and for the very same reason (when an actor and director *both* don't care for the project it's not a good thing). Both *Frankenstein* and *Sanda vs. Gairah* begin with terrific opening scenes, but unlike *Frankenstein*, Honda was not able to maintain this starting-gun momentum in *Sanda vs. Gairah*, and the movie bogs down almost immediately.

Honda's best work in the film is the pandemonium at the Haneda Airport; frantic and well-choreographed, with shots of terrified air-traffic controllers screaming and tables being tipped-over with food spilling everywhere, and stewardesses even dropping their purses in panic. As the terrified citizens flee for their lives—their screams answered by the screams of the gargantua—Honda films them dashing from every which way from many different directions, emphasizing the chaos.

When Stewart and the general find themselves on opposite sides of a large table debating whether or not to kill the gargantuas, the scene lacks any dramatic bite as the old "military vs. science" argument now seems to have lost its tincture. As in *Baran*, Honda clutters the film with numerous scenes of military preparedness; so much so that after a while one feels he is watching a recruiting advertisement. Honda's unique touches are rarely in evidence except for an occasional scene such when Akemi runs through a squad of soldiers heading in the opposite direction, and the appreciative nods from the audience watching the nightclub singer's performance (this was not the first time an entertainer came to an unhappy end in a Honda film). The live-action scenes are so ultimately pointless and uninteresting that, for the first time, the effects sequences truly dominate a Honda fantasy film.

To some, it seems inconceivable that the team of Kimura/Honda could have possibly had anything to do with the writing of this film, but there is one undeniable clue: The film's ending, one so hopeless and forlorn that it could justifiably be considered even more poignant than the one in *Matango*; the death of a woman's unfailing optimism. The severe sadness of this scene—painfully mirrored in the film's final close-up of Akemi silently closing her eyes in defeat and despair, knowing that all her efforts to keep Sanda alive have failed—unknowingly portended a real-life misfortune. Honda and Mizuno had just made their final film together.

By now, Honda was more-than discouraged with the direction

his career was taking, and while the co-American production of *Frankenstein* had gone smoothly, the director reflected years later that the collaboration on *Sanda vs. Gairah* had not been quite so smooth. There may have been another concern as well: Honda was now 55 years of age. "Ordinarily," he commented years later in *Godzilla and My Movie Life*, "50 years is the normal retirement age, but in my opinion, you can make movies at any age. After you reach retirement, you are contracted for each film, and Toho believed that utilizing a younger staff was more economical."

Honda's work on *Sanda vs. Gairah* was his worst since *Dogora*, and he now found himself in something of a quandary: Never particularly interested in directing films that stressed creatures over characters, he longed to return to the kind of sweet, sentimental pictures he was fond of directing that stressed human values. After making his wishes known to Tanaka, the producer—perhaps out of gratitude for his long-suffering employee—assigned Honda a non-genre film called *Will You Marry Me?* However, when *that* film was completed, there was no turning back for Honda, as he then returned to directing fantasy films; this time, for good.

SECTION VI:
"CHILD'S PLAY!"

KING KONG'S COUNTERATTACK (1967)
(KING KONG ESCAPES)

ALL MONSTERS ATTACK (1968)
(DESTROY ALL MONSTERS)

LATITUDE ZERO: THE GREAT MILITARY BATTLE (1969)
(LATITUDE ZERO)

GODZILLA, MINYA, GABARA: ALL GIANT
MONSTERS ATTACK (1969)
(GODZILLA'S REVENGE)

GEZORA, GANIME, KAMEBA: DECISIVE BATTLE!
GIANT MONSTERS OF THE SOUTH SEAS (1970)
(YOG, MONSTER FROM SPACE)

KING KONG'S COUNTERATTACK (1967)
(KINGU KONGU GYAKUSHU)
KING KONG ESCAPES

Cast & Credits

Film Register No. 14903
Release Date: July 22, 1967
Running Time: 104 minutes, 7 seconds

<u>Staff</u>: Producer: Tomoyuki Tanaka; Director: Ishiro Honda; Screenplay: Kaoru Mabuchi; Technical Advisor: Arthur Rankin; Cinematography: Hajime Koizumi; Art Director: Takeo Kita; Recording: Shoichi Yoshizawa; Lighting: Toshio Takashima; Music: Akita Ifukube; Sound Arrangement: Hisashi Shimonaga; Assistant Director: Ken Sano; Editor: Ryohei Fujii; Sound Effects: Sadamasa Nishimoto; Developing: Toyo Laboratory; Production Manager: Yasuaki Sakamoto; Still Photos: Jun Yamazaki; Special Effects Techniques: Director: Eiji Tsuburaya; Cinematography: Sokei Tomioka and Yoichi Manoda; Optical Cinematography: Yoshiyuki Tokumasa; Art Director: Yasuyuki Inoue.

<u>Cast</u>: Akira Takarada (Lt. Jiro Nomura); Mie Hama (Madame Piranha); Rhodes Reason (Commander Carl Nelson); Linda Miller (Lt. Susan Watson); Hideyo (Eisei) Amamoto (Dr. Huu "Who"); Yoshibumi Tajima, Sachio Sakai, Nadao Kirino, Toru Ibuki, Naoya Kusakawa, Susumu Kurobe, Kazuo Suzuki, Yasushi Matsubara, Haruo Suzuki (Huu's Henchmen); Ryuji Kita (Chief of Tokyo JSDF Headquarters); Ikio Sawamura (Elderly Mondo Island Native); Shoichi Hirose (*Explorer* Crewman); Andrew Hughes (UN Newspaper Reporter); Haruo Nakajima (King Kong/Man in Crowd at Shiba); Hiroshi Sekita (MechaniKong/ Defense Official); Kei Taguchi (Voice of Rhodes Reason); Akiko Yamato (Voice of Linda Miller); Ryu Kuse (Stuntman); Rinsaku Ogata, Yutaka Oka, Koichi Sato, Osman Yusef (*Explorer* Crewmen); Eizaburo Komatsu (Who Subordinate/*Explorer* Crewman); Hideo Shibuya (*Explorer* Crewman/Defense Official); Masaki Shinohara (*Explorer* Crewman and Crewman on Kong Recovery Ship!).

The Film

After completing *Will you Marry Me?*, Honda returned exclusively to the world of fantasy films, a return marked by a reunion with one of the monsters who had given him his greatest commercial success: King Kong. As a legendary figure, Kong was still going strong, particularly on American television, with a Rankin/Bass cartoon series produced in 1966. The US-based production company co-produced a new Kong film for Tanaka, providing additional funding in exchange for the exclusive worldwide distribution rights.

Kong was still a captive; when the giant ape wakes up in his cell in Huu's subterranean complex at the Pole, he finds himself in chains for the first time since his Broadway debut 34 years earlier. At one point, military helicopters fly above Kong's head—perhaps giving him bad memories of being transported to Mt. Fuji to fight Godzilla—but this time they merely fly away in a lovely shot (apparently there is no longer any Soma Berry juice left over from Kong's initial trip to Tokyo from five years earlier).

Takeshi Kimura was somehow persuaded to write a screenplay along lighter lines, although he had not been involved with *King Kong vs. Godzilla* (nor would he have wanted to have been), and he was certainly not the sort of writer keen on adding comedic elements into his films. As it happens, *King Kong's Counterattack* not only lacked the comedic flavor of *KKvG*, it is actually a much-more violent film. The film's greatest irony is that the acquisition of Element X—talked about throughout the entire film—is never ultimately possessed by anyone. Nelson refers to Dr. Huu as an old acquaintance, but their previous relationship is never expanded upon. Nelson, Nomura and Susan rendezvous with a Japanese PBY patrol plane piloted by two of Huu's men, and after boarding the craft, Nomura whispers to his colleagues that he doubts the pilots are really Japanese, although they certainly *look* Japanese, nor does he give them a reason for his suspicions and suggests no alternate plan.

Actor Rhodes Reason told *G-Fan* writer Brett Homenick that when he was first called in on the project, "It was rather a Saturday morning cartoon script as far as I was concerned" (not surprising, given the Rankin/Bass connection). Kimura's script falters when it tries to be "hip" with the times, betraying James Bond influences (although whether this was Kimura's doing is uncertain). The film is peppered with secret agent elements: Bondian dialogue (when Piranha offers Nelson a drink he laconically replies, "Sure, why not?"), the beautiful femme fatale, hidden communication devices, fantastic machines and a flamboyant villain (coincidentally, both Dr. Huu and Dr. No are diabolical Asians who wear black gloves and tinker with deadly radioactive materials). An even clearer tie-in with Bond occurs near the film's conclusion: When Huu's men make their last stand on the ship, firing away in a last-ditch effort to fend-off Kong, it bears a striking similarity to a scene near the end of 1965's *Thunderball*, when Emilio Largo's lackeys fire machine guns at their pursuers while perched on an immobile sea craft.

Since Tsuburaya's inspiration to work in the field of special effects came after seeing the original *King Kong*, it seems he felt indebted to pay a tribute the film that had meant so much to him by recreating Kong's battle with the Tyrannosaurus (or Allosaurus) by having his Kong fight a Gorosaurus—arguably the most-beautifully designed monster costume in the entire Toho universe. In paying his respects to O'Brien's *magnum opus* however, Tsuburaya confirmed the limitations of using costumed actors as monsters in a battle that is poorly-choreographed, clumsy, unconvincing (and even silly when Kong breaks the dinosaur's jaws to the accompaniment of a creaking noise, with frothy soap bubbles emanating from the dead reptile's mouth). Kong's fight with the snake is even less impressive, despite Nakajima's frenetic attempts to give the lifeless prop a sense of life; on the other hand, Kong's melee with MechaniKong is brief and well choreographed, while the battle on the Tokyo Tower is very effective—one feels the robot is really pummeling the ape. The scene where Huu's helicopters abduct Kong is the best scene in the movie, filmed with various pans, interesting camera angles, crisp editing and helped enormously by Nakajima's convincing performance as Kong.

Ryohei Fujii's editing was another indication of Honda's interest in the project, as there are considerably more edits and camera movements in *Counterattack* than in the director's recent films. In the scene when Piranha is conversing with Huu on her hidden transmitter, Honda cleverly superimposes inserts of the actors, giving the impression that they are actually seeing each other, and during their conversation in Huu's suite, Honda films the actors looking almost directly into the camera in an effort to involve the audience in their discussion. However, there is a missing ending to the scene when Piranha implores Huu to not send MechaniKong after Kong, fearing that a worldwide scandal might expose her country's clandestine intentions. Huu then suggests they talk it over, but the scene ends without a resolution (whatever was said evidentially did not please Piranha, as the very next time we see her she is freeing Nelson).

There were flaws in the camerawork as well, including the occasional close-up with slightly out-of-focus actors. As it turned out, *Counterattack* was the last film Koizumi would shoot for Honda in an association that went all the way back to 1957's *Defense Force*, covering a remarkable string of 16 consecutive fantasy films, an uninterrupted association unparalleled in the realm of fantasy films. The breakup is significant because in many ways the most-trusted collaboration on a movie set is the one between a director and his cinematographer, and the trust Honda had with Koizumi had been total and complete. As to why Honda decided to dispense with Koizumi's services from that point on has never been adequately explained, although the official Toho position has been that the studio wanted Honda to give other cameramen experience; however, it seems likely that Honda had been disappointed in Koizumi's recent work and—feeling he had reached the point where he felt it was necessary to replace him—simply did not request the cinematographer's services any longer.

Takeo Kita's sets are impressive, such as the interiors of Huu's complex (which look massive, solidly built and expensive) as well as Madame Piranha's attractive suite. The interiors of the *Explorer* have the proper look of functional military hardware, but, as was typical of Kita's control panels, there is not a single identifying label for any of the buttons, lights or switches.

Akira Ifukube's score for *Counterattack* begins with an amplified strumming of a pianoforte's strings, followed by a pounding tom-tom drum so as to give the music a native flavor. Strings and a plaintive oboe take over as woodwinds play in a minor key, concluding with subdued brass (this cue contains some of Ifukube's "Infant Island" music from *Mothra vs. Godzilla*). "The Base at the North Pole" starts with pounding drums as the camera zooms in on a drawing of a ferocious Kong, followed by an emotive clarinet solo backed by shimmering strings describing the bleak and lonely base at the North Pole; then, an impressive five-note descending motif on strings merges with sinister brass as MechaniKong is introduced.

One of Ifukube's more-impressive pieces is "Starting up MechaniKong," beginning with brass, pounding piano and a gong before gliding into blaring trumpets as relentless drums are pounded and trombones play in a descending pattern as if echoing Huu's diabolical laughter. Gong, ominous brass and strings play a counter-melody as the robot starts its operation, with shrieking trumpets and flutes adding to the excitement. "The Appearance of King Kong" was a variation on the King Ghidorah theme, opening with two ascending notes on trombones joined by shrieking trumpets (for some reason, Ifukube decided not to recycle his earlier Kong theme music from *KKvG*).

"King Kong vs. Gorosaurus" was essentially a ten-note theme for blaring trumpets ending with a four-note theme on horns (heard as early on as *War in Space* when the astronauts are nearing the Natalian Moon Base). The most-moving piece is easily "Kong and Susan," beginning with a mournful nine-note melody played on violins and augmented with a gentle, repeated single note played on a softly-tapping piano key. Muted drums follow (mirroring Kong's beating heart) as a haunting oboe enters playing a lovely 21-note theme gradually descending before being followed by faint drums. Then, lyrical violins enter, playing a rising and falling eight-note theme as drums complete the musical phrase, with horns playing a subdued six-note theme emphasizing the majestic Kong's deflated dreams (this sensitive music gives the potentially-ludicrous premise a touching credibility).

The part of Commander Carl Nelson—a leader of men, strong and decisive yet also tenderhearted and thoughtful—was essayed by B-movie leading-man Rhodes Reason. Physically imposing and blessed with a deep voice, his James Bond-inspired scene with Madame Piranha suggested that he may indeed have made a very credible 007. Lieutenant Susan Watson—the first American actress to star in a Honda film—was played by Linda Miller, a petite young lass with great legs who was living in Japan and making a nice living as a photographers' model. Watson is a capable physician, and having a female as the ship's medical officer was a bit of a novelty and a sign of changing times; however, she ultimately becomes the stereotypically-helpless female who must be rescued and protected by the males in her life (one 60-feet tall). Despite the actress's lack of experience (*Counterattack* would be one of only two films in which she would ever appear) Miller gave an excellent performance in a physically demanding and complex role of a woman whose initial fear of Kong turns into sympathy and adoration.

Akira Takarada played Susan's *paramour*, Lieutenant Commander Jiro Nomura, and although Takarada was an accomplished actor capable of great range, his abilities were often discounted due to his handsome and gentlemanly manner; in spite of this, he seems strangely uncomfortable in his love scenes with Miller. Mie Hama—who followed in the footsteps of Fay Wray as Kong's love interest in *KKvG*—plays the mysterious Madame Piranha and gave a competent performance as the lethal but vulnerable enemy agent (and, as typical of Honda's villains, she and Dr. Huu are not exactly on the same page). She was not however terribly convincing as a vamp, due mainly to her wholesome "girl-next-door" looks, despite the various Eastern Bloc outfits she dresses-up in (Piranha's origins are never disclosed, but the implication is that she hails from a Communist nation, although her obvious Asian ancestry narrows the field down a bit; when Nelson tries to find out where she comes from, he rattles off the names of various nations then with Communistic ties, telling her: "You're *not* Japanese." As it happened, actress Hama was actually born in Tokyo).

The film's most-interesting character was the larger-than-life Dr. Huu ("Who" in the U.S. version), played with smirking malevolence by Eisei Amamoto. The actor had certainly paid his dues as he had previously appeared in a number of "blink-and-you'll-miss-him" parts: A drunk in *Gorath*, a Mushroom Man in *Matango*, a sassy safecracker in *Dogora* and a grim-faced butler in *Three Giant Monsters*. Amamoto did have a showy part as the High Priest in *Submarine Warship*, but it was his Dr. Huu that would become the actor's signature role. Dr. Huu was one of the most flamboyant of all of Honda's villains, as he is not only mad as a hatter, but is also a common thief, a cold-blooded killer, an engineer, an inventor, a big-game hunter (of *really* big game), a hypnotist, a military tactician and skilled in the martial arts (as with all great screen villains, Huu has a wonderful sense of humor, always laughing at his own jokes). Undeservedly receiving fifth billing, Amamoto is the star of the show.

King Kong's Counterattack's pacing is excellent and overall a vast improvement over Honda's bland handling of *Sanda vs. Gairah*. The director added his usual little touches: Nelson nodding his head in understanding when hearing the dieing native's last words, Susan's shocked reaction in Kong's hand upon seeing MechaniKong arriving in Tokyo and a wonderfully-inventive shot of Susan screaming "Kong!" while in the grasp of the robot as the landscape blurs in the background. Honda's staging of the panic scenes in Tokyo are up to his usually fine standards, with numerous quick edits of military personnel and civilians reacting to Kong's battle with the robot, and Susan's predicament as she hangs onto the Tokyo Tower for dear life.

Another beautifully-handled scene is the pandemonium onboard Huu's ship as Kong swims toward it, with crazy camera angles, rapid cuts, frantic action and actors being washed away (although when the mortally-wounded native dies with his eyes staring vacantly into the camera, it is an unsettling moment). When Kong catches Susan after she had been dropped by MechaniKong, she sags her head as she slips into unconsciousness in precisely the same manner as had Akemi in the grasp of Gairah a year earlier.

On the other hand, the seduction scene between Piranha and Nelson is one of Honda's worst; awkward and not in the bit least interesting, partly due to the dialogue (why is she planning to double-cross Huu?) but also due to the fact that Hama simply lacked the poisonous allure so necessary for her part. And while Jiro's rescue of Susan from the Tokyo Tower (trimmed down in the U.S. version resulting in a number of jarring edits to the music) was elaborately planned and performed, it goes on for far-too-long, drawing attention away from the grander struggle at the tip of the Tower between the two Kongs (when the crew of the *Explorer* arrives at the island and comes upon the shrapnel remains of Huu's ether bombs, actor Osman Yusuf—playing one of the crewmen—is first to arrive on the scene. After he stops and stands, he looks down and notices he is off his mark, doing a nice little jig so as to place himself in the proper position for the remainder of the shot).

Throughout the entire film it is obvious that *King Kong's Counterattack* is intended as a diverting experience, fun for kids, pleasing for adults, and overall enjoyable to watch; but during the scene when Kong attacks Huu's ship, Huu is seen sneaking away while his minions empty their ammunition at Kong, so it is presumed he will live to fight another day. Instead, Honda films a horrific shot of Huu gargling up blood as he is slowly crushed to death by his control console. It certainly stands out as the grimmest and bloodiest death in any Honda film, even more so in this case, since Huu's gory and grisly demise is completely out-of-place in a movie that is fundamentally family faire (incredibly, the film received a "G" Rating when it was shown in America, despite the fact Huu's sickening death was retained).

Why Honda ever insisted on ending *Counterattack* on such a ghastly note is difficult to fathom, as it was so atypical of the director's usual trend toward good taste; perhaps he was determined to end the film with a dramatic flourish or was subconsciously advertising his own frustration and disgust in having to direct yet another senseless monster movie with little emotional substance and considerable violence: Two deaths by gunfire, one from internal injuries and two separate scenes where a man grabs hold of a woman's face. There was however one moment that beautifully characterizes the glory of the genre and it happens just after MechaniKong has slid down into the crevice at the North Pole to begin his search for Element X: As the machine stands at the ready, it suddenly raises its arms and shrieks triumphantly. Why the robot would be instructed to perform such a frivolous act is open to question—it is not the sort of thing Huu would have permitted—yet the moment is entirely indicative of the spirited and free-wheeling nature of Toho's fantasy films.

Honda was fascinated with the film's central theme, not the pursuit of Element X, but Kong's pursuit of Susan; When interviewed about the film by a French fantasy film journal shortly after the movie was completed, Honda denied that there was any kind of serious love affair between the two, insisting their relationship was more along the lines of a deep friendship before adding with a smile: "After all, if Kong and Susan really *do* fall in love, then I can make a sequel, right?"

Honda had directed his final film to star King Kong, but the King of the Monsters was still in his future, as Tanaka requested he helm the next one in the series. Honda's interest in the project may have been stirred by two rumors: The first that the film would set an all-time monster attendance record and another that the film might be the last in the series. By this time Honda knew better than to get his hopes up; he may have had those same hopes tinged with the unhappy possibility that, if Toho stopped making Godzilla movies, *he* might stop making Godzilla movies. In any event, it all became a mute point that whatever happened from this point on, Honda and Godzilla were a team—seemingly, forever.

ALL MONSTERS ATTACK (1968)
(KAIJU SOSHINGEKI)
DESTROY ALL MONSTERS

The Film

Film Register No. 15240
Release Date: August 1, 1968
Running Time: 89 Minutes

Staff: Producer: Tomoyuki Tanaka; Director: Ishiro Honda; Screenplay: Kaoru Mabuchi (Takeshi Kimura), Ishiro Honda; Director of Photography: Taiichi Kankura; Art Director: Takeo Kita; Sound Recording: Shoichi Yoshizawa; Lighting: Kiyohisa Hirano; Music: Akira Ifukube; Sound Arrangement: Hisashi Shimonaga; Assistant Director: Seiji Tani; Editor: Ryohei Fujii; Sound Effects: Sadamasa Nishimoto; Production Manager: Yasuaki Sakamoto; Still Photographer: Jun Yamazaki; Special Effects Techniques: Supervisor: Eiji Tsuburaya; Director: Teisho (Sadamasa) Arikawa; Assistant Director: Teruyoshi Nakano; Directors of Photography: Sokei (Mototaka) Tomioka, Yoichi Manoda.

Cast: Akira Kubo (Captain Katsuo Yamabe); Yukiko Kobayashi (Kyoko Manabe); Kyoko Ai (Kilaak Leader); Jun Tazaki (Dr. Yoshida); Yoshio Tsuchiya (Dr. Otani); Kenji Sahara (Chief of Moon Base Nishikawa); Susumu Kurobe (WSA Control Center Technician Shin Kuroiwa); Hisaya Ito (Major Tada); Yoshifumi Tajima (Defense Headquarters Commander General Sugiyama); Nadao Kirino, Naoya Kusakawa, Kamayuki Tsubono (International Secret Police); Ikio Sawamura (Elderly Farmer); Chotaro Togin *(SY-3* Crewman Okada); Ken (Kenzo) Echigo, Yutaka Sada (Mountain Area Policemen); Kenichiro Maruyama (Moon Base Engineer); Toru Ibuki (WSACC Technician Tetsuo Ise); Minoru Ito (WSACC Technician Minoru Kudo); Hideo Shibuya, Yutaka Oka, Keiichiro Katsumoto (Reporters); Yoshio Katsube (U.N. Scientist); Tadashi Okabe (TV News Reporter).

The Film

For the first time in three years Ishiro Honda found himself again directing a Godzilla and teamed-up with screenwriter Takeshi Kimura, but was working for the first time with someone other than Tsuburaya on the special effects: Tsuburaya's longtime cinematographer, Teisho (Sadamasa) Arikawa.

It was Honda's hope to work-in an environmental theme in *All Monsters Attack*, telling David Milner:

> Originally, the idea was just to show all of the monsters. Then, we started thinking about undersea farming. Eventually, these two ideas were combined and the idea for an island, on which all of the monsters had been collected for scientific study, was born. You see, we imagined that undersea farming would be required to feed all of the monsters. I really wanted to explore the idea of undersea farming in the film, but because of the financial situation, it was not allowed. Only the idea of an island of monsters survived.

The movie borrowed a number of elements from Honda's earlier science-fiction films; extraterrestrials controlling the Earth's monsters was not new (having been done previously in *War of the Monsters*), with the concept of aliens manipulating humans to do their bidding going back as far as *War in Space*, even with the same actor (Yoshio Tsuchiya) playing the man being controlled. The saucers in *All Monsters Attack* were reminiscent of those used in *War of the Monsters* and General Sugiyama's idea to use cold as a weapon against the Kilaaks echoed *Submarine Warship's* Zero Cannon. Having the aliens hailing from a planet (or satellite) between Mars and Jupiter was a plot element harkening back to *The Defense Force of the Earth*; although the Mysterians had a low-resistance to heat and not to the cold as do the Kilaaks.

Another element lifted from *Defense Force* was having an alien base reveal itself by air rushing-up from underneath the ground, and while there were no female Mysterians, the Kilaaks have no males. In keeping with a theme earlier expounded upon in several films, although the Kilaaks are an advanced and powerful race, they are easily destroyed by a relatively small number of saboteurs. *All Monsters Attack* has a remarkably linear screenplay; after the gassing of the Monster Land employees, every sequence that follows is in direct response to the previous one as there is no parallel story or subplot of any kind. The movie gets off to a rousing start; scarcely has it begun when the Ogasawara staff is overcome by gas fumes and there is very little wasted footage in the film (although the scene when Yamabe, Ogata and Tada encounter the aliens in the cave is one of those illogical and pointless scenes than poses more questions than it answers, adding nothing to the film other than to pad the running time).

The final skirmish between the beasts—occurring 75 minutes into the 89-minute film—includes no less than 11 monsters with nine actively participating in the battle. Godzilla, Gorosaurus and Anguirus fight the brunt of the battle, with an assist from Radon, Mothra and Kumonga, while the Monster Land personnel manipulating the Earth's monsters keep Baragon, Manda and Baran on the sidelines, presumably to be used if any of the frontline monsters faltered (while keeping Manda and Baran in the background made sense due to their limited capabilities, Baragon's tunneling and leaping ability—to say nothing of its fire-breathing ray—would have been valuable assets in fighting King Ghidorah). The four and a-half minute battle between the beasts is something of a disappointment as the Kilaaks send in the Space Monster to face literally 10-1 odds. Since it is obvious early on that Ghidorah cannot possibly win, the fight lacks any drama or suspense (ironically, the alien spacecraft called the "Burning Monster" was a potent weapon in and of itself; impervious to the Earth's monsters a fleet of such craft could have caused greater carnage than a dozen King Ghidorahs).

Arikawa's work on *All Monsters Attack*, although acceptable, was not up to the standards previously set by Tsuburaya. Some of it is slipshod: When the fog barrier is used to keep Mothra on the island, it is first seen as an orange mist, then red in a subsequent shot. When Godzilla sets fire to a ship at sea, the vessel comes to an abrupt stop— an impossibility—but the mechanism at the ship's bow used to churn the water is still running. The dolphin caught by Radon is stiff and unconvincing, and when Radon flies over Moscow, the buildings do not blow away as in *Radon* but simply explode. When Godzilla uses its atomic ray on the United Nations, Nakajima bent down so low that the optical animation had to be curved upwards so as to reach the exploding section of the building.

Several camera angles were impressive (not surprising as this was always Arikawa's *forte*) such as an overhead shot seen from behind a helicopter showing the army closing in on Godzilla, and another elevated shot seen shortly thereafter from behind Godzilla as it fends off rockets (one of the best shots in the entire series shows Manda destroying a monorail track in the foreground while Godzilla simultaneously blows up a gasoline refinery in the background). Arikawa's ground-level pan of a desolated Tokyo recalls Tsuburaya's similar pan from *Godzilla*, and when the *SY-3* takes off from the Moon after stealing the Kilaak remote control, a high-angle shot shows explosions detonating in the crater below. The wire works were occasionally visible and although the miniature Tokyo set itself is very impressive, it somehow lacks the convincing detail that made Tsuburaya's work so unique.

Cinematographer Taiichi Kankura was making his first film for Honda and his work is adequate, although not a noticeable improvement over the photography of Hajime Koizumi (happily, Kankura managed to keep all of the actors in focus throughout the entire film). Kankura's color photography was outstanding; the film is filled with bright, vibrant colors from the astronauts' yellow outfits to the dress blues of the Defense Force personnel. One inventive shot occurs during Dr. Otani's interrogation, when the heads of all three actors are framed within the circular panels of a hotel room's partition. There were other creative shots, such as when Kyoko and Yamabe run into the gas fumes, the eerie introduction of the Kilaak Queen and an effective two-shot of a horrified Yoshido and a sickened Yamabe looking down at the dead Otani. Honda filmed more than his usual amount of close-ups of actors looking directly into the camera: A determined Yamabe, a saddened Kyoko and a confident Kilaak Queen. The director also creatively uses a rack-focus shot of police escorting fleeing citizens in the background with a close-up of a smiling Kyoko as she enters the shot.

Ryohei Fujii's editing was very inventive as after Otani jumps out of the hotel window, there is a cut to a reaction shot of Yoshido and Yamabe, the subsequent shot showing Otani's dead body lying on the sand as the astronaut and doctor arrive on the scene. Typical of Honda's use of rapid cuts and close-ups occurs when Yamabe tries to sever the Remote Control Unit, with the director filling the frame with intense close-ups of the astronauts' twitching and sweating faces intercut with shots of the laser beam hitting the stand and the wavering Control Unit.

One particularly effective series of edits occurs just after the burning monster has appeared: After a shot of the distorted viewing screen, Honda cuts to a medium shot of the Defense Force personnel while zooming in on Sugiyama and Tada looking up to see an unsettling close-up of the smiling Kilaak Queen, which then turns into shock when she hears Godzilla's roar; then, a medium shot of the Defense Force personnel (with Yamabe entering the frame from underneath as he utters Godzilla's name) before cutting back to a close-up of a now-worried Kilaak Queen staring into the camera as the picture becomes distorted.

Set designer Takeo Kita seemed to finally be getting with the program (for one thing, the large reel-to-reel computer tapes in the Control Room are now spinning in the same direction); the designer even taking the time to label some of the control panel switches in the rocket ship (regrettably, these labels were crudely applied and even misspelled; one indicator labeled in English reads "Turgin temp" when it was probably meant to read "Turbine Temp"). The sets are impressively expansive, but once again belay their low-budget trappings; as the astronauts prepare to take-off after the gun battle with the base personnel on Monster Land, a crewmember is climbing a ladder wobbling under his weight.

By now composer Akira Ifukube had settled into a predictable pattern of incorporating a modicum of original melodies extensively supplemented by repeated bits of music used in earlier films, and *All Monsters Attack* is no exception. The "Main Title" music is introduced with a gentle oboe accompanied by a softly-tapping gong, joined by a quivering organ key and a crashing cymbal; thundering tubas and shrieking trumpets follow and the theme ends with a resounding gong and a sustained note on strings portending an unseen danger. Ifukube's "Title Credits" music begins with a military-style drum rift, strident strings and confident trumpets segueing into an optimistic string section playing in short, rapid strokes as trumpets blare in the background, before ending with shimmering violins (the music has the sound and feel of a military advance and an unwavering, determined optimism).

"Monster Land" is musically portrayed with a gentle piano and subtle gong, answered by impressive brass as the monsters are being introduced while a muted, *staccato* piece played on woodwinds mimics the everyday business of the beasts as they traverse around the island. "Unusual Changes on Monster Island" was an impressive number heralded by tinkling piano and shimmering violins playing in an agitated manner as the danger intensifies; the ubiquitous gong, organ and pounding piano are accompanied by low brass playing in a descending four-note motif (signifying a sinister element) and the selection ends with trembling strings (indicating an uncertain resolution).

The scene when Godzilla, Radon, Manda and Mothra attack Tokyo is scored with "The Missile War to Protect the Capital," essentially King Ghidorah's theme from his 1964 film appearance, with minor alterations (ironically, this same music comprises the majority of the score for "Major Battle at Fuji," a battle that the Three-Headed Monster is destined to loose). Ifukube's short pieces are always absorbing, such as when the *SY-3* is descending through the clouds to land on Monster Land, depicted with short bowstrings and drums indicating determination, with a tapping cymbal and sustained violins adding an element of mystery. Ifukube rarely employed choir music in his monster scores, but in *All Monsters Attack*, the composer used this element to color the scenes with the Kilaaks, introduced by a single note tapped on a vibraphone and a splendid use of the theremin, as well as muted oboe and electone to lend the aliens an air of mysterious dread.

Akira Kubo essays the role of the heroic Captain Katsuo Yamabe as a daring, bold and decisive leader who perseveres in the face of enormous odds. Yamabe is not only fearless, but is also unstinting in his determination to defeat the Kilaaks, an alien race he hates with such apparent passion that on at least one occasion his impetuous behavior borders on insubordination. The astronaut gets so worked up about the Kilaaks that he feels compelled to rip his sister's earrings out of her ears, suspecting they might contain the Kilaaks' remote control device (of course, he could simply have *asked* Kyoko to remove her earrings—but that naturally would not have been quite so dramatic). Honda lent little character touches to Yamabe to make him more than a one-dimensional hero, such as a certain squeamishness the astronaut displays when gazing down at the dead Otani on the beach or when a scalpel is employed to remove Otani's remote control device from behind his ear.

Dr. Yoshido was played by Jun Tazaki in his final performance in a Honda film with considerably more vitality than he had in *War of the Monsters*. Newcomer Yukiko Kobayashi (Kyoko Yamabe) was an actress whose exotic features gave her a mysterious quality, and she did a particularly nice job in the scene where she regains consciousness after Yamabe has freed her from the Kilaaks' control. Yoshio Tsuchiya's role as Dr. Otani was all-too-brief, returning as it did the actor to his familiar role of a man weakened by outside forces who turns against humanity. Despite the relatively minor part, Tsuchiya endows it with his usual charisma; in fact, Otani is arguably the film's most-interesting character; after he dies the film looses a considerable amount of steam.

Kyoko Ai played the part of the Kilaak queen with the usual arrogant confidence that had long been the hallmark of Honda's alien commanders. A beautiful woman with a creepy countenance, Ai was both fascinating and frightening to watch; even so, Honda gives her a helpless quality when she watches Godzilla destroys her headquarters. Tried-and-true performers such as Kenji Sahara (as Moon Base Commander Nishikawa) and Ikio Sawamura (the old farmer who for some reason is collecting rocks by the river) made brief appearances, but two minor yet recognizable characters were bidding the Honda series *adieu*; one was perennial newspaper reporter Koji Uno (whose one-line appearance warranted a nice close-up) as well as newscaster Saburo Iketani, who went as far back as 1954, when he played one of the journalists reporting the deployment of the Oxygen Destroyer in the original *Godzilla*.

Honda's introduction of the Kilaak Queen was subtly artistic as the woman materializes out of the mist with the director utilizing a considerable amount of close-ups to emphasize her intimate threat to humanity. One of Honda's best moments takes place when the Queen faces her defeat—the director tracks his camera around with flashing lights—until, with a look of resignation, she sinks out of sight (dying as did the Empress of Mu with a certain dignity). However, the manhandling Kyoko receives from her brother was another unnecessarily brutal moment (incredibly, none of the men watching the attack lift a finger to help her as Yoshido keeps them back); a brutality matched only by the slaughter of King Ghidorah.

One odd piece of directing is seen when the Defense Forces take flight upon Godzilla's arrival at Mount Iso; Honda places the camera at ground level, then has his principal actors enter the frame as they run sideways facing the camera. As usual, Honda inserted little touches such as when Yamabe and Yoshido simultaneously approach the doctor from behind as he holds up Otani's "hearing aid," and a brief bit of dialogue when a policeman asks his farmer friend how his astronaut son is doing on the Moon; another example of Honda inserting human comfort and warmth to reassuringly counter monstrous events. While not by any means a bad film, *All Monsters Attack* is not a terribly great one either; though packed with a great deal of visual action—gunfights, trips to the Moon, battles with aliens and monsters in a free-for-all fight amongst themselves—it is a curiously listless film, overly ambitious but emotionally empty.

The film hints at hope and perseverance, yet paradoxically there is now a distinct note of pessimism concerning the United Nations. There was a time when Honda had envisioned the U.N. as embodying the world's greatest hope for salvation and survival, but by the end of the 1960s, the director had seemingly lost faith in the institution; the world was still in turmoil and little progress had been made achieving global harmony. It was not so surprising then that after Godzilla surfaces in New York City, the first thing it does is destroy the United Nations.

All Monsters Attack was not the panacea to the Godzilla series that

Tanaka hoped it would be as audience attendance continued to decline. Earlier box-office receipts seemed to indicate that neither adults nor teenagers were terribly interested in the giant reptile's travails any longer, even if a film was touted as the last one in the series. But for Honda, *All Monsters Attack* had set another unpleasant precedent: For the first time in his career, the film he was making was all about aliens and the monsters, with humans little more than concerned spectators. As Tanaka mulled the future of the series over, he handed over to Honda another film assignment, a wild and woolly affair that resulted in the strangest film he would ever direct.

LATITUDE ZERO: THE GREAT
MILITARY BATTLE (1969)
(IDO ZERO DAISAKUSEN)
LATITUDE ZERO

Cast & Credits

Film Register No. 15644
Release Date: July 26, 1969
Running Time: 89 minutes, six seconds

Staff: Producer: Tomoyuki Tanaka; Director: Ishiro Honda; Screenplay: Shinichi Sekizawa and Ted Sherdeman; Cinematography: Taiichi Kankura; Art Director: Takeo Kita; Recording: Masao Fujiyoshi; Lighting: Kiichi Onda; Mixing: Hisashi Shimonaga; Music: Akira Ifukube; Soundtrack: Toshiba Records; Assistant Director: Seiji Tani; Editor: Ume Takeda; Sound Effects: Sadamasa Nishimoto; Developing: Far East Laboratory; Production Manager: Yasuaki Sakamoto; Still Photos: Jun Yamazaki; Special Effects: Director: Eiji Tsuburaya; Cinematography: Sokei Tomioka and Yoichi Manoda; Optical Cinematography: Yoshiyuki Tokumasa; Art Director: Yasuyuki Inoue; Lighting: Fumiyoshi Hara; Wire Works: Fumio Nakadai; Matte Processing: Hiroshi Mukoyama; Assistant Director: Teruyoshi Nakano; Still Photos: Takashi Nakao.

Cast: Akira Takarada (Dr. Ken Tashiro); Joseph Cotton (Captain Craig McKenzie/Commander Glen McKenzie); Cesar Romero (Malic/Lt. Hastings); Masumi Okada (Dr. Jules Masson); Richard Jaeckel (Perry Lawton); Mari Nakayama (Tsuruko Okada); Patricia Medina (Lucretia); Akihiko Hirata (Dr. Sugata); Tetsu Nakamura (Dr. Shogoro Okada); Kin Omae (Kobo); Linda Haynes (Dr. Anne Barton); Hikaru Kuroki (Kroiga); Susumu Kurobe (*Black Shark's* First Mate); Yasuhiko Saijo (Recovery Ship Crewman); Haruo Nakajima (Griffon/Giant Rat(Mouse?)/Bat Creature/Lion); Hiroshi Sekita (*Fuji* Crewman).

The Film

Latitude Zero was written by Ted Sherdeman, author of a popular radio adventure series in the 1940s by the same name. Warren Lewis contributed additional dialogue, and between them, the two men wrote the dialogue for the scenes with the English-speaking actors, with the balance of the screenplay falling into the hands of Honda regular Sekizawa who wrote the action sequences, proliferating the scenario with his usual James-Bondian touches. The incredible weapons, the deadly women and outlandish villains are again present and accounted for, and there are once again direct references to previous Bond films: Just as the evil Dr. No looked out at his large undersea aquarium, so does Malic, and in *From Russia With Love*, Blofeld witnesses a fight to the death between two Siamese Fighting Fish just as Malic watches two mortal eels in close combat.

The ending of *Latitude Zero* is perhaps the most-disappointing of all of Honda's films: Lawton meets the descendents of not only McKenzie but also Malic; oddly, no one seems overly concerned about the disappearance of Drs. Tashiro and Masson. What is even more difficult to understand is why the Japanese captain looks exactly like Dr. Tashiro, since Tashiro did not have a descendent on Latitude Zero. Having doubles for Malic and McKenzie was intended to show proof that LZ really existed, but why Tashiro has a double on deck is something else altogether, unless he simply neglected to mention that he had a twin brother with a moustache serving in the Japanese navy.

Just as in *King Kong's Counterattack*, Sekizawa's script implies a history between the two main adversaries, but again goes no further to explain why Malic hates McKenzie with such relish. There is an interesting subplot hinting toward a previous relationship between Kroiga and Malic—a relationship Lucrecia clearly resents—but the specifics are never explored. Both Malic and McKenzie are eccentric opposites, with Blood Rock the antithesis of the squeaky-clean LZ. Comprised mostly of rocks and sheer cliffs, there does not seem to be much of a population on Blood Rock; however, just as the island blows up, keen eyes can spot what appears to be housing units on the sheer cliffs. As to why Kroiga, once changed into a griffin, never attacks McKenzie is a question Malic was not the only one wondering about, as many viewers wonder about the same thing, as the beast seems content merely to rest on the rocks. As it turns out, Kroiga was more interested in killing Malic than McKenzie, but if so, why didn't she kill Malic the moment she was transformed into a griffin?

While there are effects works in *Latitude Zero*, calling them "special" would be a generous description. Fumio Nakadai—now working as head of the effects department—did what little he could with what he had, such as several effective overhead shots of the *Black Shark* being pelted by the landslide, with the griffin waving its wings clearly visible on the sub's hull. The sequence ends with a fine elevated tracking shot of the island blowing up (as if being viewed from the *Alpha*'s perspective), but the establishing shot of the city of Latitude Zero was flat, uninspired and lacking in the kind of details and convincing perspective Tsuburaya was so capable of, such as having miniature vehicles skirting about.

The scenes taking place in the bathysphere, on Latitude Zero and the running battle between the *Alpha* and the *Black Shark* are acceptable, but all bets are off once we get to Blood Rock; Malic's home is comprised of little more than dull and unconvincing matte paintings of cliffs and boulders, and while Latitude Zero is free from exotic beasts, Blood Rock is crawling with critters. Regrettably, the giant rodents—to say nothing of the pathetic condor and lion—rank as the most unconvincing animal costumes ever to populate a film. The griffin was so hard to manipulate that Honda was forced to "cheat," filming the costume from behind in a close-up as it "walked" toward Malic (in fact one of the worst moments in the film occurs when the griffin flies away; it did not look very lifelike, and when Malic laughs off-screen it seems as if he is laughing at the crude effect. Calling Malic's creation a "griffin" is a bit of a stretch, as an authentic griffin has the head, forepart and wings of an eagle and the body, hind legs and tail of a lion. Interestingly, Ray Harryhausen used a more-accurate representation of a griffin in *The Golden Voyage of Sinbad* four years later).

Cinematographer Taiichi Kankura did a capable job of filming *Latitude Zero*, but at best it represented an impassioned detachment on the part of the director as to what was being filmed. Kankura did manage some interesting images such as filming Malic from a low-angle to accentuate the villain's larger-than-life personality. In one of the few creative shots in the film, Honda tracks-in on Lawton as he leans in to tell McKenzie: "But I'm not *sick*. You're all so hung-up on exploring space, you're not even interested in learning about a miracle that exists on our own *planet!*" and shortly thereafter when Hastings reads aloud a telegram sent to Lawton from a New York bank, informing the photographer that 600 karats of diamonds sent by an unknown party wait for him upon his arrival; Honda inserts a zoom-in on a discouraged Lawton sitting on his sickbay bunk, unaware of his impending wealth.

The interiors of the bathysphere and the *Alpha* were characteristic of Takeo Kita's often mediocre sets, all sequential lighting and multiple switches, without any identifying labels (when McKenzie as his team climb up a ladder in preparation for their assault on Blood Rock, once again a ladder shakes as if it could collapse at any moment). Kita's "Great Hall" is simply a vast and open space, while Malic's hideaway shows a bit more imagination; the madman seems to have an affinity for bats (both big and little) and parades around like some bizarre animal lover, sitting in chairs covered with hides. He also has a parrot for a pet and walks through archways outlined in eagle profiles, while the walls of his Observation Gallery are covered in serpentine drawings

Ume Takeda's editing is very proficient: After Lawton has begun filling his tobacco pouch with diamonds, we see Malic's amused reaction in a close-up, and when we cut back to the pouch, it is now overflowing with the precious gems. As McKenzie zaps the steel door with his laser, Takeda alternates rapid close-ups of Malic and the beam cutting through the door, and after McKenzie hauls out the first of the rocket belts, we next see a close-up of the belt already strapped-on the back of one of McKenzie's team.

Kiichi Ichida and Linda Glazman designed the film's elaborate costumes, which still manage to belay their 1960's origins (when we first see Anne Barton she is dressed like a "go-go" dancer in a Vegas nightclub). The golden clothing worn by the citizens of Latitude Zero mirror the battle gear the rescuers wear, but the addition of the goggles and caps was to give the costumes an anachronistic look. Malic is dressed like a medieval superhero, whereas McKenzie's costumes are unconventional to say the least; the last of which—a pinstriped number with a jaunty cap—would be more-appropriate for an ice cream vendor on Mars.

Akira Ifukube's score for *Latitude Zero* was unlike anything he had previously written for Honda; while there are the usual bellicose touches for dramatic moments, the music is generally quite subdued (a pattern which would continue in Ifukube's few remaining scores for the director). For example, his "Main Title" theme is slow-paced and somber, beginning with French horns and softly tapping drums hinting at an island motif. Violins are followed by woodwinds, then trumpets play a six-note theme as if in a salute to past glories; the piece segues into "Diving Bell" as a piano gradually plays in lower octaves mirroring the bathysphere's descent. Trumpets play in *staccato* measures, with pounding piano keys and low brass indicating the danger of "The Undersea Volcano."

Dreamy and atmospheric music colors "The Submarine *Alpha*" with vibraphone and strings playing a sustained note until a contrabassoon enters joined by an eerie organ and shimmering violins, with an interesting combination of xylophone and coronet finishing each measure. Ifukube's score for "The 164-Year Voyage" was a curious choice depicting the futuristic submarine *Alpha*, with harpsichord and strings for added texture (the harpsichord plays in ascending and descending notes with distinctness when Tashiro and Lawton discuss the ship's plaque). The use of the harpsichord reflects the LZ society as one that is advanced, yet with strong ties to its past.

"The *Alpha* vs. the *Black Shark*" is introduced with an effectively dramatic seven-note theme punctuated by a crashing cymbal as a trombone and piano play simultaneously. Strings then enter playing a circular 11-note theme that is constantly repeated, as trumpets join in before the music rises in intensity; the spherical nature of the music suggesting the eternal struggle between McKenzie and Malic. As the *Alpha* docks in "The Entrance to Latitude Zero," Ifukube reintroduces the *Alpha* motif, segueing into warm and comforting French horns with reassuring bassoon, and when Masson is taken away in an ambulance, Ifukube introduces a flute to lend the scientist's situation a vulnerable quality.

Ifukube's music for the "Immunization Bath" is sinister and mysterious, beginning with a flurry of spooky strings joined by serious brass. As Anne enters, a quivering organ and shimmering cymbal accompany her introduction with a flurry of four quick notes played on piano, and a tap on a vibraphone when she walks into the bath. It is a long time before the composer's music is heard again when the *Alpha* surfaces near Blood Rock, a score comprised mainly of quivering strings supplemented by the maestro's signature single, pounding piano key (a sustained note on violins ending with a lower note at the end of each measure mirrors the explorers' cautious steps).

Heading *Latitude Zero's* cast was the last American to play a leading role in a Honda film: Joseph Cotton as Captain Craig McKenzie. Cotton was a true Hollywood icon and easily the most-respected American actor Honda would ever work with. One example of Cotton's restrained delivery is the moment when he announces that—if the modifications were correctly made to the *Alpha*—"We're going to fly," spoken by the actor with a softly-determined confidence. Another moment that typifies Cotton's low-key acting is when he gives Kubo the order to move the *Alpha* along at "flank speed;" the actor's voice is not raised in either pitch or volume, and there are no dramatic gestures, but his serious tone convinces the audience that the order he has given is an important one. Just what McKenzie's exact status in LZ is not made clear other than he is the trusted captain of the *Alpha*. He is a gracious host, has a laconic sense of humor, but is quick to make critical decisions (his choice to have modifications made to the *Alpha* so it could take flight was indeed a providential one; although just when he received his pilot training is never brought to light).

Cotton had some juicy lines to work with, such as: "Politics are only needed by people incapable of running their own lives" and "*Everything in Latitude Zero is real*," but he was 64 years old at the time of filming and arrived in Japan nearly too sick too work (as if to compensate for this, Honda shot most of Cotton's scenes with the actor sitting down). Nevertheless, Cotton's illness is clearly evident; he sounds terrible in the scene after the *Alpha* has docked in LZ, and he *looks* terrible when issuing commands on the *Alpha* after he and the others have rescued Okada and his daughter from Malic.

Caesar Romero was quite another matter as he gave Malic a dynamic flair; it's not often an actor gets to say lines such as: "Apply the anesthetic to the condor!" A true scientific genius who regards the transplanting of organs as mere "child's play," Malic is wasting his time brooding on Blood Rock as he could have made a great living as a brain surgeon. Capable of turning people into animals by the simple expedient of inserting a human brain into an animal's skull does not take a number of anatomical issues into consideration, but unlike H. G. Wells' Dr. Moreau, Malic's creations are not half-human/half-animal, but transformed mythical creatures and monsters. The premise is a promising one, but budget restrictions limited Malik to a handful of bat creatures and one uncooperative and ultimately useless griffin.

Romero had been one of the great "Latin lovers" of the movies whose career was eclipsed by his frenzied Joker on the "Batman" TV series in the mid-sixties (the scene when McKenzie's team becomes immobilized by a magnetic field affecting their utility belts is right out of *Batman—The Movie* (1966), which also co-starred Romero as the Joker). Romero deliberately overplays his part, widening his eyelids as far as he can, resulting in Honda's hammiest heavy; also effective was the *Black Shark's* Captain Kroiga, played with evil exuberance by Hikaru Kuroki, who seems to resent the presence of her First Mate and vice versa.

Patricia Medina was slinky and seductive as Lucrecia, and the actress even gets a bit misty-eyed in her death scene with Malic. Tetso Nakamura gives a fine performance as the vulnerable Dr. Okada, as did Mari Nakayama as Tsuruko—although most of her screen time is really "scream time." Perhaps the film's most-believable performance was given by Richard Jaeckel as the cynical reporter Terry Lawton; short, muscular and energetic, Jaeckel is cut right from the William "Star Trek" Shatner mode. Akira Takarada played Dr. Tashiro, but was given little to do; as it happened, Takarada—who had so brilliantly essayed the part of Ogata in *Godzilla*—gave his final performance in a Honda film.

Masumi Okada competently played the French scientist Jules Masson as a man who initially makes an enlightening comment regarding the red light used for better vision underwater, and then manages to say nothing even remotely intelligent during the remainder of the film (instead, he makes inane remarks such as when saying about Dr. Barton: "Look who's been taking care of *me!*, "and whistling like a schoolboy when told about Okada's radiation serum). Without question however the worst performance belonged to Linda Haynes, utterly hopeless as Dr. Anne Barton; her scenes have no energy and her dialogue is delivered without any inflection or change in tone (in desperation, Honda gave her scenes what little vitality he could by filming her in a number of intense close-ups). The actress did not seem to enjoy the experience of making *Latitude Zero*; the clearest evidence of this is her scene in the Bath of Immunity, where she seems very uncomfortable and anything but alluring.

Latitude Zero was one of Honda's most inadequate films; the continuity and sound recording are not up to his previous standards and the minute the bathysphere begins its descent into the deep, the film seems to stop before it has even started (although the underwater rescue scene is very moody and atmospheric). The director's lack of interest is reflected in his direction: When Lawton turns to find himself face-to-face with a man pointing a gun at him (a very bored-looking Osman Yusuf, also making his final appearance in a Honda film), McKenzie catches the bullet before turning to Lawton and saying: "Maybe, you'd—better test you, too." Cotton was no doubt supposed to say: "Maybe *we'd* better test you too" but had trouble getting the words out; Honda kept the muffed line in anyway.

Honda's distinct style of overheating the tension is evident when Malic and Lucrecia visibly "twitch" as they stare into the camera while watching the *Black Shark* pursuing the *Alpha*, but Honda's directing is most effective during a tense close-up of Okada and Tsuruko as they cower in Malic's "Guest Room," as well as Tsuruko's off-camera screams during the grisly goings-on in the Observation Gallery, which include a number of intense close-ups of her sweating and agonized face. However, Honda's staging of the moment when McKenzie stops Lucrecia from stabbing Okada—although adroitly edited—was clumsily staged. Instead of grabbing the hand Lucrecia held the needle with, Cotton grabbed the wrong arm, but fortunately the action is so fast it is not too noticeable (what is all-*too*-noticeable is Cotton's smiling face as he throws Lucrecia at Malic).

Ironically—after longing to live on a peaceful planet and failing to find it in the real world, Honda filmed it as a fictional cinematic utopia. Latitude Zero is indeed a peaceful place (even its treasured *Alpha* carries no offensive weapons) and as was customary for a Honda film, none of the heroes needed to bloody their hands as all three villains wind-up destroying each other while all the rescuers returned safely. Honda had always maintained that he watched his films as much as he directed them, and if this were indeed true, it's no wonder that *Latitude Zero's* illogical and muddled plot confused him as much as his audience. Years later the director considered *Latitude Zero* to be his greatest disappointment and deepest regret as a filmmaker, citing a troubled production which included a certain sense of betrayal felt on the part of Toho toward its American collaborators regarding the expense of hiring, feeding and transporting the American cast which had to return home by a certain time. Although undeniably imaginative, it is not a particularly interesting film to watch and too implausible to be taken seriously (it is also the only one of Honda's fantasy films to be shot almost exclusively on sound stages, giving it an artificially-contrived look).

Latitude Zero was Honda's final fantasy film and a disappointing departure to a genre to which he had contributed such films as *Mothra* and *Undersea Battleship*; it is not so surprising then that Honda's dismissive attitude toward the production resulted in a film that lacked cohesive direction. As it happened, Honda's next film would be a far-happier experience, as he was to tell a tale nearly as strange as *Latitude Zero's*, told this time from the point-of-view of a lonely, oppressed and misunderstood boy who escapes his troubles by creating a fantasy world where his hero is a monster—a monster that once terrified children around the world.

GODZILLA, MINYA, GABARA:
ALL GIANT MONSTERS ATTACK (1969)
(GOJIRA — MINIRA — GABARA:
ORU KAIJU DAISHINGEKI)
GODZILLA'S REVENGE

Cast & Credits

Film Register No. 16110
Release Date: December 20, 1969
Running Time: 70 Minutes

<u>Staff</u>: Producer: Tomoyuki Tanaka; Director: Ishiro Honda; Screenplay: Shinichi Sekizawa; Director of Photography: Sokei (Mototaka) Tomioka; Art Director: Takeo Kita; Recording: Norio Tokai; Lighting: Fumiro Hara; Sound Arrangement: Hisashi Shimonaga; Music: Kunio Miyauchi, "March of the Monsters" Lyrics: Shinichi Sekizawa, Music: Kunio Miyauchi, Arrangement: Jinzo (Nizo) Kosugi, Sung By: Riri (Lily) Sasaki); Special Effects: Supervisor: Eiji Tsuburaya; Ishiro Honda (Uncredited); Assistant Directors: Masaaki Hisamatsu and Teruyoshi Nakano; Editor: Masahisa Hyomi; Matte Processing: Hiroshi Mukoyama; Wire Works: Fumio Nakadai.

<u>Cast</u>: Kenji Sahara (Kenkichi Miki); Machiko Naka (Tamiko Miki); Tomonori Yazaki (Ichiro Miki); Eisei Amamoto (Shinpei Minami); Sachio Sakai (Senbayashi); Kazuo Suzuki (Okuda); Ikio Sawamura (Elderly Man at Food Stand); Shigeki Ishida (Manager of Apartment Building); Yutaka Sada (Kenkichi's Co-Worker); Yoshifumi Tajima (Detective); Chotaro Togin (Assistant Detective); Yutaka Nakayama (Billboard Painter); Junichi Ito (School Bully Gabara); Toru Mori, Toshiya Kurokawa, Hiroyuki Miyaoka, Nobuto Takahashi (Gang Members); Hidemi Ito (Sachiko); "Little Man Machan" (Minya, Voice By: Midori Uchiyama); Haruo Nakajima (Godzilla); Sachiko (Yukiko) Mori (Sachiko's Mother); Osman Yusef (Airplane Passenger); Yoshiko Miyata (Tamiko's Employer); Yoshio Katsube, Haruo Suzuki (Reporters).

The Film

All Giant Monsters Attack was that rare Honda film which focused on one character; in this case, Ichiro, a lonely preschooler bullied by a kid named Gabara (first seen wearing his cap off to one side as an indication of his disassociation with society). Even more unique is that—similar to a brief moment in Mothra when we are able to hear a character's thoughts—the viewer is taken directly into Ichiro's subconscious. *Monsters Attack* is also a one-of-a-kind Godzilla film in that, strictly speaking, Godzilla never really makes an appearance other than as a dream in the boy's imagination.

Ichiro's parents are upset that they cannot spend more time with their son, yet neither is able or willing to do anything about it. Kenkichi's co-worker asks if he knows of a solution and Kenkichi has it: Money. Strangely, screenwriter Sekizawa does not have Ichiro receive a large reward for helping to capture the two criminals, which would have enabled his parents to either move to a better area or allow one to quit their job so as to spend more time at home with their son.

It makes little sense the criminals would worry about Okuda's missing wallet when they are already on the run from the police, and why they bother to take him with them is even more difficult to understand, as it will obviously add a kidnapping charge to their ever-growing list of offensives; even more inconceivable is that the police never even think to search the abandoned warehouse for them (in one intriguing moment, Ichiro offers to show his landlord Okuda's license which the man refuses to look at; had he done so, he almost certainly would have recognized the fugitive who shows up a minute later to inquire about the car for sale).

Honda took it upon himself to direct both the live-action and special effects scenes for *All Giant Monsters Attack*. Arikawa had been Tsuburaya's cinematographer for a long time, eventually taking over the position of Effects Director, since Tsuburaya was spending less time at the studio working on his television productions (additionally, Tsuburaya had taken ill during the Fall of 1969 when *All Giant Monsters Attack* was in development). In any event, Honda would not require Arikawa's services on *All Giant Monsters Attack*; it may have been that Honda was not entirely satisfied with Arikawa's work and felt the job rightfully belonged to Tsuburaya's assistant, Teruyoshi Nakano (in later years, Honda claimed there was no need to call in somebody else to handle the effects work since there would be very little new footage to be shot for the film—but this attitude appears to have been a smokescreen disguising the fact that Honda never felt comfortable in having anyone other than Eiji Tsuburaya handling the special effects for his films).

Nakano later told Brett Homenick: "I was First Assistant Director of Special Effects; Director Honda told me he wasn't sure of the details of the special effects, so he would look to me. I drew the story boards and added the flavor of fantasy to it." A number of studio photos show Haruo Nakajima as well as Honda coaching the two actors playing Minya and Gabara in preparation for their battle scenes. Honda's effects supervision may have involved the brief segment where Godzilla teaches Minya how to breathe fire in a reworking of the same bit from *Son of Godzilla.*

The film's premise that Monster Island is a figment of Ichiro's imagination is the rationalization often given to the wide-disparity of the Godzilla costumes seen in the film, but the fact was that stock footage was used from the previous films to save money, which did not compensate for the jarring differences in their designs. Even more inconsistent than the costumes is Honda's own effects footage, which tended to look flat and static, especially when compared to Arikawa's fluid camera work.

Cinematographer Sokie Tomioka filmed a number of long and medium shots showing Ichiro walking alone on the dirt road emphasizing the boy's lonely existence, and his location shooting is excellent as he utilizes various handheld camera shots, also achieving a wonderful "dusk" effect in the scenes with the car for sale. The sequences in the warehouse were effectively filmed, including some spooky close-ups of Senbayashi searching for Ichiro. The opening shots are perhaps the dreariest in all of Honda's fantasy films: A city submerged in smog with congested traffic snarling on the streets. The shots of the traffic—taken with a telephoto lens and shot at ground level for added visual impact—puts the viewer right into the middle of the congested street, and while the idea of industrial pollution is not central to the picture (unlike 1971's *Godzilla vs. Hedorah*, where the viewer is repeatedly hit over the head with similar repellent images), Honda shows us just enough of these shots to get the point across as to the kind of environment Ichiro lives in.

Honda was always trying new techniques in his films—to keep himself interested if for no other reason—and used slow-motion to emphasize the film's dreamlike qualities. In the scene where Ichiro is about to be caught by Senbayashi, Honda intermittently advances the film on the boy before freezing the images, while at the same time intercutting slow-motion footage of Senbayashi lunging menacingly at the camera while being lit from underneath (in a bit Honda had earlier used in *Mothra*, Okuda slaps Ichiro in the face with a document the thief has been looking for).

Another innovative method is seen during the fight between Ichiro and Gabara, when Honda uses a series of stationary and blurred images of the boys tussling about. While an interesting visual technique, it indicates that Honda shot the film in this manner in order to make the shot more convincing, rather than having the boys trying to wrestle in a sustained take. Editor Masahisa Himi's work lacks the fine crispness of former Honda editor Ryohie Fujii, as Himi lingers too long on certain shots after the actors have exited the frame, resulting in an automatic shifting of the focus. The dilapidated warehouse was one of Takeo Kita's best sets, as— for the first time in many a movie—they did not contain a single control panel or computer-driven mechanism (although the switches on Inami's embryonic PC typically lack any identifying labels).

For a film such as *Godzilla's Revenge*, Akira's Ifukube's urgent music— so prominent in the last eight Honda's films—would not be needed, so Honda turned to Kunio Miyauchi, whose score was deliberately flavored to reflect the film's adolescent nature. The opening theme begins with a gently tapping piano and cymbal gaining in tempo, until reaching a crescendo of brass, percussion and electrical guitar that culminates in a trumpet fanfare before segueing into the "Monster March" (unpleasantly sung by a raspy-voiced Lily Sasaki). Brass, augmented by percussions and saxophones accompanied by an annoying electric guitar and a flurry of notes on a xylophone, comprise "Godzilla vs. Kamacuras," a motif that surfaces repeatedly during the monster fights to follow. Moments of suspense and fright—such as when Ichiro finds himself at the bottom of the pit or when hiding from the villains—are merely brief and intermittent notes played sharply on percussion and organ; an odd combination of instruments registering neither fright nor suspense.

The majority of Miyauchi's score is employed for sequences involving Ichiro's imagination, with very little music used during the "real-world" situations; although when Senbayashi is lunging at the boy, the composer uses grim trombones, muted coronets and a wavering organ, supplemented by a tapping cymbal and trilling flute. A vibraphone finally ends the moment on a humorous note when the criminal falls headfirst into a box, but as Senbayashi is being pelted with bottles thrown by Ichiro, Miyauchi scores the scene with plucking guitar and tapping cymbal when the crook opens his pocketknife, at which point Miyauchi turns up the volume with a tapping drum and plucking guitar before a flurry of flutes and brass enter when the crook closes in on the boy. As Ichiro opens up on the villain with the fire retardant, organ and cymbals are introduced before woodwinds—accompanied by descending trumpets—lighten the mood, joined by a steady drumbeat (essentially a reworking of the beasts' battle music heard on Monster Island). Wavering organs mimic the sprayed retardant as flutes play off-key as the gangster gets plastered with the foam, then a drum solo adds an upbeat flavor before sustained notes on trumpets signify Ichiro's success.

The monster battle music is again heard in "I Can't Stand Bullies" as the boy tees-off on the bully Gabara, with saxophones playing at a slower tempo while off-key flutes sound individual notes indicating a skewed situation, before a military-style drum rift enters as Ichiro walks away victoriously. The "Ending" music once again introduces the flutes playing Ichiro's theme—only this time with greater definition and volume—before triumphant trumpets and assertive flutes perform with crashing cymbals. Miyauchi scores much of the film with flutes, guitars, organ, xylophone and muted trumpets, but the bizarre blending of percussion, saxophones and guitar give the film an atmosphere more appropriate to an informal jazz session than a monster movie.

All Giant Monsters Attack had one of the smallest casts ever to grace a Honda film; in fact there are only four principal characters: Ichiro, Inami and the two criminals. The part of Ichiro Miki was done by Tomonori Yazaki, the youngest actor ever to play a lead in a Honda film. Honda always worked well with inexperienced actors, and his casting of Yazaki was interesting in that Yazaki is by no means a "pretty boy" but just an average-looking kid (Yazaki was an appealing youngster, not at all like the whining brats who would follow him in subsequent Godzilla films). The young actor successfully registers fear, vulnerability and joy; although at times he seems to be enjoying himself a little too much, such as when he and Minya are being splashed by water from Godzilla's fight with Ebirah, and particularly in the scene when he is being chased by Senbayashi.

Veteran heavy Eisei Amamoto was another example of Honda's casting against type as Amamoto plays toy consultant/inventor Shinpei Inami (first seen absentmindedly smoking in front of Ichiro). The inventor is shown working on an early variant of a PC and initiates a program discussing the Moon with the screen displaying an image of the Moon Base from *All Monsters Attack*. In later years, Amamoto claimed he was totally wrong for the part—giving in his estimation a very bad performance—but in fact the actor very credibly plays a kindly eccentric and mild-mannered inventor. The skilled actor was able to endow his part with interesting touches; after Inami explains Ichiro's fascination with Minya to the press (who then burst out laughing), Inami regards their laughter with an expression that seems to say, "You dopes don't know anything about anything."

Kenji Sahara played the minor role of the boy's father with Machiko Naka playing the part of the overworked mother. Both actors had only two scenes apiece in the film, but Naka shares only one scene with the boy; Sahara and Yazaki have two scenes together but are rarely photographed in the same shot and never on an equal level, stressing the gap in their relationship. The two thugs were played as a comedy team by Sachio Sakai (Senbayahsi) and Kazuo Suzuki (Okuda). Suzuki had played minor thugs in some of Honda's films, while Sakai (who unconvincingly drinks the "alcohol" from his flask as if it were pineapple juice) went all the way back to Honda's glory days of the fifties and early sixties. *All Giant Monsters Attack* would be the final appearance in a Honda film for Yoshibumi Tajima, whose role as a detective nearly brings him full-circle in his career with the director, beginning with his role of a reporter in *Radon* before following it as a hard-boiled detective in *The Beauty and the Liquid People*.

The reason behind Honda's desire to film *All Giant Monsters Attack* may have stemmed not simply as a desire to interest young people in the Godzilla series (which was no doubt Tanaka's intention), but to warn working parents of the dangers of becoming alienated from their children by working too hard and putting business before family. Honda still plugs away at his favorite dream of world unity, but now with a discordant tone: When Ichiro is watching a televised news program announcing the signing of a "World Treaty," the boy changes the channel immediately. There was also the kind of moment that so typifies Honda's desire for a stable society and warm human contact, perhaps best exemplified in the dinner scene between Inami and Ichiro; as Ichiro chows down his hot, steamy food, the look of satisfaction on Inami's face is heartwarming.

The core of the film is when Ichiro has beaten up his bully and honks the motorcyclist's horn, which inadvertently causes the man to fall off his ladder. Some have speculated that this bold act of bravado indicates Ichiro will turn out to be a bad kid, but Honda assures us this will not be the case; after all, Ichiro was forced to defend himself when Gabara made a threatening advance toward him, and so Ichiro responded accordingly and significantly, defensively. After Ichiro tosses Gabara down for the last time, he does not gloat or taunt the former bully, but walks away with newfound confidence. However, many feel that Ichiro crosses the line when he honks the motorcyclist's horn in a deliberate act of civil disobedience—a possible indication that the railroader's son will eventually end up on the wrong side of the tracks. It seems more likely that Ichiro, flushed with victory, honked the horn to sound a note of personal triumph, and, after the painter falls, Honda's handling of the next few moments are crucial: First, he shows the man getting covered in paint for comedic effect, then he cuts to a reaction shot of the laughing kids, then to a shot of a grimacing and embarrassed Ichiro indicating his shock and surprise at an event he never intended to make happen (Honda was also careful not to show Ichiro rejoicing over the incident).

The movie's ambivalent ending showing the kids tromping off to school amidst their polluted surroundings is classic Honda, embodying the trademark "happy/sad" endings of his finest films. The finale was unusual for a Honda film in that it is somewhat open-ended, with the ultimate outcome of Ichiro's situation left to the viewer's discretion; perhaps the father will now have that long-overdue "heart-to-heart" talk with his son to better instruct him on what is acceptable behavior. It is also possible that Ichiro's incident with the painter will be the turning point for his mother, convincing her to give up working her long hours so as to keep her son out of trouble—but then again, perhaps not (there is also the question as to the what the effect Ichiro's victory will have on Gabara and his former gang; will Ichiro become their new leader, converting them into leading a life within the rules? My daughter feels the moral of the film is simple: "Be a jerk").

Honda's stresses our empathy with Ichiro to the point that whenever the boy is being threatened, his persecutors look directly into the camera lens, putting us into his precarious position and making us identify with his fear (perhaps we remember exactly what he is going through). It is a surprising moment when the two detectives barge in on Inami and the boy without first knocking—apparently a not uncommon situation in Japan—but Honda probably wished to communicate the fact that the police are only trying to prevent the criminals from escaping by advising the inventor to lock up his car, which actually does no good (in a forced bit of comedy—as the two men begin to leave—one of them touches a gloved hand, activating the prop, Sekizawa having done an earlier variation on this gag in *Latitude Zero*).

The most frustrating aspect of the movie however is Honda's handling of the two bank robbers, as their scenes are infused with a number of silly sight gags; the first time they are seen together hiding in a locker, Honda has them bumping their heads. They then proceed to bump into boxes, fall through holes and bop each other over the head, all the while whining and snarling at each other. It seems inconceivable that they can even cross-the-street together let alone commit a daring daylight robbery (in an impossibly corny moment, Honda has Senbayashi kiss a portion of his stolen loot; stranger still, Senbayashi's sunglasses—which the villain wears in a darkened warehouse at night—are not covered by Ichiro's fire retardant, nor does the villain even think to remove them to better see the boy).

Even with all the silly sight gags the film still has a nasty bite to it, such as when Senbayashi shows Ichiro a knife before driving it into a box, and even the monster scenes have an sadistic quality. In one of the cruelest moments in all of Honda's fantasy films, Minya—coming out on the bad end of a tussle with Gabara—runs to his dad for reassurance, only to be pushed away and turned to face Gabara who is as that moment laughing menacingly, eager to have another crack at Minya. Caught between a rock and a hard place, Minya turns once more to his dad, who callously kicks him away.

Yet the brutality, sinister moments and silent-movie-style comedy is concluded by one of the most-poignant scenes in Honda's career: When Ichiro prepares to leave for school, his mother assures him that she will not be working late again, prompting the boy to ask: "But don't we need the money?" In response, his mother has no answer other than to exhale with embarrassment before helping Ichiro with his backpack. After the boy leaves, she lowers her head to weep in her apron in a heartbreaking moment.

All Giant Monsters Attack is routinely dismissed as not only the worst Godzilla film Honda ever directed, but possibly the worst Godzilla film ever made (if this were to be taken as fact, it would place Honda in the distinctive position of having directing both the best and worst films in a long-running movie series). Curiously, despite the director's penchant for sentimentality, the film itself has little charm, bouncing as it does between Ichiro's lonely life, the ridiculous robbers and the savage monster struggles. Nevertheless, the film contains classic elements found in many a Honda film: Relaxed social contact despite imminent danger, terror without teeth, corny crooks, skeptical journalists and fighting a defensive battle against enormous odds (the film clocks in at a mere 70-minutes—the shortest running time of all the Godzilla films—and even at that, nearly ten minutes of it is stock footage).

Seen today, *All Giant Monsters Attack* is difficult to evaluate objectively due in no small part to the emotions it stirs with viewers, particularly parents. Some feel the film's message leads kids down the wrong path, while others have voiced their approval of Ichiro's necessarily-drastic solution toward his problem. Perhaps the movie's most-enduring legacy is that it was not just a reflection of a new direction the Godzilla series was taking, but the ultimate embodiment of the personality and philosophy of the man who created it.

The sixties had brought many changes for both Honda and Godzilla. At the beginning of the 1960s, Godzilla was an unstoppable engine of destruction and a warning of the Atomic Age; but by the end of the decade, Godzilla's character had softened to the point where its main concern was teaching its son how to breathe fire—which had now significantly lost its radioactive bite. Having *All Giant Monsters Attack* as the first film in the series to paint the monster as a kind of hero to kids was a risky precedent, but Tanaka, desperate in his desire to make money on a series rapidly loosing its appeal, obviously believed the concept would renew the series' popularity. The film's subsequent failure at the box office thus came as a major disappointment to Tanaka, but especially for Honda, who had great hopes for it and considered it as being one of his favorite films to make; its lack of commercial success convinced him that his days of directing Godzilla films had finally come to an ignominious end.

It had been a long and bumpy road—seven Godzilla films in 15 years—but Honda had been happy to direct them providing there were important social issues to be discussed; now, it seemed that no one was listening to what he was saying, only watching. As a result, Honda quit the series for nearly six years, and when he returned, he had to be talked back into it.

GEZORA, GANIME, KAMEBA: DECISIVE BATTLE!
GIANT MONSTERS OF THE SOUTH SEAS (1970)
(KESSEN! NANKAI NO DAIKAIJU
GEZORA, GANIMAE, KAMEBA)
YOG - MONSTER FROM SPACE

Cast & Credits

Film Register No. 16236
Release date: August 1, 1970
Running time: 84 minutes, six seconds

Staff: Producers: Tomoyuki Tanaka and Fumio Tanaka; Director: Ishiro Honda; Screenplay: Ei Ogawa; Art Director: Takeo Kita; Recording: Kanae Masuo; Lighting: Toshio Takashima; Music: Akira Ifukube; Assistant Director: Seiji Tani; Editor: Masahisa Hyomi; Sound Effects: Sadamasa Nishimoto and Toho Dubbing; Production Manager: Yasushi Sakai; Still Photos: Issei Tanaka; Special Effects Director: Sadamasa Arikawa; Cinematography: Yoichi Manoda; Optical Cinematography: Yoshiyuki Tokumasa; Art Director: Yasuyuki Inoue; Lighting: Fumiyoshi Hara; Wire Works: Fumio Nakadai; Matte Photography: Hiroshi Mukoyama; Assistant Director: Teruyoshi Nakano.

Cast: Akira Kubo (Taro Kudo); Atsuko Takahashi (Ayako Hoshino); Yukiko Kobayashi (Saki); Kenji Sahara (Makoto Obata); Yoshio Tsuchiya (Kyoichi Miya); Tetsu Nakamura (Ombo); Yu Fujiki (Promotion Division Manager); Noritake Saito (Riko); Yuko Sugihara (Airline Stewardess); Sachio Sakai (Magazine Editor); Chotaro Togin (Yokoyama); Wataru Omae (Sakura); Yukihiko Gondo, Shigeo Kato, Rinsaku Ogata (Islanders); Haruo Nakajima, Haruyoshi Nakamura (Monsters); Soji Ubakata, Akira Kitchoji (Airline Passengers); Yoshio Katsube, Tadashi Okabe, Koichi Sato, Yukiko Mori (Magazine Employees); Eizaburo Komatsu (Magazine Employee/Villager); Seiya Kondo (Company Employee).

The Film

Giant Monsters of the South Sea's screenplay was written by Ei Ogawa, and even though he had previously never written a monster movie script for Honda, Ogawa was intimately familiar with Honda's previous films as the movie is a virtual catalog of previously used plot devices: Natives bowing before a fire-lit altar, the exploration of a cave, aliens wishing to control the Earth, a rocket launch at the beginning of the film, a space capsule being controlled by an alien substance, natives warning outsiders not to offend their god, a man and woman being pursued by a monster before seeking shelter in a cave, the illumination seen under the surface of the water before a monster appears, sandy footprints of the beast leading to the ocean, telepathy being connected with a monster, a man being dragged under the water to his death, a man suffering from amnesia, industrial spies, the stealing of important documents, intense cold being associated with the invaders, a native assisting the Japanese and suffering admonishment from the native chief for doing so, a native chief screaming at the outsiders' interference, scuba divers examining a sunken capsule, a weapon being fired inadvertently, the wind picking up as the monster approaches, natives weeping while watching the destruction of their village, Japanese trespassers causing a monster to appear, gasoline being used as a trap to catch the monster, tall bundles of reeds being set aflame to ward off a monster, a girl being chased by a monster as she slips and falls and screams, a journalist being laughed at by his colleagues, a person hanging onto a cliff branch for dear life, a man being possessed and given orders by aliens, a creepy substance invading a man's body, a volcano destroying the monsters, a flashing light bringing an amnesia victim out of his trace, a woman screaming upon seeing a prostate native and a man who aids society and destroys an evil force by committing suicide.

Ogawa's script is the barest of bones, containing little in the way of surprises, and is eminently predicable as it is obvious from the outset that the existence of a monster supported by the natives will be doubted by the "civilized" outsiders; however, the "god" of Selgio Island never really shows up, since Gezora was created by the aliens from random sea life. Another departure from what had been the norm in a Honda film was that none of the natives in *South Seas* are killed by the monster, although their village is damaged and some do get roughed-up a little. There was a minor subplot regarding the destruction of natural beauty for industrialization and profit, but this concept is not stressed or debated, merely a premise for a story and nothing else.

At one point it seems the film is leading to a classic Honda climax: Obata, battling over the control of his very soul, has an opportunity to save mankind by letting the bats go free from the cave before they are burned alive. Typically, in moments such as this, one would have expected him to run into the cave after allowing the bats to fly safely away before closing the door behind him, thereby shutting himself off from any possible aid and destroying himself and the aliens in the process. Instead, Obata frees the bats and then wanders off into the jungle; when he shows up later, it is merely as a spectator to the battle being waged between Ganime and Kameba. After the monsters have fallen into the volcano, Obata then rather nonchalantly jumps in—the moment brings to mind the Empress of Mu's death at the end of *Submarine Warship*, only this time without any poignancy or pathos.

Teisho Arikawa's effects work in *South Seas* is uninspired, unimpressive and unconvincing as none of the three monsters populating the film have any of the memorable characteristics or personality shared by Tsuburaya's classic creations (indeed it is a rare fan who can even remember their names). Gezora's attack on the native village is a direct swipe from *Baran*, but on this occasion is a dreary and boring four-minute affair that falls far short of the dynamic destruction seen in the earlier film. Arikawa was terrific at filming effects shots, but his execution of the effects left a great deal to be desired. Gezora's ability to walk on land is a ludicrous concept—regardless of how smoothly the effect was accomplished—and while Ganime hacks its way through the jungle with appropriate ferocity, the scene somehow lacks excitement.

The idea of animals being changed into giant mutants by aliens was an interesting one, although their designs left much to be desired. The Ganime costume was interesting with nice detailing, and Kameba's ability to extend its head was a unique feature, but Gezora missed the mark completely; staring ahead with vacant eyes while making chirping sounds, it was simply too cute to be creepy and was possibly the sorriest-looking monster in all of Honda's *oeuvre*. There were some nice effects shots such as the launching of the space craft (probably the finest of its type in a Honda film), but the human dolls of Sakura and Obata look exactly like the stiff, lifeless puppets they are. Arikawa also seems to enjoy rubbing his audiences' noses into the gorier aspects of the film, such as when he zooms in on Ganime's literally bloodshot eyes.

Gezora's capture of Yokoyama is action-packed and very well staged, but it lacks the darker aspects of the octopus's attack on the sailor in *Sanda vs. Gairah*; however, the most disappointing moment in the film is the supposedly climatic battle between Ganime and Kameba.

Tsuburaya's ability to bring costumed monsters to life is sadly missing in this scene, as was its pacing and execution; Tsuburaya's battle scenes were typically well-paced, easy to follow and built nicely to a crescendo, but Ganime and Kameba's fight was without question the least-interesting of all the Toho monster battles, with no beginning, hardly any middle and not much of an end; one is hardly concerned as to which monster will win or loose.

One of the highpoints of *South Seas* is Taiichi Kankura's outstanding location photography on Hachijo Island (an amusing moment happens when Obata shares a "two-shot" with a background Tiki god as both stare ahead with bulging eyes when Gezora approaches). Honda utilizes a great many effective close-ups such as a dramatic one of Ombo with clouds billowing behind him as he warns Yokoyama not to anger Gezora (the village elder is seen later in an unsettling fire-lit close-up condemning the Japanese visitors). Honda and Kankura's work is particularly outstanding when Obata warns everyone of the aliens' intentions; lit from underneath and with subtle makeup, the scene is quite chilling (at one point—as Ayako begs with Obata—the light slightly dims on Obata's face as if the alien influence has been weakened by her insistence). Other notable shots are a nice crane shot following the Japanese as the natives escort them to the storage unit, and a succession of close-ups of the prostrate Obata being taken over by the aliens.

Masahisa Himi's film editing keeps the movie moving at a brisk pace; after the *Helios 7* splashes down, he cuts to a close-up of the scowling newspaper editor with background laughter filling the soundtrack. The movie gets off to a very fast start as the initial scenes move with a rapidity rare for a Honda film: The rocket launch, the overtaking of the space capsule, Kudo's plane ride, his meeting with the editor and with Ayako, the briefing in the headquarters of Asia Development Company, LTD., the tragedy of the Japanese fishermen and the initial meeting with Obata all take place within the film's first dozen minutes for roughly one scene per minute (sadly, as soon as the first monster appear, the movie's pace drags down considerably).

Akira Ifukube's "Main Title" music lends a native feel to the proceedings, beginning with a softly-tapping combination of tom-toms and organ (also heard during "The Wedding Ceremony" between Rico and Saki) before segueing into a crash of organ keys, low brass and pounding piano emphasizing the furious power of the three monsters. Violins and trumpets then enter in a motif that is repeated to indicate an ongoing battle, until finally the piece ends on a sustained note played on trumpets. The composer's "Launching of the *Helios*" piano music is similar to his rocket-launching music used for the beginning of *Baran*; only on this occasion, the music seems disjointed and muddled, with an occasional cymbal crash for punctuation.

A tinkling of piano, organ, flutes, vibraphone and violins all playing sustained notes colors "The Helios Heads into Outer Space," while a tinkling piano and low woodwinds are followed by low brass and an interesting—if somewhat incongruous—use of a slide flute to distinguish the alien life form. "Gezora Attacks" begins with a tinkling of piano keys, slide flute and low brass, while raspy trumpets play in ascending chords in tandem with trombones playing in descending chords; the trombones are then joined by violins and piano in one of the few interesting pieces of music in the movie (a fortunate happenstance as this music is heard during all of Gezora's wearisome scenes).

A brief piece prosaically entitled "Background Music on Board" is very enjoyable—a *samba*-like piece scored for tom-tom and piano—while "The Prayer of Selgio Island," written for drums and native flutes, is merely a re-orchestration of Ifukube's native chant music from *King Kong vs. Godzilla*. Ifukube seems to have preferred Ganime over the other two monsters, as "The Appearance of Ganime" is a lengthened version of his "Main Title" music, opening with pounding piano and tremulous trombones, violins and organ, with trumpets blaring with the now- familiar crashing cymbal.

Organ, gentle tom-toms and quivering violins introduce "Remains of the Dead Bats," an effective and subtle piece comprised of a tapping organ cleverly mimicking the moisture dripping from the roofs of the caves. Pounding piano and low brass herald the appearance of the third and final monster in "The Appearance of Kameba," with descending coronets and strumming piano strings playing in a stop-and-go manner. Perhaps the most-disappointing piece of music was "Obata's Resistance," heard in the key scene when Obata hesitates to set fire to the bats. Scored with soft violins and electone, it should have been emblematic of the sad, sweet music Ifukube was known to compose for such moments; however, the melody contains no significant structure or discernable passion and lacks the necessary clout needed to increase the scene's dramatic impact.

Reassuring French horns color the "Ending" music, followed by the usual violins and coda of trumpets; oddly, Ifukube chose not to score the initial scenes of Obata being possessed by the aliens; even more incredible was the composer's decision to leave unscored the moment when Obata jumps into the cave; this, combined with Honda's distant recording of the event, makes it all seem a rather routine incident of no special significance.

In addition to the lovely location photography, the film's other main asset is its excellent cast, populated with familiar and welcome faces. Akira Kubo excels in the lead as the sardonic journalist Taro Kudo, while pretty newcomer Atsuko Takahashi was very believable, giving a sincere performance as the naïve and enthusiastic Ayako Hoshino. The part of the smarmy industrial spy Makoto Obata was handled by Kenji Sahara in a delightfully-hammy performance in a role originally intended for Yoshio Tsuchiya (Dr. Kyoichi Mida). Tsuchiya had made a bit of a career playing either aliens or persons possessed by aliens, and so he offered Obata's part (with Honda's approval) to Sahara, who gives a tremendous performance. Tsuchiya plays Dr. Mida with great gravity and conviction and in many ways set the tone for the convincing performances which carry the film. Yukiko Kobayashi—who earlier essayed the role of the Kilaak-controlled Kyoko in *All Monsters Attack*—was nicely cast as the exotic native girl Saki, while her betrothed, Rico, was played with earnest naturalness by Noritake Saito. Also ably-filled were the minor roles played by such able hands as Sachio Sakai as the newspaper editor, Yu Fujiki as the promotional division manager and Tetsu Nakamura as Ombo in the last in a long and noble line of angry native chiefs.

Nakamura was one of the more-underappreciated actors in Honda's films, and the performer must have enjoyed the wide disparity of roles he was given to play, from a Third-World drug dealer in *Liquid People* to a ship's captain in *Submarine Warship* to a Nobel Prize-winning scientist in *Latitude Zero*; but he will most-likely best be remembered as Clark Nelson's spokesman in *Mothra*. Even Chotaro Togin—usually an uninteresting actor—does a fine job as the happy-go-lucky resort agent/turned wacko Yokoyama; but the ending of an era was in sight as many of these fine actors were making their last appearance in a Honda film, including Kubo, Tsuchiya, Fujiki, Sakai and Nakamura.

After directing 23 genre films over a period of 16 years, Honda had every right to be bored, and yet—possibly due to the beautiful location scenery and working with dedicated actors—Honda's direction was actually his best since *King Kong's Counterattack*, with the film itself the most-satisfying since *All Monsters Attack*. There is an undeniably tongue-in-cheek atmosphere and spirited humor to the film (indeed, the film's trailer made the film seem quite the comedy). Of particular note is the cave scene where Sakura's watch gets washed up, showing a Honda fantasy film scene at its best: Atmospheric; beautifully photographed, eerily scored, poetic, mysterious and suspenseful, it ends on a note of grim humor as Yokoyama goes bananas. However, the moment where Dr. Mida attends to Rico with the natives peering through cracks in the hut walls while drums drone-on ominously in the background, somehow lacks the usual tension and claustrophobic feel Honda normally imparted to such scenes.

Honda's best scene was probably the moment when Obata issued the aliens' warning, a creepy scene filmed with spooky close-ups and eerie lighting. As Ayako tearfully begs him to reconsider, it lifts the movie to a higher peak that regrettably would not be ascended again in Honda's career (when Obata jumps into the crater—destroying himself and the aliens within him—Ayako, in a tender moment, softly thanks Obata for his sacrifice). One of the biggest mysteries in all of Honda's work however was why the director did so little with Obata's death scene, as the actor was not even given the obligatory close-up as he makes his mortal decision. Normally a moment of great significance, instead Obata simply leaps out-of-frame in a long-shot. Shot in a more intimate fashion, the death-dive would have lent the film a fine finish and a certain substance; but as filmed, it is familiar, anticlimactic, detached and on a slightly-bitter note of disappointment.

The once-marvelous Toho fantasy film division had long become a factory, with Honda as its chief foreman; it was to no one's surprise when he decided to retire from directing feature films. Honda not only missed the compelling stories, original plotlines, reasonable shooting schedules and decent budgets, but what he no doubt missed the most was the friendship, partnership and work ethics of Eiji Tsuburaya.

As it happened, *South Seas* was not to be Honda's final monster film as there was one more to be made—but that would not happen for quite some time. When he did allow himself to return four years later, it would give him one last opportunity to reestablish himself as the genre's definitive director (an accolade he would probably have preferred be granted to another), and the best man to helm a monster movie starring the monster that had given him so much fame and frustration: Godzilla.

SECTION VII:
"THE DIE IS CAST!"

MechaGodzilla's Counterattack (1975)
(Terror of MechaGodzilla)

Reverberations

Bibliography

MECHAGODZILLA'S COUNTERATTACK (1975)
(MEKAGOJIRA NO GYAKUSHU)
TERROR OF MECHAGODZILLA

Cast & Credits

Film Register No. 18255
Release Date: March 15, 1975
Running Time: 83 Minutes

<u>Staff</u>: Producer: Tomoyuki Tanaka; Director: Ishiro Honda; Screenplay: Yukiko Takayama; Director of Photography: Sokei (Mototaka) Tomioka; Art Director: Yoshifumi Honda; Recording: Fumio Yanouguchi; Lighting: Toshio Takashima; Music: Akira Ifukube; Sound Arrangement: Toho Recording Center; Sound Effects: Toho Sound Effects Group; Assistant Director: Kensho Yamashita; Editor: Yoshitami Kuroiwa; Still Photographer: Issei Tanaka; Associate Producer: Kenji Tokoro; Production Manager: Keisuke Shinoda; Processing: Tokyo Laboratory, Ltd.; Special Effects Techniques: Director: Teruyoshi Nakano; Directors of Photography: Toshiro Aoki; Kan Komura.

<u>Cast</u>: Katsuhiko Sasaki (Akira Ichinose); Tomoko Ai (Katsura Mafune); Akihiko Hirata (Dr. Shinzo Mafune); Tadao Nakamaru (INTERPOL Chief Tagawa); Goro Mutsumi (Alien Commander Mugal "Mugar" "Mugan"); Masaaki Daimon (Kusagari); Katsumasa Uchida (INTERPOL Agent Jiro Murakoshi); Tomoe Mari (Yuri Yamamoto); Toru Ibuki (Alien Lieutenant Tsuda); Makoto Roppongi (Yuichi Wakayama); Kotaro Tomita (Professor Ota); Ikio Sawamura (Mafune's Silent Servant); Kenji Sahara (JSDF Commander); Yasuzo Ogawa (Man on the Pier); Shizuko Azuma (Woman on the Pier); Hiroya Morita (Captain of *Akatsuki No. 1*); Taro Yamada (Yamashita); Shoichi Hirose, Haruo Suzuki, Shigeo Kata, Kazuo Imai (*Akatsuki No. 2* Crewmen); Toru (Kawane) Kawai (Godzilla); Kazunari Mori (MechaGodzilla); Tatsumi Fuyamoto (Titanosaurus).

The Film

In 1974, Toho released Jun Fukuda's *Godzilla vs. MechaGodzilla*, a film which marked the 20th anniversary of the series. *MechaGodzilla* was a decided improvement over Fukuda's two previous efforts—1972's *Earth Destruction Directive: Godzilla vs. Gigan* and 1973's *Godzilla vs. Megalon*—due in no small part to the introduction of a dynamic new monster called MechaGodzilla. After Fukuda declined to direct any future Godzilla films, Tanaka asked Honda to return to filmmaking after a four-year absence. Honda found himself working with Sokei Tomioka as cinematographer, editor Yoshitami Kuroiwa and a new scriptwriter, Yukiko Takayama, the first female scenarist ever to work on a Godzilla film. Nakano had since replaced Arikawa as head of the special effects department, and there would be one important familiar face rejoining Honda for the last time: composer Akira Ifukube.

For the sequel to *Godzilla vs. MechaGodzilla* a number of plot elements were repeated from the previous film, such as having aliens from the Black Hole disguised as humans trying to repair MechaGodzilla with the help of an Earth scientist. INTERPOL is once again trying to stop the aliens while saving the lives of targeted Earth people, and the aliens utilize a base beneath a mountain for their headquarters which can only be reached by a subterranean entrance; also, a tied-up human is able to free himself while the aliens are busy watching their viewing screens showing the battle between Godzilla and MechaGodzilla. In addition, a number of actors appeared in both films, such as Masaaki Daimon; although in *Counterattack* he was not the lead and instead regulated to the minor role of INTERPOL agent Kusakari, a man who somehow survives a disastrous attack on his submarine by Titanosaurus only to taken prisoner, having his tongue cutout and being slaughtered by aliens (Hirata and Mutsumi essentially reprised their roles of a scientist forced to repair the robot and the alien leader).

One anomalous scene involves two small boys—inconsequential to the plot—who play hooky from their evacuation group and spy on Titanosaurus, which is then alerted to their presence. As they run away, they actually call out Godzilla's name and the monster soon arrives to presumably save them. Although such moments were no longer new to moviegoers—Godzilla had been a hero of sorts ever since *Three Giant Monsters*—but this was the first and last time in a film directed by Honda that the King of the Monsters deliberately went out of its way to save human beings.

Honda's return to the Godzilla series seemed to inspire those around him, including Teruyoshi Nakano, whose work of late had been unimpressive. After Titanosaurus seizes the *Akatsuki No. 1* and brings it to the bottom of the sea, a sudden flash of light and smoke explode which silhouettes the monster, followed by a close-up of the beast bellowing bubbles while it roars triumphantly as smoke from the explosion trails behind it; easily the best effects sequence in a Toho monster film in seven years (Honda skillfully cuts the monster in mid-roar, emphasizing the shock and horror of the moment).

Another impressive scene was MechaGodzilla's assault on Tokyo blowing up miniature buildings (in a nice bit of detail, windows were loosely-placed inside the structures so they would fly off during the explosions); there was even an eye-pooping shot worthy of Tsuburaya when a miniature street is hurled upward by the force of the robot's rotating missiles. Equally effective was Godzilla's introduction; its ray coming in from off-camera stunning Titanosaurus, followed by a long-shot shot of a strobe effect back-lighting the beast before a light slowly brings it into view. The battles were cleverly edited with brief and frantic close-ups of the monsters' heads intercut with shots of the battle, filmed with a combination of slow-motion, fast-motion and real-time footage.

Nakano developed a number of unique opticals such as a close-up of Katsura's eye revealing the submarine, and an impressive downward pan of MechaGodzilla as seen through a window in the aliens' control room; another inventive shot zooms through the submarine's porthole to a close-up of an approaching Titanosaurus. Nakano's greatest asset was his use of pyrotechnics, and *Counterattack* contains several scenes of impressive explosions, but his battle scenes leaned toward the comic side with little regard for physics, such as when Titanosaurus bites Godzilla's mouth before punching it up into the air like a paddle-ball.

Tomioka's photography was bland and not particularly noteworthy, although there are occasional sparks of interest such as when Murakoshi is framed through a circular opening in the cell door as he shoots off its lock. There is also a nicely-composed shot of Mugal and Tsuda laughing in the foreground while a crestfallen Mafune hunches-over in the background. Two curious moments occur when Katsura—incongruously dressed in a zebra-patterned shirt, form-fitting black leotards and flowing white scarf—and Mafune's servant seem to disappear into thin air. This was due not to an accident or flaw in the film, but done intentionally during the post-editing process as the intention was to show the pair being teleported, as it was through this fashion they were able to gain access to the sound-transmitter (although the range of the teleportation device is evidentially only a few yards).

Akira Ifukube had not scored a Godzilla film since *All Monsters Attack*, and the difference between that score and *Counterattack* is evident from the very beginning. Unlike the up-tempo military-style music which starts-off *All Monsters Attack*, the composer's "Main Title" music for *Counterattack* is a modest drum rift, augmented by a wavering organ and electronic effects, followed by a gently-tapping gong.

Katsura's theme—first heard when the woman meets Ichinose and Murakoshi in "The Female in the Mafune Family"—is a sad, gentle piece beginning with a vibraphone (representing the aliens) and a flute (Katsura) which plays a seven-note theme that holds on its final note, indicating her uncertain and frail condition. A clarinet takes over, joined by a softly-tapping piano, before emotional violins enter with a rising-and-falling four-note theme (heard later on the electone organ signifying the aliens' intrusion into her life). A somber and sinister contrabass follows playing a section of the MechaGodzilla theme predicating Katsura's connection to the robot, while violins and flutes play in tandem the same seven-note theme, now joined by a quivering organ. This music—used again during her second surgery in "Cyborg Surgery"—indicates not only Katsura's demeanor but her demise as well (a portion of this music is heard in "Ichinose Gets Tailed" when Ichinose is watching her walking through the countryside; on this occasion scored with shimmering cymbal, organ and vibraphone).

The touching moment when Katsura covers up her damaged arm begins with her theme—only this time, played with violins instead of flutes indicating a forthright and moral decision, as an organ enters playing her motif while she struggles with her emotions. Flutes and violins play in greater volume when Katsura begs Ichinose to destroy her, and as she reaches for the space gun and shoots herself, the organ plays in a muted key with violins playing in an upper register, mirroring a muted and feminine horror. Subdued horns and violins play the MechaGodzilla theme for the last time as both machines—Katsura and MechaGodzilla—are rendered inoperative forever.

The "Ending" music begins with a mournful yet reverential French horn as Katsura's body is gently placed upon the ground; the horns holding on their final notes playing in their upper registers as the camera films her beautifully-calm expression. As Godzilla roars for the last time in a Honda film, piano, violins and a unique native flute—as if recalling Godzilla's island origins—brings the piece to a surging and emotive conclusion. Ifukube ends the cue with his characteristically sustained, two-note coda on violins and horns, and although triumphant in tone, the music is somber and subdued in its orchestration as if Ifukube was lovingly acknowledging the end of a remarkable film series.

For his final film Honda was allowed to handpick certain members of his cast; not surprisingly, he choose Akihiko Hirata to play the embittered Dr. Shinji Mafune. Hirata's performance has garnered much underserved criticism over the years for what many have viewed as a hammy performance, but in frank contrast to previous Honda villains, Hirata's interpretation of the enigmatic doctor was remarkably restrained. Normally, the actor was almost exclusively playing bland officials, and as such, the part of Mafune was a radical departure for Hirata in what was probably the most-dastardly villain in a Honda fantasy film. Mafune is a man who removes himself from society, using his intellect not for the benefit of the Mankind but to further his evil purpose and please his own ego. At the end of the day, his research will come to naught and his selfish aims will cause destruction and the death of not only hundreds of innocent people, but his own and his daughters (in fact he gets to watch her die not once but twice).

The actor gives his role a dimensionality not usually accorded to Honda's evil characters as the actor conveys not just rage but a smug satisfaction that his efforts have finally been recognized. He also expresses deep affection toward his daughter, shock at her death and disbelief when he is told the aliens have connected her with their titanic creation (when Ichinose makes a last-minute appeal to Mafune to reject the aliens, the doctor responds by saying: "The die is cast," encapsulating the fatalistically-unrepentant attitude of all of Honda's villains).

The film's leading role belongs to Katsuhiko Sasaki as Biologist Akira Ichinose, and Sasaki was an earnest if unremarkable actor who was nonetheless very convincing as the idol-worshipping and love-struck Ichinose. Undoubtedly his most-challenging moment comes when he declares his love for the robotic Katsura; his emotive invocation of her name as she dies, brings to mind Yamane's utterance of "Serizawa" in *Godzilla* and Kozumi's "Jinguchi" in *Submarine Warship*. Katsura Mafune is played by Tomoko Ai, and she is an interesting choice for the role; while not exceptionally beautiful, she nonetheless radiates a mysterious sexuality. Ai adeptly shows fear when confronting the aliens and vulnerability when she begs Ichinose not to go on his submarine mission. As with Kumi Mizuno's Miss Namikawa, Ai had to play an emotionless machine which still is able to feel passion.

Essentially reprising his earlier role as the alien leader from *MechaGodzilla* is Goro Mutsumi as Mugal; however, rather than the colorfully swearing, cigar-smoking and cognac-sipping Kuronuma from that film, Honda has the actor play Mugal with much-greater subtlety. The role of Mugal also called for a certain dimensionality as the alien not only exhibits the usual sly confidence which had long been a hallmark of Honda space villains, but also of concern and compassion for Mafune, as well as a certain wariness of the doctor's mercurial temper.

The supporting cast was also excellent, including Toru Ibuki as Tsuda, Katsumasa Uchida as the "shoot-first-and-ask-questions-later" Interpol agent Murakoshi, his dour boss Tagawa (Tadao Nakamaru), Tomoe Mari as the sad-faced Yuri Yamamoto and Shin Roppongi as the harried inventor Wakayama. Also notable were Kotaro Tomita as Ota and the ever-reliable Kenji Sahara, here playing the minor role of General Segawa (Sahara was yet another holdover from *MechaGodzilla*, where he appeared in a cameo as a cruise ship captain).

The film's most enigmatic casting was Ikio Sawamura as Mafune's silent manservant in a role probably never in the original script but added by Honda. Sawamura had appeared in numerous small roles for Honda such as *Great War In Space, Three Giant Monsters* and *Submarine Warship,* and his inclusion in the film as a non-speaking and shadowy background figure was an intriguing afterthought on the part of the director (*Counterattack* was to be Sawamura's final film role; he would die six months later at the age of 70).

As to the reason why Honda returned to the screen after having been away for so long has been a subject of much speculation, although it could have been that Honda felt a certain responsibility toward the series which had given tremendous momentum to his career, and may have wanted to end it with the same character that had in so many ways had started it. Sentiment and a responsibility toward his employer may also have played parts in the decision, and there may even have been the temptation for Honda to see if he still had the ability to make a good film, having never been totally satisfied with *Giant Monsters of the South Seas.*

Honda knew the task would be an arduous one; after all, he was 64-years-old and hadn't directed a film in four years. "It was the whim of the studio heads that I was even chosen to direct the film," he admitted years later to Milner, "I just didn't know if I was going to have the energy to get through it." The film begins with a protracted sequence onboard the *Akatsuki No. 1* and it is fully three minutes before the first monster appears, which was typical of Honda's approach to begin his films off gradually and let his audience get settled in to better involve them with the situation (originally the film was to start with the sub being readied for its departure, but Honda decided to start with the submarine's journey already underway).

Although Honda was pleased with the fact that a woman wrote the screenplay, he later lamented the fact that he was not more involved with the film's preproduction, later claiming that the story had gotten away from him. Initially, Honda wanted to place greater emphasis on the issue of nature's exploitation by man, but Tanaka's insistence that the director focus on yet another Earth takeover attempt by aliens killed that concept. Honda also seemed to finally resent Tanaka's perpetual butting-in; to what extent the producer interfered is unclear, although budget and time constraints were factors already familiar to a weary Honda.

The best moment in the film comes when Ichinose finally meets up with Mafune. It is a scene every viewer knows is coming, yet it is so effectively filmed and edited that it still packs a considerable wallop. Honda shows great economy of movement in the scene where Ichinose proposes the increased sonar capabilities for the *Akatsuki No. 2* in a single "take" lasting one minute, and filmed with only slight pans; the scene ends with Murakoshi looking up as if suspecting trouble—a technique Honda was fond of using to end a scene on an uncertain note. When Ichinose discloses the existence of the sound-transmitter device to Katsura in the cafeteria, Honda—for the last time in his career—tracks-in on an actor's close-up.

Yet, Honda's films still contained scenes of brutal violence, but now of a more sadistic kind, with some of it filmed in slow-motion, close-ups or accompanied by unpleasant gurgling sounds; there is talk of executions and of tongues being cut-out, there are on-screen whippings, a strangulation and Ichinose gets cold-cocked not once but twice with space guns. There is an electrocution and no less than four close-ups of people's dead faces, not to mention four shootings and a suicide (when Ichinose is freed from his bonds, he uses his rope to sneak up from behind Tsuda and strangle the alien to death, when—in a strange, confusing and unnecessary bit of business—Tsuda's last act is to remove his mask and reveal his hideously scarred face).

There is a strange conundrum occurring at the film's end: After the villains have been vanquished—exhibited by the typical Honda montage of celebrations among the victors—Honda cuts to the INTERPOL office where sharp eyes can spot Tagawa in the background grabbing his coat before beating it out the door. The reason for this becomes clear when Tagawa soon meets up with the others standing vigil over Katsura; although one wonders how he was able to make it to the site so quickly.

267

Eventually, five mourners are gathered around Katsura: Tagawa and Yuri on one side and Ichinose, Ota and Murakoshi on the other; the film's surviving principal characters lining up in the last of Honda's cinematic curtain calls (significantly, Honda films Ichinose and Yuri with a visible gap between them, implying they will never become a couple).

Ichinose declares his love for Katsura, saying: "Even though you're a robot, I still love you! You're not to blame, none of this is your fault!" Then, seeing her shed a tear: "You're human! You'd never lose the heart of a human being!" This kind of scene was a tall-order for any director to handle in a serious manner, but Honda pulls it off due to his sincere approach to the subject matter and his concern for his characters, regardless of their outrageous situation.

Honda's directing of *Counterattack* was a vast improvement over the Fukuda efforts, but the film could not help but suffer from the same imperfections that had hampered the most-recent Godzilla films: Sloppy optical work, unconvincing miniatures, off-scale composites, poor continuity and the overuse of stock special effects footage from earlier films—not to mention the inane plots and ridiculous monster battles (then there is the scene where Katsura is given her second operation: While the prosthetics doubling as her breasts are very lifelike, the vein-painted balloons representing her heart looked like the vein-painted balloons they were). Even more detrimental is the film's final moment after Murakoshi covers Katsura with his white coat (symbolizing purification); after a lovely close-up of the dead girl's face, Honda cuts to a grieving Ichinose looking off into the distance—but this touching *tableau* is soon shattered by a horrendous shot of a Godzilla promotional costume roaring on the beach, with the creature standing and grinning like some dreadful Cheshire cat; Honda's career had ended on a dreadful exclamation point.

Not even Honda's hope to recreate the magic he had woven so creatively in the past could overcome still another juvenile and predictable script, although he managed to lend the film a certain *panache* it had lacked for some time. Regrettably, it was not enough to regain or sustain interest in the series, as *MechaGodzilla's Counterattack* was yet another financial failure for Toho. With Honda's fondness for instilling romanticism and sentimentality in his films, it now seemed he was a bit behind the times; if fantasy films had not yet become an anachronism, perhaps his approach to making them had. Gone now were sentiment and sensitivity; now all was cynicism and cruelty. The director must have been amazed how his original conception of the beast as the visual embodiment of radiation had been transformed into a champion of justice, defending the very humans it once seemed destined to destroy. Godzilla—who only 21 years earlier was the reason a mother had to tell her terrified children that they would all soon be with their dead papa—was now being beckoned by children to save them from harm. The fiend had become a friend.

But the phenomenon of the Godzilla film series had reached its apex in *Mothra vs. Godzilla*. *MechaGodzilla's Counterattack*—the 15th film in the series and the eighth and last to be directed by Ishiro Honda—appeared to have finally reached the end of the line. A number of potential projects were announced over the coming years in a frantic effort to keep the series going: *The Resurrection of Godzilla, Godzilla vs. Gargantua, The Return of Godzilla, Space Godzilla* and most intriguingly, *Godzilla vs. the Devil*. As it happened, Toho would put the big beast into semi-retirement; it would be nearly a decade before the monster's mighty roar would be heard again.

And when it was, Honda would have nothing to do with it. "After that," Ryuji told Yutaka Ichimura years later, "he did not talk about Godzilla so much."

REVERBERATIONS

"Godzilla is *passé*."—TV Producer Haruki Kadokura in
*Godzilla, Mothra, King Ghidorah: Giant
Monsters All-Out Attack* (2001)

In writing about the Warner Brothers cartoons in 1943, film critic Manny Farber wrote: "The surprising facts about them are that the good ones are masterpieces and the bad ones aren't a total loss," a sentiment that can accurately be applied to the fantasy films of Ishiro Honda; they may not all be classics but they are never boring. For many, the feeling one gets after watching a Honda monster movie is like not having quite finished a sumptuous meal; one feels satisfied, yet wants more. It is no accident that, some 35 years after he made his last film, we still want more.

The woman who knew him better than anyone else on Earth—his beloved wife, Kimi—told Hiroshi Takeuchi seven years after her husband's death:

> It was his dream to become a movie director since he was in the 5th grade. Someone once called him an artist and I believe that to be true. He knew how to work with the materials he was given, knew his limitations and always gave his best effort. There were some movies where he had to work with that had a very limited budget and others where he had to use stock footage; nevertheless, despite these conditions, he always knew how to make good movies.

The world today is a very different place than it was when Honda entered the world of filmmaking; when he first joined P.C.L., Japanese militarists were well on their way to inducting Japan into a global conflict which resulted in unimaginable destruction and the loss of millions of lives. As Honda's career flourished, Japan found itself in the crosshairs of a nuclear-confrontation between America and the Soviet Union; his fantasy films stressed international harmony at a time when

270

the real world's destiny seemed on the edge of doom (the optimistic *Mothra* was released one month before the building of the Berlin Wall, and during the tense weeks of the "Cuban Missile Crises" in October of 1962, *Gorath*—Honda's ultimate cinematic treatise on worldwide cooperation—was released to Japanese theaters).

Happily, Honda lived to see the start of international bans on nuclear testing as well as the beginnings of global disarmament, although his treasured ideal of a united world was a concept he never lived to see. He also lived long enough to see himself become a cult figure, and gained enormous satisfaction knowing that so many of his films have been enjoyed by so many people around the world, a fact that both amused and humbled him (Honda's birthplace is currently the location of the "Yamagata International Documentary Film Festival," a bi-annual event held every October since 1989, which showcases new <u>documentary filmaking talents</u> from around the world. The festival *should* be named after Honda, but sadly is not; however, the Grand Prize *is* named after one of Honda's favorite directors and is called "The Robert and Frances Flaherty Prize."

It has been suggested that if Ishiro Honda had never directed another movie after *Godzilla*, his significance in the annals of cinematic history would in no way be diminished, and there is more than a modicum of truth to the suggestion; indeed, Honda never made another film that would have a greater impact on his career than *Godzilla*. It is interesting to speculate then on how Honda would be remembered today had *Godzilla* never been offered to him; what if the original director considered for the project said yes? Would this then be a book about the fantasy film work of Senkichi Taniguchi?

When Simitar Entertainment released several of Honda's Godzilla films on DVD in 1998, the liner notes on the cases described him as "... the first and the best of the Godzilla directors," which in all-likelihood is how he will always be remembered. It is a bittersweet remembrance not unlike the ambivalent endings to his fantasy films; for better or worse, Honda's career will always be in the shadow of the King of the Monsters (in one of Honda's last interviews, Stuart Galbraith asked him if he considered *Godzilla* to be his best film; Honda shrugged and smiled wearily before answering: "Probably"). It is one of the great ironies in movie history that such a non-confrontational and gentle man is known today as directing films of intense carnage and violence.

It was a double-edge sword to be remembered as the best in a long-line of directors of a series that itself is not normally highly regarded by mainstream movie critics; perhaps no one else has summed up Honda's career more-eloquently than Godzilla film director/writer Kazuki Omori, who told *Markalite* magazine: "No matter what we do or how we do it, it can never be as good as Honda's work." Certainly *Godzilla's* moody magnificence will forever keep it at the top of any film listing Honda's contributions to world cinema, but it is unfair to mention *Godzilla* exclusively when discussing Honda's career, without taking into consideration his many other fine films; fantasy or otherwise. *Godzilla* should be remembered then as not simply Honda's finest achievement, but merely part of a much-greater career. History has recently repeated itself with South Korean director Joon-ho Bong's brilliant *The Host* (2006), a film, like the original *Godzilla*, that was produced in an Asian country not known for its cinematic output, focusing more on a family in crises than on the monster, while at the same time commentating on environmental, social and political issues; in short, a film which embodies everything Honda stood for as a director.

Honda admitted that the war was the biggest influence on his life, giving him a unique perspective on human existence and its values. As he reflected back on his career in *Godzilla and My Movie Life*:

> Many people who came after me passed me by as directors while I was in the army, and although it took a long time for me to do what I wanted to do, I have no regrets about the movies I have made. However, as I look back, if I were to score my movies, they are all between 70-to-75 percent. It's a shame that I was never able to make a perfect movie that I could be completely satisfied with. I always worked hard on every project, so I do not have any regrets about my work; but after looking at a film I have made I often think, 'I could have done *this*' or 'I should have done *that*!

Despite the years of frustrations and cancelled projects (and projects that should have been cancelled), Honda pressed-on with calmly-determined intent. To some film historians the book is closed on Ishiro Honda, who consider him merely as a "clock-puncher" and a good company man who did what he was told and went through the motions; but the majority of his films tell a very different story; of a man concerned with the merits of his movies and who had something to say and cared deeply about how he said it. Never an outwardly-passionate man, Honda saved his passions for the movies he made with an almost palpable sensitivity. The fantasy films of Ishiro Honda comprised the Great Triumphate of Fantasy Film Makers of the late fifties and early sixties (along with George Pal and Ray Harryhausen) and will continue to entertain fans and influence filmmakers for generations to come. He was no "hack."

When considering Honda's career, one has the same mixed-feelings that shades the endings of so many of his films; joy at what he ultimately achieved, yet also disappointment of what might have been; but if Honda has left us any legacy at all, it is that of a man who never lost his childlike innocence and sense of wonder of what amazing images could be projected by that same marvelous machine he first saw one magical summer evening as a boy, and of a man whose gratitude toward his profession, personal integrity and love of filmmaking fills every frame of every film he ever made.

Such legacies last through the ages.

BIBLIOGRAPHY

BOOKS

Clarens, Carlos, *An Illustrated History of the Horror Film*, Capricorn Books, 1967.

Callow, Simon, *Orson Welles—Hello Americans,* Viking Penguin, 2006.

Kalat, David, *A Critical History and Filmography of Toho's Godzilla Series*, McFarland & Company, Inc., 1997.

Galbraith IV, Stuart, *Japanese Science Fiction, Fantasy and Horror Films*, McFarland & Company, 1994.

_____, *Monsters Are Attacking Tokyo!*, Feral House, 1998.

Honda, Ishiro, *Ishiro Honda—Godzilla and My Movie Life*, Yoshikazu Masuda (Editor), Kabushikigaisya Jitsugyono Nihonsya, 1994.

Kalat, David, *A Critical History and Filmography of Toho's Godzilla Series*, McFarland, 1997.

Maltin, Leonard, *Of Mice and Magic—A History of American Animated Cartoons*, A Plume Book, New American Library, New York, 1980.

Rovin, Jeff, *The Fabulous Fantasy Films*, A.S. Barnes & Co., Inc., 1977.

Ryfle, Steve, *Japan's Favorite Mon-Star*, ECW Press, 1998.

Sakai, Saburo with Caiden, Martin and Saito, Fred, *Samurai!*, E. P. Dutton and Company, Inc., 1957.

Smith, Steven C., *A Heart At Fire's Center—The Life and Music of Bernard Herrmann*, University of California Press, 1991.

Taleuchi, Hiroshi (Editor), *The Complete Works of Ishiro Honda*, Shiro Kimijima, Sonorama, Asahi, 2000.

Tanaka, Tomoyuki (Editor), *The Complete History of Toho's Special Effects Films*, Toho Company, Ltd. Publishing Division, 1983.

Tucker, Guy Mariner, *Age of the Gods*, Daikaiju Publishing, 1996.

Youngkin, Stephen D., Bigwood, James and Cabana Jr., Raymond, *The Films of Peter Lorre*, The Citadel Press, 1982.

PERIODICALS

Biondi, Robert, "Godzilla: the Filmbook," *G-Fan*, No. 12, November-December 1994.

_____, "The Evolution of Godzilla," *G-Fan*, No. 16, July-August 1995.

Biondi, Robert and John Rocco Roberto, "Godzilla in America, Part 2," *G-Fan*, No. 11, September-October 1994.

_____, "Godzilla in America, Part 8," *G-Fan*, No. 20, March-April 1996.

Biano, Mike, "The Ultra Bizarre World of Ultra Q," *G-Fan*, No. 62, May-June 2003.

Bouge, Mike, "King Kong vs. Godzilla," *G-Fan*, No. 64, September-October 2003.

Bradley, Chris, "Half-Japanese," *Kaiju Review*, 1995.

Brothers, Peter H. and Ed Godziszewski, "Rodan—A Commentary," *Japanese Giants*, No. 6, 1980.

Bubois, Andre, "Godzilla Meets Zone Fighter," *Japanese Giants*, No. 7, December 1985.

Chan, Kevin and Ragone, August, "An Interview with Director Ishiro Honda," *G-Fan*, November-December, 1994, Issue #12.

Cooper, Mike, "Godzilla Scrapbook," *Cult Movies & Video*, Videosonic Arts, No. 4, 1992.

Chan, Kevin and Ragone, August, "An Interview with Director Ishiro Honda," *Screen Special*, 1991.

Debus, Allen A., "Kaiju Conjure: A Russian Ghidorah?," *G-Fan*, No. 80, Spring 2007.

England, Norman, "Toho Tunes 4," *G-Fan*, No. 30, November-December 1997.

Filoni, Dave, "Ogasawara Sketchbook," *G-Fan*, No. 40, July-August 1999.

Galbraith IV, Stuart, "The Japanese Film Industry—Circa 1954," *Japanese Giants*, Vol. 1, No. 10, September 2004.

Gingold, Michael, Godzilla, "The Japanese Adventures," *Fangoria*, No. 173, June 1998.

Godziszewski, Ed, "Akira Ifukube—A Profile," *G-Fan*, No. 18, November-December 1995.

_____, "*Atragon*: A Toho Classic Revisited," *G-Fan*, No. 21, May-June 1996.

_____, "The Making of Godzilla," *Japanese Giants*, No. 10, Sept. 2004.

Godziszewski, Ed and Imamura, Michiko, "Ifukube on Ifukube," *G-Fan*, No. 18, November 1995.

Gudmundson, Bill, "Monster Sizes," *Japanese Giants* 1976.

Harrington Clifford V., "Japan's Master of Monsters," *American Cinematographer*, August 1960.

Homenick, Brett, "Akira Ifukube: More Than Monsters," *G-Fan*, No. 60, January-February 2003.

_____, "Death Takes Maestro Akira Ifukube," *G-Fan*, No. 75, Spring 2006.

Homenick, Brett, Lees, J.D., Field, Robert Scott, "Nakano's Other Side," *G-Fan*, No. 72, Summer 2005.

Homenick, Brett, Foster, Damon, and Field, Robert Scott, "The Man Who Made Godzilla Fly," *G-Fan*, No. 73, Fall 2005.

Imamura, Michiko, Godziszewski Ed and Kuni Takikawa, "Godzilla Speaks! A Conversation with Haruo Nakajima," *G-Fan*, No. 22, July-August 1996.

Ichimura, Yutaka, "Tokusatsu Studios Were My Playground," *G-Fan*, No. 88, Summer 2009.

Inouye, Jon, "Godzilla and Postwar Japan," *The Japanese Fantasy Film Journal*, No. 12, 1979.

Ishizuka, Daisuke, "Mr. Explosion," *G-Fan*, No. 68, Summer 2004.

_____, "Sayonara Arikawa-san,"` *G-Fan*, No. 74, Winter 2006.

Johnson, Bob, "Mighty Jack: The TV Movie," *Markalite*, No. 1, Summer 1990.

_____, "Short Takes," *Markalite*, No. 2, Winter 1991.

Johnson, Bob and Ragone, August, "The Ultra Series: 25 Years of Science Fantasies from Tsuburaya Productions," *Markalite*, No. 2, Winter 1991.

Johnson, Teddy, "When Roman Centurions Attack," *G-Fan*, No. 54, January-February 2002.

Kalat, David, "Inside Story: The Americanization of Godzilla 1985," *G-Fan*, No. 20, March-April 1996.

_____, "The Disney-Toho Conspiracy," *G-Fan*, No. 25, January-February 1997.

_____, "Mad Science," *G-Fan*, No. 35, September-October 1998.

Lees, J.D., "Visit to Monsterland," *G-Fan*, Special Collection, 1994.

_____, "G-Calendar '96," *G-Fan*, No. 19, January-February 1996.

_____, "G-Mail," *G-Fan*, No. 21, May-June 1996.

_____, "Godzilla's Ray: Frequency of Use," *G-Fan*, No. 30, November-December 1997.

_____, "Godzilla's Serious Side," *G-Fan*, No. 32, March-April 1998.

_____, "Godzilla's Serious Side," *G-Fan*, No. 68, Summer 2004.

_____, "Box Office Blast For Godzilla!," *G-Fan*, No. 68, Summer 2004.

Lethem, Roland, "Inoshiro Honda," *Midi/Minuit Fantastique*, No. 20, October 1968.

Lingua, Rosemary, "Video Reviews—*The Human Vapor*," *Cult Movies*, No. 7, 1993.

Majer, Jay, "Toho's Monsters Speak Out," *Cult Movies and Video*, No. 7, 1993.

Milner, David with Shibata, Yoshihiko, "Ishiro Honda Interview," *Cult Movies*, No. 9, 1993.

Min, Soo Lee, "Mothra's Song Revisited," *G-Fan*, No. 30, November-December 1997.

Ono, Akiko, "Memories of Godzilla," *G-Fan*, No. 12, November-December 1994.

Pusateri, Richard, "The Mysterians," *G-Fan*, No. 27, 1997.

_____, "The H-Man," *G-Fan*, No. 34, July-August 1998.

Pusateri, Richard and Lees, J.D., "Frankenstein Conquers the World," *G-Fan*, No. 30, November-December 1997.

Ragone, August, "Godzilla: Toho & Film Trends," *Markalite*, No. 1, Summer 1990.

_____, "Giants of the Kaiju Genre," *G-Fan*, No. 45, May-June 2000.

Ragone, August and Tucker, Guy, "The Legend of Godzilla—Part One," *Markalite*, No. 3, Fall 1991.

Rainey, Stephen Mark, "*Atragon* DVD Review," G-Fan, No 75, Spring 2006.

Rebello, Stephen, "Selling Nightmares," *Cinefantastique*, Vol. 18, No. 2/3, March 1988.

Roberto, John Rocco, "In Memory of Ishiro Honda," *G-Fan*, No. 12, November-December 1994.

_____, "The Other Side of Toho," *G-Fan*, No. 23, September-October 1996.

Roberto, John Rocco and Tucker, Guy Mariner, "Bigger than Life!—An Interview with Henry G. Saperstein," *G-Fan*, No. 15, May-June 1995.

Roberto, John Rocco and Biondi, Robert, "Godzilla in America, Part 5: Monster Island!," *G-Fan*, No. 15, May-June 1995.

Ryfle, Steve, "Reminiscences of the Vapor Man," *Japanese Giants*, No. 9, 2002.

Ryfle, Steve with Galbrath IV, Stuart, "Teruyoshi Nakano," *G-Fan*, No. 27, 1997.

Ryfle, Steve, with Sakahara, A. & Godziszewski, M, "Final Notes: Interview with Composer Akira Ifukube," *G-Fan*, No. 41, September-October 1999.

Schultz, Mark A., "Horror—Toho Style," *G-Fan*, No 19, January-February 1996.

Shoemaker, Greg, "Editor's Notes," *The Japanese Fantasy Film Journal*, No. 12, 1979.

_____, "The Toho Legacy," *The Japanese Fantasy Film Journal*, No. 13, 1981.

_____, "The Toho Legacy," *The Japanese Fantasy Film Journal*, No. 14, 1982.

_____, "The Toho Legacy," *The Japanese Fantasy Film Journal*, No. 15, 1983.

Tsuburaya, Hideyo, "*Gorath* Retrospective," *The Japanese Fantasy Film Journal*, No. 15, 1983.

Tucker, Guy, "Takeshi Kimura: God's Lonely Man," *Markalite*, No. 1, Summer 1990.

_____, "Akira Kurosawa's *Dreams*," *Markalite*, No. 2, Winter 1991.

_____, "The Earth and the Stars: Notes on the Human Vapor," *Cult Movies*, No. 35, 2001.

ADDITIONAL SOURCES

Anderson, Jeffrey M, "Teaching Our Children Well," *Combustiblecelluoid. com*, October 2000.

Coleman, Dave, "Human Vapor aka The First Gas Human,", *Bijouflix*, August 2003.

Culver, Brian R., "Jujin Yokiotoko/Half Human," *Kaiju-Fan, dalekempire. com*, 1998.

Eaton, Matthew J., "The Nandi Bear: Ferocious Killer from the Past," *Cryptozoology.com*, 2003.

Burton, Ronnie and Elam, Christopher, "The Kaiju Detective," Owari Publishing, December 1999.

Homenick, Brett, Interview with Rhodes Reason, recorded during "G-Fest 14," July 7, 2007.

Marshall, Fred, "The Emperor of Film, No, Not Yet!," *Kinema, November 2002.*

Milner, David, Shibata, Yoshihiko and Honda, Ryuji, "Kimi Honda Interview," *cinescape.com*, July 1994.

"Mothra's Song (1961-1998)," *geocities.com/Tokyo/Island* 2004.

Petsev, Nik, "Yeh-The: 'That Thing There,'" *cryptozoology.com*, 2003.

Reality Software, "The Bear Ritual of the Ainu," www.bears.org/spirit/ainumyth, 2003.

Thomason, Andy, "The Ainus of Japan," *Suite University, Suite101.com*, 2003.

Todd, Mort, "Godzilla, King of the Monsters!—Monsters Attack!," *Globe Communications Corpse*, No. 4, Sept 1990.

Tuczynski, Lawrence, "Review of *Daikaiju Baran*" CD Soundtrack, www.godzillamonstermusic.com, 1998.

_____, "Review of *Battle in Outer Space" CD Soundtrack,* www.godzillamonstermusic.com, 1998.

_____, "Review of *Gorath*" CD Soundtrack, godzillamonstermusic.com, 1999.

_____, "Music in the Key of Godzilla," *G-Fan*, No. 44, March-April 2000.

Walman, Nancy, "The Daimajin Trilogy, *G-Fan*, No. 49, January-February 2001.

Walsh, David, "Akira Kurosawa's Achievement," *World Socialist Web Site*, September 1998.

3767124R00164

Printed in Great Britain
by Amazon.co.uk, Ltd.,
Marston Gate.